WORLD'S
EDGE

Also by David Hair

THE MOONTIDE QUARTET

Mage's Blood
Scarlet Tides
Unholy War
Ascendant's Rite

THE SUNSURGE QUARTET

Empress of the Fall
Prince of the Spear
Hearts of Ice
Mother of Daemons

THE RETURN OF RAVANA

The Pyre
The Adversaries
The Exile
The King

THE TETHERED CITADEL

Map's Edge

WORLD'S EDGE

THE TETHERED CITADEL BOOK 2

DAVID HAIR

Jo Fletcher
BOOKS

First published in Great Britain in 2021 by

Jo Fletcher Books
an imprint of
Quercus Editions Ltd
Carmelite House
50 Victoria Embankment
London EC4Y 0DZ

An Hachette UK company

A CIP catalogue record for this book is available
from the British Library

TPB ISBN 978 1 52940 205 6

10 9 8 7 6 5 4 3 2 1

Typeset by Jouve (UK), Milton Keynes

Printed and bound in Great Britain by Clays Ltd, Elcograf S.p.A.

Papers used by Jo Fletcher Books are from well-managed
forests and other responsible sources.

This book is dedicated to all you 'creatives' out there, in this strange and scary time. We've all had to endure lockdowns and shortages, and some of us have faced loss, and many of us have had to live with the fear that our careers are very precarious, as our publishers, promoters and producers grapple with their own problems.

But it turns out that some of the big things that got a lot of us through all the stress of 2020-21 were music, movies and TV, and books. Thank you to those who produced the shows and songs and writing that got me through – and I hope that for some of you readers, this piece of escapism helps you to relax and, well, *escape . . .*

TABLE OF CONTENTS

INTERLUDE (1): SURVIVAL INSTINCTS

PART 2: USURPER

INTERLUDE (2): SOMMAPORT

PART 3: SHIRO KAMIGAMI

What Has Gone Before

The World of Shamaya

Shamaya, a world orbited by planetary rings, is in the grip of an Ice Age, brought about by misuse of magic. The polar caps have encroached thousands of miles beyond their normal bounds, engulfing huge tracts of land and constricting humanity into a narrower band of life, two thousand miles either side of the equator.

This magical catastrophe occurred five hundred years ago, when the dominant elites, powerful sorcerers known as the Aldar, went to war. They may (or may not) have been a different race who ruled over humanity. They wore masks in public to add to their mystique, used a destructive form of magic called *mizra* and lived long lives of decadence and cruelty.

The collapse of Aldar rule coincided with the discovery of a new form of magic called *praxis*. The antithesis of the unpredictable mizra, it emphasises discipline. The credit for discovering praxis is given to a woman, Gerda, a messianic figure within the dominant human religion revering the god Deo. Gerda is said to have slain the last Aldar god-king in his palace at Rath Argentium, triggering the wars in which the Aldar unleashing massive destructive forces that saw their own race destroyed and caused the onset of the Ice Age.

Recent History 1000-1530ME (Magnian Era)

At the beginning of the Ice Age, millions of people were displaced as humanity crowded onto the equatorial continent of Magnia, the largest

1

landmass free of ice. Three centuries of barbarism ensued, until the 1400s saw a renaissance in which the study of the sciences and arts were renewed and political institutions took on increasing democratisation. Personal freedoms grew, accompanied by new wonders, from telescopes to clocks to gunpowder, through the alliance of education and the praxis.

But in the 1520s, those freedoms collapsed when the large (if backward) kingdom of Bolgravia sought dominance. Using assassination, corruption and military might, the Bolgravians defeated the Magnian royal house, then conquered their vassal kingdoms of Norgania, Ferrea, Pelaria, Otravia and others. By 1534, the Bolgravian Empire not only dominates the Magnian continent, but has imposed a culture of fear and exploitation based on sorcery and a mineral called *istariol*.

Istariol and Sorcery

Istariol is a naturally occurring substance which, when processed into a blood-red powder and utilised by a sorcerer, vastly increases magical output. Any sorcerer can start a fire, but with istariol, that fire can be an inferno; a magical breeze may become a hurricane; a small wave a tsunami. Istariol cannot be manufactured and natural reserves are few; the Bolgravian Empire now controls all mining and distribution, although there is a thriving and lucrative black market.

Both forms of sorcery, praxis and mizra, require a sorcerer to bind with a 'familiar' spirit which channels and enhances magical energy; they communicate using language, symbols and gestures. These bonds are formed when the sorcerer first manifests power in their teens. Choosing a benign spirit accesses the praxis, but choosing a wild spirit results in mizra, which is illegal. In Magnia, all mizra-witches exist in secret, for fear of execution.

The Events of Spring and Summer, 1534 (as told in Map's Edge)

In Teshveld, at the western edge of the Magnian continent, an imperial party newly returned from the recently settled land of Verdessa demands aid from a local healer. One of them, a cartomancer (a sorcerer and map-maker), is suffering from a mysterious ailment. The Bolgravian lord commanding the mission menaces the healer and his daughter, demanding they save the dying cartomancer or suffer violent consequences.

The healer is Raythe Vyre, an exiled sorcerer-lord from conquered Otravia. Surreptitiously reading the cartomancer's encrypted journal, he discovers that traces of istariol have been found in Verdessa. He sees this as a chance to restore his fortunes and strike back against the empire. Realising he can't save the cartomancer, Raythe kills the Bolgravians and steals the journal.

The istariol will need to be mined, so Raythe recruits among the local villagers, refugees and soldiers of fortune, many of them also fugitives. Soon after, a caravan of three hundred souls quietly slips out of Teshveld, taking the northeastern coastal road (the Ghost Road). Accompanying Raythe are his daughter Zarelda, a potential sorceress, and some trusted comrades: the Shadran blademaster Jesco Duretto; the Deist priestess Varahana, and Vidar Vidarsson, a bearskin, or shapeshifting berserker.

The travellers comprise three factions: a third are Teshveld villagers led by Varahana and the midwife and healer Kemara Solus; who have vital skills but lack military experience. Another third, trappers and hunters, are loosely led by Cal Foaley. The remaining third are merce-naries in the pay of duplicitous knight Sir Elgus Rhamp. Conflicts soon arise, mostly involving Rhamp's men.

However, their flight hasn't gone unnoticed. Toran Zorne, a sorcerer-assassin of the Ramkiseri, the Bolgravian Secret Service, was already on Raythe's trail. He commandeers soldiers and ships and sets off in pursuit, catching the travellers just as they are crossing into Verdessa. As the ships' cannons and marines prepare to annihilate the fugitives, all appears to be lost.

But the day is saved when Kemara reveals an unsuspected power: she is a sorceress, not of the praxis but the illegal and deadly mizra. Link-ing her magic to Raythe's in a bonding called a *meld* expands their power, enabling them to destroy one imperial ship and drive the other away, saving the caravan. A meld between opposing forms of magic is supposed to be impossible; it's certainly far deadlier than any bond Raythe has experienced before. To allay fears, Raythe and Kemara keep her mizra secret by pretending she used the praxis.

The expedition follows the trail of the istariol out of Verdessa into the northern ice wastes, following a river that's been frozen for five hundred years.

They believe they've eluded the empire, but Toran Zorne has disguised himself as a wounded sailor they fished from the sea and is using praxis magic to guide the pursuing imperial forces.

Nevertheless, the travellers manage to stay ahead. They find a vast patch of fertile land deep within the ice wastes: a clear sign that istariol is present. At the heart of this region is an ancient ruined city built on an old mountain – and the spectacular sight of the peak floating in the air above the base, tethered to the ground by giant chains. There is a castle atop it.

To Raythe's shock and amazement, they have found Rath Argentium, the Silver Citadel, once the heart of the Aldar civilisation.

But no sooner have they found this legendary place than they are beset from all sides, for the imperial forces have caught them up. Spotting campfires away to the east, Zarelda and her boyfriend Banno Rhamp go to seek aid, but they're captured by a hitherto unknown tribe of people who call themselves the Tangato, pre-Ice Age humans, trapped here for five hundred years: they believe themselves to be the last people alive on Shamaya.

Meanwhile, at the height of the imperial attack, Toran Zorne tries to kill Raythe and Kemara, who he believes are both mizra-witches.

But Raythe and Kemara defeat Zorne, who falls into the canyon river and is swept away, once again believed dead. While Raythe leads his people across the ancient bridge into the ruined city, the Bolgravians, out of gunpowder and taken by surprise, are annihilated by the Tangato . . . who then encircle Rath Argentium.

Raythe's expedition has found the istariol, and so much more. But will they ever be able to leave again?

Prologue

The Long Road Home

Toran Zorne woke to the sound and feel of words tumbling from his own mouth and realised from the dry rawness of his throat that he must have been babbling for hours, 'Ruscht, consano, consano a multo, quaeso, lanista . . .'

Ruscht – heal me, heal me of it all, I beg you . . . repeated, over and over again.

And Ruscht, his familiar, had been dutifully doing exactly that.

I'm alive . . .

For a time, everything blurred but the sound of the churning river, the moaning wind, the call of birds and hum of insects, and the painful rasp of his own breath. Then taste and smell returned: the bitter tang of blood in his mouth and the aroma of damp earth.

Then came pain, the agony of still raw damage to his torso, the rending that steel had wrought on flesh, the exquisite torture of even the subtlest movement. He knew his own body well enough to know that despite waking, his survival was hanging by a thread.

But the worst ache of all was that of defeat. He'd been vanquished, cast down and washed up here to die alone.

But I am never alone, for my empire is with me.

That reminder, that pride, overrode defeat. He opened his eyes and found himself in a gorge, cast up in the shallows of a river, lying half out of the flow on the stony shore beneath high cliffs.

This river carries traces of istariol, he remembered: a river that flowed into a lake that became a glacier that inched towards the sea before becoming another lake, another river, meandering through Verdessa to the sea. This miraculous journey was only possible through the strange geography of Shamaya, where a motherlode of istariol could sustain life-supporting climate-zones hundreds of miles inside the frozen wastes.

A fragment of memory returned: Raythe Vyre, battered but somehow able to plunge his sword into Zorne's gut. He rolled over, peeled aside the sodden remnants of his shirt and examined a livid, newly sealed wound.

It should have been fatal.

But I have you, Ruscht: you kept me alive.

A familiar keeping their host-sorcerer alive, even without instructions, wasn't unique, but it was rare. The spirits weren't terribly intelligent, but one thing even their wayward minds could grasp was that the human they'd bonded with *must not die*. And if there was one thing Ruscht was well-versed in, it was in putting his master back together again.

'Abeo, Ruscht,' Zorne breathed. Rest now.

The familiar squirmed in pleasure at his approval, then left his body. Magic was draining, and they both needed to recover. The familiar, invisible to everyone else, flew off, while Zorne lapped at the river-water until his thirst dissolved, then closed his eyes and let the tranquillity transport him into darkness.

He woke the next morning, or so he estimated, and found Ruscht inside him again. The wound was still painful, but it was sealing, entirely thanks to his familiar's ministrations. It was nigh on impossible for a sorcerer to heal others using magic, but repairing oneself was instinctive. He drank again, then clambered painfully to his feet. It was time to leave.

He found a trail beneath the cliffs that went up and out of the ravine to a low rise at the south end of a plateau. When he'd recovered from the exertion and got his bearings, he realised that he'd stood here before, just a few days ago.

He'd been Moss Trimble then, one of the three hundred souls led here by the infamous Raythe Vyre. Trimble had been a simple person, a man of base habits. He'd been courting the healer, Kemara Solus, trying to get close enough to plunge a stiletto into her black mizra-heart, but her familiar saved her, just as Ruscht had saved him.

Only hers pulled her back from having her heart impaled – and then turned her into a killing machine . . .

Such was the potency of a mizra-witch – and Raythe Vyre had to be one too. It wasn't through cunning or skill that they'd eluded the empire, but through the deepest evil known.

It occurred to Zorne that for the first time in his life, he was overmatched.

That notion haunted him all morning as he walked north, back towards an impossible city growing against the skyline: *Rath Argentium*, a place he'd never believed existed, let alone survived the Ice Age. But there was Shiro Kamigami, the legendary floating citadel of the god-kings, chained above the Silver City. It could be nowhere else.

He came in sight of the camp his Bolgravian allies had set up before assailing Vyre's position, a hill-fort at the edge of the ravine, and a chill ran through him. The Bolgravian encampment had been *utterly* destroyed, as if a hurricane had blown through it, strewing bodies all about. There were dozens of the giant flightless phorus birds, each taller than a man, as well as thousands of vultures, picking over the carcases – but there were men present too, brown-skinned savages with black hair brandishing primitive spears and clubs, calmly looting the place. Remarkably, they were being directed by garishly robed women mounted on phorus birds.

How could a group of savages defeat a Bolgravian regiment? he wondered, shocked to the core, and then, *Who are they?*

He circled the destroyed camp, heading for the bridge spanning the ravine to Rath Argentium. Climbing a low hill, he found a troubling scene: arrayed on this side of the bridge were thousands more of the brown-skinned warriors, facing the city. They were singing some barbaric song, beating their chests and shaking their weapons, but making no direct attack.

On the bridge where Vyre and Solus had slain four imperial sorcerers and forced Zorne to throw himself into the river were even more of these savages, gathered before a throne surrounded by vivid banners. Around the throne were what looked like courtiers in brightly coloured robes and, of all things, masks.

Across the bridge, in the fortified gatehouse, he saw movement, and the distinctive silhouettes of long flintlocks: Raythe Vyre had clearly got his people into the city, while this tribe of primitives – who surely must be some forgotten remnant of the Aldar Age – had slaughtered the Bolgravians. He pictured a surprise attack at night, taking from behind men who'd run out of gunpowder. It was difficult to believe and harder to stomach, but he'd seen the aftermath and had to reckon with it.

I'm the only empire man here – which leaves me with two choices.

For two years his sole mission had been to find and kill the treacherous Vyre, so duty demanded that he find a way into the city and split the man's black heart. But that no longer made sense – not because he couldn't do it, but because the stakes were now so high that failure would be unacceptable. He knew the tales about Rath Argentium, of its wealth and power. More importantly, for a swathe of warm land to exist this deep into the ice, the istariol lode here must be *immense*, the kind of power that could change history.

I can most likely kill Vyre, but if I fail, there will be no one to report back. The emperor will remain unaware of this motherlode – until it turns up in the hands of our enemies. That cannot *be permitted.*

Given that, his course was clear: he must return to his masters and report. That meant retracing his journey, alone and unsupported: thirty miles south, right to where this unfrozen land lapped against the glacier, then down the ice for another fifty-odd miles, a hundred miles or more through the Verdessa wilds to Rodonoi, the imperial port. From there he would need to sail hundreds of miles to Sommaport on the Magnian coast, and finally, two thousand miles by carriage to reach someone with the rank to deal with this.

A daunting journey, but Vyre did it, to bring his people here. I can do no less.

Zorne didn't believe in Deo, so he didn't bother to pray before setting out. He did believe in the innate destiny of the Bolgravian Empire, though – and his own superiority – so he turned his back on the incredible panorama of the mythic city, faced south and took one step, then another. One small man, on the long road home.

PART ONE

Across the Divide

1

Who Are These People?

'Who are these people?' Raythe Vyre wondered, gazing from the gate-house tower along the stone bridge to the far side of the ravine that was protecting his small group of travellers from annihilation. Below him, behind a hastily thrown-up barricade of broken timbers and wagons, a thin line of mercenaries and hunters aimed flintlocks and bows along the span. Dozens more had found vantage points on the walls, while the women, children and old folk readied reloads and stretchers.

There's just three hundred of us – and there are thousands of them.

For now, all he could do was squint through his spyglass and try to work out what they were facing. He'd never seen people like them, and he was widely travelled. They were all brown-faced, with plump lips and wide nostrils, and dark markings of some sort on their faces. Their bare arms were also decorated with patterned symbols. Their breast-plates looked like boiled leather and their weapons were primitive for the most part, spears and bows, although the officers had curved swords, possibly of bronze, judging by the colour, and elaborate hel-mets of leather and metal. Right now, they were all singing a warlike chant that involved a lot of thigh-slapping and pulling faces. It was undoubtedly unsettling.

At least a quarter of the warriors were women, which was virtually unheard of except during the last, desperate days of the Bolgravian Conquests, when anyone who could hold a weapon had been con-scripted, regardless of age or gender. But these women looked every bit as fierce and athletic as the men.

Even stranger, the two dozen advisors clustered about the throne of their female ruler appeared to be women. Their black hair was coiled in elaborate piles, they all wore brightly coloured robes and masks of shining red and black. They reminded him, chillingly, of mosaics he'd seen of Aldar women.

'I count two thousand, give or take,' said Jesco Duretto. A light breeze teased the black hair that framed his handsome, olive-skinned face. 'And there's nothing but smoke coming from the Bolgravian camp – I reckon these folk have killed them for us.'

'They might have, but not for us,' Raythe replied, returning his spyglass to the pale figure kneeling before the queen's throne. Once again his heart nearly stopped at the sight of that slender fair-haired girl.

Zar.

Feeling his anguish, his familiar Cognatus, perched unseen on his shoulder in parrot form, shrilled angrily.

He'd been told many times that he was heartless and calculating, that he kept his feelings buried too deep, and perhaps that was just. Maybe the Revolt, with all the senseless slaughter and the loss of so many friends and allies, had killed something within him. But seeing his daughter like that made him howl inside.

How she was there, Raythe had no idea, but so much was still unknown right now . . . Was this ruined city actually deserted? Were there other ways in and out apart from the bridge below? And were any Bolgravs still alive out there?

And most of all, where had these tribal people come from, and what would they do?

He was doing his best to conceal his anguish: people needed *composure* from their leaders, not histrionics. But inside, his stomach was roiling with nausea and fear.

'Is Cal Foaley back?' he asked Jesco. The hunter had set off at first light with a group of scouts to reconnoitre this ruined mountainside city.

'He can't be far away,' Jesco replied. Looking up, he shuddered and added, 'This is the strangest place I have ever seen, bar none.'

Raythe followed his gaze past the ruins of multi-storeyed stone buildings that crowded above their position, many with strange curves and crenulations more akin to art than architecture, to the huge floating rock half a mile above the ground, tethered in place by four giant chains, every link bigger than a man. Atop that, partially visible, was a fortress.

'Rath Argentium,' Raythe breathed. 'The royal seat of the last Aldar King – and Shiro Kamigami, the floating citadel. I never believed either was real.'

'Nor I,' Jesco replied. 'They say that when he realised that his reign was doomed, Tashvariel the Usurper locked himself and his courtiers in the banquet hall up there, and for three days and nights they ate and drank and screwed until they were utterly sated – then they took their own lives, rather than yield. They say he murdered his lover Shameesta before he killed himself, and that he haunts the castle still, raging against the gods . . .'

'Enough with the ghost stories.' Raythe grinned. 'It's quite scary enough already.'

Across the bridge, the fierce song and dance of the warriors ended and Raythe tensed, anticipating attack. But instead, another song began, this one mournful rather than a rousing call to arms.

'It's got a weird beauty to it, don't you think?' Jesco remarked. 'I wonder who they are?'

'They must be survivors of the fall of the Aldar,' Raythe answered.

'Holy Gerda! But if that's so, why aren't they in here?'

'No idea.' Raythe turned as boots thumped on the stone steps behind them and Cal Foaley, a lupine hunter with weather-beaten skin and tangled grey hair, appeared with his flintlock slung over one shoulder.

'Boss. All the scouts are in.'

'And?' Raythe found himself instinctively matching his gruff tone.

'Everyone's accounted for, except your daughter and Banno Rhamp. We lost six, with thirteen wounded, in the hill-fort engagement with the Bolgies. Everything we could carry is inside, including all the large gear – we hauled it over in handcarts. We've got enough powder and balls for half a hundred volleys, and about as many arrows. Food for a week. No fuel for fires, but there's trees we can cut down, and we've found steps to the river below. Varahana's organising water containers and my cousin Skeg swears he's seen fish.'

'Do we have any way of catching them?'

'Skeg was a fisherman – he's working on it.'

'Good. What about the city? Is it empty? Secure? Are there other ways in?'

'Gan Corbyn's scouted the periphery. He says the rivers completely encircle the city – it's actually an island – and this is the only bridge. There was another one on the north side, but it's collapsed, ages ago, looks like. The cliffs are sheer, but there's half a dozen sets of steps leading down to the river, and some old stone docks. No boats, though,' Foaley added, when Raythe looked alarmed. 'They don't look like they've been used for many decades.'

'Let's station guards at each stair, regardless,' Raythe ordered. 'The only advantage we have is that we're inside and they're outside. Let's not lose that.'

'Ahead of you, boss. I've got Rhamp's mercs at each vulnerable point.' Foaley's tones told Raythe exactly what he thought of Sir Elgus Rhamp and his men.

'About them—' Jesco began, but Raythe shook his head.

'Later,' he said firmly.

Jesco and Foaley both scowled, then the hunter went on, 'Most of the houses are wrecked and overgrown, but there are still many that are intact, enough to shelter us. Kemara's set up her infirmary over there' – he gestured behind the gatehouse – 'and Gravis Tavernier has found what he reckons is an old inn – it's still got its ovens and furnaces. And Matty Varte has found an old garden with plenty of fruit and vegetables. He didn't recognise them all, but if they're safe to eat – and why else would someone have been growing them? – there's enough food for the short term.'

'That's encouraging.' Raythe replied. 'Get Mater Varahana on it. She's a scholar – she may be able to identify them. How're the wounded doing?'

Foaley looked down. 'Vidar's the worst, I fear. The bearskin's at death's doorway. And Fossy Vardoe took a bayonet in the chest. Kemara reckons he'll make it, though. The rest of the injuries are mostly minor.'

'I'll visit them when I can,' Raythe said as the latest song ended. 'Hold on, what's this?'

A small cluster of warriors were forming up on the bridge behind a figure wearing a long cloak made of what looked to be red, green and brown phorus feathers. Raythe leaned over the battlements and shouted down to the men aiming flintlocks and bows along the arched bridge, 'Don't shoot at the group moving onto the bridge unless I order it.'

From his higher vantage, he watched the tribesmen advance. When he trained his spyglass on their leader he was surprised to see a young woman with lustrous black hair and strong, attractive features. Her face bore similar markings to the men and he wondered if it was paint, or even tattoos?

'It may be a parley,' he reported, repeating, *'Don't shoot.'*

'Aye, we hear you,' the gruff voice of Sir Elgus Rhamp called from below.

They watched in silence as the knot of warriors crested the apex of the bridge, then stalked towards them. The strange way they were holding their spears, close to the bronze heads, made Raythe wonder if they were actually spears at all. The men were clearly apprehensive, but the young woman looked completely calm.

'All right, listen,' he called out, 'Jesco's going to fire *one shot* in the air, as a warning. It is *not* a signal to open fire! Understood?'

'Understood,' the voices chorused.

Raythe nodded to Jesco, who pointed his flintlock skywards and pulled the trigger. The hammer dropped and sparked and the gun shot flame and an iron ball into the sky. The sound reverberated in the ravine, scattering the circling birds.

The men on the bridge flinched, looking round in alarm, which confirmed Raythe's suspicion that they'd never seen a gun before. But the woman spoke sharply and kept walking. A low murmur rose from his men below as she emerged from the press: she certainly was an impressive sight. Her feather cloak blew out behind her, revealing just a beaded kilt and bodice which left her waist and well-muscled thighs and calves bare.

'Do I shoot again?' Jesco asked, reloading swiftly.

'Wait,' Raythe said. When she was a hundred yards from the gatehouse, he called out, 'That's far enough—' He didn't expect her to understand, but hoped she'd infer the meaning.

She halted, and called, 'Are you . . . Rat Weer?'

He blinked in surprise. 'I am Raythe Vyre,' he shouted back. 'Do you speak Magnian?'

He saw the woman mutter to herself, then she called back, the words slow and awkwardly pronounced, 'Your Magneeyan is like our "Gengo". And my familiar can help translate.'

Below him, Raythe's gunmen whispered, '*Familiar? She's a sorcerer!*'

Or a witch, Raythe thought grimly, for the Aldar had used mizra, not the praxis. The masks the queen and her women wore suggested that if these people weren't Aldar themselves, they clearly had memories of the long-vanished race.

This isn't a conversation I want to have in front of my people, he decided.

'May I approach you?' he called.

She considered, then called, 'Ae – that is "Yes".'

He gave Jesco a wink. 'Cover me.'

'Sure . . . *Rat Weer.*'

Raythe snorted and descended, once again warning his people not to shoot anyone without his express command. Then he clambered over the barricade and walked out onto the span, feeling very exposed.

The woman came to meet him. Up close she was surprisingly young, a portrait of vitality, with an expressive face.

I wonder what kind of legend I've stepped out of in her people's mythology?

'What's your name?' he asked.

She cocked her head, listening to her familiar, a lizard sitting on her shoulder, then said, 'My name is Rima.'

'I'm Raythe Vyre,' he said, emphasising the pronunciation. 'How can you know Magnian?'

'This is not "Magnian" we speak, but Gengo,' Rima replied slowly. 'It was the use-tongue of the Aldar Kingdoms. It is not our first tongue, but we have preserved knowledge of it, and mahotsu-kai like me learn it.'

Raythe felt his wonder deepen. 'Then "Gengo" has become Magnian . . . Incredible.'

'Ae. When I heard your daughter speak, at first I did not realise it was the same tongue, for her pronunciation is strange. But I have communed with my familiar since then, and attuned to your accents. Hence, we are speaking now.'

Raythe frowned at that: Cognatus could obey simple, well-drilled instructions, but not of the subtlety required to learn a language.

This Rima is young, but she's got real skill, he realised.

He had a million questions, but one burning need, and that was to secure his people's position. To that end, he put aside the mysteries and said, 'I seek a truce.'

She shook her head. 'The city is tapu. Leave it, and we can discuss truces.'

'Tapu?' It wasn't a Magnian word.

She conferred with her familiar, then clarified, 'This word *tapu* comes from our main tongue – "Reo". Tapu means sacred and forbidden.'

Two languages . . . He was getting the impression that these were a people with two identities, one, the warrior culture; the other that of the silk and masks. Servants and masters? And they clearly recalled the Aldar.

He was careful to conceal his growing unease and awe. 'We're not leaving,' he said firmly. 'I wish to speak with your leader.'

'She who leads us is Shiazar, Great Queen of Earthly Paradise, Guardian of Death's Threshold, Empress of the Tangato and Serene Divinity of Light. You are not worthy to meet with her.'

Raythe doubted that even the Emperor of Bolgravia claimed so many titles. 'I am Lord Raythe Vyre, Earl of Anshelm. I have met with rulers of larger nations than your own. I will speak with your queen.'

'We have your daughter,' Rima pointed out. 'You do not set the terms.'

'The life of one does not override the needs of the many. Do not threaten her.'

Rima mellowed her tone. 'Your daughter is not threatened. My tribe have adopted her.'

Raythe was momentarily stunned. 'She's on a leash at the feet of your Empress.'

'No unknown may bear weapons before the throne, and magic is a weapon. The cord resists sorcery. It is necessary for any unproven sorcerer who goes before our Queen.'

Raythe was impressed: such artefacts took skill to make. *They might have primitive weapons, but that doesn't mean their sorcery will be backward,* he reminded himself. 'Release her, and we can talk.'

Rima shook her head. 'A sorcerer is sacred and must serve Her Serene Majesty. She will learn our ways and live as one of us.'

'No, she will not.'

'The alternate was to put her to death. Would you prefer we had done so?'

'I warn you –'

'Do not "warn",' Rima said sharply. 'You have come as thieves to a sacred place. Go home, never return, and give thanks that your daughter's service has obtained this for you. You have three days.'

With that, Rima turned on her heel and walked gracefully away as if three dozen flintlocks weren't trained on her back – although Raythe suspected she didn't know what a flintlock was. He replayed her words in his mind, thinking about what they revealed about her and her people.

'Wait,' he called.

She turned, head held high. 'Yes?'

'Was my daughter alone?'

The girl pulled a thoughtful face, then said, 'Her husband is with her. He is also safe.'

Husband? Well, Zar wouldn't claim to be married without reasons.

Keeping his face impassive, he asked instead, 'What is required for me to meet Queen Shiazar?'

Rima considered. 'Her desire to meet you. Perhaps it may occur.' She turned once again and strutted away.

'She's quite a woman,' Foaley breathed when Raythe got back to the barricade.

'Rather wonderful,' Jesco agreed admiringly.

Raythe stared after her as the men on the walls and below began to relax and chatter. 'Right,' he said eventually, 'we need a leaders' meeting. Cal, take charge here.'

After Foaley had saluted offhandedly and sauntered away, Jesco dropped his voice and said, 'Raythe, Elgus Rhamp tried to change sides last night, then covered it up when the Bolgravian attack failed. You've got to deal with him, once and for all.'

Raythe shook his head. 'It'll have to keep for now. We need every man, and if I turn on Elgus, his men will defend him. But I will act, I promise, when the time is right.'

Sir Elgus Rhamp stared along the bridge, quietly simmering. He should never have joined this cursed expedition. *I should've knifed Vyre and claimed the bounty instead.*

The dream that had lured him was now right here: Rath Argentium, and above it a rock so riddled with istariol that it floated, a miraculous place indeed.

But this expedition has cost me two of my sons – maybe three, 'cause no one knows where Banno is – and it'll probably be the death of me.

His two lieutenants, grey-bearded, calculating Crowfoot and swarthy, belligerent Bloody Thom, joined him. Raythe Vyre wanted a meeting, but he needed their thoughts before that. He found a secluded court-yard and waved his seconds in.

'How're the lads?' he asked the pair, once he'd assured himself they were alone.

'Their heads are spinning,' Crowfoot replied. 'Floating castles, lost tribes, Aldar ruins? It's like we've fallen off the edge of the world.'

'But most of all, the lads don' know what side we're on,' Bloody Thom added. 'Last night, we were about to help the damned Bolgies, then we kragged 'em instead. Deo knows we hate those bastards, but Vyre needs to go down – so damned right our heads are spinning.'

That was fair. Changing sides twice in one night was a first for them, but it'd been a crazy situation, and as it turned out, he'd made the right choice.

'You were there: Jesco Duretto and his lot had the Bolgies cold – and then those savages hit their rear. If I hadn't two-stepped us out, we'd have gone down with them.'

'You didn't know that was coming, Elgus,' Crowfoot replied. 'You made that call purely on gut.'

'And my gut got it right,' Elgus boasted, slapping his ample girth. 'Sometimes it ain't the logic but the *feel*, and that attack din't feel right. Vyre's people had the high ground and the Bolgies wanted *us* to charge into their guns. I pivoted, and I was right to.'

Bloody Thom got it, he could see. He understood that while large bat-tles were decided by numbers and firepower, skirmishes like last night got settled by luck and cosmic energy. And three times now, Vyre had led his caravan safely out of the empire's jaws.

The gods are with him, my Pa would've said.

Focusing on Crowfoot, who was all about numbers and tactics, Elgus said, 'Vyre has the upper hand, and Duretto suspects us. We play along and wait our moment.'

'Elgus, even if that Bolgrav force was wiped out, they must've told their superiors where they were going,' Crowfoot replied. 'They'll be back and we need to be gone – with a shitload of istariol – before they do.'

'Maybe, but it's just as likely that Bolgrav force was operating on their own. Who's to know if they left adequate directions? Verdessa's a new settlement and things are loose in such places. And in case you've not noticed, there's an army of savages out there,' he replied. 'Until we know more, we play along. Got it?'

Both of his lieutenants grumbled into their beards, but at last they grunted assent.

'Look, I'm chewed up over it too,' he told them. 'But I'll see us right. I always have.'

With that, he headed for Vyre's meeting, readying the lies he'd need to hide what he'd done last night. But his thoughts constantly returned to his one remaining son.

Banno was last seen with Zarelda Vyre and she's a prisoner – so where's my boy?

'Well?' Crowfoot growled.

Bloody Thom hunched over, seething. 'Elgus is deluding himself. I reckon we've got two, maybe three months before the empire returns. By then, we've gotta be gone.'

Crowfoot considered. 'Aye, a month for anyone who escaped to reach Rodonoi, a month to get their shit together and muster, then a month to get back here. Three months.'

Thom leaned in and murmured, 'You reckon he's still got the balls for this?'

'I don't know,' Crowfoot admitted, and that was painful to say. They'd all been through so much together, all the chaos of the imperial conquests and the rebellions. 'He's got to assert himself with Vyre or that slimy Otravian will sell us all out, you watch.' He enumerated their enemies, finger by finger. 'Jesco Duretto. Vidar Vidarsson. Kemara Solus. Mater Varahana. Cal Foaley. Vyre himself. Six backs, six knives.'

'Aye. And maybe seven, if Elgus don't see us right,' Thom growled.

2

Prisoners of the Tangato

Hour by hour, the day passed. Zarelda Vyre's knees first ached, then degenerated into throbbing agony, while the Tangato queen sat above her, masked and draped in silk, a regal doll who never moved. Her courtiers fluttered about the throne, elaborately accoutred and alien in their masks. At one point, Rima went across the bridge. When she returned, she held a whispered conference with Hetaru, the ancient sorcerer, after which he spoke to a masked woman who whispered in the Empress' ear.

And the massed Tangato warriors waited patiently.

Please, Father, she thought, *I beg you, get me out of here.*

Yet again, she tested her bonds, but the leash round her neck was strong, and it had a binding effect on her praxis. Adefar was inside her, translating if she asked, but when she tried to burn the leash away, the spell fizzed out like a candle thrown into water.

All the while, the Tangato men sang in their sonorous voices, alternately martial and aggressive, then sorrowful. But then it began to rain, the first cold drops on her skin making her shiver, then the skies wept, as grey clouds swirled in, almost concealing the impossible floating fortress above the city.

In moments she was soaked.

Men came running in and held giant woven fans over the Queen's head while they lifted her throne – with her still sitting on it – and manhandled it into her palanquin. Then Rima darted in, her feather cloak streaming with rain, plucked the leash from its ground peg and wrapped it round her arm before hauling Zar to her feet, having to support her when her knees screamed and refused to bear her.

She commandeered a warrior's cloak and draped it over Zar's shoulders, saying in accented Magnian, 'Come, we return to the village.'

Their initial conversations had been held with Rima's familiar intermediating – a sophisticated use of a familiar; Zar hadn't thought them to be so capable. But that morning, Rima had arrived speaking Magnian, saying she'd now realised that Zar's language was the same as Gengo, an archaic language her people used in ceremony. It was a remarkable thing, and a real relief to be able to communicate at all.

Zar looked around to see the massive Tangato force, two thousand men at least, were on the move, trotting east towards the low hills that divided this place from their village. Even though she was being led away from her own people, right now all she wanted was to be out of this freezing rain and reunited with Banno.

She made it half a mile before her legs cramped up and she fell, howling in pain, and this time Rima had some men hoist her into a roofed palanquin that appeared from Deo knew where.

The rocking of the conveyance had her asleep in seconds.

When Zar woke after what felt like seconds, the rain still fell down, reducing the ground to thick mud, and the palanquin was being lowered. Four strong young warriors were chuckling over her, and when one offered her a hand, she wasn't too proud to accept.

Rima appeared, her black hair soaked flat and her cloak turned inside out to protect the feathers, revealing the lining to be some kind of hide. They were amongst a sea of pole-houses made of wood with timber-slatted roofs and huge, dramatic red-daubed gables and ridges, many carved with dragons or demonic faces. Wooden walkways ran between gardens and bigger buildings – communal halls or temples, maybe – dotted amidst the hundreds of smaller dwellings, and smoke rose from every chimney. Brown-skinned Tangato were everywhere, the bedraggled warriors being greeted by women in colourful gowns. They all had facial tattoos and mostly dark brown eyes, peering curiously at Zar as she was lowered.

All she'd seen last night was the odd fire and silhouettes; now she realised that had she seen the village in daylight, she'd have had a completely different impression of these people. *This place is properly old*, she realised, *the way things at home in Otravia are old.*

Rima helped her up the steps into a tidy little house and even in her exhausted state, Zar could see it was beautifully constructed, with whitewashed, well-sealed outer walls and a carved doorframe stained red. Inside, the wooden walls were polished. There were carved pillars, like the pou-mahi poles they'd seen in the countryside, intricately detailed. Everything screamed of craftsmanship and house-pride.

A young girl had pots of something simmering on a fire burning in a central pit. There were mats on the ground and blankets of hide and feathers, and against the walls were stacked crockery, cooking implements, clothing, footwear and more blankets. While Rima wrung out her hair in the doorway, Zar collapsed onto a floor-mat beside the fire.

'Where's Banno?' she asked.

'Next house,' Rima replied calmly. She dismissed the young girl and once they were alone, she removed Zar's leash, then called Adefar and somehow *sucked* the little familiar into a jade pendant around her neck.

'Hey, give him back!' Zar gasped – she'd never seen such a thing. To be stripped of her familiar, and therefore her access to magic, was terrifying.

'To remove temptation,' the young Tangato sorceress replied. 'Prove your loyalty and it will be returned.'

Zar jabbed a finger to her own newly tattooed chin. 'You brand me like a slave, then speak of *loyalty*?' But when Rima didn't rise to her anger, she sagged again, exhausted.

At least we can talk, she thought numbly. It was still stunning to think that after five hundred years of separation, she and Rima shared the same language, although with hugely different accents and some vocabulary mismatches.

'Where's Banno?' she asked again.

'Your husband is in the next house, recovering.'

Zar had lied about being married to Banno, but it was possibly the only reason he'd not been killed already. If she didn't warn him, the deception would unravel. 'May I see him?'

'Of course,' Rima replied, as she shrugged off her cloak. 'First, you need to understand your situation. You are accepted here as a mahotsu-kai – your word is "sorcerer" – and you are free to be with your husband. Should you leave us without permission, or turn against us, then your husband must die.'

'Then we're both prisoners!'

'No, you are both Tangato now: you, because you are a sacred mahotsu-kai; he, because he is your husband. No other foreigner would be treated so generously.'

From what Zar had seen, what 'mahotsu-kai' really meant was 'mizra-witch', for that was what Rima and her master Hetaru were surely using. Zar had heard them speak Aldar words – *mizra* words – to their familiars, and that was terrifying.

But they didn't want to kill her right now, and her father was still alive, so knowing that, her duty was clear. *I have to survive and learn about these people. Father will come for me.*

That thought gave her heart, and when Rima ladled stew into a wooden carved bowl and handed it to her, Zar found she was ravenous – she'd not eaten since midday yesterday. There was no cutlery, but she followed Rima's example, rolling the meat and vegetables in the rice, then eating with her fingers. The stew was gently spiced, nourishing and tasty – and gone in moments. She was beginning to feel just a little more human.

'You have suffered today, but you stayed strong,' Rima praised. 'Hetaru was proud of your demeanour.'

Zar didn't care in the least about their approval. She was exhausted, but she had some urgent questions she needed to ask, starting with, 'Who are you people?'

'We are the Tangato,' Rima answered proudly, 'and these lands are our fenua – our home. But who are you?'

Dear Gerda, Zar thought, realising how much they had to catch up on. She'd never been the most academic of students, but she tried to summarise five hundred years of history. 'When the Mizra Wars triggered the Ice Age, people fled to the equator, where there is no ice—'

'What is "equator"?'

'It's the band around the middle of our world that's free of ice,' Zar replied. 'How can you not know? You're only three weeks' walk from Verdessa and the sea!'

'Truly? Long ago, we sent explorers, but few returned and those who did found only ice. We believe – *believed* – that we were the last people left alive.'

Zar swallowed. 'There's millions of us.'

Rima's whole demeanour changed to something like dread. *'Millions?'*

Is this something I could exploit? Zar wondered. But the warmth, the food in her belly and her exhaustion were making her yawn, despite her amazement. 'Please can I see Banno?' she begged. *Before I collapse.*

Rima immediately understood. 'Of course. We can talk more tomorrow.'

Zar sagged in relief: she felt like she was falling into a pit, overloaded with shock and trauma. She needed to reassure herself that Banno was alive, and then she needed to sleep.

Rima helped her to get up and led her through the rain to a neighbouring house. When Rima went to enter first, Zar dared to pull her back. 'I need to see him alone.'

Rima hesitated, then said, 'Of course. How long have you been married?'

Worried that she was trying to catch her out, Zar answered, 'Not long,' hoping nothing Banno had said contradicted that. *If they realise we're not married, they might kill him.*

Rima patted the pendant containing Adefar. 'I'll look after your friend, I promise.'

Zar's hackles rose, but sensibly, she restrained her temper. *They tattooed me like a branded cow and they've stolen my familiar. I can't fight her, not now . . . but I will, when the time is right.*

So she turned, glowering, and entered the pole-house.

Zar knew something was wrong the moment she walked through the doorway, for Banno was lying on his side, cradling his head and moaning. She flew to his side and kneeling on the mat beside his thin mattress, she took his hands. For all he was sweating profusely, his fingers were cold to the touch. He barely responded to her presence.

She'd seen this before. 'Rima,' she called over her shoulder. 'Rima!'

The Tangato girl appeared in the doorway. 'What is it?'

'Look at him!' Zar yelped in fright. She grasped Banno's face and pulled up his eyelids, but even then he couldn't focus on her. 'I helped the doctors during the wars – head injuries like this can kill.'

Rima wavered. 'This is known . . . our men sometimes have such head injuries, but seldom does it kill.'

'You hit him—'

'He used his weapon on me! What was I meant to do?'

Banno had levelled his gun at Rima, but she'd battered it aside as it discharged, then crashed her wooden club into his skull. She doubted Rima had realised what the flintlock was, or how close she'd come to death. But she did look genuinely distraught.

'Help me get him closer to the fire,' Zar said, trying to remember what the army surgeons had done in such cases.

They mostly hacked off shattered limbs and cauterised stumps, then moved on, leaving the nurses to do what they could, even though they were mostly just camp followers, with their babies squalling a few feet away. She remembered the way the blood had pooled in lakes and the grisly piles of severed limbs, and how everyone had been screaming at once . . .

It had taken her two years to push those memories away, but now they had come back in visceral force. Fighting for calm, she pulled Banno closer to the fire, saying, 'More blankets, and cold water. Dear Gerda, help me.'

Rima shot away, returning with a pile of blankets, a pail of water and another woman to help make him more comfortable.

But by dawn, Banno had slipped into unconsciousness.

Raythe looked round the solidly built house, which they'd found some four blocks behind the gatehouse. There was an intact stone table in the downstairs room, though no usable chairs, but it would do as his office and meeting room for now. Everyone had arrived, all save Vidar Vidarsson, who was still unconscious from the wounds he'd taken saving Raythe's life the previous night. Mater Varahana, Jesco Duretto, Kemara Solus and Sir Elgus Rhamp were sipping from water flasks, all wishing it was wine – but water was their friend right now, for when the heavy rain poured down, the Tangato tribesmen had all marched away.

'After all that song and dance, a little rain puts them off?' Elgus chuckled. 'Wait 'til we give them some musketry. They'll run for a week.'

'Somehow, I doubt it,' Raythe answered, wondering how far he could trust Rhamp. Jesco was convinced the Pelarian had changed sides the previous night and Raythe believed him.

But he'd be mad to try anything now.

Mater Varahana looked exhausted. She'd spent the night at Vidar's bedside, helping Kemara keep him alive, but she'd found five minutes to shave her head again. Priestesses did it to reject vanity, but Raythe was pretty sure she kept it up because it suited her.

Kemara looked utterly spent too, but in her case, it was the result of the extreme sorcery they'd performed the previous night, followed by hours more tending the wounded. Raythe was amazed she was still conscious.

'So, what's our situation?' Varahana asked, not looking at Elgus.

Raythe gave them the rundown: apart from Banno and Zar, everyone else was accounted for. All known entrances to the city were under watch, and there was good news about provisions, for the ruins were stuffed with surprising quantities of wild food, including some chicken-like birds Foaley's hunters had found which would provide them with meat. The ivy-like vines everywhere were woody enough to burn for cooking, and there were plenty of buildings intact enough to provide shelter.

'This city was abandoned, but it was never plundered,' Raythe told them. 'Valuables were removed, but there are the remains of furniture and crockery everywhere. The decay is from time and weather.'

'Why is it empty at all?' Elgus wondered. 'This is an istariol mine of unsurpassed capacity, judging by that damned floating rock, not to mention it was the seat of the Aldar God-Kings – so why are those primitives out there, not in here?'

'The messenger of the Tangato called it "tapu" – it means "sacred and forbidden". So basically, these Tangato have banned themselves from the city for religious reasons.'

'That's crazy,' Jesco remarked.

'Is it?' Varahana asked. 'The Mizra Wars destroyed the Aldar and brought about an Ice Age that would have destroyed the Tangato too if they hadn't been on an istariol motherlode. So it's not really surprising they'd make this place forbidden ground.'

'But they could have conquered the world,' Elgus said incredulously.

'But as far as they knew, there was no world left,' Raythe replied. 'Surrounded by ice, with no one but themselves to fight, and knowing what war could do? I'm not surprised they rejected it.'

'They're living heirlooms of another age,' Varahana marvelled. 'If I could study them, I'd forego all the istariol in the world.'

'Fine, Mater, I'll take your share.' Elgus guffawed.

The priestess rounded on him. 'I'm sure you would – just as you'd take the Emperor of Bolgravia's coin. I heard what went on in your tent, Sir Elgus.'

The Pelarian knight snorted dismissively. 'What you heard was the sound of a fish biting a hook. I played that Bolgrav komandir like a fat trout, led him onto our guns and cut him down from behind.' He pulled out a Bolgravian sabre, the hilt and scabbard studded with semi-precious stones, from beneath his cloak. 'I took his sword from his dead hand, right after taking his head from his shoulders.' He glared at Varahana and drawled, 'You're welcome.'

'You laid a bet either way,' said Jesco.

'You weren't there.'

'No, I was aiming my flintlock into the enemy lines and seeing your men among them.'

'Mmm. Brilliant, eh?' Elgus looked around defiantly. 'I got our arses out of the fire.'

Raythe had to restrain himself from punching the knight in his large belly, because he was almost positive that Rhamp had intended betraying them before getting cold feet. But they were in no position to have this out, so yet again, he would have to accept Rhamp's word.

The man's got the survival instincts of a damned rat.

'I think we need each other more than ever,' he said, looking firmly at Jesco and then Varahana. 'Let the results speak for themselves: the Bolgravians have been eliminated and a traitor has been unmasked.'

'Traitor?' Elgus asked. 'What traitor?'

'Moss Trimble – the sailor we saved from the shipwreck back in Verdessa? His real name is Toran Zorne and he is a Ramkiseri agent. Or rather, *was*. Kemara and I killed him.'

Or so I pray.

He had to assume Zorne was dead, but with a Ramkiseri, one could never be wholly sure. The Bolgravian secret service agents were notoriously hard to kill, and famously dedicated to their service.

'There's a Ramkiseri on your trail?' Rhamp grunted, looking at him like he had leprosy.

'Aye, but he's gone. My point is, we're all in this together. Let's work as one and let the past lie.'

Jesco and Varahana scowled, but grudgingly agreed. Kemara was looking as if the only thing that mattered right now was sleep. 'So what now?' she yawned.

They all looked at Raythe.

'Now? We secure our position, restock and explore. We need to dig up as much istariol as we can carry while we're finding a way out of this corner we've painted ourselves into. Even if all the Bolgies here perished in the massacre, there may well be more coming. We've got three or four months, I'd guess, to make this trek worthwhile.'

'My lads fought hard for this,' Elgus growled. 'We want to see the rewards.'

'We've *all* fought hard and we *all* want to reap the rewards,' Raythe replied, restraining his temper, 'but I doubt the Tangato are going to just let us out. We have a three-day truce, so I'll try and get us more time, but let's not forget: they have my daughter and I want her back.'

Elgus jabbed a finger at him. 'You'll not surrender our position for the sake of one girl.'

Varahana stared at him in shock. 'You're unbelievable –'

'Your own son's with her,' Jesco reminded him, his handsome features contorted with disgust. 'You'll be wanting to abandon him too? Was losing your other two not enough?'

Elgus stood and reached for the hilt of the Bolgravian sword lying on the table, but Raythe interposed himself, facing Elgus. 'That's enough! I can assure you all that I will not be exchanging the futures of three hundred people for Banno and Zar. But I'll do all I can to get them back.'

And as for him being her 'husband', I'm not saying a word.

Elgus harrumphed, but he backed down. 'Fair enough.'

Neither Jesco nor Varahana were happy, but both acquiesced.

Raythe directed their minds to other matters. 'Let's get properly settled in. We'll establish patrols and perimeter guards, set up foraging and scouting.' He turned to Elgus. 'There will be no more segregation. Every patrol will be a mix of your people and Teshveld folk. Create a roster and show me. And we need to find a strong, well-fortified building somewhere behind us to be our fall-back position if we're breached.'

'Sure, I'll do that,' Elgus replied. 'What about the istariol?'

'Istariol mines are dangerous: the dust is flammable and the istariol itself is complicated to deal with, so I'll need to explore the mines first.' He wondered if he dared risk Kemara in such a place. *No, not when she's really a mizra-wielder. Who knows how her magic would react to it?* 'I'll take Jesco with me – he can pull me out if anything goes wrong.'

No one looked overly happy at that, especially Jesco, who hated confined spaces. But having been awake for the best part of two days, they were all exhausted and anxious to avoid another flare-up.

With that decided, the meeting ended. Elgus was the first to leave, and Kemara, yawning widely, got up to follow suit. Jesco gave her a courtly bow. 'I'll see you to your bed, Mistress Kemara. I'm not sure you'll make it alone.'

'I'll be fine,' Kemara mumbled defensively, but then she softened and said, 'but you can see me to my door.'

Jesco, who everyone knew was a man's man, took her arm and they departed, leaving Raythe with Varahana. They'd known each other for years and he was something of a secret admirer. Her delicate bone structure and high cheekbones were accentuated by her bald scalp, which didn't in any way diminish her elegant beauty.

'Jesco and Kemara . . . the unlikely couple?' he suggested drily.

'I very much doubt it, unless she's had a ball sack in her skirts all along,' the priestess laughed. 'And I've been wondering – without any proof – if she's more interested in women than men.'

Raythe felt his eyes bulged. *'Kemara?'*

'It's not illegal, darling. Well, it wasn't . . .'

Before the Bolgravian invasions, the reigning Liberali party in Otravia had decriminalised homosexuality; that was what had brought Jesco to Otravia in the first place. Those laws had been among the first repealed by the Bolgravians' puppet government.

'None of our business, I guess,' Raythe muttered. He didn't care to recall trying to kiss Kemara the night they reached the city and being punched in the face for his trouble. They'd just shared a sorcerous meld, which had lowered their inhibitions momentarily – *very* momentarily, in her case. He changed the subject. 'Anyway, how's Vidar?'

'Kemara says it's looking hopeful. The shot punctured a lung, but it missed his heart. She says that if the great shaggy bear hadn't tried to fight on, he'd already be out of danger.'

'Bearskins are known for their resilience,' Raythe commented. 'His battling on saved us.'

'He's a good man.'

'And an ardent admirer of certain priestesses,' he teased.

Varahana didn't smile. 'Please Raythe. I've taken vows, and in any case, there's only one man who's ever really tempted me.' She looked him in the eye. 'But you were still in love with your ex-wife.'

'Aye, and I still am,' he sighed, although he was no longer sure that was true.

Mirella was married to Luc Mandaryke now, a man he'd sworn to kill for betraying Otravia to the Bolgravians. Raythe had been forced to run, and he'd taken Zarelda with him. *Does Mirella hate me for taking our daughter?* he wondered. *Is she a pawn of the Bolgravians, or resisting from within?* Her actions and motives remained a mystery to him.

Varahana's quicksilver mind had evidently moved on. 'Water,' she remarked airily. 'That's what's been puzzling me.'

He frowned. 'Water? It's a clear liquid, falls from the sky and gets everywhere.'

'Yes, dear,' she said. 'Think: we're standing at the confluence of two rivers which encircle this island, then flow south and freeze again. This patch of habitable land is miles inside the permanently frozen Iceheart. So where does the water come from – and where does it all go?'

He yawned widely. 'Intriguing, I grant you, but too much for my poor brain just now. Ask me tomorrow.' Then he grinned and added, 'Or better yet, work it out yourself and tell me.'

She laughed. 'Get some rest, Raythe dear, you've earned it.'

Once she was gone, all his levity ebbed away.

I lost my wife and now I've lost my daughter. Dear Gerda, give me the strength to get them both back . . .

35

3

Rath Argentium

Kemara Solus peeled the bandage from Fossy Vardoe's chest, making him inhale sharply. 'Kragga mor,' he groaned, as she revealed the wound, caked in blood and seeping. 'Gentle, woman!'

'Harden up,' she told him.

He patted his groin. 'You climb up on this, I'll show you how hard I can get.'

'Fossy – that's short for "Foreskin", right?' Kemara said slyly. 'You'll never get so lucky.'

His actual name was Fosterkin, a traditional orphan's name, but he was twenty-something now, and grown into a rugged trapper who'd taken a bayonet in the chest during the Bolgravian attack.

The other patients chuckled, while Vardoe scowled, not liking his new nickname one bit.

Kemara sniffed the wound and smelling no corruption, slathered on one of her herbal ointments. 'It'll keep weeping for a while yet, but it needs some air, so we'll keep the dressing light from now on.'

'Thank kragging Gerda.'

She patted his arm, and went on to Vidar, her toughest case. The Norgan bearskin's breath rattled wetly with each inhalation and he still hadn't regained consciousness, but hopefully that was down to the oil of kermeer she'd dabbed under his nose, to keep him under. His hairy chest rose and fell in fits and jerks, but each passing hour, she felt more confident.

Any other man would have died, she reflected, but the durability of a bearskin, who became something both more and less than a man when enraged, was legendary.

Thinking of that reminded her that she and Raythe had survived worse on the bridge the previous night, thanks to their familiars, who clearly didn't like to let their masters die. *Although quite who's the master in my case, I'm not sure.*

She changed Vidar's dressings, then waved in Sister Bea, one of the mousy Sisters of Gerda who were helping her to tend her patients. 'All yours, Sister Bea. I need a break.'

She left the improvised sick-ward and wandered out to the street, thinking about those fresh scars on her chest. Buramanaka had pulled her back from death itself after Toran Zorne, who'd gulled her with his lies, had all but murdered her.

How can I ever trust anyone again after that? she wondered.

Trust in me, that's all you need, Buramanaka whispered into her mind. His scarlet gigaku mask was concealed in her gear, but he was always with her. If she closed her eyes, she could see him: a demon-masked man who moved like a panther – if man he was: she'd taken the mask from the grave of an Aldar, after all. She found herself wondering if that decision would damn her for eternity.

She thrust that thought aside and looked round her in awe. This vast, ruined city had swallowed all three hundred of them without a trace. Vines covered many of the buildings near the river, but they were less pervasive upslope. Some of the houses were several storeys high; taller than any she'd seen. She couldn't begin to calculate how many people might have lived here – and were they all Aldar, or human as well? What had the living city been like?

Do you really want to know? Buramanaka whispered. *I can show you.*

No, she replied. *Leave me alone.* She was grateful that he'd pulled her back from oblivion, but she feared being little more than his glove puppet. *I just want to get out alive, with wealth enough to live free.*

She couldn't escape the thought that they'd walked into something far bigger than all of them, like ants crawling onto an anvil just as the hammer fell, so maybe that particular dream was already dead.

'Why did you pick me?' Jesco grumbled. 'You know I hate going underground.'

Raythe grinned. 'Perhaps I enjoy torturing you?'

'Knew it.'

'Don't worry, O mighty Blademaster,' he laughed. 'I'll protect you from the dark.'

Raythe had seen Jesco face cannons and muskets without flinching, but he was claustrophobic, so bringing him here was cruel. But with Vidar down, Jesco was the only one with the skills and true loyalty for the task.

They'd descended into the crater left by the immense rock now floating above them. At the bottom was a shallow, slimy pool overflowing into a ditch that drained away underground. But the mine entrance Raythe had chosen was only halfway down and he was hoping to find the mine itself dry. It hadn't smelled damp, and Cognatus had found no obstructions.

He glanced up at the rock above. The underside was jagged, where it had torn away from the earth, and water dripped constantly – seepage from recent rain, he guessed. 'I'm really hoping that thing doesn't fall to earth while we're underground,' he commented wryly.

Jesco flinched. 'Thanks for adding that to my burdens!'

At the mine entrance, Raythe conjured a globe of light and sent it bobbing ahead, illuminating a rough-hewn tunnel descending into the rock. 'Cover your nose and mouth with a scarf,' he told Jesco. 'Istariol dust can be hallucinatory.'

'Oooh, fun!' Jesco winked, but he covered up before following the conjured light down into the cold dark. The outside noises faded until all they could hear was the echo of their footsteps and voices and the trickle of water through stone. The tunnel was gently curved, and wide enough for half a dozen men to walk abreast. Every so often they came upon a narrow side entrance, but each had a symbol etched above that Cognatus, Raythe's familiar, translated as *Closed*.

'I wish the whole damned place was closed,' Jesco muttered.

'No, you don't – if it was, we'd have come all this way for nothing.'

Jesco jabbed a finger skywards. 'I bet there's plenty of istariol in that floating rock.'

'We'd still have to dig it out.' Raythe chuckled. 'And if we mined it all, it wouldn't float – imagine being on it when it fell.'

Jesco went pale. 'Dear Gerda, I never thought of that. I've heard some horror tales about mining for istariol—'

'Ignore them,' Raythe interrupted. 'People have been mining istariol for many centuries. The accidents are the exceptions – that's why people talk about them.'

'They say giant shingar lizards ten times the size of a man nest underground. And the ghosts of the Aldar haunt istariol mines, devouring men's souls, and—'

'If that were true, the Bolgies wouldn't have any istariol, would they? Relax, my friend, the only ones down here are us. And look – this one's still marked as open,' he added, as they reached a flat chamber with a hole descending into the ground. The wooden scaffolding around it looked rotten, although somewhat drier than he'd expected. There was no way to climb down that he could see.

Examining the shaft, he felt a subtle warmth. 'Feel that?' he told Jesco, who was peering cautiously into the square-cut tube of emptiness at their feet. 'It might indicate istariol.'

Jesco shuddered. 'It's hideous, Raythe. And look, the lift's gone. It's all been for nothing. What a shame, let's go.'

Raythe clapped him on the shoulder. 'Nice try – but we've got carpenters who can fix up a new lift. And we've seen flax; Varahana says it'll make excellent rope.' He looked round the chamber and spied another tunnel, this one apparently running level, heading in a northeasterly direction. 'Let's see what else we can find down here.'

A little way down the new tunnel they found another closed shaft, and then another, this one with the entire lift mechanism completely rotted away, and there the cross-tunnel ended. The only other way out was up, via another sloping tunnel, this one more naturally formed.

'This tunnel stinks,' Jesco muttered. 'There's something up there . . . maybe stone spiders? They infest istariol mines, everyone knows that. Let's go back the way we came.'

'There's no such thing as stone spiders,' Raythe told him. 'You need to stop listening to Norrin Harper's ghost stories.'

'Sweet boy,' Jesco sighed. 'So sensitive and pretty.'

Raythe started up the exit-tunnel and winced. There was a definite animal smell here. If a predator was still lurking, preying on the animals living in the city above, then it was his duty to find it before he could ask his miners to work down here. 'You loaded?' he asked.

'Aye,' Jesco gulped. 'What is it? A murk-goblin? Or maybe a nashrek?'

'Deo's Balls, Jesco,' Raythe snorted. He conjured brighter light and inside him Cognatus quivered in anticipation. 'It's probably nothing.'

'You could return tomorrow with someone else,' Jesco suggested. 'Let's go back the way we came—'

'Shh . . .' Raythe, told him, listening hard. Something above had scraped, like claws on stone. 'Be ready,' he breathed, drawing his blade.

Jesco swore and stepped in front. 'I'm supposed to be protecting you,' he said, without a trace of irony. 'Shine that light of yours ahead of us, about ten feet, and bring it back to cover us if anything happens.'

Raythe did as he was bid, sending the light bobbling ahead. This tunnel sloped sharply upwards, with occasional stairs. A central gutter flowed with water, maybe the result of the previous day's rain.

The smell of animal was growing stronger. When Jesco pointed out some rotting reptile skin, Raythe whispered, 'Praesemino, Cognatus,' and his familiar went into full readiness. It could be sustained for only a few moments, but something was imminent. 'Be ready, Jes.'

The stink of dung and waste as they entered the chamber was almost too much to bear. In the centre was a pile of gnawed bones – phorus birds, Raythe guessed – then he realised that the rock floor was strewn with other detritus too: human skulls and bones. He picked a couple up to examine.

'This was a mass grave,' he choked out, gagging from the stench, 'maybe from the Mizra Wars. These are *very* old.'

Then something moved in the gloom above and he flashed his praxis-light into the stalactites that knifed down from above.

Perhaps if he hadn't, they'd have been allowed to pass . . .

The light glinted off many eyes, looking down from cracks and perches in the broken ceiling: at least half a dozen shingar lizards, with bodies larger than a man, angrily waving tails as long again. Vicious claws gripped their precarious perches.

Then the one above him screeched through jagged teeth, and dropped –

– but the praxis-light thrust up into its face dazzled the lizard and jaws that could have crushed Raythe's head instead clashed together just inches away as Jesco hauled him aside and thrust his sword up into the reptile. He impaled the skull, then wrenched the blade free to let the shingar fall, striking the rocky ground and thrashing out its death-throes among the bones. But already, more were shrieking as they dropped to the ground, ready to fight for their territory.

Gripping their swords, the two men waded forward, driving sharp steel up and under long, snapping jaws, slicing through throats and severing neck-bones, until Raythe shouted, '*Impetu, nunc* –' He thrust out his hand and Cognatus sent a wave of force into the faces of the beasts. The five remaining went reeling back, two slamming into the far wall and rebounding, stunned.

'*Iterus!*' Raythe shouted – *Again!* – and another wave of power smashed into the beasts, then he and Jesco advanced, dodging the reflexive death-bites of those they'd slain.

There were now just three left, and two of them were dazed. They died a moment later as Jesco punched his blade through one while

Raythe beheaded the other with a swing of his heavy falchion. The last tried to run, but Raythe blasted it with flame, then Jesco's blade trans-fixed the chest.

'Nice,' Raythe panted at Jesco. 'Good to see you're over being afraid of the dark.'

'Oh, no I'm not,' the Shadran answered. 'But I'm fine with enemies I can see.'

Raythe sent his light bouncing back up to the ceiling so they could examine each crevice. In one they found a dozen tiny lizards, no more than a foot long, clinging to a narrow ledge, hissing down at them. 'You know,' Raythe said, 'I've heard of people taking baby shingars as pets.'

'What, so they can get eaten by them a few years later?'

'Mostly they just escape the moment they can.'

Jesco scowled up at the baby lizards. 'Kill the little snits, please. No good'll come of letting them live down here, not if we have to work these mines.'

'Fair enough. They do grow fast, and we've got our own children to worry over.' Grimly, Raythe traced Ignus, the fire rune, before sum-moning Cognatus again. '*Cognatus – fumus, nunc.*'

A torrent of smoke shot from his hand and the lizards began to drop, gasping for breath and helpless. Jesco deftly impaled each. 'Necessary, I suppose,' he grunted, before adopting a damsel-swooning pose. 'Take me away from all this death or I shall faint away . . .'

Raythe laughed. 'Ah, ever the deadly warrior with the heart of gold.'

'And don't forget my delicate constitution. This place *stinks*.' Jesco turned to go, then stopped suddenly and picked up something from among the bones. He rubbed it on this thigh, then held up a ring, gleaming gold where he'd scraped off some of the muck. 'Ha! My score.' He pocketed it, then started. 'Did you hear that?'

'What?' Raythe had heard nothing.

'It was like a woman's sigh.'

'When have you ever made a woman sigh?'

'Ha! I know my way around women. Where I grew up, men are

expected to be stud-bulls, and Deo help you if you don't conform. So yeah, I can show anyone a good time, but only in Otravia was I free to be me.' He looked round, puzzled. 'There it is again!'

'You're imagining it,' Raythe said, after listening. 'I've heard nothing, and let's not forget I'm the one with the sorcerer's senses.'

Jesco looked unconvinced, but he wasn't keen to remain in this foetid chamber and there were several more shafts they needed to explore.

They found no more shingar nests, to Raythe's relief; the lizards had large territories, and they'd not found a lot of game in the city, so there was a good chance this nest was the only one in the mine.

'It's an excellent start,' Raythe remarked, as a welcome gleam of daylight appeared ahead, 'but until we've checked them all, the other mines are out of bounds.'

'And this one?'

'I'll set Relf Turner and Lynd Borger to repairing those lift platforms. We need to find out if there's any istariol as soon as possible – worst case, it's been mined out, so we'll need to find a new place to dig.'

Jesco frowned. 'So what exactly would happen if we mined the istariol in that floating rock?'

'If we took all of it, the rock would fall from the sky,' Raythe answered. 'But don't panic – it's only activated istariol that's able to defy gravity like that, and it's quite distinctive. As long as we don't touch the activated stuff, it's fine. People could live up there with no problems – well, apart from the lack of water, food and so on.'

'You're not selling it. I'm even less inclined to go up there than down these holes.'

They emerged from the mine a hundred yards from where they'd entered and Jesco struck a triumphant pose. 'Once more, we conquer the eternal darkness!'

'My hero,' Raythe chuckled, gazing up at the chained rock above. The shifting clouds above gave the eerie illusion that it was moving. Then they heard footfalls and saw a runner pelting down the path towards them: young Ando Borger, the blacksmith's son.

43

'Lord Vyre,' the boy called, 'that native woman's shown up at the bridge again. She's asking for you.'

Crowfoot watched Raythe Vyre and Jesco Duretto emerge a few hundred feet below, a quarter-turn around the crater from where he was leaning on an ancient wall. Someone had met them – Ando Borger, by the look.

'I wonder what they found?' he said to Bloody Thom.

They were outside a big house, as much castle as anything, that they'd identified as the best fall-back position if the tribesmen broke in – although if that happened, they were all screwed anyway. They were calling it Rim House, because it was built right at the edge of the crater.

'The Aldar lords can't have been terribly trusting,' Bloody Thom remarked, patting the bastion-thick walls.

Crowfoot was gazing up at the chained rock, wondering about the castle up there. He wasn't so jaded that he couldn't appreciate the miraculous view. *What a place . . .*

As an added bonus, the afternoon sun was pleasantly warming, which his ageing joints appreciated. Time was a slow killer, and this place was too damned cold.

'Let's find that damned istariol, then go somewhere warm,' he muttered.

Bloody Thom's eyes were fixed on Raythe Vyre. 'If my eyesight were better, I'd shoot that prick from here.'

'Ain't a flintlock in the empire can shoot that far with any accuracy,' Crowfoot snorted. 'I wonder what they found in those mines?'

'If it weren't blood-dust, we oughtta cut their throats.'

'And if it was, we will,' Crowfoot answered.

'Elgus won't sanction another strike,' Thom griped. 'He ain't got the balls any more. An' if'n he does get hisself killed, no way will we have his boy Banno as the new company leader. Those natives'll be doing us a big old favour if they butcher him.' He laughed. 'Prob'ly have already, and et his lily-coloured liver.'

'Aye,' Crowfoot agreed, 'when the time comes, you take over. I'll be yer second.'

'You telling me you don't want command?' Thom snorted.

'Number Two has always been good enough for me,' Crowfoot replied, absolutely honestly. 'I'm not one for giving speeches or prancing round wind-bagging with nobs, and that's Deo's own truth. Right now, my eyes are on the istariol – I get me enough to retire on, I'm out. Getting too old for this shit anyway.'

'Nah, never happen – this is the only life you know.'

'You watch me. Gimme a villa on the Shadran coast and some willing fanny and I'll be out and laughing.' Crowfoot knew the very mansion he wanted. Right now it belonged to an earl, but gold would deal with that. 'Whereas you, Thom – you don't know how to stop.'

In a rare moment of introspection, Bloody Thom nodded. 'Aye, yer probably right. I'll be doing this 'til the Pitlord calls me name.'

'Then we're agreed: you'll lead and I'll back you . . . if *tragedy* should strike.'

Thom licked his lips. 'Yeah, and who knows when things might get *tragic*.'

It was Rima the Mizra-Witch again, Raythe noted as he walked onto the bridge, conscious of the two dozen flintlocks trained on the span.

Or on my back . . . half those men answer to Rhamp.

Putting aside that uncomfortable thought, he walked towards the distant silhouette waiting at the apex of the span. There was someone else with her, a male warrior. It was possible that they were both mizra-witches and this was a trap, but he wasn't getting that sense.

They've been on their own here for a long time, on a very small patch of land, he reflected. *That says they've got restraint, and probably an honour code. So* he was cautiously optimistic there'd be fair play. When he got within twenty paces, he called, 'Rima?'

'Koni'ka,' she greeted, before switching to Magnian and introducing the burly warrior with her. 'This is Kamo, warleader of our tribe.'

Kamo looked to be in his thirties, and had a certain barbaric majesty: he was bare-chested beneath his cloak of hide and feathers, wearing only a beaded kilt, with a sword in a shoulder scabbard and a bronze-tipped spear-club cradled in his grip. As he got closer, Raythe realised it wasn't just a spear; the haft was shaped for striking. An unusual weapon.

'You asked for me?' he called.

'I wish to tell you that Shiazar, the Light of Heaven, has granted you audience,' Rima announced. 'She will bless you with her presence here, when the sun is highest, two days from now. In the intervening time you may not pollute yourself with a woman, nor partake of sacred spirits.'

Raythe snorted. 'Chance would be a fine thing.'

Rima frowned. 'What say you?'

'I'm sorry, it was a jest. We have no sacred liquor and my wife is lost to me.'

Surprisingly, the girl said, 'We grieve for you,' in tones that actually sounded sincere.

'It was some time ago,' Raythe answered. *But damn, it still hurts.* He peered at Rima curiously and asked one of his more burning questions. 'Do you use mizra or praxis?'

She looked puzzled, before replying, 'We wield maho,' which Cognatus translated as 'magic'. Then her face wrinkled up in concern and she said, 'There's another thing. Your daughter's husband has a head injury. He is unconscious. We have tried our best, but he hasn't recovered. Zarelda says you have a healer among you. Queen Shiazar, as a gesture of trust, has agreed to return him to you.'

Raythe swallowed. *Three days he's been unconscious? That's not good.* 'Kemara may be able to help, but he should have been returned sooner.'

Rima sounded genuinely concerned. 'He was recovering. But now he cannot wake.'

Raythe peered towards the far end of the bridge, where a contingent of men had gathered. They were bearing a stretcher. Then his heart thumped as he saw Zar among them. 'Then please, bring him – and may I speak with my daughter?'

'If you swear that you will not seek to abduct her.'

He was momentarily taken aback, not thinking his request would be agreed. 'Of course,' he lied.

Rima's expression suggested she saw through him, but she signalled and the Tangato came forward: two men, apparently unarmed, bearing Banno's stretcher. Zar walked with them, holding Banno's hand.

He called to the gatehouse, 'Cal, Jesco, come up. Just the two of you. No weapons.'

Jesco and Foaley trotted out and once the situation had been explained, took over the stretcher, while Zar rushed to his arms, tears streaming down her face. For a long moment all they could do was cling to each other.

Finally, he brushed his tears away, clasped her shoulders and pushed her to arm's length to look at her – and saw what had been done to her face. On her chin was a curved pattern etched in dark ink, still raw and scabbed: a primitive kind of tattoo carved into her skin. Body tattoos were rare in Magnia except among sailors – to brand another human on the face was beyond the pale.

'What have they done to you?' He looked angrily at Rima.

Zar realised his mood and grabbed at him. 'No, Father,' she whispered.

'I'll burn their faces off,' he snarled, while Cognatus shrilled angrily.

'Please—' She suppressed a sob as she explained, 'Rima says it was necessary to protect me – by identifying me as a sorcerer. They see it as doing me an honour.'

'Explain.'

Hurriedly, she told him everything: how she and Banno had been captured, but treated fairly – so far, at least. Rima and her master, a man called Hetaru, were mizra-witches – she called them mahotsu-kai – and that as a sorcerer she'd been deemed sacred and adopted into the tribe. 'Otherwise they'd have killed us both.'

'And what's this about "marriage"?'

'To save Banno, I had to pretend we were married.' Her eyes trailed to the stretcher, now held by Jesco and Cal. The Tangato had drawn back watchfully, but Rima and Kamo were clearly alert for trouble.

No problem, I'll handle them, Raythe thought grimly. 'Are you all right?'

'I'm fine,' she insisted. 'It's scary at times, but I'm okay. Rima's look-ing after me. She says they will train me in their kind of magic.'

'In the mizra? But . . . *how*?'

'I don't know. But they're scarily good.' She leaned forward and whis-pered, 'Rima can pull my familiar out of my body and trap it in her necklace. He's in there, right now. So I *can't* leave them yet.'

Raythe glanced at the wedge-shaped jade pendant dangling in the Tangato girl's cleavage. 'Then I'll be sure to take it off her corpse. Listen, here's what we'll do –'

'Dad–'

'On three, you run, and I'll take them down–'

'No,' Zar said firmly, 'I'm not going. I need to learn how they're so strong – and I gave my word.'

When he realised she was serious, he rocked back on his heels. 'Of course. We'll think of another way. Where are you being held?'

She described a village in the next valley, behind the low brown hills to the east. 'There's maybe three, four thousand people there – and they aren't primitive, Dad. They have communal bathhouses and ablu-tions blocks and temples to the Aldar gods, and many beautiful things. There are allied tribes in the neighbouring valleys too. They thought they were alone in the world,' she added, sounding amazed. 'Rima says that their ancestors served the Aldar, but after the Mizra Wars, they abandoned the city. They live off the land.'

'It's hard to believe,' Raythe mused, 'but it must be true.' Reluctantly, he put on hold his half-formed plans to regain his daughter. 'Stay safe, and keep your wits about you. I'll find a way to get you out. I'm a praxis sorcerer – they'll not stop me.'

She looked up at him, her eyes rimmed with tears, and smiled bravely. 'Can I just say goodbye to Banno?' she asked. Rima nodded, and she went to the stretcher, ignoring Jesco's murmured exhortation to make a run for it, and hugged the unconscious man.

'Kemara will get him right,' Raythe muttered awkwardly. Banno wasn't worthy of her, in his view, but he knew enough not to voice that opinion.

Zar hugged him again, shaking with grief.

'You are finished?' Rima called, her tone of voice suggesting she'd guessed much of their conversation. 'Queen Shiazar is merciful. Your daughter is one of us now.'

'She belongs with me.'

Rima put a hand on her shapely hip. 'With daughters, there must always be a letting-go. She belongs to her husband, and to my tribe, now. She will find happiness in her new life.'

'She was abducted and is being held against her will. But I'll meet with your queen.'

With that he let Zar go and made a little hand gesture: they'd learned the Vossland finger-cants together during Colfar's rebellion. *Patience,* he sent, and she replied, *I'll be ready.* With that, Raythe nodded to Rima and Kamo, then turned on his heels and marched back to his own people with all the dignity an Otravian lord should display, Jesco and Cal bearing Banno along behind him.

Elgus Rhamp was waiting; now he bent over his son's stretcher, anguish on his face. He barked, 'Get him to Mistress Kemara, *quickly,* krag it! That's my son you've got there –'

'Kemara will heal him, I'm sure,' Raythe assured him, but Rhamp, muttering doubtfully, was already hurrying after the stretcher.

'How's Zar?' Jesco asked.

'Fine,' Raythe answered, gazing across the ravine at the retreating Tangato. 'They didn't have to return the Rhamp boy. I think they place great stock in honour.'

'Good,' Jesco drawled. 'That'll make them easier to screw over.'

4

On the Bridge

After a shaky, tear-filled afternoon, Zarelda pulled herself together and resolved to learn as much as she could of these people.

Before Father destroys them . . .

She started by allowing Rima to draw her out into village life in the coming days. Each morning she sat at the door of her tiny pole-house, people-watching, trying to accustom herself to Tangato ways. This morning she cradled a gift from Rima, a carved stone sphere she could cup in her palm, a marvel of intricate carving: the outer layer was a bird like an eagle, with fiery wings and tail, and coiled around it, a long serpent or dragon. There were at least six inner balls of latticed stone which could be moved, aligned and realigned, revealing a different design every time. It had been carved from a single piece of stone like marble, Rima said, using delicate tools like toothpicks. It was called a gong-qui, which translated as puzzle ball.

It's like the Tangato themselves, Zar thought. *It has mysteries within secrets, it's beautifully crafted and quite alien.*

All the houses in the village – or town, for it wasn't a small place – had their own little garden containing both flowers and root crops, fertilised, she found out, with a mix of bodily, garden and food wastes. The maize and wheat fields and cultivated orchards surrounding the village were a collective responsibility. Hunting parties went out daily, but meat was a minor part of their diet, judging by the food she was given.

The biggest difference was that so much of Tangato life was communal. The houses were just a place to sleep; the real living went on in shared facilities like the big cooking halls and ablution blocks, which had a sophisticated plumbing system piping hot water straight from the ground. She glimpsed humming looms in the big work-houses turning out the most beautiful, lustrous fabric; according to Rima, the Wakatoa and Puketapu tribes to the north had large silkworm plantations, and centuries of cloth-making skills. And there were potters, carpenters and blacksmiths, too, all plying their trades as well – or better – than anything she'd seen at home in Magnia, which was food for thought.

But it was in the people that Zar saw the biggest contrasts. There seemed to be two opposing traditions: an earthy warrior culture which saw the men trooping round bare-chested, usually on their way to or from weapons-drills in the fields outside the village; while domestically she saw elaborate politeness, careful grooming and a reverence for tradition. Everything took place under the light-handed supervision of the queen's masked female courtiers, and there wasn't the atmosphere of oppression she'd felt in imperial lands, where nobles and officials hammered people the way smiths tempered iron, bending them into the shapes they wanted: men as serfs and women as docile breeders.

She soon became fascinated, especially with the facial tattooing. It was almost as if the ordinary Tangato were etching versions of the Aldar masks onto their own faces. Now she had time to study them, she could see that they were all unique and often delicately beautiful.

Yesterday, Rima had taken Zar to the temple, where the shaven-haired priests and priestesses – kannushi, Rima called them – were chanting prayers. The large wooden building had carvings of the twelve Aldar Gods and incense burned continuously, but unlike a Deist Church in Magnia, there were no sermons telling people what they ought to be doing.

Another difference Zar had noticed was how they were for ever touching each other. They always had their arms round each other's shoulders or held hands, male or female, young or old. A Deist priestess would be having apoplexy, raging about sin and perversion. She wondered how Mater Varahana would cope with it . . . and decided she'd be fine, being a free spirit herself.

Rima appeared, swaying along the path through the close-packed pole-houses, her elaborate beaded flax shirt and striking feather cloak standing out among the beautifully embroidered clothes worn by the villagers. The young sorceress was popular among the ordinary people here, and given respect beyond her years.

'Are you ready?' Rima called. 'Hetaru wishes to see you perform.'

'Perform? What do you mean?' Zar exclaimed.

'Nothing difficult,' Rima replied. 'He wishes to see you conjure so that he can gauge your training. First we wash, for Hetaru is a sacred mahotsu-kai and you must purify. Second, you haven't washed since you got here, and heaven knows how long before that.' She sniffed loudly, as if to make the point.

Zar blushed, but she followed Rima meekly to the nearest bath-house, which was on stilts over the stream flowing north towards Rath Argentium. It was surrounded by a beautiful garden, dotted with stat-ues of the Aldar gods, and there were dozens of Tangato women bathing in four large pools. Each was a different temperature, Rima told her, before upbraiding her fellow tribeswomen in her own tongue as every face turned to stare at Zar.

Rima reverted to Magnian. 'I told them you are a sacred mahotsu-kai and to show respect.'

Rima clearly had authority here, because the women went back to their own washing. Zar disrobed, feeling extraordinarily self-conscious beside the lithely muscular Rima, whose back and buttocks were cov-ered in swirling black tattoos. With her bone-white skin, apart from her tanned forearms and neck, Zar felt like a snowman.

Rima handed her a cake of smooth white stone. 'Use this to clean yourself.'

Zar accepted it in puzzlement, then realised that it was volcanic pumice which had been soaked in something scented that lathered in water. She followed Rima into one of the pools of warm water and immersed herself before rubbing the pumice gently over her skin, replacing the dirt with a pleasant herbal smell. 'It's like soap,' she commented, but Rima's familiar didn't know the word.

'Wash, hurry,' Rima urged. 'Hetaru awaits.'

When Zar returned to the seating area, she found her own clothing gone and a Tangato bodice and skirt left in their place. 'No way!' she exclaimed.

'One, your clothes are filthy; two, you are a Tangato mahotsu-kai now and must dress according to tradition. Wear them, or go naked. Up to you.'

Zar gave Rima a filthy look, but seeing no way out of this trap, she dressed awkwardly, feeling dreadfully exposed. 'I don't like this,' she complained.

'You're one of us now, and need to respect our ways,' Rima said, fiddling with Zar's blonde hair. 'Too short for braids,' she *tsked*.

She called out something to a girl nearby, who shyly handed over a dyed woven flax headband. Rima fitted it, tucking Zar's hair behind her ears and studied her, muttering about her 'looking like a child', before shrugging. 'So, when we enter the lodge, you will kneel, touch your forehead to the floor and then sit cross-legged. Make sure the skirt covers your puta.' She patted the front of Zar's beaded flax kilt. 'Understand?'

Puta – my fanny? Zar blushed. 'Fine – just keep your hands to yourself.'

Rima snorted with amusement. 'Come.'

They left the bath-house and wound through the village to a lodge on the edge – there were no fortifications, not even wooden fences like those surrounding the hill-fort outside the ruined city. The lodge had an entrance arch of carved red pou-mahi, decorated with depictions of dragons coiled around each other. Rima led her into a long hall lit by firelight and dropped to her knees on the matted floor. Zar followed suit, then they went to the central firepit, where a lively fire burned.

They sat, and Zar discovered the strings of beads forming her skirt had an irritating way of parting in embarrassing places, exposing her white thighs, while the strands she sat on were digging into her, but she tried to keep her dignity as she faced the man on the other side of the fire.

She'd met Hetaru the morning after her capture; he'd tattooed her chin, claiming her for the tribe. He had a shock of white hair and a thin white beard which didn't quite conceal his own facial tattoos. He was naked to the waist and completely covered in tribal markings. She'd seen sailors' tattoos in Magnia, but none like these, actually carved into the flesh. The ridges of scarring on her own chin were still tender to the touch.

As soon as I can find a healer who can do it, I'll have them removed, she'd resolved. But for now, she was all deference, because Hetaru held her life in his hands. He had a gentle, jovial face, with a glint of mischief in his eyes; of all the Tangato she'd met, he was the least intimidating.

He signed to Rima, who drew out the jade pendant and chanted some words. Suddenly Adefar emerged and exploded back into Zar's body, and for a moment she was subsumed in love and fear as the little spirit tried to express its joy and terror. It took a few moments before she could think straight.

Then Hetaru spoke in stilted Magnian, 'By what name are you known, young one?'

'Zarelda.'

'Za-rel-da? An awkward name; but we will manage. How do you fare?'

She fixed him with a defiant look. 'You've taken me prisoner, stolen my familiar and *branded* me.'

'What is "branded"?'

She tapped her still-painful chin scars. 'This. In my home, we mark cattle for ownership, but never people.'

'Ah, I see. Then I apologise for the need, but you had to be claimed, or Kamo would have killed your man and taken you as a trophy-woman.'

Zar's heart thumped, but she refused to appear grateful. 'That doesn't make it right.'

'It is a mark of great honour,' Rima lectured. 'You are mahotsu-kai. All give you respect.'

'They stare at me all the time,' Zar retorted.

'Because you are different,' Hetaru answered, in his gentle voice. 'Just as you stare at us.'

Maybe, Zar acknowledged inwardly. 'I can't be one of you. I'm an Otravian.'

Hetaru frowned again. 'What is "Otravian"? My turehu does not know this word.'

The context told Zar that "turehu" his familiar. 'It means I am from Otravia.'

'Otravia is your tribe?'

Close enough. 'Yes.'

'But one can be both of a tribe and a mahotsu-kai,' Rima said. 'And a mahotsu-kai belongs to all tribes. We walk freely in all of the Fenua Tangato.'

'Where I come from there's always war, and sorcerers are the deadliest weapons.'

Hetaru looked genuinely pained at the notion, and Rima was visibly appalled. 'You are at perpetual war?' she exclaimed. 'How can you survive like that?'

'Did your people learn nothing from the Mizra Wars?' Hetaru added.

'It's how the world is,' Zar replied, remembering a conversation when she was eight and her father had tried to explain the Bolgravian conquests to her. *Nations contend*, he'd said. *Even in peacetime, we fight by other means: trade, exploration, industry. Just watch the way animals compete – even plants fight for light and water. It's not how I like things to be, but the truth is that life is an eternal struggle.*

When she related this, the reaction of these two Tangato made her feel like she was lecturing her six-year-old self – and somewhat ashamed, as if she were the barbarian here.

'War must be a last resort,' Rima told her, her lively face distressed.

'But your people make war! You wiped out those Bolgravians – you're planning to kill my people.'

'But both parties violated tapu land. We warned your "Bolgravians", but they attacked us. And we will not assail your father's people until all else fails,' Hetaru replied. 'War is waste. Were your people of our kind, we would resolve this through champions.'

'What?'

'Where there is a dispute between tribes, champions contend,' Rima replied, once again puzzled by her ignorance.

'That's bizarre,' Zar replied. 'That's not war, that's . . . sport.'

'I do not know this word.'

'Games. Play.'

'Play? Champions often die,' Rima retorted.

'Often?' Zar snorted. *Deo, but these people are innocents.* 'Don't try taking on my people – we'll slaughter you. You don't even know what war is, but we sure as the Pit do.'

Hetaru, looking bewildered by her aggression, changed the subject. 'Show me your maho.'

Adefar translated maho as magic. Zar gathered herself, commanding Adefar to draw in energy and be ready, wondering for an instant if she could fight their way out of here. But she discarded the idea, remembering how casually Rima had pulled the familiar out of her and imprisoned it. Instead, she focused on tracing the rune of fire, *Ignus*, and said, *'Adefar, praesemino . . . nunc.'*

A tongue of flame appeared above the palm of her right hand, just as she wished.

'Ah,' Hetaru breathed. 'Now, douse the hearth fire.'

That required water. Zar looked round, saw a gourd and told Adefar, *'Submergo quod flamma, nunc,'* while tracing Aqua, the rune of water. A spray of water rose from the gourd and flowed towards the fire.

But Hetaru had begun muttering and gesturing, and suddenly a barrier was imposed. Zar pushed against it, snapping, *'Adefar, plus amplius! Fortior!'* She felt her familiar batter against the old man's barrier, but it never moved. *'Iterum! Fortior!'* Again, stronger.

Still she barely pushed him back – then Hetaru said, *'Shiimasu yameru!'*

and suddenly they were contending mind to mind for control of her familiar, and she didn't know how to fight it. *'Adefar, saru!'* the suddenly scary old man rumbled, and Adefar quailed, then vanished.

Her dousing spell collapsed and she saw the pendant around Rima's neck pulse. Adefar was trapped in there again. 'Hey,' she blurted, 'give him back!'

But the two Tangato weren't listening. They leaned together, muttering in their own tongue, until Rima turned back to her and said, 'Hetaru is concerned at your weakness.'

Zar flushed. She was breathless from the exertion, but the old man wasn't even panting. 'I'm new to this,' she admitted. 'It's only been two months since I gained the praxis.'

'The problem is your turehu,' Hetaru replied. 'What is wrong with him?'

'There's *nothing* wrong with him,' Zar cried, deeply hurt. 'He's mine – he's perfect! Give him back.'

Rima shook her head. 'He is malformed. No turehu should be so weak.'

'There's nothing wrong with him,' Zar retorted. 'Father would have said.'

Hetaru held out his hand to Rima, who removed the pendant and handed it to him. He examined it, his eyes gleaming unnaturally as he brought his magical sight to bear, then he said, 'Ah,' and turned to Zar. 'He is not whole, but he can be. We can make him stronger, restore him to what he should be.'

'No – *leave him alone!*' Zar exclaimed.

'It will make you more powerful,' Rima told her. 'Much stronger.'

'But Father says I'm *fine*. I'm as strong as I should be at this stage,' Zar protested.

'Then your father is equally ignorant,' Hetaru replied.

'What would you know?' she snapped. 'No one reaches their full magical strength until they're adults. We grow with our familiars – everyone knows this!'

'I reached my full magical strength this year,' Rima snorted, nose in the air.

'No boasting, child,' Hetaru chided her. 'Strength is not maturity.'

'Yeah,' Zar glowered.

Rima looked abashed at Hetaru's comment, but snorted at Zar's.

Hetaru lifted the jade pendant again. He chanted over it, gesturing with his fingers, and a heartbeat pulse began. Then to Zar's surprise, he handed it to her. 'Wear it,' he told her.

She peered into the depths of the jade. 'What have you done?'

'The pendant is pounamu, a sacred stone. I have set a calling over it to bring your Adefar strength. Wear it, and do not be afraid. When we are done, your maho will be made whole.'

Zar suddenly was afraid, but she didn't want to look like a coward in front of Rima, so she slid it over her head, even as a new hope dawned.

Maybe he's right and Adefar and I will truly grow stronger. She pictured herself, performing feats even her father baulked at. *And once I'm stronger, I can escape.*

Much later, she lay alone in her pole-house while the village settled in for the evening. Distant song was resonating from some far-off communal hall. She'd been invited to go with Rima to the gathering, but she hadn't felt ready for that. Too many eyes.

Sleep was slow in coming, because she couldn't resist picking at the spells in the jade pendant. Even though she couldn't get Adefar out, he was aware of her, and chafing at this imprisonment.

I could escape without using magic, she thought. *Then Father could release Adefar . . .*

But somehow, that felt like the wrong move when the Tangato sorcerers had shown trust in her – and anyway, she doubted she'd get away; they'd posted sentries around the village, because of her people.

Somewhat relieved that she wasn't going to try it, she fell into a restless slumber, tossing and turning . . .

. . . until some hours later she woke, shivering in the cold, hearing a snuffling sound. She went to the entrance, pulling aside the canvas flap that served as a door in keeping out the cold and giving her a measure of privacy. Kneeling in the doorway, she peered up. The sky was clear and the planetary rings bright as a scimitar, cleaving the night in two. Stars glittered on either side, diamonds in the firmament.

There was a small creature beside one of the poles of her house, cocking a leg and pissing. She smelled the unpleasant tang and hissed at it, but far from fleeing, it growled back – a reddish-brown fox cub with over-bright eyes . . . *'Adefar?'* she called.

. . . then she woke properly, alone inside her room, the Tangato settlement now silent.

She sat up, heart racing and thoughts muddled.

Just a dream . . .

The night she'd found Adefar, dozens of spirits had presented themselves, but she'd been told to wait until there were just two: one would be attuned to praxis, the other to mizra. She had chosen well: Adefar, who appeared to her as a brown fox cub, was perfect – while the other red cub had tried to bite her.

The fox cub in my dream wasn't Adefar, but his shadow twin . . .

Had Hetaru had summoned Adefar's dark shadow back? That opened up an uneasy line of thought: were the Tangato sorcerers really trying to help her? Or were they trying to turn her into a mizra-witch?

Raythe looked left and right before asking his companions, 'Are you ready?'

'Sure,' Jesco drawled, and Mater Varahana nodded distractedly. She was in her best robes, her freshly shaven scalp gleaming in the bright sunlight. Right now she was a bundle of nerves at the thought of the impending meeting with the Queen of the Tangato.

It was noon, the planetary rings a pale light arch against the brilliant blue skies, an echo of the bridge over the ravine. Behind them were armed men ready to leap into action if required, and Cal Foaley was returning from the apex of the bridge, where he'd met with Rima to ensure nothing was amiss; they'd been acting as go-betweens for the past two days.

'All clear,' Foaley said. 'Her Stroppiness says to bring a seat – just you, Raythe; mere attendants have to sit on mats or stand.'

'Suits me,' Jesco replied, although Varahana looked vexed.

'How's Vidar?' Raythe asked her.

'Recovering.'

'And Banno?'

'Still unconscious, but Kemara says she's eased the swelling in his head,' Varahana reported. 'She drilled a hole in his skull and drained the fluids – truly hideous, darling. But it does appear to have helped.'

'Trepanning, it's called,' Raythe said. 'I've had to do it myself, during the Rebellion.' He looked up as a burst of singing heralded activity at the far end of the bridge.

'That's the queen arriving,' Foaley reported, peering across the ravine.

'Gerda Alive, I'm nervous,' Varahana squeaked.

'You'll be fine,' Raythe told her. He looked about and spotted a small barrel. 'That'll do as a seat.' He went to pick it up, but Jesco got there first.

'Wouldn't do for our king to look like he's a servant,' the Shadran remarked.

Raythe led Jesco and Varahana out along the bridge, his full attention on the approaching Tangato party. Four muscular men carried the queen's palanquin shoulder-high. She wore regal blue silks embroidered with gold lace, and a blue mask of serenity decorated with silver stars. Once the conveyance was lowered to the ground, they removed the throne and placed it facing Raythe, unrolled a sitting mat for her attendants, then left.

Her companions were both male: one was Kamo, the burly, truculent warrior Raythe had met before, now clad in leather armour and carrying an elaborately carved Tangato spear-club. The other, a kindly-looking old man with white hair and a beard, was wearing a beaded kilt and a body-length cloak of feathers. Both men were heavily tattooed and carried themselves with lordly gravitas.

Raythe led his companions, chosen so that each party contained a fighting man, a sorcerer and a woman, to the appropriate spot, and Jesco set his barrel down opposite the queen's elaborately carved throne with its inlaid gems and padded cushion.

The contrast could not have been greater.

'Just who are the barbarians here?' Jesco murmured.

Beside them, Varahana was drinking in every detail.

The old man spoke first, addressing Raythe. 'I am Hetaru,' he said, in stilted Magnian, aided by his familiar. 'With me is Kamo, shoganai of the Hiriwa, which is our tribe.'

Raythe introduced Jesco as his own shoganai, or warleader, and Varahana as a priestess and advisor.

Hetaru bowed in thanks, then said, 'I now introduce Shiazar, Great Queen of Earthly Paradise, Guardian of Death's Threshold, Empress of the Tangato and Serene Divinity of Light. She speaks for the Voices of Heaven, and the Ancestors of All, her word is Law and her will is Fate.' He knelt and kissed the queen's slippered feet, before taking a seat cross-legged on the mat, facing Raythe. The warrior Kamo took up a more casual stance, leaning against the parapet of the bridge.

'I trust he doesn't expect us to kiss her dainties,' Jesco murmured. 'She's better dressed than you, mind.'

'You're just jealous that they're ruled by a queen,' Raythe replied.

'Oh, you're not so bad. Wouldn't kiss your boots, though.'

Shiazar made a graceful gesture and said something in a voice that had a strange cadence to it, rapid-fire and higher than sounded natural, then Hetaru translated. 'Queen Shiazar welcomes the foreign lord to the Fenua Tangato, her realm.'

All very polite, Raythe mused. He'd been wondering if she might be some kind of sorceress, but if so, her familiar wasn't apparent and her aura didn't indicate any powers. He wondered what her rule was based on.

'I am Raythe Vyre, once of Otravia,' he replied. 'I lead the travellers inside' – he looked up – 'what do you call this city?'

'We call it Kinji Haikyo, which means Forbidden Ruins. But before that, it was called Rath Argentium, and the castle above was known as Shiro Kamigami.'

Varahana positively quivered with excitement.

Hetaru went on, 'Among our people, it is customary before a debate to state the particular history that has brought us to the matter in dispute. In our case, it has been five hundred years since anyone has come to this place from outside. We must begin there.'

Varahana sucked in her breath. 'Oh yes,' she breathed.

What followed was a unique retelling of the Mizra Wars and thereafter. Raythe got the impression that Hetaru was having to cut down what was for him a beloved saga, usually related for entertainment and education, complete with artistic flourishes. But the tale that emerged was still incredible.

Five hundred years ago, as the Mizra Wars reached their dreadful, destructive climax, the Aldar faced an uprising among the people who served them. The destruction wrought by the wars had damaged the environment beyond repair: storms now raged uncontrollably, as did forest fires and plagues destroying crops and people. The tiny number of Aldar now remaining faced the hatred of those who had once loved them, and they underwent a schism, some Aldar siding with humanity against their kin.

The Aldar of Rath Argentium retreated to their mighty floating citadel, while the Tangato and their Aldar guardians besieged them, enduring rains of fire and death from above. Finally though, the citadel fell silent, and the Tangato realised that Tashvariel the Usurper and his court must be dead.

'*Tashvariel*,' Jesco and Varahana breathed in unison: the legendary brother and betrayer of Vashtariel, the last true God-King of the Aldar. 'So he truly dwelt here?'

'Tashvariel reigned for the entire decade of the Mizra Wars,' Hetaru replied. 'It is said he was driven mad, for the prize he most desired, his brother's wife Shameesta, fled him to be with her lover. Tashvariel recaptured her, raped and murdered her – and for that crime, the gods turned against him and his reign failed.'

That sounded like poetic nonsense to Raythe, but the wider tale intrigued him. 'Who defeated him?'

'A shoganakai – your word would be "Supreme General" – named Kohiro Buramanaka, and his Aldar mahotsu-kai followers.'

Raythe almost fell off his seat. *Buramanaka? Holy Gerda!* That was the name of the spirit Kemara used to access the mizra. 'What happened then?' he asked, trying to mask his shock.

'Before he committed suicide, Tashvariel resolved to end the world,' Hetaru replied. 'Using istariol, he and his sorcerers conjured the greatest storm ever created, which he called "Ago no Kori" – the Jaws of Ice. From north and south, two storms grew until they blacked out the sky, ravaging the land and then freezing it. Men fled, but the Ago no Kori met and closed tight. None survived.' Then he smiled wryly. 'Or so we believed.'

'Few enough did, of the millions who sought refuge,' Raythe told him.

'Ae, but here you are,' Hetaru said. 'Kiiyan is merciful.'

Kiiyan: the Aldar goddess of Mercy, Raythe remembered. 'How did you survive?'

'We realised there was nowhere to run, so we took shelter in the mines beneath the city. When the world froze, we endured, thanks to those Aldar who had sided with humanity. They, and the istariol here, created a small circle of warm, habitable land in the sea of ice.'

Varahana looked utterly rapt. 'What happened then?' she asked.

'It was realised that we could no longer live in the city,' Hetaru replied. 'The citadel above is under an interdict – none may enter it. Use of istariol became forbidden, lest it destroy us. All agreed this ruling, handed down by those Aldar who remained – all of them women. We evacuated the city and declared it tapu. It is that prohibition you have broken.'

'We weren't aware of it – all we sought was shelter from harm.'

'But you know now,' Hetaru remarked sharply, before resuming his tale. 'We believed ourselves the last people left alive and that knowledge has shaped us. Warfare was prohibited, with all disputes to be settled by debate, or at worst, trial of arms by chosen champions. Rulership was passed into the hands of the surviving Aldar women, because we knew that the old ways of ruling by force had to be abandoned.'

'How wonderful,' Varahana breathed.

'How did the men feel about that?' Raythe asked wryly.

'A few men of violent nature rebelled,' Hetaru replied. 'The champions of the first Queen – being her shoganai and her mahotsu-kai, my forerunner, and Kamo's – stood strong and prevailed, winning the love and loyalty of the people.'

Raythe shifted his gaze to the expressionless mask of Queen Shiazar, an impossible suspicion forming. 'Your Majesty, are you descended from the Aldar?' *If there were only females left, they must have bred with Tangato men . . .*

'Our Queen is indeed a direct descendant of one of Tashvariel's rebel Queens,' Hetaru answered for her.

Varahana gave a strangled squeak, blurting, 'Then Queen Shiazar –'

'Is part Aldar,' Hetaru confirmed.

All manners were forgotten – Raythe and his companions stared unashamedly at Shiazar's mask, wondering what lay behind it. Right now, he would have given everything he owned just to see.

'I think I'm going to faint,' Varahana murmured.

Raythe couldn't untie his tongue to reply in the light of such a revelation.

Fortunately, Hetaru hadn't finished his tale.

'So much was lost,' he was saying. 'Many crops and materials were devoured by the ice, and people with unique skills were now dead. Creatures we once knew were no more, and those left had to be preserved, so meat became a sacred delicacy. But gradually, things eased, and we have managed to preserve our tribe and our way of life down through the centuries,' he concluded proudly.

Raythe considered, then asked, 'How is it, after all this time, you have only just been found? You are only a few hundred miles north of the ocean and ice-free lands.

'Many have gone looking,' Hetaru replied. 'One great hero went all the way to where the sea had been – and found a frozen expanse. That was two centuries ago. From that, we concluded that we were alone.'

Verdessa was only uncovered relatively recently, Raythe mused. *That's what the explorers who passed through western Magnia said. It's plausible . . .*

'Have you changed, in all that time?' he asked, thinking of how Magnia had evolved, and what the scholars had to say about *progress* and *enlightenment,* about *technology* and *science* and *change.*

'We have not changed,' Hetaru replied proudly. 'We have remained the same.'

But people don't remain constant, Raythe reflected. In the desperate struggle to survive and prosper, people changed – all the time. 'Why do you think that that is?'

Hetaru had a lengthy exchange with his Queen. Her voice had a fluting, musical quality that was almost exaggeratedly feminine to Raythe's ears. He wondered how old she was.

Finally, Hetaru looked back at him and said, 'We were the last humans left alive. We were few, and grew fewer. Our land – a circle of life in a world of ice – gives us all we need. We have no need to change.'

Raythe bit his lip, for this didn't address his real question, but he turned to Varahana. 'What do you make of this, Vara?'

The priestess leaned in and murmured, 'Raythe, I'm a philosophic and general scholar, but I've studied a little into how societies develop. Remember the tales of how Magnian explorers found the Sheraic Isles in the far east? The islanders had only wood and stone tools, while we had guns and steel, and we all wondered how two societies could have developed so unequally. Some fools spoke of "racial superiority", but my professors concluded that progress requires certain factors: a growing population creating shortages and conflict; mineral wealth to be exploited and a dynamic society with opportunities for individuals to make their fortune. The Tangato don't seem to have those factors. The land provides enough food, they don't appear to mine, and from what Zarelda said, they have no money because they work communally, so individuals can't dominate. Moreover, they live in the shadow of destruction, and have a deep collective horror of that history.'

'But surely someone, somewhere would have wanted to do things better?'

'And would have no doubt been dissuaded. Look at their clothes, their weapons, their accoutrements: all of them are beautifully crafted, but old-fashioned and primitive to our eyes. These are signs of a society frozen in time.'

'I can't imagine that lack of curiosity and ambition.'

Varahana smiled. 'You were raised to privilege, educated and trained to excel, in a competitive world that venerates wealth and dominance. Whereas this is a small, precarious mini-world that has a horror of change, lest it rekindle that which destroyed them.'

'And it's ruled by a half-Aldar,' he breathed, glancing at the doll-like Shiazar in her elaborate silks and mask.

'Exactly; a rulership based on *preservation*, mandated by heaven and history, with no external threats to force them to progress. We have stepped onto the face of a stopped clock – and perhaps our presence here will start it ticking again.'

'The Magnians destroyed the tribes of the Sheriac Isles,' he noted. 'They were defeated, ravaged by plagues and the survivors enslaved.'

'Yes, they were.'

He swallowed. 'I do not wish us to be the harbingers of such a fate for the Tangato.'

'That's to your credit, but these things rarely end well,' Varahana replied gravely.

With that weighing on his mind, Raythe turned back to Hetaru and said, 'It is a miracle that you survived at all. So many things could have ended your culture – and your tribe.'

'Kiiyan was merciful,' Hetaru agreed. 'With the guidance of our wise Queens, we learned to embrace harmony, so that all might survive.

Gradually we prevailed, though we are still few, compared to the days before the Mizra Wars. We cannot outpace what the land provides sustainably, but we preserve the ancient skills and are at peace. Or we were, until you came.'

Raythe took a deep breath. His eyes were drawn again to Shiazar's mask, wondering about the woman behind it. The Aldar were said to be surpassingly beautiful, so that beside them the loveliest human was as if rendered in clay. And every one of them was said to be a mighty magician.

His thoughts looped back to the present. The Aldar used mizra, the most destructive form of magic known, and according to Zar, so did these Tangato sorcerers. How could they be the peace-loving people they professed to be when they cultivated such a power?

He wasn't sure how to pose that question, so he asked another: 'Is your history finished?'

The old mahotsu-kai opened both hands. 'Please, we are eager to hear your own story.'

'They're so genteel,' Jesco murmured. 'I kind of feel like an arsehole just for showing up.'

'I know what you mean,' Raythe confessed. 'But we didn't know they were here – and someone was always going to find them. They may not believe it, but they're lucky it was us, not a full Bolgravian regiment.'

'Ignoring the fact that we kind of brought one along with us,' Varahana noted.

'Stop being factual,' Raythe chuckled, then he raised his voice. 'Thank you for your tale, Hetaru. Now, let me tell you ours.' He went on to relate the hard years on the equatorial continents after the Ice Age brought life to its knees; then the rebirth of civilisation with the Magnians, and the recent Bolgravian conquests. It was, depressingly, a tale of constant war.

History is written blood, his childhood tutor used to say.

Then he related a little of his own tale: the flight from Otravia with his daughter; the failed rebellion; their life as fugitives. 'Finally, we found clues about a place where we might find istariol, to make better lives for ourselves. We came here, knowing nothing of your existence, but we were unknowingly pursued by soldiers of the Bolgravian Empire – they were the men in grey you fought a few days ago. I fear they will return – Bolgravians never give up.'

At this, the warleader Kamo spoke for the first time. 'Then we will kill them again.'

'You don't understand: that Bolgravian force was small and weakened – they were out of supplies, their commander and more than half their men were dead, and they were taken by surprise. The next battalion will be fully prepared. You won't stand a chance.'

He withheld any mention of modern weapons: the Bolgravians had been out of powder when they were wiped out, so the Tangato might not know about that crucial factor. Although he felt sorry for these people, he had to think of them as likely enemies.

The two Tangato men muttered a few words to each other in their own tongue, then both fell silent as the queen spoke to them. *I'm listening to a real Aldar – well, a half-Aldar,* Raythe thought. *It's almost worth the journey on its own.*

Finally, Hetaru said, 'These are the words of Shiazar, Sacred Queen of the Tangato: We come now to the matters between us. You are interlopers who have seized a place which is both sacred and forbidden, and also perilous. Your reasons are venal, and you have brought enemies and danger to us. We decree that you must leave the city without taking anything from it. You must return to your own land, where you will deny knowledge of us and prevent others from coming. It is the only honourable path for you.'

They listened in silence, and then Jesco muttered, 'That's not going to happen.'

Raythe turned to Varahana. 'What do you think, Mater?'

'Well, I think you're right: the Bolgies will come back with ten times the manpower and they'll enslave whoever they don't kill, mine this place to death, then turn it into a summer palace for their emperor.'

He nodded grimly. 'Absolutely – but that's out of our hands. It's shitty for these people, but it was bound to happen eventually. We've got to mine some istariol, fast as we can, rescue Zar, then slip away. I wish them luck with the Bolgies, but there's nothing we can do.'

The priestess sighed heavily. 'Sadly, I agree. But you can't tell them that.'

'I know.' He quickly reviewed his options, then turned back to the Tangato. 'Queen Shiazar, we came here as honest explorers, unaware of your presence. I've got a thousand men' – deliberately inflating his numbers – 'trapped in Rath Argentium, and we need to build up supplies for any return journey. That'll take weeks, not days.'

Especially as we've got some mining to do.

'As for the Bolgravians, they *will* return. Your people will either be enslaved or wiped out. The Bolgravians believe people with brown skins are "subhuman". And you, Queen Shiazar, they will capture and take back alive as an exhibit for their emperor: "The Last Aldar". He may even use you as a concubine, to amuse himself. That is the nature of these people.'

Hetaru and Kamo reacted in shock and then anger at his words. The war chief advanced a few steps, clearly offended, and Jesco swung into readiness.

'Easy, fella,' the Shadran breathed.

'Kamo,' Queen Shiazar herself said sharply.

The big Tangato didn't back down, facing up to Jesco just a few paces away, his long spear-club cradled with deceptive calm. The Shadran blade-master subtly shifted weight. Kamo snarled something in Tangato, which Hetaru translated as, 'Kamo wishes to duel your champion. He stakes temporary sovereignty over the city.'

'Sure,' Jesco drawled, his hand going to his sword hilt.

'No,' Raythe snapped. 'There will be no duel. I must confer with my advisors – and then there is the matter of my daughter. Until she's released, no one is going anywhere.'

Kamo said something derisive aimed at Jesco which Hetaru didn't translate.

The Shadran responded with a teasing smirk.

'Jesco,' Raythe warned, 'I don't want trouble here. Let him think what he will.'

'You're no fun, Raythe,' the Shadran said lightly. But he did take a step back, and honour satisfied, Kamo did the same, although they were still dangerously close.

'Queen Shiazar,' Raythe called, 'having champions duel as a method of settling disputes died out centuries ago. No one civilised does it any more.'

'Aye, we "civilised" people send thousands of soldiers to die instead,' Varahana murmured sarcastically.

Raythe ignored her. 'Majesty, might I propose that we extend our truce, so that I may confer with my people. Then we can meet again to agree the path forward?'

Hetaru consulted, then nodded. 'Three days.'

Already they give ground, Raythe noted. *They really don't want to fight.* 'Then we thank her Majesty,' he answered. 'Jesco, take another step back.'

Neither the Shadran or Kamo moved.

'Jesco.'

The blade-master half-turned – then for some reason decided he needed to make a point to Kamo, because he turned back suddenly.

What happened next defied sight: Kamo's spear-club spun in his hand and suddenly the thick haft was blurring towards Jesco's temple, cracking the swordsman across the brow before he could twist away, and then the big Tangato was leaping forward. Varahana gave a small squeal, as Raythe cried out, '*Cogna*–'

A moment later Kamo's weapon smashed into his midriff, he staggered and lost the spell he'd been trying for, the warrior's right foot swept his legs away and he slammed down on his back, winded.

The bronze spearhead poked him in the throat, not quite breaking the skin. 'Yurushite, no Joo?' Kamo rasped, preparing to ram the sharpened metal into Raythe's jugular.

'*Iie!*' Shiazar shrilled, stamping her right foot once. 'Kamo, yameru ima!'

Raythe saw the exact moment that Kamo decided to obey his Queen and *not* to kill him anyway. Instead he stepped back, twirling his weapon again with deft precision, fell into a crouch and poked his tongue out, first at Raythe and then Varahana. But he did back away, moving past Jesco to his Queen's side.

Raythe sucked in air. '*Cognatus, praesemino,*' he muttered, just in case, and clambered painfully to his feet, wincing at the agony in his belly. 'If he comes at us again, shoot him,' he told the priestess, who had a concealed pistol in her robes.

'I'm sorry,' he called deferentially. 'Jesco acted without sanction.'

Hetaru stood. 'The Queen will overlook this unfortunate incident. Consult with your people, then we will speak again in three days.'

Raythe thanked him, hoisted Jesco over his shoulder, then he and Varahana made an ignominious retreat. Halfway back, Jesco stirred, thankfully, but Raythe doubted he'd be fit to walk for a while. Varahana informed him that the Tangato hadn't moved, but the four palanquin bearers were jogging up to join them. By the time they'd reached the gatehouse, the Tangato Queen was being borne away.

Cal Foaley emerged. 'What happened? We saw a scuffle, but were too far away to intervene.'

'Just a misunderstanding,' Raythe answered, handing Jesco over. 'Take him to the infirmary, will you?' *Damned show-off nearly got us killed.* He pulled Varahana aside. 'Well? What do you think?'

'We met a half-Aldar!' she enthused. 'And their tale is incredible – a miracle.'

He enjoyed the way her love of learning overrode all other concerns. 'Ay, but we've only got three days to agree what we're going to do. We'd better call a meeting.'

5

Red Fox Cub

Zarelda jerked awake for the second time that night. It was the same dream: she was a little brown fox being stalked through a dark wood. Her hand sought the jade pendant around her throat and she felt Adefar's warm, adoring presence inside her. She'd been held in quasi-captivity for almost a week now; in a day, the latest truce would end.

Perhaps that's why I'm having nightmares?

She wondered again if she should have broken her vow and tried to escape, but realistically, it had never been possible. The Tangato didn't post guards, exactly, but she was never alone, except in here, and without access to her praxis-magic, she couldn't see a way out. It was wearing her down, especially as she worried constantly for Banno. Had Kemara been able to help him? Rima hadn't spoken to her father since, so there was no fresh news, and the uncertainty was a torment.

Dad will come for me, she reminded herself. *He always does.*

Another hour passed, then dawn's light crept through the canvas covering her doorway, so she gave up on sleep and went out, clad in just her Tangato bodice and skirt, some slippers and a hide blanket. The chill in the wind off the mountains made her breath steam.

Already, groups of Tangato were heading along the raised wooden walkways to the ablution blocks. She joined them, and after relieving herself in one of the semi-private cubicles, she was making for the nearest bath-house when a phorus bird emerged from a garden she was passing, towering over her and fixing her with a glaring eye.

Then she realised that Rima was riding it.

'Ah, Zarelda,' she said, 'have you washed yet?'

'No,' Zar replied, once she'd overcome the shock. 'Are you mad?'

Rima laughed. 'This bird is a "kikihana" in our tongue. Riding them is fun. Come, I know a good place on the river, perfect for bathing and totally private. The water there is *divine*.' She patted the space behind her on the bird's long back. 'Climb up.'

The phorus gave her a malevolent glare and Zar looked doubtful, but she was determined not to look timid before the Tangato girl. 'All right.'

Rima helped haul her up, ignoring the phorus squawking in annoyance, but when Rima clicked her tongue, it walked obediently through the waking village. A few young men called out jests or taunts as they passed, and Rima replied in caustic tones.

Then they reached the fields and the giant bird burst into a loping run. Zar clung to Rima's back, the bird's spine mashing her nethers uncomfortably, but the woods flew by in an exhilarating way. 'How do you control it?' she shouted in Rima's ear.

'Through the maho,' Rima answered, whooping as the bird blurred through a clearing, then bringing it to a halt beside a steaming rivulet. 'Here we are!'

The phorus screeched at them as they dismounted, eyeballing them menacingly, but Rima just snickered and sent it off. 'They're all mad,' she laughed, throwing an arm round Zar's shoulder, 'but such fun to ride.'

'Yes, it was fun,' Zar replied, removing her arm. 'But our people don't touch strangers.'

'Strangers?' Rima gave her a puzzled look. 'You are the one who is strange.' She turned away with an insulted air, shed her clothing silently and waded into the stream. As her intricately tattooed back sank into the water, Zar hesitated, then stripped and followed her through icy-cold water and into a hot patch. She groaned in pleasure as bubbles rose from the stony riverbed.

'The skin of the earth is thin here,' Rima said. 'The heat bleeds through.' Then she sighed and sank beneath the water, lying on her back with her black hair floating about in a cloud.

Zar did likewise, drowning in the warmth, and for a few minutes she let her stress subside, closing her eyes and sinking into herself . . .

. . . and she was padding along a forest track, her whiskers twitching and her bushy tail waving, wary of danger. Then she heard a throaty cough and realised that she was being hunted, and slunk into the dark . . .

. . . and gasped as she burst back to the surface and thrashed about.

Rima caught her shoulders and steadied her until Zar found her feet and shoved her away. She immediately felt embarrassed at her own ingratitude. 'Sorry – I thought I was drowning!' she panted, feeling her face go hot. 'Ever since Hetaru did whatever he did, I've had nightmares of my familiar being hunted.'

'Your Adefar is safe inside the pendant,' Rima assured her, 'but it is not whole.'

'You say that, but I don't understand. We did everything right, and Father says he's fine.'

'Then your father is also ignorant.'

'My father is a soldier, a politician, a nobleman and a sorcerer. He knows *everything*.'

Rima's lively face took on an amused smirk. 'You love him. That's good.'

'He got me out when the Bolgravians invaded our home, after Mother deserted to the enemy. Since then, we've been travelling, fighting, trying to raise armies to win our homeland back. That's why we're here – for the istariol, so we can use it to make magic and sell some to buy soldiers.'

'To make war and death,' Rima said, her voice condemnatory.

'Should we just roll over and die?' Zar shot back.

'I did not say that,' Rima replied. 'But the istariol is not yours, and it is tapu – forbidden by the gods. And if it belongs to anyone, it is us, not your father. We're not part of your war.'

'We didn't know you were here.'

'But you do now: yet he still refuses to leave.'

'Why should we? You're not using it and we need it – for our freedom,'

Zar snapped back, surprised at her own passion, for she'd mostly regarded this whole trek as just another of her mad father's grand gestures.

'Just because we do not use it, does not make it less ours,' Rima answered. 'But that is for the Queen to resolve. Hetaru and I are more interested in you.'

Zar didn't want Rima's curiosity right now. 'Is there news about Banno?' she asked, to mask her anxiety.

Rima shook her head. 'Nothing new. It must be hard for you to be here, without your husband, but I am sure he will want to re-join you once he is recovered.'

Zar hadn't thought of her current situation as anything more than a temporary inconvenience. 'I suppose,' she replied. She couldn't imagine Banno as part of this tribe, though. He was utterly Pelarian, and had no aspirations beyond living among his own kind.

'How long have you been married?' Rima asked.

'Not long,' Zar replied. 'We met on the journey here.'

'Ah. How does marriage work among your kind?'

'It's sacred and holy. A priestess must bless it, and a justiciar register it, and then you're married for life. "Whom Deo has joined, let no man set apart", the Holy Book says.'

To her surprise, Rima shuddered. 'How awful. And who can marry?'

'Anyone . . . um, well, any man and woman, obviously. What about your people?'

'For us, it is quite different. Liaisons are easily made and simply broken. If a couple nail their tokens to the lintel of their farai – their house – then they are considered married. Either can chose to break up the relationship; but both must then abstain from others for a full cycle, to ensure the provenance of any child is known. Any disputes are settled by the Queen's Yokei – her officials.'

Zar was staring. 'You just marry and unmarry at the drop of a hat? That's . . .'

'Barbaric?' Rima sniffed. 'The Aldar, whose mistakes are the things that guide us, had lifelong oaths of fidelity and faithfulness, but broke them all the time, lying and cheating and even murdering to free themselves from the "eternal love" they'd sworn, creating feuds that lasted for generations. *That* was barbaric.'

Zar went to defend her people's ways, but found herself wondering if they were indeed better after all. 'Are you saying people don't get jealous and fight over lovers?'

'Ha!' Rima guffawed. 'No, no, it is the thing we argue about most, especially when young. But the thing is, we are all heartbroken at some time. I have jilted lovers, and been jilted. You get over it and grow up. And some couples constantly unite, part, reunite, part ... There is always hope. We are one tribe, so that person you love is always there, even if you are not currently sleeping with them. You can enjoy their company, even so.'

'I'd break the face of anyone who tried to steal Banno,' Zar growled. 'But does no one love forever, among your kind?' That was a depressing thought.

Rima smiled wistfully, 'There are many couples who have been married for years and years, sometimes only once in their lives. Love is still love. But most people need time and experiences before they find the right person to grow old with. Our way makes that easier, and guilt-free.'

'What about children?'

'They remain the joint responsibility of the parents, to care for, raise and educate. And all belong to the tribe anyway. No one is abandoned.' She frowned. 'Ideally. Not all do their duty, but the Yokei deal with that.'

This felt so alien that Zar couldn't begin to envisage it. But her father still loved her mother, Mirella, even though he'd had an affair with Tami Janvoli during the wars. *And Dad always looks at Mater Varahana with calf-eyes, which is embarrassing.* So perhaps there was something in what Rima said.

Though I will love Banno for ever, she thought fiercely. But she had a more urgent question. 'What is happening to me? What did Hetaru do to Adefar?'

'Your turehu – your familiar – is not whole – so he has called on the spirits to heal it.'

'So you say, but ever since Hetaru did that, something is hunting me in my dreams.'

'Then let it find you.'

'I can't do that.' Zar exclaimed fearfully. She wondered if Rima and Hetaru's misunderstanding was because their magic was different. 'How did you gain your familiar?'

Rima grinned and her lizard-familiar manifested, draped round her shoulders. She stroked it amiably. 'This is Mokomoko, my dear heart. When my time came, Hetaru took me to a holy place and we made the calling. All manner of spirits came, but Mokomoko called loudest to my soul. He slid inside me and we became one. It was a thing of beauty, like lovemaking and spiritual awakening all at once. Bliss.'

That was so different to the terrifying ordeal of winning Adefar that Zar couldn't relate to it at all. 'But what about the final pair, the praxis and the mizra spirit, and choosing the right one?' she asked.

Rima gave her a baffled look. 'I don't know what you mean.'

Do they only have mizra familiars here? Zar wondered. *That might explain it.* Her fears that they were trying to turn her into a mizra-witch deepened.

'When I gained Adefar, the spirits all contended, until two remained,' she told Rima. 'Both were like little foxes, one brown and one red. But the red one was the dark twin of the brown – the mizra familiar. I had to reject it and take the brown one. Then Father banished the mizra spirit and I was safe.'

Rima gave her a troubled look. 'That's very strange.'

Hearing the young Tangato woman admit to not knowing something was a surprise – she wasn't modest about her prowess. 'Are you and Hetaru the only sorcerers your tribe have?'

'Apart from you. But the other tribes also have two each; we share ourselves around.'

'Other tribes?'

'There are five others, but we are the largest – the Hiriwa. One day when Hetaru passes on, I will become chief mahotsu-kai of the Hiriwa and advise the Queen. And then there are the Queen's people, the Yokei. They also do magic.'

'Those are the masked women, yes?'

Rima gave her a proud look. 'They are the descendants of the last Aldar Queens, and human men.'

'*Half-Aldar?*' Zar's heart thudded. 'So Queen Shiazar is a half-Aldar, and all her ladies?'

'Ae, all the Yokei are of Aldar blood,' Rima replied. 'After the Mizra Wars, the surviving Aldar were all women, and they remained with us, using their powers to save us from the ice. Now they guide us against the forces that destroyed the Aldar – warfare, greed and the ruination of nature.'

Does Father know? Zar wondered. *This is incredible – the Aldar still live, in a way. He really needs to know.*

'What do they look like, behind the masks?' she wondered.

'I haven't seen. Very beautiful, people say. Ask Hetaru.' Rima rose, warm water streaming from her. 'Come, I want to show you something.'

Zar felt a sharp pang of body envy as she too rose, skinny and pale beside such muscular athleticism. 'Do you have a husband?' she wondered.

'No, I've never married,' Rima replied, for the first time a little coy. 'I'm selfish – I like my independence too much to be tied to others, especially a needy little baby.'

'But I'd love a baby!'

'Of course,' Rima snorted. 'So did my last partner, but I'm not ready to be a parent. Anyway, there's been no one for a long while. Learning magic consumes me.' She indicated the shore. 'Shall we go?'

It was clear that Rima didn't want to talk about relationships, so Zar let the question lie. They made their way back to the riverbank and rubbed down their skin briskly with the soft cured shingar-skin lining of their cloaks before dressing again, while Rima chatted about the other tribes. Hers, the Hiriwa, was the royal tribe, and the others were all formed by Hiriwa settlers as the tribe recovered its numbers. All remained subject to Queen Shiazar.

'With most we have good relations, but the Manowai – the Thousand Water tribe – have grown hostile in recent years. It's rumoured that they ignore the limits on children – the Queen forbids a woman to have more than three, to ensure we don't grow too fast and use up all the land.'

'Is Shiazar concerned about the Manowai?'

'Ae, but we are four thousand strong, and they are only two thousand.' Rima sniffed. 'Any disharmony is bad, though, so the Yokei keep them under control.'

It felt strange to think of a society in which a woman – albeit one of Aldar lineage – could wield such authority. In Magnia, there were few woman rulers, and those were inevitably undermined by the men around them. But here, Shiazar's control sounded absolute.

Rima put her fingers to her mouth and whistled shrilly, and her kikihana, the phorus bird, appeared a few moments later from the misty trees, beady eyes fixed resentfully on the two young women. But he submitted to them mounting up.

Instead of taking her back to the village, Rima took the bird out onto the plains. They rode all morning across the land south of Rath Argentium, then entered a rugged woodland. It was a tiring, uncomfortable ride, but Zar was intrigued, especially when they came upon an ancient, overgrown stone road leading into some wooded hills.

'It's an Aldar road,' Rima remarked.

'You find them at home, too,' Zar replied, 'but mostly they've been ripped up for building materials.'

They broke the journey and ate a late breakfast, then remounted and rode the kikihana into the trees. The ancient road took them into deeper forest, until they found a clearing beside a lake, surrounded by cliffs. Looking about, Zar was startled to see the outlines of tall, blockish stonework among the trees, walls and old ruined buildings.

'What is this place?' she asked.

'It was the summer palace of the Aldar King,' Rima told her. 'In ancient times, when the lands were warmer, the city in summer could be unbearable, so the Aldar court would come here, where it was cooler.'

They followed the road through the trees, which were alive with birdsong, and entered more ruins, all overgrown and decrepit. 'This is a tapu place,' Rima told her, 'sacred and forbidden. Normally people can't come here, but as a mahotsu-kai, I am permitted.'

Zar did feel like they were intruders, especially when they entered a courtyard the size of a tournament arena and found a massive stone bust of an Aldar woman, built over a fountain. Her mouth was open, clearly an aperture for water, and her face was streaked with green mould that made it look half-alive, the visage at once serene and menacing, the facial planes too perfect for humanity.

'Let's walk,' Rima murmured.

They slid from the kikihana's back and Rima led the complaining bird as they wound through the ruins, admiring old carvings on what remained of the buildings and walls. Eventually they came to a big plaza beside a deep blue-green lake, which Zar guessed was now higher than it had been, because much of the plaza was underwater.

They walked out on an old stone jetty jutting into the lake – Rima named it as Waiotapu, or 'Sacred Water' – and Zar saw many big fish in the clear waters. Then they worked their way around the shoreline to another open space, a circular auditorium with banks of seating, overgrown and covered in detritus.

Is this where Gerda slew the Aldar King? Zar wondered. But when she asked, Rima didn't know the tale, which was puzzling.

Everyone knows about Gerda, surely?

'Vashtariel was murdered by his brother, Tashvariel, not by some imaginary woman,' Rima corrected her offhandedly. 'Come see; this is what I wanted to show you.'

She led Zar through the arena and another narrow cutting to another riverside plaza, this one filled by a strange metal contraption that, alone in this ruin, was intact – and surprisingly free of rust, though it was weathered and coated in mould and windblown detritus. It was in the shape of a metal sphere, held by a semi-circular arch, like a globe, but on a giant scale. There were many holes in the sphere, and Zar glimpsed inner spheres, also riddled with holes.

'It's like the puzzle ball you gave me, the gong-qui,' she exclaimed. 'It's amazing.'

'It's said that the Aldar could use it to create a rainbow bridge and walk the skies,' Rima told her, her face reverent. She pointed northwest, and there was the floating citadel, Shiro Kamigami, fully ten miles away, a silhouette against the horizon. 'It was known as the Bridge of Izanami.'

Father's underneath that rock, Zar thought with a shiver.

'Tangato stories are filled with rainbows,' Rima went on. 'The Mother and Father of Creation descended a Rainbow Bridge to create our world. Some say that if you find the end of a rainbow, you can walk to Heaven.'

'Why did you show me this?' Zar asked.

'Because you are one of us now, and should know of this place. And to show you that we are not entirely backwards: we are the heirs of the Aldar, and they live among us still. Our land is a place of miracles.' She faced Zar and added, a little shyly, 'You can be happy here; I know this.'

'Maybe, but you're not giving me a choice in the matter.'

'I know. But Kamo would have killed you and your husband if I hadn't acted, and life is precious, especially when you are another mahotsu-kai.'

Zar nodded, putting her grievances aside, for she needed allies among the Tangato, and Rima did at least wish her well.

Just then, the kikihana bird hissed warningly, and they turned to see a small woman in a scarlet tunic and an elaborate gold and blue mask, standing at the entrance to the courtyard. She was holding a carved, metal-shod staff, which she hammered against a flagstone, glaring at Zar and snapping out angry words.

'Rima, what are you doing here with this . . . *creature*?' Adefar interpreted. Behind her, a young Tangato warrior appeared, helmed and armoured, with a bared bronze sword, the blade elaborately carved and decorated.

Rima knelt, pulling Zar down with her. 'Honourable Jinkatia, I didn't know you were here.'

The masked woman stalked forward, tapping the stones with her staff as she came, shadowed by the warrior. 'This place is tapu to all but we Yokei, and to such as you,' she said. She stopped in front of Zarelda. 'Who – *what* – is this creature?'

Zar flushed angrily and might have retorted, but Rima interjected, 'Zarelda is also mahotsu-kai. She is a traveller from afar, one whom Hetaru has adopted into the Hiriwa. Perhaps you haven't heard this, dwelling as you do with the Manowai.'

Manowai – the hostile tribe, Zar thought.

'A traveller from *outside* the Fenua Tangato?' exclaimed the Yokei – a half-Aldar, if Rima was to be believed. 'Impossible!'

The rapid-fire argument in the Tangato 'Reo' between the peremptory Yokei and Rima, who was uncharacteristically subservient, was too fast for Adefar to translate, but Jinkatia was clearly upset by Rima's news. But after a few minutes, the heat went out of the exchange and the warrior abruptly sheathed his sword, then stepped before the kneeling Zar and offered his hand.

Zar stared, then took it and rose.

He removed his helmet, revealing a deeply bronzed and heavily tattooed face, surprisingly youthful – and strikingly handsome. His hair was strange, shaven on either side of the skull but with a centre strip of long, thick hair running from forehead to the back of the skull. They stared at each other for a long moment, and he said something in Reo.

'Use Gengo,' Rima advised him. 'She can understand if you speak slowly.'

The warrior looked startled, but then smiled, an infectious, confident grin that changed his entire visage, and said, in a deeply musical voice, 'Will you walk with me, foreign lady?'

Zar tried to imagine how she looked to him – pale, blonde, freckled, with a Tangato tattoo on her chin, clad in a bodice, flax skirt and little else. She looked at Rima uncertainly.

'Protect her, Onkado,' Jinkatia told the young warrior. 'She has been accepted by Hetaru and is sacrosanct.

The young man – Onkado – bowed. 'I will guard her as I do you, Great One.' He turned back to Zar. 'My mistress and this mahotsu-kai must confer, and I would hear of you. Will you join me? I have food and drink.'

Zar's stomach rumbled, which sealed the deal. 'Yes, please.'

Onkado led her back to the plaza before the jetty, where another pair of kikihana were now tethered, but these had saddles and leather baggage. He unpacked and laid out a breakfast of honey-cakes and cured spiced meats, and flasks of water.

Zar was very conscious that she was alone with a strange man, but at no time did he make her feel uneasy, though he was clearly studying her avidly whenever she wasn't looking directly at him – and there was no wonder in that, she decided. She must look like a creature from myth to him.

Once she was done eating, she let him gently question her: Where had she come from? How did she get here? What were her people doing here? How could she be a sorcerer *and* a foreigner? How did she know his language?

She made a point of telling him she was married, but that Banno was currently convalescing, in case he thought she was available. 'Kemara – our healer – is very skilled. She'll save him if anyone can.'

Onkado made a respectful gesture. 'Then I wish him well.'

When she told him of Magnia and the vastness of the Bolgravian Empire, he went very quiet. 'So many millions of people?' he breathed, his face going slack with disbelief. 'Truly?'

'More than the stars of the sky.'

He sagged against the wall and gazed heavenwards. 'You fill me with fear.'

And so you should be afraid, she thought. *Bolgravia will destroy you when they find you.*

But she was enjoying speaking with someone other than Rima. With Banno gone, she had been missing masculine company. 'It's not all bad, though,' she told him. 'There's so much we could show you. Sailing ships bigger than palaces, gunpowder and steel and clocks and paper and books and everything! You'll be amazed.'

He didn't look reassured. 'You'll eat us up,' he muttered.

'No,' she insisted, 'we're not all like the Bolgravians. My father and Mater Varahana, our priestess, put learning and peace above every-thing else. We just want our homeland back. We're not here to stay.' Even to her ears, that sounded naïve, so she changed the subject. 'What are you doing here? Don't you Manowai live far away?'

'Only two, maybe three days' travel,' he replied. 'We live west of here, right up against the ice wall. Yokei Jinkatia wished to inspect this place. I was selected as her bodyguard, though no one would dare assail a Yokei, so I'm really just here to serve her.'

'Is she truly part-Aldar?' Zar asked, unsure how he'd react to the question.

'Truly,' Onkado replied reverently. 'They saved us, after the Fall.'

Part-Aldar . . . how incredible. I have to tell Father.

Just then, Rima called, 'Zar, Zar! It's time to go.'

Onkado rose to his feet gracefully and again offered her his hand, but this time didn't immediately let go, instead bowing over it, and say-ing formally, 'It is a pleasure to make your acquaintance. I pray that we will not have to be enemies in future.'

It was a sobering end to what had been a pleasant conversation.

'I hope so too,' she replied, sincerely.

Rima called her kikihana bird, they mounted up under the eyes of Jinkatia and Onkado, then she nudged the bird into motion and they rode back through the ruins. The midday sun breaking through the clouds lit up the old stones and the vivid greens of the forest, trans-forming it from sad and mysterious to a glorious palette of colours.

Zar realised that she'd enjoyed the morning, despite all her fears and worries. It felt like she'd made two friends, even with all their differences.

'What were they doing here?' she asked.

'I don't know, but Jinkatia is the Archivist of the Yokei, so there'll be some deep reason. She's lived among the Manowai for all my life.'

'Onkado seemed nice . . .'

Rima snorted. 'He is Manowai, so he is a savage. But he does have a nice arse.'

Zar's eyebrows shot up. In Magnia, such things weren't ever said. 'I never noticed.'

'No, of course not. You're married to another man, after all.'

Zar was offended that Rima might think she had been flirting with Onkado. He'd been nice, but Banno was her love. 'I am married, and I give all my honour to my husband.'

Rima ducked her head apologetically. 'I am sorry I had to strike your Banno so hard, truly. But I felt endangered, even if that silly weapon of his only made a loud noise.'

That 'silly weapon' would have killed you if you hadn't moved so fast, Zar thought. But she said nothing, because if push came to shove, guns might be the only thing that kept her father and their people alive.

They returned to the edge of the Hiriwa valley by mid-afternoon, dismissed the kikihana bird at the edge of the village and walked towards the arched gates.

But just as they were about to enter, a low-slung dark shape stepped from the undergrowth and blocked their path. At first Zar thought it was a dire-wolf like those on the Bolgravian steppes – then she froze. It was a red fox, the size of a pony – and not just any red fox, but *her* red fox cub: Adefar's dark mizra twin, grown impossibly immense.

It was both here and not here, she realised, and were she not a sorcerer, it would have been invisible. But when it bared its teeth and growled, she heard it clearly.

'What does it want?'

She felt terrified, but Rima was excited. 'Zarelda – the pendant – give it to me –'

Zar was scared to move, in case she provoked it – spirit beasts could be just as deadly as real ones. But she pulled the necklace over her head and handed it to Rima.

The Tangato girl held it to her lips and whispered something – and mist poured out and became a quivering, terrified Adefar, huddling on the ground at Rima's feet.

'Adefar!' Zar squeaked, lunging to scoop up her familiar, but Rima blocked her.

'No, wait!' she commanded.

Adefar mewled as the giant fox advanced, making a rumbling sound that could have been hunger, a warning, or even a purr. But then it dropped its head and sniffed, licking the fox cub, then patting it with one massive forepaw.

Zar sagged in relief.

Adefar went up on his hind legs, stroking the larger beast's face—

—and with a terrifying wrench of its head, the giant fox's jaws opened, it clamped its massive teeth around Adefar – and *swallowed*.

Zar shrieked as the fox *flowed* – changing before her eyes into a crouching man in a fox mask, naked and smeared in blood and ash, with a bushy tail and an erect phallus.

He reached for her—

Zar's knees gave way, something battered her mind like a fist, and the world fell away . . .

6

All in This Together

Raythe convened his daily meeting with his co-leaders after breakfast. He was feeling a growing sense of urgency: there was so much to do, and time was running short.

To his right was Mater Varahana, elegant and dignified in her religious robes. Beside her, Kemara Solus was giggling with Jesco Duretto; he'd recovered from the blow he'd taken on the bridge, but there was an uncharacteristic brittleness about him. He and Kemara had always got on well, but since the head injury, he'd started hanging round her like a besotted boy, which was highly unlike him.

At the far end of the table, Cal Foaley was picking his teeth with a knife, the picture of calm. Elgus Rhamp had the other side of the table. His sons Osvard and Banno had been part of the command group, but with Osvard dead and Banno still unconscious, Elgus had asked if Crowfoot, his grizzled, cunning captain, could attend. Raythe had agreed, hoping Rhamp's right-hand man might start to see the bigger picture and realise they were all in this together. It was probably naïve, but it had to be worth a try.

He rapped the table for silence, then turned to Kemara. 'First up, how are things in the infirmary?'

'Busy, but well,' the healer replied. 'Vidar Vidarsson and Fossy Vardoe both have bad chest wounds; they're the most seriously injured. They are improving, but Vidar's still weak. Banno's doing well – I think he'll make a full recovery, but it'll take time. A few women are due, and one idiot boy speared his own foot while fishing.' Then she turned on Elgus Rhamp. 'And one of your thugs – that cretin Skavid – broke the jaw of another of yours – Jos Petz – then bit him in the throat. He almost crushed the boy's windpipe.'

Elgus scowled. 'Skavid's a bearskin.'

'That doesn't excuse it.'

'No, but it explains it,' Crowfoot growled. 'All the lads know not to get Skavid riled, but Jos was screwing him round and got what he earned. I expect Vidarsson is just the same.'

'He is not,' Varahana retorted.

'I know you've taken a shine to the Norgan,' Elgus replied, making the priestess colour, 'but bearskins are all the same, more animal than man, at least until they get some grey in their beards. I'll have a word with Skavid.'

Varahana was fuming, but Raythe spoke over her retort. 'Will Jos recover?'

'Aye,' Kemara said, 'I'll see him right.'

'We appreciate it.' He turned to the priestess. 'Varahana, how is morale holding up?'

She stopped glaring at Elgus and sighed. 'Everyone's frightened, of course. We're trapped, and this ruined city is unnerving people. But that floating rock above proves that there's istariol here, so at least they know there's a good reason for them being here.'

Raythe thanked her and turned to the knight. 'What of your men, Elgus?'

'Also pleased to be here, anxious to leave.'

'We all want the same thing: to get out alive and rich,' Crowfoot added.

'Your mercenaries move to a different drum than the rest, we all know that,' Raythe said, 'so how are they *really* taking all this? What does Bloody Thom think?'

'Crow and I are with you,' Elgus maintained. 'So's Thom – he's my man, and he'll follow orders. They all will. And don't forget, we're still the best fighting men you've got.'

Nothing but platitudes, but that's all I'll get.

He moved on. 'Jesco, what's our defensive situation?'

'We're getting a clearer understanding of the city,' the Shadran started. 'As you know, we've got a natural moat formed by the rivers, and there's only one bridge in, so we've stationed watchers in every tower and everyone's been taught how to signal danger.'

'My lads are manning most of the towers,' Elgus put in. 'We've been working hard.'

'If sentry duty is your definition of hard work,' Cal Foaley grunted.

Jesco ignored the interruptions and went on, 'We've found seven postern gates in the walls, with stairs leading down to various jetties and fishing holes. We're guarding them, but they're a potential weak spot.'

'What about a fall-back point if we're breached? Have you found one, Sir Elgus?'

'There's only one real option: a big castle-like place right up on the crater rim. It's a twenty-minute climb from here, which ain't good, but it's got strong walls and good fields of fire. We're callin' it "Rim House". We've started shifting some dry stores up there.'

'Ideally, we'd move everyone up there,' Crowfoot put in. 'Given our numbers, the outer walls are indefensible.'

'I'm aware of that,' Raythe replied, 'but it's the only barrier we can defend, so we can't withdraw, and we need to be close to the river, as no one's found a functioning well yet.' He turned to Foaley. 'Cal, how's the exploration of the city going?'

'We've found dozens of old garden plots running wild, with plenty to forage,' the hunter said. 'We've killed and cooked or dried seventeen phorus birds and three more shingar lizards. But we've searched barely a third of the buildings in any detail so far – it's slow work when you're also hunting for food – and we need to take care we don't become the prey.'

'Good work,' Raythe told him. He gave them a quick precis of his venture beneath the ground with Jesco, describing the shafts that needed lifts repaired, and the shingar nest. 'I didn't get a great sense of istariol dust in the air, so whatever's left down there is buried deep. It could be that the mines were mostly cleared out – and maybe that rock above us is where most of it now lies.'

'Then you and Kemara need to get up there,' Elgus said. 'Have you found a way?'

Raythe shook his head. 'Those chains might be big enough to climb, but they're coated in some sort of oil which makes them slippery as an eel. It'd be suicidal.'

'Well, the Aldar got up there somehow,' Jesco said.

'The tales always spoke of them flying to their cloud castles,' Varahana put in, 'but they must have had servants up there, so they'd have needed some other means of getting up and down.'

I wonder if the Tangato know? Raythe thought. *Though I doubt Rima or Shiazar would just tell me.* 'We'll get there,' he said, 'but our priorities are food, shelter and security: those always come first.'

'What about those primitives outside?' Crowfoot growled. 'There's only two days until your truce expires.'

'Aye. We need to stall them, and I think we can. They want us to leave, but they believe life is precious and that they don't want bloodshed. It sounds as if the Mizra War instilled a deep horror of war in them. So as long as we keep our walls secure, I believe they'll give us more time. I'm going to ask for a month's extension – that should give us time to explore the mines fully and find a way up to the citadel.'

They digested that in silence, then Elgus looked up. 'I understand your daughter prevented me having to bury Banno. I thank you for that.'

'Don't thank me, thank her,' Raythe answered. 'She told them they were married, and they showed him mercy.'

'Well, they've grown close, true enough,' Elgus rumbled. 'When we get her back and he recovers, I'd be content to see them wedded, if you would be?'

Raythe blanched inwardly, but kept his face schooled. *I do need some way to tie him to me – perhaps this is it?* 'If Zarelda and Banno are in love and that's what they truly want, then perhaps you're right and we should let it be. Elgus, we've had our fallings-out, but if our children can find peace, so should we.'

Elgus looked at Crowfoot, then back at him. 'We back you, Raythe.'

'That's to the hilt,' Crowfoot added, just a little too quickly for Raythe's liking.

But it was a positive step and in this uncertain world, he supposed Sir Elgus Rhamp wasn't the worst man to be related to. *One day Zar and I will be back in Otravia, and if Banno's stuck by her through however long that takes, he'll have earned my respect.*

'So, brother-in-law,' Elgus drawled, 'how exactly do we get Zarelda back?'

'Honestly? I don't know,' Raythe confessed. 'If we try something and botch it, we risk her life. But I've spoken to her and I think she's safe enough for now. Let's find the istariol, then see what our options are. Once we're armed with some blood-dust, I'm sure Kemara and I can find a way to bring her back safely.'

'So in the meantime you'll just leave her a prisoner?' Crowfoot asked.

Is he trying to goad me into doing something foolish and getting myself killed? Raythe thought in annoyance. *Well, it's not going to happen.* 'You think I'm happy about it?' he replied. 'We'll do all we can when the time's right. But I've been assured of her safety – by Queen Shiazar, and by Zar herself.'

'I guess you have the right of it,' Elgus commented.

'Excellent. Then let's move forward together. Jesco and Elgus: security. Cal, exploration and food supply. Varahana, community and disputes. Kemara, health – and when we've got time, you and I need to find a way to the upper citadel.' He rapped the table again, in closure. 'Let's get busy.'

'Well?' Bloody Thom said to Crowfoot. 'How's the supping at Lord Vyre's table?'

Crowfoot snorted. 'He's a weakling. Everything he says and does is a compromise. He tries to lay down the law, but the moment he's challenged, all the weasel words come out. Wouldn't last ten minutes leading our lot.'

'Thought so – always reckoned his reputation was overblown. Reminds me o' them Bolgie nobles struttin' about in their fancy uniforms but knowin' krag-all about war. It's soldiers what wins victories, not jumped-up lordlings like Vyre.' He gestured around the room they were using as a mess-hall for the company, now down to fifty men. Elgus was downstairs, arbitrating complaints among the few remaining camp women and their brats.

'What struck me,' Crowfoot said, 'is that because our situation is perilous, he imagines no one will risk upsetting the apple cart by going after him.'

'Then now's the time to strike.' Thom made a fist and thumped it into his other palm.

'I see two options.' Crowfoot held up one finger. 'Either we wait until we're all safely out and on the way home with the loot' – he raised a second – 'or we do it now. The benefit of waiting is that we wouldn't have to worry about those savages, and we'd have the istariol.'

Thom grunted. 'Aye, but the cons are that Vyre will only have us to worry about by then, so he'll be watching us like a hawk, and with all that istariol he'll be more dangerous – 'specially if he makes the first move.'

That was how Crowfoot saw it, too. 'But if we strike now, while Vyre's attention is on the barbarians and his daughter, he'll have no istariol, and he won't see us coming.'

Thom scratched at his beard thoughtfully. 'But it leaves us still stuck in here, with that lot outside and no istariol. What if there's none down there? If it's all up in the kragging rock up in the sky, we'll need him to get it.'

Crowfoot was well ahead of him. 'That's why I got some of the lads to sneak into the mines on the quiet. Even Elgus don't know.'

'You cunning bastard.' Bloody Thom snickered. 'What'd they find?'

Crowfoot smiled crookedly. 'They found the mine-shaft Vyre reported finding, the one he's going to get the carpenters to repair, and went down on ropes. They came back up with their pockets full of istariol nuggets, a small fortune – and they reckon there's loads more.'

They shared savage, greedy smiles.

'That proves that there's istariol down there,' Crowfoot went on, 'and we can bring the rest up after we've seized control. Because, let's face facts: those primitives won't let us go, and we can't fight our way out. So when we leave here, it'll be a stealth operation: you, me and a few chosen lads, laden with as much istariol as we can bring up.'

'It won't be the riches we dreamed of,' Thom sniffed.

'But still enough to retire on,' Crowfoot assured him. 'And we'll be alive.'

'Aye, that's the way it has to be, I guess,' Thom admitted. 'Then let's do it as soon as possible – though we'll have to keep it quiet, so the barbarians don't realise something's up and use the chance to attack.'

Crowfoot looked worried. 'Aye, that's a danger for sure. But if we do it fast, without disrupting the sentries, we'll be fine. My main worry's that some of the lads have made friends among the hunters and Tesh-veld folk – I reckon if we noise it round that we're going to strike against Vyre, someone could rat us out.'

'*Who?*' Thom demanded.

Crowfoot was shaking his head. 'Nay, they're all good lads, just mis-led. If the hard core of us strike, the rest'll fall into line. The key's in not givin' 'em time to think.'

Thom didn't look happy, but he muttered, 'Fine. We'll lead with the hard nuts, those we can be sure of: Skavid, Eilfin, your Kallesburg clan, my Norgan reivers . . . that's a good two dozen we can trust right there.'

'That's enough to do it,' Crowfoot calculated. 'Once the mayhem starts, we'll spread the word that Vyre's betrayed us, Elgus too – then the rest'll pile in. We cut down the ringleaders quickly enough, there'll be no one'll gainsay us.'

Thom grinned. 'An axe in the back'll settle the Shadran pansy. Lucky that Vidarsson's still bedridden. Assign a few to corner and gut Cal Foaley and the hunters will come round to our way of thinking.'

'Just so long as Vyre takes a musket ball in the back of the head right at the start, we won't need to worry about sorcery ... oh, and then there's the healer.'

'Shame, but she dies same time as Vyre.' Bloody Thom licked his lips. 'You can have the priestess, if you want, or throw 'er to the lads.'

'Ain't had a priestess since the rebellion,' Crowfoot chuckled. 'But first up, we deal to Elgus, right?' He paused, then added, 'And his boy. Banno don't get to wake up.'

'Fair enough,' Thom grunted. 'When?'

'Sooner the better,' Crowfoot replied. 'Let's do it tonight at dusk, when most folks are gathered in the food-hall. That way we can confront the lot with a done deal. When the sunset horn blows, we strike.'

Vidar Vidarsson was floating in a river of memories. Some were of his childhood in Norgania, and of his lost wife, slain by the milk-plague, but interspersed were more recent events, like clasping the unconscious, dying Mater Varahana to his chest and storming alongside a river, roaring for help.

'Save her,' he shouted, thrusting the stricken priestess at Kemara Solus. 'It's verdeghul poison – save her!'

Varahana's face, so clever and serene, had haunted his dreams ever since. Seeing her in peril had ripped something free inside him, something buried since his wife died.

Is it wrong to fall in love with a priestess?

It's the height of stupidity, his dead mother told him. What can ever come of it?

I miss you, his wife's ghost added. How dare you forget me?

But I haven't forgotten, he protested. I'm thinking about you right now.

But Varahana's voice was the melody he clung to when he drifted in and out of consciousness, to hear her talking, praying or softly singing. She was the comfort in each nightmare, the thread that drew him back up . . .

. . . into wakefulness.

His encrusted eyes opened painfully and the dreams dropped away, but her voice went on, '—push on to the shafts on the north side and—'

He heard her suck in her breath, then gasp, 'Vidar? Dear Gerda, you're awake!'

He blinked, his vision cleared and there she was, sitting on a stool, starkly beautiful, her angular features truly a gift from Deo.

'Vara—' He started coughing, but managed, 'I could hear you, I followed you up . . .'

The priestess grabbed his right hand, her expression both relieved and joyous, and for a moment they gazed at each other, as they had when she was the recovering patient after the verdeghul attack and he'd watched over her.

'You're looking better,' she blurted at last. 'I'm so glad.'

Because of you, he went to say, but she'd turned her head and was shouting, 'Kemara! Kemara, Vidar's awake!'

A wizened Sister of Gerda rose from where she was kneeling over another patient. 'I'll fetch her,' she said, throwing him a grin as she waddled away.

They were in a weather-stained room, the stone walls lined with crumbling plaster; a dull crimson light was shining through the one window. Four other patients were lined up along the walls; the nearest was Banno Rhamp, with a bandaged head and starkly pale skin. Somewhere near, a woman was moaning through what sounded like labour.

'Where are we?' he panted.

She squeezed his hand. 'You'll never believe it. We're inside Rath Argentium.'

More memories returned: the fight on the bridge to the impossible city; Toran Zorne. 'We made it across?' he croaked. 'What about Zorne? The Bolgies—?'

96

'Hush,' Varahana said, beaming down at him. 'All in good time. You just concentrate on getting well.'

He smiled weakly. 'I heal fast – it's a bearskin thing. You just watch me. I'll be fit enough to rescue priestesses again in no time.'

She gave him that arch look he enjoyed most. 'I'm sure that'll be a huge relief to my Sisters of Gerda. But don't overtax yourself. We've got everything in hand—'

Outside the ward they heard hurrying feet, and from somewhere nearby, a watch horn blew, just as the sunlight outside vanished and the sky darkened . . .

Madelaine Groff was in labour, her contractions down to four minutes apart, but Kemara had three Sisters fussing over her in the birthing room beside the infirmary, a half-ruined manor near the gatehouse, while she took a breather. Since the expedition had fought its way into this ruined city, she'd been bombarded by the health concerns of three hundred people and had had barely a moment to herself.

Aside from Maddy, she had five seriously injured patients to worry about: Vidar; Banno Rhamp, who looked to be recovering after she'd trepanned his skull; Jos Petz, one of Rhamp's men who had a smashed face; the farmer Lew Fulter with a newly fractured leg; and Bessa Tyne with a worrying fever.

She'd scrubbed out the room below the infirmary and made it her own; it had a balcony where she could bask in the golden light of the setting sun. The views were incredible: the rock floating above, anchored to the ground by those immense chains, silhouetted against the planetary rings, which were growing brighter as the sun set. The towers of the ruined city gleamed rose-gold in the glow of dusk, while the music of the rivers blended with the sound of a harp – Norrin, the young trainee bard, was somewhere near, practising his scales.

Beautiful, but eerie.

Then the music fell silent and someone coughed behind her. She turned to find Val Groff, Madelaine's husband, a furrier from Teshveld, at the doorway. 'Just checking up,' he said apologetically, 'but the Sisters won't let me in. Is Elaine all right?'

Kemara was too tired for company, but she understood expectant fathers and forced a smile. 'She's fine, Val. I wouldn't be down here otherwise.' Then she frowned. 'I thought her name was Madelaine?'

Val grinned. 'Actually, it's just Elaine. Her friends added the "Mad" bit.'

Kemara, taken by surprise, found herself laughing. 'I'm sure we're all mad, or we wouldn't be in this crazy place. Your girl's fine, Val. Get some rest. We'll fetch you when something happens.'

He touched his brow in salute. 'Thank you, Healer. I'm grateful.'

Boots sounded on the pavement below, moving purposefully. She leaned out to see who it was, but the setting sun both dazzled and dimmed her vision, throwing the city into shadow, and those below into anonymity. From the gatehouse, the watchers blew the signal horn for the change of the watch – but a moment later, she heard a sound she knew all too well: the rattle of distant flintlocks echoing about. The distance and direction were impossible to gauge, but the men below thudded into a run and the entrance door to her infirmary, a flight below, burst open.

'Lord Vyre?' a rough but respectful male voice called from Raythe's door.

Raythe looked up from the map he'd begun of the Fenua Tangato and found Larch Hawkstone at the door. The sight of the former imperial borderer always brought a rush of conflicted thoughts: Hawkstone had pursued them all the way from Teshveld, scouting for the Bolgravian army, but when the desperate travellers had tried to break out of an imperial trap, Hawkstone had changed sides. Not only had he allowed the caravan to escape the Bolgravian cordon, but he'd also given the warning which had ultimately saved Raythe's life. And without Hawkstone, they'd never have known that the Ramkiseri agent Toran Zorne was masquerading as a fellow traveller. But he'd changed sides to save his own skin, not out of altruism.

'Master Hawkstone,' Raythe greeted him neutrally.

'Milord,' the man said with nervous deference. Hawkstone was a burly, brusque man, and the borderers, wardens appointed by the imperial governors to keep the peace, were universally loathed. He had few friends here, despite his part in saving the caravan. 'You asked to see me?'

Raythe faced him. 'I did. I'll be frank, there's many here who don't feel happy that you're with us. Is there anyone who'll vouch for you?'

Hawkstone ducked his head awkwardly. 'There's Angrit, Milord. I'm the father of her wee girl, Rosebud, though we've never wed. Truly, Milord, I only wanted to keep Rosebud safe. I paid her upkeep, back in Teshveld.'

'And what does Angrit have to say of this?'

The borderer ducked his head again, colouring. 'She'll tell any who'll listen that I'm a no-good waste of air, Milord, and maybe I deserve that, but a man's gotta take work where he can, an' the imperials were the only ones could pay high enough for me to look after my girl. I been tellin' her this, an' I think she's comin' round.'

'Was it consensual, when you conceived Rosebud?'

Hawkstone coloured. 'Well, it was fairly paid for, Milord,' he mumbled.

Sometimes that's the best you can hope for. Raythe straightened and looked out of the window at the setting sun. 'I'm remembering Teshveld, when you and your men tried to kill me for the crime of answering back.'

'Milord, you know if I'd backed down, I'd have lost my rank, my job – maybe even my life. An' I was right about you – you *were* up to something.'

'That might be so, but I always thought you took a little too much pleasure in your role,' he pointed out. 'But that said, every man deserves a second chance. I'm willing to –'

The blast of the watch horn interrupted his flow and as Raythe waited for it to subside, hope grew on Hawkstone's face. He was about to resume when he heard a faint *click* from outside, a sound he knew too well.

The cocking of a flintlock's hammer . . .

'Nice playing.'

Norrin Harper, a slender, pale young man with big eyes and a delicate face, looked up from his instrument and smiled his shy smile as Jesco entered the small tower room.

'Glad you liked it,' he replied, giving Jesco an admiring look as the Shadran perched in the window box.

'I really like your fiddle playing, too.' *Such a lovely boy.* 'Don't stop on my account,' Jesco said. 'I'll just listen.'

They shared one of those looks that told him he was on the right trail here, and Norrin far from unwilling. Then the boy gave himself back to the harp, closing his luscious eyes and setting his elegant fingers dancing over the strings. Notes rose, blending with the river below.

The watchtower was a few hundred yards east of the bridge and the gatehouse, not far from Kemara's infirmary. The sun was going down and a cool, still night was about to unfold, perfect for strolling beneath the ring-light, for secret trysts and the magic of moments.

The precarious state of the caravan, trapped in this magical place, had sharpened Jesco's desire. He'd been feeling off-kilter recently, not understanding his recent fixation on Kemara Solus. He wasn't drawn to her sexually, but for some reason, found himself constantly hankering for her company – that was partly why he'd sought out the young bard, to remind himself of who he was.

He suddenly remembered the little ring he'd picked up in the shingar chamber below and pulled it out, wondering why it mattered. He examined it, then went to pocket it again – but instead found himself slipping it onto his little finger.

There's something about it, he thought. *Something I need to know.*

Then Kemara's face intruded on his thoughts again, which irked him, so instead he concentrated on the lips and hands in front of him, imagining the first kiss – and that swept away thoughts of others. Norrin's playing was as enchanting as the dreamy look on his face.

And when the harper finished the tune and opened those glorious eyes again, they were full of come-hither promise.

He's ten years younger than me, but he's old enough – I want him, and I'm sure he wants me too.

'Don't move,' Norrin murmured, rising to his feet. 'You look amazing, framed by the sunset outside. Like a god come to life.' His gentle face was enraptured, his expression vanquishing all doubt. The rosy gleam of the setting sun turned the harpist's eyes to pools of liquid as he came to Jesco and kissed him fiercely, stroking his face as they tasted each other for the first time . . .

Outside, the watch horn blew from the gatehouse tower and the sun dipped below the horizon.

Jesco slid his hands under Norrin's tunic, seeking warm flesh, while the harpist did the same, and all the while they drank in the promise of the pleasure to come –

– then something creaked on the stairs, right outside the door, then it swung open –

– and fire blazed from the muzzle of a flintlock.

Elgus Rhamp was in his improvised mess-hall, a block west of the gatehouse, when Eilfin, a young mercenary with sharp features and dead eyes, approached.

'Eilfin – what is it?' he asked.

'Boss, got a message for ye,' Eilfin replied. 'From Crowfoot.'

Brego, one of his distant relatives, was Elgus' bodyguard today. He eyeballed Eilfin while everyone in the hall glanced up, but this was routine and they had little interest.

Eilfin was young, handsome and cocky, with a reputation back in Magnia for getting village girls into trouble. But recently, he'd been making himself a new reputation: as their best young swordsman. Admittedly, they'd lost a few good ones, but just now, everyone was singing Eilfin's praises.

Elgus decided to feed his ego. 'I hear you're the best blade in the company these days?'

'Reckon I am,' Eilfin answered. 'Been training hard, getting my footwork sorted. Only bugger I don' fancy taking on is Skavid – because he don't know how to lose without going mental.' Then he tapped his temple respectfully. 'And yourself, of course, Boss.'

'Don't flatter unless you mean it. What's Crow want?'

'Wouldn' say. He's at the house by the Lion's Well.'

Elgus swilled the water that was all they had to drink these days and decided he needed some fresh air, so he'd go and see what Crow wanted. 'With me, Cousin,' he told Brego, then he clapped Eilfin on the arm and added, 'Get yourself a bite, lad.'

'Cheers, but I've another job Crow wants doing,' Eilfin replied, his smile not reaching his eyes. 'Reckon he's pipped 'cause I kicked his arse in training.' He hurried away.

Elgus grunted in amusement, then faced the room. 'Gilly, Cassyr, you two come with Brego an' me. Rest o' you lot, behave,' he added, eliciting a jovial chorus of, 'Krag off, Boss.'

They headed through the lower-level streets for the Lion's Well, a dried-out fountain in front of what might have been an old guildhall.

I was right to make peace with Vyre, he mused, *but Crow and Thom don't like it. So what's this about?*

The sun was almost down and the streets of the ruined city were taking on an eerie feel, as if they remembered a time when they had teemed with people. The wind whispered in the tangled ivy and the broken towers and their footfalls echoed strangely.

Elgus glanced at Brego, Gilly and Cassyr. 'Stay alert.'

The man guarding Crowfoot's door was Ned Bock, one of Crow's by-blows, who showed Elgus into the old guildhall. He left Brego, Gilly and Cassyr outside and walked into the smallish room where Crowfoot waited alone. The only furniture was a table, on which a cloak was laid over something lumpy.

'What's up, Crow?' Elgus asked.

In reply, the grizzled veteran pulled the cloak off, revealing a pile of rocks. Every one of them was shot through with scarlet veins. Elgus felt his mouth go round. 'By Deo, is that what I think it is?'

Crowfoot grinned wolfishly. 'Sure is. We found 'em in the northern mines, the unexplored ones. Vyre's been holding out on us. If I hadn't sent some lads down, we'd never've knowed.'

Elgus held up the largest nugget and gazed at it hungrily. The last rays of the sun lit the ruddy seams of istariol so that they glowed like hot lava. *Istariol . . . Thank Gerda.* There was relief too, that Crow had come to him with this, instead of concealing them.

But his lieutenant's words didn't quite add up. 'Crow, you sent lads down them holes ahead of Vyre, so we don' know he wasn't going to play this straight.'

Crowfoot *tsked*. 'And there you go, defending your "brother-in-law" again.'

Instantly, Elgus felt uneasy. He had his big, old-fashioned sword, but Crow was armed with his battle-axes, as well as a captured Bolgravian pistol.

Perhaps I'm just paranoid: he's showing me what he found and he didn't have to do that.

So he masked his tension and just asked, 'How much did you find?'

'This and more,' Crowfoot replied. 'But we need to take control, before Vyre tries to screw us over again.'

He wants to move against Vyre . . .

If Crowfoot – and therefore Thom – were this advanced in their planning, then his life was at stake. *Even if I cave and sanction this, they've usurped my authority.* Either he quashed this now, or he died. *It's them or me.*

But Crowfoot was fully alert, so he pretended to fall into line. 'Kragging good work, Crow.' He tossed the istariol-riddled stone from hand to hand. 'You're right, and you've seen things clearer than I have. Are the lads in place?' He glanced through the window at the rapidly fading daylight. 'What's the signal?'

'The evening watch horn,' Crowfoot replied. 'We've got Skavid ready to smash into the infirmary; Eilfin's stalking Jesco Duretto, and Thom's got eight with him to take down Vyre. I'm about to go to the mess-hall and proclaim the new order. It's all ready to go.'

Holy Gerda . . . that horn's goin' to blow any minute . . .

Elgus was suddenly struck by how badly he wanted to hold his grandchildren, the ones Banno and Zarelda would make. How badly he wanted to *live*. But a plan this advanced was clearly going ahead, whether he gave his sanction or not.

I'm no longer in command . . . This is as much about deposing me as Vyre . . .

As he stood there paralysed, the watch horn sounded from the gatehouse tower and echoed sonorously through the city.

'That your signal?' Elgus asked, resigning himself to Fate. 'Then let the wagons roll!'

With that, he turned on the *faithless bastard* he'd believed his friend and hurled the rock, shattering Crowfoot's nose and smashing out his front teeth. He had his sword out in a flash, but there was already yelling outside the door, and a frantic yelp of surprise.

Pausing to finish off Crowfoot would likely mean being trapped in here, so he barged out of the door as the hallway filled with the crack of flintlocks, flashes of fire and billowing smoke. Gilly was already on the floor, his throat cut – and it was Cassyr standing over the body, bloody knife in hand. Brego was staggering backwards, his chest a bloody mess, then he fell too.

Fury and grief smote Elgus, but he drove his sword into Cassyr's chest, and as he yanked the blade back out, he snatched up Cassyr's flintlock from against the wall, glimpsed one of Crow's mates peering in the window and shot him in the face.

Then Elgus stormed out into the courtyard, thinking he might just make it—

—until a flintlock spat and a lead ball punched into his left shoulder, making him stagger drunkenly. He reeled as Ned Bock came at him: a lad he'd held at his naming and seen grow into a worthless thug. He parried – just – then his clumsy old family sword all but severed the boy's head.

He staggered towards the well in the middle of the small square, seeking cover and a way out – but another ball hammered into his back and pain blazed through him. He lurched to the Lion's Well as Crowfoot came out through the guildhall doors, his face a scarlet ruin but his throat venting hate. His dreaded twin axes were gripped in his bloody hands.

Elgus propped his arse against the well, planted his sword and drew his pistol as Crowfoot raged towards him, thumbed the hammer and pulled the trigger.

But the gun failed to fire, the packed powder jolted loose in the scuffle, and Elgus cursed and dropped the useless weapon. He managed to get his broadsword up to parry Crow's right-hand axe, but the left one arced down unchecked, crunching into his shoulder blade.

Numbed by shock, he fell backwards, flipping over the lip of the well and smashing into a pile of debris a dozen yards below – then unexpectedly crashing through that into running water with a mighty splash. Dark water swept him under as the numbness gave way to pure, unadulterated pain.

7

Crowfoot

The dry rattle of musketry haunted Varahana's worst memories: in her mind she saw visions of men and women she'd blessed and prayed over being mown down by the rolling volleys of the Bolgravs, then trampled into the mud.

She pulled her hand free of Vidar's anxious grip and darted to the window of the infirmary, but echoes distorted distance and direction, and darkness was closing in. The patients were all sitting up, babbling questions; Maddy – Mad Elaine Groff – even stopped her shrieking and was instead clutching her friend Gerdina's hand.

'What is it, Mater?' blurted young Bessa Tyne, whose flushed face was sweaty with fever. 'Are the tribals attacking?'

That was one explanation, but someone had crashed open the main door three floors below and Varahana could hear boots on the stairs. *If it's an attack, where are the alarm bells?*

Quickly, she evaluated the building from a defensive viewpoint, hard-won experience coming to the fore. On this floor there were a kitchen and washroom and four rooms, with two staircases, front and rear. Everyone was in this room, so, worst case, they could barricade themselves in.

I'm calling this a worst case . . .

She spun, snapping orders at the three Sisters of Gerda on duty. None of them were younger than sixty. 'Agnes, stoke the fire.' She wasn't sure why yet, but she knew there'd be a why. 'Bea, Marta, stay with Maddy.' Then she assessed the patients. Banno was only just out of his coma and still weak from blood-loss. Jos Petz, one of Rhamp's men, had a broken face and damaged throat; he'd had to be sedated. Lew Fulter had a broken ankle. And moving Vidar with his punctured lung would be insane. *At least their weapons are all here*, she thought, checking to ensure they were still stacked against the wall.

'If you can, arm yourselves,' she told them as she hurried to the main door.

'You sure?' Lew Fulter wheezed, trying to rise on one leg. 'Might be nothin'.'

'Better wrong than dead. *Let's move!* Gerdina, help me with this table.'

The burly farmer's wife, as wide as she was tall but strong as any man, helped her drag the big old stone table to the door. There were bloodcurdling howls that sounded barely human coming from below, and she heard something hit the ground – a body, she assumed. Then someone came pounding up the stairs and Varahana realised it might be Kemara, fleeing for her life . . .

'Wait!' she told Gerdina, reaching for the door handle, her nerves shredding because it might not be Kemara at all. But fighting in Colfar's rebellion had taught her that fear was paralysis was death, so she acted, nudging the door open and peering through . . .

When the door crashed open one flight below, followed a moment later by the distinctive rattle of gunfire, Kemara's first thought was of Ionia, the woman who'd initiated her into the forbidden mizra. When the tavern they were staying in was raided, the older woman had thrust Kemara out the window; but before she could follow, she'd been seized. Kemara escaped . . . but Ionia burned.

That trail of thought took her to the mizra and Buramanaka's mask, concealed in her bedroom down the hall. '*Buramanaka*,' she whispered, '*Kaneska alla mizra*.'

Through the aether, she felt her familiar's dark presence, but without the mask on her face, the connection was tenuous. Sorcery was slow, but life wasn't. She hurried out into the hall to retrieve the artefact.

Val Groff was ahead of her, peering down the stairwell. 'Them trib-als must be attacking,' he was saying. 'I'll go see.' Then boots thumped below and he called, 'Hey, who's there?'

Kemara didn't wait, a premonition of mayhem impelling her towards her room – but before she got there, a wild-looking figure barrelled up the stairs, swinging a battle-axe in a silver arc that ended in Val's skull with a sickening wet crunch. The farmer collapsed as his killer roared like a beast. He was bare to the waist, revealing his immensely muscled chest and arms, with matted long blond hair and a forked beard: Skavid, probably the worst of Rhamp's men. He wrenched his axe free in a spray of blood as more men pushed up behind him, raving and snarling.

The long-festering, always imminent rampage had finally erupted.

Kemara spun and fled, skidding along the hall as Skavid closed in, grinning maniacally, his battle-axe raised. She threw herself sideways, a desperate dive into her room, just as the heavy wedge of steel slammed into the door frame, missing her by an inch. It stuck there, buried deep, but muscles bulging, Skavid was there, tugging at the haft.

That small delay was all she needed to slide to her bedroll and scoop up the rolled cloak containing her mask. If Skavid had just pulled a knife and charged, she'd have died right there, but he wanted his pre-cious axe. He wrenched it free, then charged – just as she threw herself out of the open window.

The axe-blade caught her skirt as it slammed into the lintel, right beside her ankle, ripping the fabric as she crashed down onto a sloped tile roof and skidded into the gutter. Above, Skavid was screaming in incoherent fury, eyeballs bulging, as he tugged at the axe again.

Then he was shoved aside and a pistol muzzle appeared –

Kemara rolled off the gutter as the gun roared and something tore a furrow in her right shoulder. Then the ground rose to meet her, a tan-gle of ivy and bushes that filled the back yard. She crashed into the foliage, scratched and bruised, winded but unbroken, clutching the rolled-up cloak containing the mask.

'Get her,' someone snarled above. 'Kill the kragging sorceress!'

Yes, she remembered, trying to ignore the hot blood soaking her back, *that's right. I am a sorceress . . .*

Feet crunched across the tiles above as she wrenched the spirit mask free, shrieking for Buramanaka.

To the man with the flintlock, Jesco and Norrin were just silhouettes against the setting sun, but Jesco could clearly see the gunman standing in the doorframe, a blade in one hand and a pistol aimed right at him in the other. There were two more shapes behind him.

He shoved Norrin one way while hurling himself the other.

The silver circle tracked left and belched flame, the other men firing an instant after, barrels jerking as they adjusted aim. Three lead balls tore through the air, one whistling into the space between the two falling men.

But Norrin gave a small, agonised, *'Oof!'* and hit the ground awkwardly, while the third ball punched into Jesco's right bicep and hit bone, knocking him off-balance and sending him tumbling to the stone floor.

Despite the blaze of pain, he kicked off and rose, drawing backhanded and flinging the blade across his body, catching what should have been a death-thrust from a straight sword, rolling clear as his attacker came at him, a pretty boy with dead eyes – Eilfin, who fancied himself to an obscene degree. Jesco jack-knifed from the waist and slashed at his thigh, but the mercenary darted clear.

One of the other men raised his flintlock butt, obviously intending to hammer down on Norrin's head, while the other, standing next to him, was fixing a bayonet to his smoking gun barrel. The harper wasn't moving. Blood was pooling on his chest.

'Finish him off,' Eilfin snickered, 'then let's take this bitch down.'

Jesco feinted right then went left, diving and rolling right into the feet of the two men, reversing the blade in his left hand and thrusting up into the gunman's groin in one smooth movement, before kicking clear as

Eilfin slashed at him. The tip of the sword carved a furrow down his back, but the bulk of the blow went crunching into Eilfin's own comrade.

The gunman collapsed and Eilfin snarled, more in frustration than loss, Jesco suspected. But the other man had finished ramming his bayonet onto the barrel of his gun and was circling to Jesco's blind side . . .

Jesco began to lunge at him, but Eilfin came in too fast, forcing him to give ground beneath a flurry of blows that he barely parried, then the bayonet-man stabbed at his ribs, but he spun away, taking another slash to the side, and managed to get his back to a wall.

On the floor, Norrin was bleeding out . . .

But death was an old dancing partner and though his soul was wailing, all Jesco really saw now was the movement of feet and blades. The cut to his side was incidental, but the ball in his right arm was numbing. For the rest of this fight, he'd be left-handed.

Eilfin chuckled as he came to the same conclusion. 'Hey, you know what we call scum like you back home?' he jeered. 'Tindersticks.'

'Let's light 'im up,' the bayonet man growled, stepping back and pulling out a pistol.

'Oh, I'm going to teach him a lesson first,' Eilfin crowed. 'Out with the old, as they say.'

He came in hard, but Jesco had spent his whole life training for just this situation: he'd been determined that he would never end up in a position where he couldn't fight. His defence held, despite Eilfin slashing and cutting and hacking with dazzling speed, driving him against the wall.

Damn, but the snit really is good . . .

The second man, getting bored, raised his pistol and thumbed the hammer back . . .

Time to do the impossible. Jesco crouched, then feinted and *leaped*, kicking off the wall, planting his foot on a decorative curlicue of plaster and pushing himself higher again, launching himself over Eilfin's left shoulder with his blade interposed to block the obvious slash at his thighs – which came and was deflected – then he was cartwheeling straight at the pistoleer . . .

. . . who panicked and *missed*.

Flame and smoke filled Jesco's sight as his sword spitted the man's heart a moment before he slammed into him, sending them both crashing to the ground, when he'd counted on landing on his feet. That failure was fatal, for even as he hit the stone floor, Eilfin lunged, a perfect thrust that finished in Jesco's belly. He smirked. 'Gotcha, you old po–'

His voice broke as Jesco caught his wrist. There was just time for those dead eyes to spark to life in horror, then Jesco's roundhouse slash took him across the throat, severing the main arteries. Eilfin lost grip on his sword, grabbed at his neck as his legs went from beneath him, collapsing and kicking his way to stillness.

Jesco's fingers went numb as the punishment he'd taken caught up. He dropped his sword, yanked Eilfin's blade from his belly, then fell sideways.

There were no more pounding footsteps outside, no one calling, but distant shooting reached his ears, the far-off rattle of flintlocks, so this wasn't an isolated attack. Rhamp's men were making their move.

I knew those bastards would try it on, he thought dizzily. The wound in his belly was critical, and he couldn't seem to staunch the blood as darkness swarmed in.

Raythe, he thought, *I'm sorry, but you're on your own* . . .

Hot blood pouring through his fingers, he found himself staring at the ring on his finger, the one he'd plucked from the mass grave . . . as it became an eye, and then a mouth – that swallowed him whole.

The sound of flintlock hammers cocking, barely heard but instantly recognised, jolted Raythe into motion. 'Down!' he shouted, and Larch Hawkstone, survivor that he was, was with him as three flintlocks cracked in unison from a building opposite.

Lead balls tore through the space the two men had occupied and pinged off the walls.

'*Cognatus, animus nunc!*' Raythe was shouting even before he hit the floor, and his familiar burst into being, plunging into him as he rolled into the lee of the wall. Hawkstone shouted something incoherent as they heard running footsteps in the hallway outside.

'Larch, cover me!' Raythe shouted, while tracing *Tenebrae*, the sigil of darkness. '*Cognatus, praesemino.*'

·Three doors burst open in the far wall, revealing six men, led by Bloody Thom wielding a giant sword.

'Get him!' the Pelarian mercenary roared, and his men fanned out, brandishing their weapons.

Hawkstone cursed, drawing his sword, although each of the five were aiming pistols.

'Get out of the way, Hawkstone,' rasped Bloody Thom. 'Count of three.'

Inside Raythe, Cognatus was inhaling energy like oxygen, but it was still too soon.

Hawkstone gulped audibly, throwing down his sword ... but he didn't *quite* step aside ...

Bless you, Raythe thought, as his familiar readied itself. '*Cognatus, obscurum.*'

Like the opposite of a candle flaring in a dark room, darkness swallowed the light.

Raythe rose as the spell took effect, grabbed Hawkstone's shirt and hauled him to the ground, then slithered away, hearing the borderer follow a moment before a hammer fell and a lead ball went shrieking over Raythe's shoulder to punch into the wall. That panicked shot triggered three more, the cursing gunmen firing blindly, but not even the muzzle flashes were visible in the utter blackness ... except to Raythe, who pressed his mouth to Hawkstone's ear and whispered, 'Quietly now.' He nudged him down the room, away from the attackers, then slipped his boots off.

At Bloody Thom's order, everyone went still. They might be blinded by the dark, but to Raythe, they were hazy shimmers in the darkness ...

'Back up!' Bloody Thom barked. 'Back up to the doors.'

Raythe silently slipped his falchion from his well-oiled scabbard.

'Who's that?' someone whimpered.

Raythe smiled and padded silently forward on socked feet.

'We should reload again,' someone said.

'No one shoots!' Bloody Thom snapped. 'Back out – carefully.'

One of the five turned and ran in entirely the wrong way, smashed into a chair and fell noisily to the ground.

Outside the windows, someone shouted, 'Oi! Get some light on in there!'

That was followed by, 'We're coming over!'

'I've found a lamp on the wall,' the closest man babbled, but Raythe reached him and plunged his blade deep into the chest. He grabbed the mercenary, who whimpered, choked and fell silent, then lowered him to the ground and circled away.

A voice called, 'Ferdi?'

'Where're the kragging doors?' another voice bleated, stumbling along with arms outstretched. Raythe stepped in front and pushed his sword into his heart. The man shuddered and fell.

'*Two*,' Raythe whispered audibly, then slipped quickly away.

'Oh Deo,' a man bleated. 'Thom? Thom–?'

But Bloody Thom had gone silent.

'I've got a lamp lit, but it's not lighting anything!' someone wailed.

When no one responded, the lamp-holder tried to run, but blundered into a corpse, slipped in the blood and crashed to the ground. Another man roared as steel hammered painfully into his flesh – then the fallen man shrieked.

A pistol roared.

Two more bodies went still.

Three and Four . . . thanks, lads.

'Holy Gerda,' the praying man bleated. 'Thom? Thom–?' Then his hands found the wall and he began working his way along, seeking the door . . . heading towards Raythe.

Feeling more like an executioner than a warrior, Raythe thrust and slew, sending the man sliding to the floor.

The black room fell silent again.

Five.

Raythe ghosted backward, seeking ... and his hand brushed a handle.

The darkness spell was a tricky one, for it couldn't be sustained for long and it was already fading. He considered renewing it, but the need to speak and the few seconds when he would be visible made it too risky, so instead, he drifted towards the big man in the centre of the room.

Bloody Thom was turning slowly with his sword raised, occasionally chopping viciously at the space around him. Raythe waited until his foe was facing the other way, then began to move ...

But the spell failed a moment too soon: light flooded the room, revealing the five corpses, and Hawkstone, huddled against the wall beneath the windows.

The sight of his murdered comrades snapped the thin thread of control in Thom's brain. Boiling with rage, he rampaged towards Raythe. His giant sword came crashing down on Raythe's falchion, which belled and vibrated madly. Raythe staggered backwards, almost losing his footing–

–as three more gunmen crashed through the doors.

With Elgus Rhamp dealt with and the teams assigned to take out Vyre, Duretto and the infirmary off on their missions, there remained only one more place Crowfoot needed to gain control of. Wiping the blood from his battered face, he gave his orders, grabbed his escort and hurried off, reloading as they went.

Their destination was the main dining hall, where virtually the whole caravan would be gathered, apart from those on sentry duty. The travellers had grown used to communal living during the trek and at night they still huddled together, holding hands against the dark.

All in one place, where we can easily control them, Crowfoot thought.

He resheathed his axes, then led his unit into the dining hall, where they found themselves muscling their way into a scene of confusion, for everyone was already on their feet, peering out of the windows into the dusky gloom. When they saw him at the head of a squad of armed men, their faces lit with every type of reaction, from relief to fright.

The children ran for their parents as a chorus of queries greeted them.

'What's happening?' many shouted. 'Is it the barbarians? Where's Vyre?'

'Do we gotta head to the bridge?' a hunter called.

Crowfoot raised his reloaded pistol and fired it into the ceiling, instantly silencing the adults – although it set most of the babies and infants screaming.

'Shut those brats up!' he roared, looking for familiar faces as he strode into the middle of the room. 'Nesto, Falgram, get out here – and Semus, Aramak, you two as well! All Rhamp men, to me!' He glared about him, angry that his men – *mine, not Rhamp's, not any more* – were mingling with these village idiots.

'What's going on?' Falgram bleated, the dumb prick.

Crowfoot faced the room. 'What's happening is that this expedition is under new management. Raythe Vyre has betrayed us once too often. He's dead now.' *He kragging better be.* 'So're his cronies, the scum who were robbing us blind.' He held up a nugget of istariol. 'See this? He's already found istariol and told none of us –'

Then he had to stop, drowned by the exclamations of shock and awe that filled the room. He saw heads turning this way and that, seeking guidance and reassurance. Incredibly, the dominant reaction was disbelief.

These fools actually trust Vyre, he realised.

'Is Lor' Raythe dead?' one fool girl blubbed. 'Is he dead?'

Oh, for Gerda's sake! 'Aye,' he shouted, stamping his foot, 'and Duretto and Vidarsson and that whore of a healer – they're all traitors and they're all dead!' He drew an axe and swung it slowly as he looked from face to face along that wedge of steel. 'So's Elgus Rhamp. Bloody Thom and I are in charge now.'

'Oh Deo,' that damned girl wailed, 'you *murderer*!'

He took a step towards her and when an idiot boy tried to interpose himself, he backhanded the kid across the face, instantly felling him.

Moving as one, the crowd gasped and recoiled – but the wretched girl fell to her knees over the boy, screeching, '*Murderer!*'

He raised his boot to kick the bitch senseless, but to his amazement, Nesto interposed himself, saying, 'Leave her be. She's but a girl, Crow.'

Fire and ice. His heart boiled, but his mind went cold. 'Aye, you're right, Nesto,' he muttered—

—and his axe flashed round and cut Nesto down, almost severing his head.

Everyone went scrabbling backwards, all white-faced and terrified.

'Be *quiet!*' he roared. 'Be *still!*'

There was silence.

He looked round again, irked to see many of *his* men were still standing among the crowd, even those he'd called out. He'd not realised how much the community had grown together on the journey.

Three months ago, none of our lads would've hesitated to do any kragging order I gave.

'Falgram, Kortenberg,' he called again, while the pool of blood around Nesto's corpse grew. 'Dando. Get over here. Side with them and you're dead to us.'

Still they didn't move, and still the babies went on wailing, shredding his nerves.

'Here's how it's going to be,' Crowfoot shouted. 'My lads rule this place now: we keep you safe from the tribals and you work the mines. We're going to strip this place, then slip away. Do your bit an' you'll get your reward.' He spread his hands, shifting from threats to benevolence. 'Nothing's changed, people. We was always the ones protecting you. And we're still going to be rich – rich beyond your dreams! Under

Vyre you'd've got nothing! And the best thing is – there'll be fewer to share with.'

Still no one spoke.

Then from the back of the hall, a shadowy figure clapped, once . . . then twice . . . in slow-handed mockery.

'That right, Crow?' asked a totally unexpected voice. 'Well, ain't you a kraggin' hero.'

8

Tipping Points

The next moments seemed to happen in some strange world where time stretched like treacle. Varahana saw the man on the infirmary stairs below throw up his flintlock. For an instant the muzzle pointed at her face – she jerked aside as flame bloomed in the barrel and the ball skimmed her nose and blasted into the door, sending splinters flying.

She'd been shot at before and those previous brushes with death carried her through the next few seconds as she slammed the heavy door and locked it, bellowing, 'Gerdina!'

Together they heaved the big table up tight to the doorway, just as someone smashed against it.

She cast a look around: Maddy Groff was clinging to Sister Marta, caught up in another contraction and Bessa Tyne, who'd been dealing with fever-dreams most of the day, looked to be near fainting. Sister Agnes was hurriedly throwing logs into the fire, Lew Fulter was hobbling towards her, using a hunting spear as a crutch, and Sister Bea hefted Banno's sword. Even Jos, the battered Pelarian mercenary, was trying to rise.

Banno Rhamp groaned dreamily, barely aware of the danger.

Vidar rolled over on his pellet and Vara felt her heart lurch. He was in no condition for this. 'Vara,' he growled, his eyes turning amber.

No – it'll kill him . . .

Then someone shot out the lock and a voice snarled, 'We're coming for you, Priestess!'

'Oh no,' Jos croaked, his broken face contorting in terror, *'it's kragging Skavid . . .'*

Lew and Jos joined them as Varahana and Gerdina threw their weight against the table, but there were more men outside shoving back, and their greater strength was beginning to tell . . .

'Push!' Gerdina howled, but the men outside were crashing against the door again, smashing the table back just enough for someone to squeeze inside. Lew rammed his spear into the intruder's guts, but the next man through smashed a hammer down on Lew's skull – then the next heave flipped over the whole table, battering Varahana and Gerdina aside – and a bipedal white wolf with raking claws burst through.

Skavid went straight for Jos, ripping out his throat and hurling him aside. Three men followed the bearskin, all of them howling like berserkers.

This is it, Varahana realised, barely reacting as a grinning attacker loomed over her –

– until an oil-lamp smashed into his face, followed an instant later by a burning log. He ignited with a scream, staggering against the wall, his throwing axes clattering to the floor. Even the savage mercenaries gaped as mild old Sister Agnes reached for another burning log.

Then Vidar's nails became claws and his jaw a muzzle. He leaped at Skavid, battering his axe away and going for the throat – but Skavid was made of the same dark materials. He ripped free of Vidar's teeth before they could grip and tear, while his other hand grasped Vidar's neck. They crashed over, Skavid on top, while behind them, the other two men went for the women.

As the sickly Bessa was backhanded to the floor, Varahana snatched up one of the throwing axes, trying to remember what Jesco and Raythe had taught her. She didn't quite nail it – what crunched into the man's face wasn't the blade, but the top of the axe – but it was enough to break his nose and knock him senseless.

The other man spun . . .

. . . and brave, sick Bessa grabbed his leg, unsettling his balance, then little Sister Bea, who had a temper few saw, plunged Jos' dagger into the man's back. He convulsed, flopped and tried to rise, but Sister Bea stabbed him again, two-fisted and shrieking, and again and again.

The man-beasts in the middle of the room took no notice. Muscles bulging, teeth gnashing as muzzles vented ferocity and hate, they wrestled for dominance. Skavid's jagged canines were coming palpably closer to Vidar's throat with each minute.

For a moment, Varahana's vision went scarlet. She grabbed the second throwing axe and stormed forward, shrieking, 'YOU! GET ... OFF ... *HIM!*'

Each word was punctuated by an axe blow. The first, which came crunching down on Skavid's furred back, severed his spinal cord – that would likely have been enough. The second, cleaving open his wolf-head skull, certainly was. The third half-severed the neck . . .

. . . and Vidar caught the fourth, closing his left hand round the haft and holding on as his own transformation dissolved. With his other hand he shoved aside the broken body and enfolded her in a bloody, shaking embrace. On their knees, they clung together for support.

'Hey, hey, hey,' he panted soothingly, 'I'm the bearskin, my love, not you.' His words were barely discernible, but not to her. 'Let it go.'

How long they remained like that, she couldn't say . . . Enough time for him to become more truly human, for her rage and terror to subside, and for her to hear the word *love* and know it ran both ways.

Frightened of the realisation, she disentangled herself and looked round.

Jos and Lew were both dead, gone for ever, but somehow Bessa was still conscious, and Sister Agnes and Sister Bea were on their knees, praying forgiveness of Deo.

Banno blinked blearily from his mattress, barely aware of what had happened. Next to him was Sister Marta, trying to restrain Maddy Groff, who was shouting, '*VAL! VAL –?*' as she ignored the increasingly strong contractions and tried to scramble free.

The reminder of what lay beyond this room brought Varahana to her feet.

Val was down there, and Kemara – what's happening to them?

Kemara whipped the mask free of the cloak just as a figure appeared on the tiled verandah roof above, pulling his arm back to hurl a knife. Another was clambering out of the window, and from the infirmary room upstairs, she could hear shrieking. The man threw his knife as she tossed her cloak into the air, blocking the blade, which fell harmlessly to the ground.

'Krag!' the man cursed, hauling out the rusty sword that gave him his nickname and leaping into the foliage where Kemara was cowering.

But she'd found her feet and was stumbling out of the tangled shrubs just as Rusty's blade swept through the space she'd just vacated. Without pausing, she threw herself over a low wall into a muddy alley – as his sword crunched into the stone and shattered. The metal tip flew past her while his hands grasped for her.

She punched him with all her strength, aiming to go *through* him, just as Ionia had taught her, and her fist crunched into his nose, snapping his head back, leaving her knuckles blazing with pain.

But a second man had dropped down in pursuit, and yet another was on the roof and aiming a flintlock, which spat just as she dropped; the ball smacked into the wall behind her and ricocheted.

She jammed on Buramanaka's mask as she pelted down the road, her shoulder bleeding but running on adrenalin. At the end of the alley, she turned downhill towards the walls and the patrolling guards.

The three men hammering after her were too fast to outrun.

In desperation, she veered into a building she'd explored while seeking a home for her infirmary: the front door was open and the lobby beyond had multiple exits. She chose one, just in time to spin and slam the door in the face of the nearest mercenary, a bruiser named Rokasson. She'd treated him for foot-rot – for which he'd sought to reward her by grabbing her tits.

His fist slammed into the door, but she'd already shoved the still intact bolt across, thanking Deo for the excellent Aldar engineering which had left a surprising number of metal fixtures in good order. His body crashed into the door a moment later, but she was already thumping up the stairs, leaving footprints in the dust – then she flipped off the balustrade and landed as gently as she could on the stone floor below and darted through the next door into the large room she'd almost selected as the infirmary ward.

Rhamp's making his move, she thought, which meant all the people she'd begun to respect, even care for, were probably dying. Then she heard the bolted door smash open and Rokasson shouted, 'I heard her go upstairs!'

They thudded up the wooden steps . . .

. . . which were rotten at the top, the reason she hadn't chosen this building.

'Kra-a-a-ag–' someone wailed as the wood gave way and a body came crashing down on the other side of the wall from her. The impact sounded pleasingly painful.

'Bezo, you all right?' she heard Rokasson call.

There was a pause, then Bezo bleated, 'My knee . . . my kraggin' knee.'
Good.

She backed up, touched her mask and whispered, '*Buramanaka, kaneska alla mizra.*' Like a comet hurtling down a tunnel of light, the mizra spirit came for her.

A muffled nasal voice called, 'Roka? Bezo?' Rusty sounded rather like his nose was broken. The three men had a quiet conversation, then they fell silent and she heard stealthy movement in the hall.

She made for the windows, but her feet crunched on the grit on the floor and she heard Rokasson say, '*Listen*–'

Then Buramanaka slammed into her like falling star, like lava coursing through her veins, a blacksmith's hammer pounding in her heart. For a moment she could barely breathe, feeling his energy flowing in – then he took control. Her torn, bloodied clothing shifted on her skin, becoming something tooled for a macabre theatre. Her breasts were barely covered by a corselet of black lacquered leather embossed with red dragons; her thighs were bare and her hair writhed like snakes into a pile of scarlet coils framing her mask. She felt like some kind of she-beast from the Pit.

Bura's curved sword appeared in her right hand. *Ready?* he breathed in her mind.

Oh yes . . .

She blended into the shadows as Rokasson burst through the door into the hall, followed a moment later by bloody-faced Rusty and skinny, limping Bezos. They were dimly lit by the twilight's last gleaming through the open windows, but to them she was just a shadow in the dark.

'Anyone got a tinderbox?' Rusty bleated, snorting blood.

The scent of it made her tongue quiver.

'Nah,' Rokasson said nervously, 'just let yer eyes adjust.'

'She ain't here,' Bezos whined. 'We should head back.'

'She *punched* me,' Rusty spat. 'I owe her – I'm gonna kill her nice and slow.'

'Nah – she's a sorceress,' Rokasson reminded him, 'so we gotta do it quick.'

'She ain't here,' Bezos repeated.

'Yes I am,' she told them, stepping into the half-light. 'Come and try me, Rusty.'

She could see dread warring with masculine arrogance, unable to contemplate fleeing a mere woman, but terrified of what they saw in her.

Then Rokasson roared and came to meet her, while Bezos fumbled up his pistol and fired.

She caught the ball in her left hand while her sword smashed against Rokasson's blade – and continued effortlessly through it and through him, sweeping forward to sever his spine.

He fell in two, but she'd already spun to lop off Bezos' hand, sending the pistol spinning away. He was blubbing, staring at the blood pumping from the stump, until she thrust her blade into his chest and he folded and fell silent.

'Now it's just you,' she purred, turning gracefully to confront Rusty.

He dropped to his knees, sobbing, 'Please, no –' as she stalked closer and placed the razor-sharp edge of the blade against the back of his neck.

'But I thought you *owed* me, Rusty?'

'Uh . . . no . . . . . please . . .'

Pathetic. She slashed, and Rusty's head leaped from his body and bounced across the bloody floor, while his body plunged forward and flopped into motionlessness.

For a few seconds, she was paralysed by the desire to seize the neck stump and guzzle the blood – she could already taste it on her tongue, the hot metallic flow that would fill her throat and belly and feed her beast – but she pushed the *need* away.

She threw back her head, wailing her refusal, then gasping for air, she staggered away.

Inside her, Buramanaka was moaning in disappointment.

Go, she was about to command, *yameru a mizra* – but before she could articulate the command, Buramanaka *felt* something he'd not sensed in the five centuries he'd lain mouldering in his sarcophagus – something he needed and desired above all else.

She tried to fight him, but it was like shouting at a hurricane. With a howl, her unwilling body bounded through the open widow, landed in more tangled shrubs, hurdled a wall and powered on, seeking that spark before it faded . . .

Three more men burst into the room as Bloody Thom charged towards Raythe – who had thrust out his left fist and was shouting, '*Impetu, Cognatus!*'

Thom was hurled away, but Raythe was already spinning, roaring, '*Habere scutum, nunc!*' at the newcomers, two of whom were levelling flintlocks.

Before they could fire, Hawkstone shot the man on the right – but he couldn't get to the second man in time.

With Cognatus' shield only half-formed, the ball should have caught Raythe mid-chest, but he was already twisting away and instead, it raked his side.

The third newcomer wavered, not sure if he should go for Hawkstone, who was aiming a second pistol, or Raythe, raising his sword – and that hesitation killed him, for Hawkstone's ball took the man in the forehead and he pitched over backwards.

Raythe levelled his left hand at the last gunman standing, readying a blast of energy, but the man dropped his flintlock and called, 'Please, I yield!'

Hawkstone rammed a bayonet into the barrel of his flintlock and stalked forward, growling, 'Yield, you bastard? I don't think so!'

'Hold,' Raythe told him. 'Reload your pistol, I'll cover you.' Then he called, '*Impetu*–' and Cognatus hurled the last man across the room to slam into the stonework next to Bloody Thom – who was rising, his face purple with wrath.

The mercenary looked fearfully at his gigantic captain. 'Thom, I din' mean I *yielded*–'

But his words were chopped off by the blade Thom had plunged into his chest.

'A Rhamp man don't yield,' Thom announced, pulling his sword free before erupting towards Raythe, all madly blazing eyes and bared teeth.

'*Cognatus, impe*–' Raythe began, then, realising there was no time, he dropped to one knee just as the massive blade swept round at waist-height. Parrying desperately, his angled blade deflected the arcing steel up and over his head in a mighty sparking crash, before he rammed the hilt of his sword up into the man's groin.

The mercenary didn't seem to feel the blow, for he'd planted his feet and now began lifting his huge blade, ready to bring it down and hack Raythe in half.

Raythe had no choice. He shoved the full length of his falchion into the giant's body, going in through the groin and pushing it through until the tip burst from his back.

Thom's blade fell from hands that had suddenly lost grip and he toppled, Raythe's sword still impaling his body.

Hawkstone stopped reloading and stared in horrified awe. '*Milord*—'

Raythe remained kneeling, dazed by the intensity of the sorcery and the carnage. *Holy Gerda* . . . It had been a long time since he'd so fully lost himself in the dance of death. But time was pressing: if Bloody Thom had been confident enough to take him on with hidden snipers and a squad of killers, what else was going on?

Where're Jesco and Vara and Kemara? What's happening at the dining hall?

The hall was closest, and that's where most of his people would be – and that's where Elgus Rhamp, who was surely behind this, would be trying to assert control.

He bent, yanked his falchion from Thom's body, wiped it clean on the dead man's sleeve, then hacked off the man's head off and bagged it.

'Larch,' he said, 'if you're with me, let's go. We need to end this before it's too late.'

Crowfoot stared in disbelief at Elgus Rhamp, bloodied, white-faced and soaked to the skin – *a well-ghost*, the superstitious part of him groaned.

Utter confusion reigned in the hall, villagers and hunters and mercenaries alike jerking their heads back and forth as if they were waiting for someone to tell them what to do.

'Is he alive or dead?' one of Crowfoot's lads bleated.

'He's alive,' Crowfoot snapped, finding his voice, 'but not for much longer.'

The old bastard must've pulled himself out the moment I turned my back. How the crag did he survive?

'One solid smack an' he'll go down,' he promised, but there was a solid wall of people between him and his old chief, and a quick head count told him just eight of his lads were left. Crowfoot felt the winds of Fate vacillating between fortune and failure.

'Nothing's changed,' he shouted, seeking to regain control. All the weapons were stacked against one wall, so no one here was armed but his men. 'Vyre's dead,' he went on, addressing those Rhamp men still among the villagers. 'Elgus is deposed, lads – he's been Vyre's catspaw all along! I'll give twenty argents to the man who strikes him down.'

That was a year's grog – but no one out there even blinked.

'Don't want yer money, Crow,' Falgram replied. 'Elgus is our cap'n; he always will be.'

'Aye,' said Semus, and Miki Brond, whose leg was in a brace, nodded.

'Get out, Crow,' shouted Angrit, one of the tavern whores. Crowfoot had had her many a time, but there was nothing but loathing on her face now. 'We don't want you here.'

'You ungrateful–' he started, but she was laughing at him.

'I should be grateful? For what, you limp-dicked backstabber?'

With that, the entire hall erupted. Clearly, if a whore could shout you down, everyone else thought they could too. The furious faces were crying out, *'We're with old Rhamp!'* and *'He can't take us all!'* – and worse, he *finally* noticed that someone had been busy scooping up the stashed weapons and distributing them among the crowd.

'Crow, what're we gonna do?' came a shaky voice from behind him: Uthir, of course, the pussy.

Crowfoot peered through the angry crowd at the swaying knight. 'We hold firm: Elgus is out on his feet and there's no one else here matters a shit.'

Then a new voice was raised, and his heart went utterly cold.

'Is that what you think, Crowfoot?' Raythe Vyre called – from the doors *behind* him.

He turned, shaking, and saw the Otravian was holding Bloody Thom's head by the hair – and blue fire was dancing on the fingertips of his other hand. Beside him was Larch Hawkstone, cradling a flintlock.

Ah, krag . . .

But there's still Skavid at the infirmary, and Eilfin should've slaughtered that Shadran tinderstick by now . . . but where the krag are they? Their absence was beginning to feel less like the boys having fun and more like abject failure. Everyone here was armed now, and the children and women had been herded to the back. *They're just village scum,* he told himself. *Not a one of 'em could face down a real warrior . . .*

But he could see Gan Corbyn had an arrow aimed at his heart, and he knew the hunter wouldn't miss.

One by one, the lads behind them laid down their arms and knelt, and then there was just him and he already knew the fate he'd be allotted – the only one he feared.

No. No – I will not be hanged.

With a wild scream, he hurled himself at Vyre, his twin axes flailing–

Hawkstone's gun boomed, the ball slammed into his gut and doubled him over, and his axes spun away. He smashed headfirst into the floor and the lights winked out.

When Crowfoot woke, it was in the shadow of an old arched bridge over a sunken street. It was full night and the planetary rings dividing the sky were partially concealed by the floating rock above. Garish flaming torches on all sides lit the scene.

He came to, finding himself tied at wrists and ankles, sprawled on the stones. Above him, Uthir was kicking frantically on a rope dangling from the bridge. Eight other bodies hanging beside him were already still, except for the piss and shit dripping from their feet. As he watched, Uthir sagged and his bowels voided too.

'Wakey-wake, Crow,' Elgus Rhamp wheezed. 'It's your turn.'

'No . . . no, not the rope – *please*, Elgus, *no*–'

'What did you think was going to happen? We'd kiss and make up?'

'Lord Vyre!' He sought the Otravian. 'Milord, please, show mercy – not the rope!'

'The sentence is passed,' Vyre said calmly.

'No,' he pleaded, 'not this way – I was an executioner once meself . . .

They're all waiting for me – all them feckers I hanged ... Deo and Gerda, not the rope!'

'All the better.' Elgus Rhamp was a mess, like a revenant returned from the grave for just this moment, but the whole community was gathered behind him, their faces stoic, disdainful or angry.

'String the bastard up,' shrieked Angrit, clinging to Larch Hawkstone's arm, and her cry was echoed on all sides.

Falgram and Lynd Borger, burly men both, dragged Crowfoot up the short rise onto the bridge. Cal Foaley looped a noose over his head and Gan Corbyn checked the knot.

Unseen by them, all the men Crowfoot had ever hanged began to appear, ghastly wraiths of his imagination, crowding in. Losing all courage, he fell to begging, 'Please, no, no ...'

Then someone hurled him over the parapet, and he flew ... then he fell ...

As he dropped, he tried to jack-knife, to make sure the sudden stop when he reached the end of the rope would break his neck cleanly – but all he contrived to do was to soften his fall, so that although his neck muscles *cracked*, he ended up dangling, kicking and blubbing like a frightened child, while the hole in his belly ripped open and blood came pouring out.

He'd been good at hangings, at engineering this very effect, to draw out his victims' terror and give the crowd a proper show. He'd always cackled dementedly as his victims danced – but now, as the rope tightened around his own neck and the air was slowly squeezed out, he danced for his ghosts as they climbed his legs and pulled him down to their waiting teeth ...

'May the Pitlords feast on his carcase,' Elgus Rhamp shouted as Crowfoot finally, mercifully, went still.

The crowd had no appetite for any of this, but they all stayed to see justice done. Gravis Tavernier opined that the real Crowfoot had been revealed in his last sobbing moments.

Maybe that's true, Raythe thought, *but who knows how any of us will face our end?*

He steadied himself against the parapet as all eyes now turned to Elgus Rhamp. What had happened an hour ago was still a mass of confusion to most, and they all knew the old knight could twist and turn like a snake. Some even wondered if he'd triggered the push before disassociating himself, but Raythe had heard Crowfoot's denunciation of his boss, and Uthir, hoping for mercy, had detailed their whole plan, describing the trap Elgus had been lured into just as the other attacks began – and how they'd thought him dead, their first victim.

'So,' Raythe murmured, 'Elgus, are we finally done with treachery?'

'This was nowt to do with me,' the Pelarian protested yet again.

'Perhaps, but you cannot deny that you set the tone for it, with your sons and their attempts to seize control; your refusal to bring your men into line, your protection when they've raped or molested villagers. They all took their cues from you, from Crowfoot down.'

Beneath his bellicose, boisterous exterior, Elgus was a bullying fraud. Raythe had known that from the first, but he'd had no choice; he'd needed the man and his company. But he was sure those mercenaries who now remained – fewer than twenty of them – were redeemable, and perhaps Elgus was too.

'You're right, I was lax,' the old knight mumbled, his shoulders dropping. 'But I swear it was them two – they've been undermining me from the get-go, but I didn't see it.'

Well, I do believe you're with us now, for Banno's sake, if nothing else.

Raythe laid a hand on Elgus' shoulder. 'You and I have been yoked together,' he said loudly, 'first by this expedition, and now by our children.' He turned to face the watching crowd and announced, 'Sir Elgus and I have agreed that Zarelda and Banno will marry when they are restored fully to us. We will be as *brothers*, Elgus.'

While those listening cheered, he dropped his voice. 'When I am restored to my Otravian estates – *which I damned well will be* – you will share in that, through Banno and Zarelda: this I swear. Your grandson – *our* grandson – will inherit my estates. So you will be loyal to me *to your last breath*. Am I understood?'

Elgus slumped and nodded. Raythe made a show of embracing him, then cast his gaze over the crowd. Almost everyone had been accounted for; even Vidar was there, badly injured and pale from blood loss, but clinging to Varahana's arm.

That left only Jesco, Norrin and Kemara still missing. *Please, Deo, let them be found*, he begged silently.

But for now, he had no time to grieve or panic; he must act like a leader. 'My friends, what happened this night was worse than the beach in Verdessa, or the glacier or the hill-fort: because this time the enemy came from within: twenty-six men – men we badly needed – turned against us. They betrayed every single one of us, including Sir Elgus Rhamp – the man who brought them here to give them all the chance of a new life. They even tried to kill his son Banno, lying helpless in the infirmary. They sank so low as to assail the sick and dying, and poor Maddy Groff, who was giving birth. Poor Maddy is now a widow and her new babe has no father.'

The whole crowd growled at the dangling bodies.

'But let me assure you of two things I know for certain: one is that Sir Elgus was never a part of this treachery – and nor were those of his men who still live: Falgram, Semus and Aramak and those standing among you now – and poor Nesto, who paid for his loyalty with his life. I can also tell you that *nowhere* did Crowfoot's men succeed. We repelled their treachery in the infirmary, in my council room, in the dining hall – everywhere they struck at people they accounted weak, they found them to be strong.'

There were murmurs at this, and someone called out, 'Were you assailed, Lord Vyre?'

'I was.' He gestured Hawkstone. 'And without Larch here, I doubt I'd have survived the attack.'

Few here esteemed the former borderer – he'd been the bane of too many people's lives back in Teshveld – but they gave him a not entirely grudging murmur of praise.

Hawkstone ducked his head sheepishly. 'Weren't much,' he blurted. 'Were mostly Lord Vyre.'

Raythe raised a hand. 'Folks, it's been a frightening evening, but look at us: we're still standing. We've lost a few – if you count Crowfoot and his conspirators, we've lost a lot. This rebellion has weakened us all. But it's made us stronger, too, because we no longer need to watch our backs, or protect our families from supposed comrades!'

'Aye!' someone shouted, although a lot were still looking sceptical.

But Raythe had finished speaking and now, as the crowd broke up, some were coming forward to express their relief that he had survived. 'We can't do this without ye, Milord,' was the prevailing sentiment, and he was moved by the sincerity.

Finally he was left with Elgus and Foaley. Varahana was helping Vidar back to the infirmary, and watching them stagger away, he envied their closeness. He badly needed the comfort of someone who cared for him – and he missed Zar even more.

'Raythe,' Foaley murmured, 'I'm sorry I wasn't here – I got called to the east side, by the river. A false alarm . . .'

'A stroke of luck, I warrant – I doubt they had any intention of letting you live,' Raythe replied. 'Young Jos Petz was killed at the infirmary, and Lew Fulter and Val Groff. They're the worst losses, I reckon, and they were good husbands.'

'And Norrin Harper's dead too,' the hunter added. 'We just found him in the watchtower east of the bridge.'

Raythe sagged, thinking of the way the young bard came alive when he played his harp. 'Any sign of Jesco or Kemara yet?'

'Well, we found three of Rhamp's men lying near Norrin, and it was blade-work that killed them. One was Eilfin, who reckoned himself the best sword in the expedition.' Foaley smiled wryly. 'Reckon he wasn't.'

'Who lives and dies isn't decided by skill alone,' Elgus pointed out.

'True,' Raythe agreed.

Foaley slapped his shoulder, a rare gesture from the normally taciturn hunter. 'There's a blood trail the lads are following, but we
mightn't find anything until morning.'

'I'll not sleep until I know,' Raythe replied. 'Come on, show me where.'

Once, when she was young, Kemara had been taken to a fair by her
parents. An old warrior was giving children rides on his warhorse for a
copper, perching them on top and leading them round on a rope.

When it came her turn, some idiot boy threw a grass snake in the
horse's face as a prank – and the stallion had reared, then bolted. Somehow, she'd held on as it thundered through the crowd, bouncing
uncontrollably but still gripping the saddle for dear life, terrified and
shrieking . . .

She was reminded of that wild ride now as Buramanaka lashed her
body along, her awareness buffeted and battered, and all she could do
was try to cling on. There were terrifying gaps in her sight and vision
as she thundered down an alley to the walls and burst into a tower
room where five men lay unmoving.

But someone still lived – the one who mattered.

Kiiyan, yaru jihibukai! she heard Buramanaka plead: Kiiyan, be merciful.

She scooped him up and then, fearful of further attacks, bore him
out into the pitch-dark and ran down a lane skirting the outer wall.
The man in her arms was breathing, but each footfall elicited a gasp
of pain and finally she shrieked at Buramanaka, *'Stop! You're killing
him—'*

Her words jolted Buramanaka out of his madness and she was
allowed to lurch to a halt. A moment to look around, then she kicked
aside a broken door and pushed through to a debris-filled room. She
cleared a space and lowered the body to the ground, and only then did
she see who it was.

Jesco Duretto.

Why Buramanaka should be so distraught about the Shadran, she had no idea, but the emotion was absolutely real. *Kyuen ka no*, he hissed: Save her.

Her? Then she remembered Varahana saying that the Aldar language didn't always differentiate according to gender.

Abruptly, her body was her own again. The garish costume she'd been wearing vanished, replaced by her own torn and bloodied blouse and filthy, shredded skirts – but she didn't pause to take stock; she knew what she had to do. She pushed away the filthy ripped cloth from around the four-inch-wide hole in Jesco's belly, knowing stomach wounds usually guaranteed a slow, agonising death, but there was a presence inside Jesco, she realised now, and she could feel Buramanaka entwining with that entity. She fed Buramanaka power, hoping that somehow the spirit could do what she couldn't . . .

She concentrated on the things she could, bathing his wound in the rainwater she found in a broken pot in one corner; sealing it with cauterising fire from her fingertips, bandaging it in strips torn from her underskirt – until Jesco's body suddenly *jolted*, and heat began to suffuse his skin, and that was nothing to do with her.

Finally, there was nothing more to do but to remove the mask and tuck it into its usual hiding place before lying down beside Jesco so she could cradle him to keep him warm as the world fell away . . .

Kemara woke to blazing torches and the sound of relieved voices. It took her a blurry minute to realise she was being hoisted onto what was a makeshift stretcher, but she was too exhausted to protest. The use of the mizra had severely depleted her: magic always had a price.

But Raythe Vyre was here, and Cal Foaley too, and other friends, and they were telling her that everything would be okay, that she could go back to sleep. Then Varahana's beautiful face appeared, alive with concern, but she said that Jesco was doing well, and so too was Maddy Groff and her newborn baby boy.

Thank Deo, she thought, rolling over and staring at the sleeping Jesco. She had no idea why Buramanaka had been so determined to save him, but she was deeply thankful that she'd been there, for otherwise, he'd certainly have died.

Perhaps Buramanaka cares for those who matter to me? But no, that didn't quite feel right.

'The mask?' she mumbled to Raythe Vyre, bending over her.

'I have it,' he whispered. 'I'll keep it safe.'

Grateful, and annoyed at once more having to be beholden to him for her safety, she relinquished her tenuous hold on consciousness and drifted down into the world of dreams.

9

Regrouping

Raythe ran panting through the ruins of Rath Argentium, hidden flint-locks and archers firing at him every time he tried to rest or hide, forcing him onwards into what he knew would be an ambush.

Then a firm hand pulled him up and out of the nightmare and Vara-hana's tired but serene face swam above him. 'Vara?' he gasped, looking around anxiously, but they were alone in his room. 'Is everything all right?'

'We think so – but there's a masked woman on the bridge, demand-ing to see you.'

Masked? He sat up blearily and saw Gravis Tavernier peering in anxiously.

'He a'right?' the publican called, almost like he cared. 'Can I get 'im owt? Brekkie, perhaps?'

Raythe looked at the window to see the sun was well up – and he'd slept through breakfast for the first time in what felt like centuries. 'I'm fine, and yes, hungry – thanks, Gravis, that'd be appreciated. How's Jesco? Kemara? And Vidar?'

'All doing well,' she assured him. 'I'm going to hold a Mass of Thanks-giving at midday. I think the Tangato might have heard some of what happened last night – and now one of the masked ones is out there.'

A part-Aldar woman wants to see me . . . 'Okay, fine, just give me a moment.'

'Of course, you take your time. You don't want to meet her looking anything less than your best. You represent us all.'

Once Varahana was gone, Raythe set about getting himself properly dressed and armed. The priestess was right: he needed to present a front of complete control and confidence to the Tangato envoy. Making people wait was always a handy way to get inside their heads, so he took his time over the food Gravis brought, then he and Varahana headed to the bridge.

Foaley was already there, with a double rank of gunmen and archers. He gestured at the distant figure at the apex of the bridge. 'One of the masked tribals – she says she's the queen's sister, Ulaka. Creepy as all the Pit.'

A thought struck Raythe. 'Listen,' he said loudly, so everyone there would hear, 'we don't use the term "barbarians" or "tribals", or any other nicknames. These people are the *Tangato*, and this is their land.'

Everyone except Varahana looked puzzled, but they murmured their obedience.

'Bravo,' she murmured. 'Do you need company out there?'

'She's alone,' Foaley noted. 'The fellas in the tower can see all the way along the bridge and there's no one else.' He paused, then suggested, 'Shall we try and nab her?'

'No,' Raythe said firmly, 'we need to maintain good faith with these people. Just shout if anything looks amiss.'

Calling Cognatus into him, he went to meet Ulaka.

As he approached, the masked woman came to meet him. She stopped ten yards away.

'Good morning,' he called.

She was a breathtaking sight, robed in heavily embroidered green, blue and yellow silk robes. Her gilded mask was shaped like a peacock head. There was not a fleck of skin visible.

'I am Ulaka, sister to Queen Shiazar,' she replied, in accented but easily understandable Gengo-Magnian. 'My Queen sends greetings.'

'Thank you, Princess,' he replied carefully. 'I return her greetings.'

'We have no "princesses",' Ulaka replied. 'The throne is not hereditary.'

He bowed and apologised. 'I was not aware. How can I help you?'

'At sunset last night, our watchers heard strange sounds,' she replied. 'A sharp sound, over and over, and much shouting. My Queen was worried for you.'

I bet she was, Raythe thought wryly. Remembering their casualties, his smile slipped away. 'All is well,' he answered. 'We thank the Queen for her concern. Was there anything else?'

'Only that you come to your senses and leave soon,' Ulaka replied. 'You told my Queen you needed to consider her proposals. What have you decided?'

That we don't know what to do, was the honest answer, but that wasn't likely to appease the Tangato. But he'd agreed to play for time, so he could start now. 'Respectfully, we need much longer to replenish our supplies. Do you know the Kirra Moon – the brightest orb of the planetary rings?'

Ulaka frowned, looking up, but the Kirra Moon – according to scholars, a giant sphere of rock that was caught in the planetary rings – wasn't currently visible. 'Do you mean the Tamago – the Egg?' she asked.

'Maybe? It's visible in the night sky for five days in thirty. Our scholar says it will reappear in twenty days. Will you give us that long to restock and be ready to move?'

That should be time enough to secure enough istariol to have made all this worthwhile so we can get out before the empire comes.

Ulaka didn't sound pleased. 'I'll need to consult with my Queen,' she said sourly.

'Sooner would condemn us to death on the road home. It's realistic.' He decided to change the subject before she pressed him further. 'How is my daughter?'

'Unwell,' Ulaka said shortly.

'*What?* May I see her?'

'No.'

He wondered if this was some power play, but he couldn't see the angle, unless it was to remind him of the leverage they had over him, should they choose to exert it. Perhaps it wasn't even true – *but what if it is?*

'Please – if she is ill, I have to see her.'

'When she recovers. We care for her as if she were our own – which she is.'

'Is her life endangered?'

'Hetaru himself cares for her,' Ulaka answered. 'There is no danger.'

He bridled, but kept his temper. 'Then I will await word,' he said. 'Please, tell Zarelda that I'm well, and so is Banno. Tell her he is awake, and thinking of her.'

She bowed her head in acknowledgement, then turned and glided gracefully away, leaving him with a whole new worry. *What's wrong with my daughter . . . ?*

Spinning stars collided as Zarelda quailed, trapped in a tiny circle of calm, the eye of a cosmic hurricane. Coruscating light blinded her, the crash of thunder rang in her eardrums, so loud it deafened her, making her whole body vibrate, rattling her bones to the marrow. Then the swirling energies became two giant serpents, eating each other's tails; then two rivers, meeting in a maelstrom, sucking her under. It was bewildering, uncontrollable, overwhelming – all she could do was coil herself into a ball and scream for it to end.

But it didn't; instead, the crisis grew, the spinning of the universe wrapping tighter and tighter about her, tearing at her, flesh and bone, ripping her apart as she howled . . .

Rima gripped her master's shoulder. 'Save her,' she pleaded, staring at Zarelda, lying on the mat before them in Hetaru's farai.

Hetaru, his gentle face contorted with anxiety, said, 'I'm doing all I can, e aroha.'

Zarelda was caught up in some inner cataclysm. It wasn't supposed to be like this – it never had been for any other mahotsu-kai. But they'd never before encountered such a strange turehu as Zar's familiar. It was as if Adefar was mutilated – and yet Zar thought him normal.

These people must be wrong in the head, Rima thought, feeding Hetaru more of her strength as he tried again to reach Zar. If he could place an oar in the spinning waters of the girl's soul, he could slow the destructive maelstrom to something she could handle.

At times she heard the voices of the Yokei, asking for updates, but there was still nothing to say.

What can we tell them? That we don't really know what we're doing . . . ?

Zarelda felt the moment when her spirit severed from her body. She floated for what felt like hours while wolves howled over mountain tops and a wind tugged at her frayed spirit, trying to sweep her away. But she clung to the vista of glittering rings of light above, refusing to blink or to look away, binding her sight to the *here*, to the *now*, and fighting to remain within it . . .

Rima pounded Zar's chest, then inhaled deeply, placed her lips over the dying girl's mouth and pushed air into her, breathing for her, watching her chest rise, then fall. She hammered again, did another round of breaths as she pleaded with Heaven.

Kiiyan, have mercy . . . Kagemori, withhold your deathly hand . . .

Something licked Zar's cheek and she opened her eyes. She was floating in the stillness beneath the planetary rings as if she were the planet they orbited. Two amber eyes peered down, and then a tongue caressed her cheek again. A fox . . . Adefar, but *not*-Adefar: bigger, wiser – *whole*. She sighed, reached up and pulled his face to hers and kissed the fur on his cheeks as tears of happiness flowed–

–then came a sudden pain in her chest and she convulsed, her eyes flying open. Rima was kissing her – no, not kissing, forcing air down her throat – and Adefar was a hot furry weight on her chest. She seized the fox and crushed him against her, caught up in uncaring relief in this moment of rebirth.

Rima's face lit up and she whooped in absolute joy and triumph. Beyond her, Hetaru's face hovered, his tattooed old visage beaming like a sun. A fire was blazing beside her and the heat was searing her side, but she didn't care: the pain was pleasure, for it signified *life*.

'I'm back,' she reassured this new Adefar. 'I'm back.'

Inside her mind, the fox-faced man gave her a vulpine smile, and then he was just her Adefar again, cute and lovable, even with eyes that were worldly and wise. When she kindled a little energy, the connection fizzed and crackled.

He's so strong now . . . no, we are so strong!

'What happened to me?' she asked.

Hetaru and Rima's faces fell as one. 'We're so sorry,' the old man murmured, bowing his head. 'I've never heard of such a thing before. We thought the merging of your existing familiar spirit with its greater kin would be safe. If we'd realised it would endanger you so, we would have done things very differently.'

Rima's face pleaded for understanding. 'We mean you nothing but good,' she insisted.

Zar found that she believed them, and with Adefar glowing inside her, she couldn't feel anger. She could forgive. 'But what actually happened?'

Hetaru gave her a troubled look. 'We don't fully know, but I have a suspicion. In your lands all spirits are either "mizra" – wild and dangerous; or "praxis" – passive but weak, yes? Our familiar spirits – what we call "turehu" – are neither: they are whole and strong. Your Adefar is now turehu – but clearly such a reuniting holds peril.'

Zar's mind reeled at the implication. In Magnia – across the whole continent – there was only the praxis – well, other than the occasional mizra-witch in hiding. Was it possible that *every* Magnian sorcerer had less than half the power they should have? To think of her own people as backwards in this matter was deeply unsettling, but the evidence, personified by Adefar, was compelling. Hugging the fox-cub familiar, she worried anew for her father.

I must to speak to him. I need to share this.

And more than anything else, she needed to stop these people from wiping out hers. And that reminded her with a jolt that she'd been unconscious – for how long . . . ?

'What day is it?'

Rima understood. 'Queen Shiazar and your father met again yesterday: they have agreed to extend the truce by twenty days, until the Tamago – the Kirra Moon, he called it – rises. And your Banno is awake and thinking of you, your father says.'

'Thank Gerda.' Zar put her hand to her chest in relief – and realised that the jade pendant that had housed Adefar was gone. She looked at Rima, who was dangling it from her index finger.

'Do we need it any more?' the Tangato girl asked her.

They've made me stronger – and think what else I might learn . . . 'No, you don't need it,' she told them. 'I'll stay here. You can trust me.'

Her words came out with the resonance of certainty and truth and she knew she meant them. A whole new vista had opened up in her mind: life in Magnia had been dangerous, and the rebellion had severed all her ties of family and friends. The possibility of never going back was daunting, but perhaps life here would be better than what she'd left behind?

I'll never see Mother again . . . but would I ever have, anyway?

Rima gathered her up in a hug, while Hetaru beamed down at her, nodding and smiling. 'Welcome to the Ngati Hiriwa,' he said. 'Welcome to the Tangato.'

INTERLUDE (1)

Survival Instincts

Toran Zorne limped to the foot of a tiny gully, not much more than a rut of stunted grass and stones, confronted the next rise – and collapsed. His entire body was begging for respite.

Every inch of him ached, stabbed, itched, oozed or bled. Had he known just how much suffering he'd have to go through, he might never have begun this trek. His estimate of how long it would take him had been badly wrong: unarmed, wounded and without provisions, every mile he walked felt like it had doubled, then doubled again.

The few berries he'd been able to forage had given out after two days, and the flightless birds that he had thought to catch were elusive, so that by the time he stood at the edge of the frozen lake in the south of these hidden lands, all he had was a bundle of dried tree branches, a knife and an empty food pouch.

Day three saw him stumbling down the glacier that would take him south to Verdessa. He was dizzy and wild-eyed, his belly groaning from hunger. A fire kept him alive that night, but he used up half his wood. The next day, the third without food, he survived by drinking snowmelt. A storm would have killed him.

Day four saved his life.

He reached the northern end of the section of the glacier that Raythe Vyre had destroyed, somehow melting the ice and drowning or sweeping away many of the Bolgravian force pursuing him. The climb down on semi-melted, refrozen ice was treacherous and he almost fractured an ankle when he fell, but that evening, he came across a Bolgravian deserter who'd somehow eluded the destruction of his regiment and started fleeing for home.

There are always deserters. Scum always floats away, he thought derisively.

They'd been as weak as each other, but Zorne, with the advantage of surprise, had managed to plunge in his dagger often enough that the other man quickly went limp. After looting his body, Zorne butchered him and built a fire from the debris of the Bolgravian bombards, which was piled up against the walls of the ravine. Then he ate a breast while he cooked the rest for the journey.

With a decent fire and a full belly, he was finally able to sleep and heal.

It was the first time he'd consumed human flesh: *just salty pork*, he decided, *nothing to be squeamish about*. That night he dreamed of roasting Raythe Vyre and Kemara Solus while they were still alive, and carving bits off them as they rotated on the spit: a pleasing fancy.

The deserter gave him the sustenance he needed to climb back onto the treacherous glacier surface and traverse the long, twisting ravine; all the same, it was three unpleasant days of gnawing dried Bolgravian while his own toes and fingers went numb with cold. He found no further fuel, but his familiar shared energy, keeping him from freezing, although frostbite gnawed at his extremities as he slept.

On the seventh day, he reached the frigid lake at the base of the glacier. He wasted half a day trying to fish, before going a little insane and running at a flock of deer that came down to the water to drink, screaming, 'I am the Emperor! I am Khagan Koreimi of Bolgravia! I demand that you let me eat you!' until he pitched onto his face and lay there shaking.

I am the Empire. There is only me.

But his equilibrium soon settled. Madness was fleeting, but his sanity was eternal – and with that return to awareness came the sudden realisation of danger: he heard a yipping sound and peered through the stubbled grass to see a wolf pack sniffing his trail. He made it to the pines before being run down – and when one leaped higher than he would have believed possible, he drove his dagger in under its snapping jaws and severed its throat.

That night the beasts feasted on their fellow, then slunk away.

He caught nothing, not a deer, or even a squirrel. He'd never learned to live in the wilds, for he'd only hunted men before, never beasts, and his prey lived in cities and towns. But the deserter's flesh sustained him for the long tramp from the lake at the base of the mountains to the coast.

By then, his boots were more hole than leather, his toes were blackened and numb, his skin and beard itched abominably. Some days he could barely recall. Too often, he'd catch himself shrieking abuse at Deo, mingled with desperate prayers.

Then he found a litany that kept him focused: 'Vyre, Solus, Duretto, Varahana, Rhamp.' He dreamed that he was roasting them all with mint and rosemary, then wolfing them down, still screaming: a feast fit for a god-king.

But today, with gulls shrieking in the distance and the surf pounding, all he had the strength to do was crawl to the top of the next rise, where he finally saw his destination: Rodonoi, the imperial port, clinging like a burst boil on the shores of the great ocean, a shambles of poorly made huts and rickety docks, a refuse pile of a town. But a Bolgravian troopship was docked there – the very one he'd commandeered months ago in Sommaport – and the Imperial Orb was flying over the only stone building in the town.

My empire, he thought, hope renewed by that all-conquering banner. *See, I am never alone.*

He rose to his feet. He no longer looked anything like a dread servant of the Holy Bolgravian Empire: he was a stinking wild man, injured and oozing, ragged and unwashed. But he knew names and passwords and secrets, so they would accept his authority – or by the Khagan himself, he would feast on their livers . . .

'I am Toran Zorne, Under-Komisar of the Ramkiseri,' he shouted to the winds. 'I am the emperor's bloodhound. I have never failed – and I. Never. Will.'

With that, he exhaled madness and inhaled authority.

Imperium.

He straightened and marched down towards the port, and the next part of his journey home.

Do you feel my footfalls on your grave, Raythe Vyre? No one escapes my empire.

PART TWO
Usurper

1

Mining for Power

Raythe stared at the tiny pile of rocks on the table. The dull seams of istariol looked like scabs of dried blood, as if some long-dead giant had bled to death, then calcified. In some legends, that was how istariol had come to be.

There's certainly blood wherever there's istariol . . .

But even this small haul was worth a small fortune, and it betokened much more to come. He lifted his gaze and assessed the reactions of his team.

Varahana was unconsciously stroking her scalp as she gazed at the nuggets, but there was unease in her eyes rather than greed. Kemara looked equally unsettled. He could understand that; she was terrified of her own powers, so anything that would enhance them was bound to worry her. Jesco looked almost disinterested, still haunted by his recent near-death experience, although he'd insisted on being here. At least he was in a better state than Vidar, whose recovery had been set back a long way by Crowfoot's attack.

But it was Elgus Rhamp's reaction he was most interested in. These nuggets had been used by his trusted lieutenants to lure the old knight into a trap. He scanned the Pelarian's battered face, wondering what it masked.

Have we purged all the bad blood, or just brewed more?

But Elgus remained inscrutable.

Raythe began, 'The Tangato Queen has extended our truce until the Kirra Moon rises – that's in roughly twenty days. She told me she's summoned the other tribes, so by then we'll be impossibly outnumbered, guns or no guns. We must decide what we're going to do.'

'We have no choice but to pillage as much as we can and get out,' Elgus said. 'After what Crow did, we're down another twenty fighting men. My lads have bled and died out here.'

'Killing us and each other,' Varahana pointed out.

'I'm not denying it.' Elgus sighed. Looking up at Raythe, he continued, 'Mercenary companies have always attracted violent men. But those who went with Crow and Thom – they were the last of the pure killers. The men I have left are decent, I swear: you saw how they stood up to Crow in the dining hall. They're with you . . . with me.'

They'd better be, Raythe thought, though he'd also seen those men stand side by side with the villagers and hunters, fighting against their own.

Vara, Jesco and Kemara had lost patience with the knight long ago; they still believed that he was the problem, but without Elgus, they'd have no control over the remaining mercenaries. Bad enough they'd lost so many during the course of that bloody night; they couldn't afford to lose any more.

'Elgus and I have agreed this constant rebellion has come to an end,' Raythe told them now, repeating what he'd said at the hanging. 'We're all in this together – as we always have been – and we can't afford to lose another man, woman or child. If Queen Shiazar knew our plight, we'd be dead already.'

'It's over,' Elgus agreed, looking around at the stern faces. 'I have sworn it.'

'You've said that before,' Jesco pointed out.

'I thought it was – truly. But this time it is. It's real. It has to be.'

It was as close to an apology as Raythe could expect. 'And you are responsible for seeing that it is – but this isn't a blame session. We need to discuss our path forward.'

'Which is what?' Varahana asked.

'We've got twenty days, and we're sitting on top of an istariol mine.' He indicated the nuggets. 'Crowfoot's men found these just lying around – if we find as much every day we have left, we'll have made this journey worthwhile.'

'And then we come back with more men and make these lands ours,' Elgus said gruffly.

'No, we don't,' Varahana snapped back. 'These lands belong to the Tangato.'

'If they can hold them, sure. This is a dog-eat-dog world, Mater. If they want to keep what they have, they'll have to fight, just like Pelaria and Otravia have had to.'

Before Vara could retort, Raythe raised a hand for silence. 'I hear you both. I regret that the Tangato have been affected by us coming, but we have to look to our own survival. The Bolgravians will come again, in strength: we all know that. It may not be for years, but one day, they'll come. So whatever else happens, we need to be safely out – and surpassingly wealthy – before that happens. So we hold together, we work day and night to mine what we can, then we get out. If some want to come back, that's their business, but I won't be one of them. I owe Queen Shiazar that much, for her forbearance towards Zar.'

The room fell silent when he was done, but eventually, with varying degrees of reluctance, they all signalled agreement.

'Then let's get to work,' he told them. 'We have twenty days.'

Raythe stood with Elgus among a small group of men with experience in mining or construction, watching Relf Turner and Lynd Borger, carpenter and blacksmith respectively, make final adjustments to the new lift they'd fashioned. Old pine trees found within the city had yielded good wood, and while the men cut it into lumber, Jak the Rope-maker had enlisted the help of half the wives and older children to twist wagon-loads of mature flax into a pile of coils of all thicknesses. It had taken them two days to get ready, an incredible effort under any circumstances.

The shafts Crowfoot's men had scoured were fully mined out, their finds little more than the leftovers after a feast, valuable in themselves but insufficient reward for all the effort and sacrifices made to get here. Every single person was working frantically, cutting timber, making rope, nails and myriad other requirements, or foraging through the city, where they'd uncovered a surprising amount of useful plunder from the past; crockery, pots and pails, perfectly ordinary things that somehow humanised the ancient, long-dead buildings: both useful, and a treasure trove of ancient history.

'Milord,' called Relf Turner, a bad-tempered perfectionist, 'we're ready to give it a try.'

'D'ye want volunteers?' Lynd Borger asked.

'I'll go myself,' Raythe told them. He turned to Sir Elgus. 'You game?'

'It's bad enough being this far down a hole,' he muttered, 'but aye, I'll do it.'

'Now you're sounding like Jesco.' Raythe laughed, though Elgus scowled at being compared to the Shadran.

Raythe selected Celric and Malkyn to accompany them down. The four men grabbed pick-axes and stepped onto the platform, secured at each corner by Jak's stiff new ropes, while the rest of the men gathered round to watch. He took a torch as Rolfus Bohrne, one of Elgus' men, and Ando, Borger's third son, applied themselves to lowering the platform.

Elgus shuddered visibly as they slowly dropped into the shaft, the rough walls closed in around them and the chamber they'd left became just a square of light above. There were symbols carved in the rock here and there, the initials of long-dead men, perhaps. They almost caught on jagged outcroppings, but they didn't get stuck.

'You should be nearly there,' Jak called down, watching the rope paying out – and sure enough, a few moments later, the platform crunched down onto a stone floor.

Raythe's blazing torch revealed a larger chamber.

'We're down!' Elgus called up to those watching above, and they cheered.

Raythe sent Cognatus skittering down one of the two tunnels leading from the chamber, but it was a dead end, so he led the way to the other. He was a little worried, for the air was cold down here, with none of the residual warmth that was said to signal the presence of istariol.

But looking around this tunnel, there were some tell-tale signs in the rock that made him hopeful.

The spirit rejoined him and he murmured, '*Cognatus, animus,*' before warning the others to stand back. Facing the cavity where the tunnel ended, he traced *Terra,* the rune of earth, pulled an istariol nugget from his pouch and showed it to Cognatus, murmuring, '*Quaerere istari sic.*'

He was the only one who saw the parrot shape dive into the stone, seeking the mineral, and he could feel Cognatus sniffing his way blindly, going first left, then right, down, then lower . . .

. . . until . . .

Yes.

Cognatus returned, struggling through the rock like a fish swimming upstream, until merging back into Raythe's body, quivering with pleasure at having fulfilled his mission.

'It's a few yards in,' Raythe announced, trying not so sound excited. *We don't know how much* . . . 'There's certainly enough to merit a proper look.'

He stepped away, took a deep, deep breath and readied himself. '*Cognatus, frangit lapis lente,*' he told the familiar.

With a slow unfolding of power, he and Cognatus weakened the stone, then he picked up one of the pick-axes and started driving it into a fracture. Twelve hefty blows took him a foot into the rock, until, as the fragments fell away, there was a perceptible rush of warmth, making them all gasp.

Trembling with hope, he looked into the gap he'd made.

Before him was a seam of pastel-red, about a finger's-breadth wide, running through the stone. It was darkly lustrous: it didn't glow itself but caught and held his sorcerous light.

Celric and Malkyn whooped, and Elgus rumbled, 'Praise be to Deo – at last!' He clapped Raythe's back.

Raythe let them enjoy the moment, but his own thoughts were darker: this was just a tendril, still not the major seam he'd hoped for. He needed to keep looking.

But for now, he smiled at Elgus. 'It's a start.'

They returned to the upper chamber and he delivered his news, which was greeted with a great deal of cheering and back-slapping. Every man there, every woman and child, had uprooted their lives on the promise of istariol. None had bargained on finding the lost city of the Aldar God-King, or a tribe none knew existed, but they'd all prayed for this moment.

Raythe said now, 'I need to continue the exploration in the northern mine shafts while you make a start here. Oh, and tonight, the drinks are on me.'

That raised a rueful laugh: they'd run out of alcohol weeks back.

But even so, the dining hall that night was a place of high spirits. There was music, thanks to Jesco, recovered enough to bring out his fiddle, and Millea Cranville, a joiner's young daughter, had shyly asked if she might use poor Norrin's harp. It turned out she was skilled, and could sing as well. Pots and ladles supplied percussion, and anyone who wasn't dancing clapped along.

'But here you are, sitting on your arse,' Varahana chided Raythe, dropping onto a bench beside him.

'I took a solemn vow never to dance until I get Mirella back,' he told her.

'No you didn't – you're just clumsy and shy.'

'Damn. You've found me out.' He raised the pewter goblet, one of those they'd found in a building near the crater rim, and toasted her; the finely polished metal and austere, delicate decorations of foliage and grapes made them almost too good for the water which was all they'd had to drink for weeks now. 'How's young Banno faring?'

'He's doing well. He'll be up and about soon.'

'And Vidar?'

'Better every day.'

'Bearskins are almost indestructible.' He nudged her teasingly. 'Don't take this wrong, I know you respect your vows – but there's a real bond between you and Vidar, isn't there? You've pulled each other out of some deadly situations, and you know he worships you.'

She gave him a troubled look. 'I know, but I have another calling – I really do. That's not to say I don't like Vidar. He's quiet, but he's wise, and he can make me laugh when I least expect it. If I weren't a priestess ... but I am, and that matters. This expedition needs someone to take care of our collective soul.'

'Our "collective soul",' Raythe echoed. 'I like that – and you do it well.'

'I try, dear. But I'm still worried for him. He insists that his kind have greater recovery powers than ordinary men, but it requires transformation, and that means battle-rage, which doesn't just come on call – and nor would we want it to. What he needs is a way of tapping into that healing power without the rage. Any suggestions, O Mighty Sorcerer?'

He gave her a sideways look. 'Haven't you heard the stories?'

She gave him a dubious look. 'What stories?'

'That for some bearskins, there's another thing that brings out their inner animal?'

Her eyes rounded. '*Oh*. He's not mentioned that ...'

'He's a polite man, so I doubt he would. Remember that Vosslander bearskin who followed Colfar? He had quite a reputation among the camp-followers.'

Her cheeks went a deep scarlet. 'Um, thank you, Raythe. I'm not sure that's helpful.'

'Well, I suppose there's always prayer,' he chuckled. 'That brings out my inner beast.'

'Krag off,' she exclaimed, laughing despite herself. 'I shall do my very best to ignore your advice, and if you mention it to him, I'll excommunicate you.' She peered around the hall, which was heaving with dancing men and women, all barriers between villagers, hunters and mercenaries finally erased. 'I doubt anyone cares that I'm about to hold Vespers?'

'Put in a good word with Deo for us.'

He watched her wind her way to the exit, smiling ruefully, and settled back into the serious business of missing people: the three most important women in his life. He had left Mirella behind in Otravia, where she was sharing Luc Mandaryke's bed; Zarelda, not far away, was a prisoner of the Tangato, and poor Tami was lying in an unmarked hole somewhere to the south, murdered by Toran Zorne.

She wasn't mine any more, but I still miss her.

All around the hall, married couples were dancing and a few of the unmarried ones were flirting. The usual patterns of Magnian life – in which courtship required formal approaches and parental permission – were breaking down, but no one looked too worried. Larch Hawkstone was talking intently to Angrit, while their daughter Rosebud played with a doll beside them; and Ando Borger was sitting *very* close to Millea Cranville, talking to her eagerly between songs. Seeing them made him smile . . . and accentuated his own loneliness.

Then he realised that he couldn't see Kemara Solus, who'd been dancing among the crowd earlier but had now vanished. He wondered where she was – not that there any chance at all that she'd want to ease his aching loneliness. She had made that very clear.

She and I should be practising our sorcery meld, he thought. *And trying to find a way up to the citadel.*

With a sigh, he decided that the best thing he could do right now was walk – that always helped him to think. So he rose, shook a few hands and slapped some backs on the way out, then wrapped his cloak around him and went off to check the watchtowers, planning on some serious cogitation along the way.

As he walked through the ruins, his eyes were drawn to the mighty rock floating above, silhouetted against the planetary rings.

If I were an Aldar, how would I get up there?

Sometime in the night, Kemara's eyes flew open and she sat bolt upright, shuddering at the sight of a shadowy shape with a scarlet, leering face looming over her.

But it was Buramanaka, not some night prowler, and in her mind he asked, *Issho ni kite, kudasai?* in his ancient tongue: Will you come with me, please?

He usually stayed away unless she'd called him, but since that awful night when she'd lost herself but somehow saved Jesco, she'd been afraid to summon him at all. At the best of times, she was barely able to control him, but that night he'd been the one in the saddle and it had terrified her.

I need to work this out, she decided, so she pulled on her boots and added a dress over her night-shift, wrapped a cloak around her, then drew the mask from its canvas bag. She didn't put it on yet; whatever tenuous control she had immediately disappeared when she wore it.

'What is it, Bura?'

The mizra-spirit bowed, then flowed out through her door. She followed, glimpsing him at the head of the stairs and following him down the hall to the room where they'd put Jesco.

She'd been avoiding the Shadran, unnerved by the strange circumstances that had led to his rescue, but she found herself thinking about him all the time. She almost turned round, but Buramanaka flashed to block her way, whispering, Kudasai – Please.

Reluctantly, she opened the door and peered in.

'Kemara?' croaked Jesco from his pallet. He was wrapped in blankets and looked hot and sweaty. 'What is it?'

'Just checking on you.'

'I'm fine, but I can't sleep. I'm having these really vivid dreams . . .'

'After what you went through, it's not surprising,' she said. She knelt beside him and placed her hand on his damp forehead. 'I'll check the wound.'

She conjured light, peeled away the blankets and set to unwrapping the bandages round his waist and right arm, but beside a little seepage, both looked to be healing passably well. 'Not bad,' she said with a smile. 'I did a good job, naturally.'

'You saved my life,' he said, catching her hand in his. 'Thank you.'

'All in a day's work.' She wondered what it was about him that brought out her soft side. 'Tell me about these dreams.'

He shuddered. 'I'm dreaming those old stories about the floating castle – remember? They say that when Tashvariel the Usurper knew he was doomed, he invited all his remaining friends to a feast of legendary debauchery.'

She harrumphed. 'No wonder you're excited by these dreams.'

'No, no, these aren't good dreams. So in the stories, at the height of the feast, Tashvariel murdered them all – and that's what I'm seeing . . .' Jesco tailed off, as if he'd lost the thread of his words, then shook himself and went on, 'In my dreams, he's butchering a living woman and serving her as a meal – but he's laced her with poison, and that's how everyone dies.'

Kemara swallowed the bile that had risen in her throat. 'Deo, Jesco – that's *hideous*.'

Jesco squeezed her hand and in a haunted voice, said, 'In my dreams, I'm *her* . . . I'm the woman he's butchering and cooking – and the worst thing is, *I'm not dead*. I watch as the cook opens up my belly and throws my entrails on the grill. It's *excruciating* – I've never felt such pain – but I can't wake up, no matter what I do.'

Kemara knew all about unrelenting nightmares: hers were of Ionia, screaming as the flames caught in her shift and she began to burn. 'Be strong,' she blurted, embracing him, which was completely out of character – and to her surprise, he hugged her right back, and kept on holding her, providing comfort and taking it as well.

Sometime in the midst of the embrace, they both fell asleep . . .

. . . until she jolted awake when someone nudged her shoulder. To her embarrassment, it was Mater Varahana, her scalp gleaming in the morning sun lighting the room, looking amused. 'Good morning, Kemara. I'd have let you sleep, but we need you in the ward.'

Kemara was sure her cheeks were the colour of her hair. Somehow, she'd fallen asleep with her head on Jesco's chest. 'Oh, Deo,' she groaned, pulling herself from under Jesco's arm. He stirred when she slithered free.

'Sleep well?' Varahana smiled.

Amazingly, she had – the best sleep she'd had in weeks. 'Neither of us could sleep, so I sat with him. We must've nodded off. Nothing happened,' she added sharply.

'I never thought so for a moment. Get yourself together, then come on up. Anna Finch has broken her toe on a water bucket, but she's your only new patient this morning.'

'I'll be right there,' Kemara said as Varahana left.

When she went to follow a couple of minutes later, Jesco woke and gripped her hand. 'Morning,' he said, in a dazed voice. 'Are you still here, or did you come back?'

She blushed again. 'I . . . um, I slept here.'

'I'll be the envy of every man in the expedition,' he laughed.

'As will I,' she said drily. 'Did you have the nightmare?'

He thought for a moment. 'No – no, I didn't, for the first time since they started. You must be good luck.'

'More likely I scared it away.'

They shared a warm smile and Kemara felt a curious feeling of kinship. Of all the men here, Jesco was the only one she felt truly safe around. Everyone else looked at her with desire, but with Jesco there was only friendship.

Because he only wants men, she supposed, wondering what that said about her.

She left and went to work, but all day, she felt strangely disconnected, as if the only place she should be was in that little room, and when she visited him to check his wounds, she stayed to help him with his dinner . . .

. . . and woke in his arms again.

It was chaste, it was comfortable, it was restful, and it made absolutely no sense. But his nightmares were kept at bay and so were hers, which was a gift both gladly accepted.

Adefar wasn't a cub any more. Zarelda's familiar prowled about her as a full-grown fox – and sometimes, chillingly, he was the lean, naked man in the fox mask she'd glimpsed, with a bushy tail and reddish-brown fur on his legs.

But the magic now at her fingertips took her breath away.

When she'd gained the praxis two months ago – *was it really only two months?* – she'd been facing years of study and practise, gradually learning the basics before she could start expanding her limited repertoire of spells. But this incarnation of Adefar could interpret her thoughts without her saying anything, and now her spells came in a dizzying, instinctive flow, as if she wasn't so much *commanding* Adefar as *channelling* him. It wasn't praxis any more, it was *maho* – and it was so much better.

She still had a lot to learn, though, because she didn't know all the commands and possibilities of her magic. Fortunately, Adefar still responded to the Magnian praxis-commands her father had taught them, but now she had to study the Aldar tongue if she was to be able to use the new orders Rima was showing her. Most of all, she had to discover her own limits, for greater power meant more drain on her own energies.

Escape wasn't something she even considered any more: this was where she had to be. The Tangato clothing and feather cloak she wore against the growing cold were beginning to feel natural, and the delicately spiced, plentiful food was winning her over. Having a farai to herself was enjoyable too, making her feel grown up. *If Father turned up today to free me, I'd tell him to go away*, she thought. She wasn't sure how that made her feel.

The task Hetaru had set her today was to find a bone pendant carved in the stylised Tangato style. She'd been using seeking spells all morning, but to no avail, despite her increased strength.

'*Yameru*,' she sighed, dismissing Adefar to let him recover. The process was exhausting them both, but their magical stamina was definitely improving.

She looked at Rima, sitting cross-legged on the mat facing her. 'What am I doing wrong?' she demanded.

'Nothing.' Rima smirked. 'You execute the spells well.'

Zar slapped her thigh in frustration. 'Then why don't they work?'

'Because this isn't just a question of maho. It is also a puzzle.'

'Gerda's Tears,' Zar groaned.

Rima frowned. 'Who is this Gerda you constantly speak of?'

Zar stared. 'Gerda? Gerda, the gladiator woman who slew Vashtariel, bringing down the Aldar Empire with the praxis, who is now the chief servant of Deo? *That* Gerda.'

'I do not know this tale. Vashtariel was poisoned.'

How can they not know of Gerda? Zar wondered again. Then the logical part of her brain suggested an answer: *Because she's a fairy-tale to explain the fall of the Aldar.*

She didn't want to think about that, so instead she asked, 'How could praxis defeat mizra?'

Rima rubbed her chin. 'Our tales speak of a new cult of sorcerers whose discipline was too much for the Aldar. New weapons are always the most deadly: a man with a new fighting move rules the training yard, until everyone learns it, or a counter is devised. It is said that those new mahotsu-kai, who you would say wielded praxis, could defeat the old Aldar easily, because the Old Ones had no idea how to counter them.'

Zar clicked her fingers. 'Of course – just like the Bolgravian rolling volley. When they invaded my land, they used this new tactic and they won all the battles, until our Otravian generals learned to fight back . . . They were just too late,' she added ruefully.

This was Magnian history, but Rima understood. 'Exactly! A new move, a new technique, buys you a moment of opportunity. The mizra in the hands of an Aldar is stronger than the maho; but the praxis was a surprise move and thus the old Aldar were defeated. But after the wars, we rejected both paths as too extreme. Instead, we turned back to the maho and we found the balance.'

'The way you "balanced" Adefar?'

'Ae. When you arrived, your Adefar was just praxis – somehow, when you first gained him, you got only half of what he is. Hetaru summoned his missing half – the mizra bit – and their reunion brought the ghost-spirit, the fox-faced man, who completed your familiar. Now you are as strong as Hetaru or me: you are properly a mahotsu-kai.'

This could revolutionise magic in Magnia, Zar mused, envisaging a whole new order: one whose power could blast the Bolgravians away. *I can't wait to tell Father – he can do this too.*

But Rima had returned her attention to Hetaru's task. 'Back to your problem,' she told Zar. 'And hurry up – I'm getting bored.'

Zar rolled her eyes. *'You're* bored? I've spent the whole damned morning trying to find it and I'm out of ideas – oh, wait! Am I allowed questions?'

The Tangato girl perked up. 'At last! Yes – but you can ask only one, so don't waste it.'

Zar started to blurt out something – but she stopped herself and instead, tried to think her question through. *Okay, I've handled the bone pendant: I know what it looks like. But the seeking spells aren't working, which means it's either buried under earth or water, or it's veiled by a spell – or both.*

She suddenly heard her father telling her, *The only way to uncover hidden objects is to find a link to them: a blood-link for a living thing, or for an object, something made from exactly the same material.*

'Whose bone was used for the pendant?' Zar asked carefully.

Rima's grin lit up her face. 'Right question. Hetaru's wife – who's dead, by the way.'

Zar groaned, then remembered a conversation a few nights ago. 'Hetaru's wife was the older sister of–?' She clicked her fingers in frustration, then it came: 'Omala, Kamo's brother's wife. Let's go and find her.'

'Thank goodness – we can *finally* get out of this stuffy room. Let's go.'

Outside, it was blustery and the wind was biting. 'How do you survive winter?' Zar complained as they hurried along, huddled in their cloaks, through the maze of wooden buildings, ignoring the rampaging children and the teenagers working on their weapons-drill. Most of the adults were in the fields, Rima had told her, harvesting the root crops and rice, the Tangato's staple foodstuffs. 'It's already freezing here!'

'You have no meat on your bones. This is warm – wait until full winter.'

Zar shuddered. 'Does it snow, even though the istariol's here?'

'It does, but never for long. But we're still confined to our houses for many days. Lots of babies are made in those months,' Rima chuckled, then her face changed to sorrow. 'But it also breaks many relationships. Sometimes, too much time with one person is not good for love.'

Zar thought of all the years she and father had spent together in exile. Sometimes she'd hated him; now she was older, she had begun to realise he probably hadn't always enjoyed her being there. Bonds flimsier than family would be even easier to break.

'How do you cope?' she asked.

'The important thing is community. Every evening we gather together, to sing, dance, tell and hear tales that remind us who we are – join us, see for yourself.'

'But I'm not Tangato.'

Rima stopped, took Zar's chin in her hand and traced the ridged tattoos on her chin with her thumb. 'These say that you are: *this* is why Hetaru teaches you our customs and history as well as our magic. You must come to the lodge tonight.'

It sounded scary: it was far easier to retreat into her own little polehouse when day was done.

But Rima was insistent, and at last, Zar gave in. 'Oh, all right,' she mumbled, to shut her up.

When they got to Omala's farai, they were welcomed in with the ceremonial pressing of noses. The old woman, the younger sister of Hetaru's dead wife, lived with Kamo's brother Hamano. She spoke in rapid Tangato, but then switched to Gengo-Magnian, allowing Zar to follow her words.

After the rituals of greeting had been observed, Omala asked, 'To what do I owe this honour?'

'I wonder if I might have a lock of your hair?' Zar asked.

Omala was taken aback, but Rima said, 'It's all right. Hetaru approves. It is part of a test for this one.'

'Ah.' Omala gave her a gap-toothed smile and cut a strand of grey-black hair. 'This pale girl is skin and bone. Is she sick?'

'You can speak to me directly,' Zar put in. 'I'm just here.'

'She's healthy enough,' Rima replied, 'but she eats like a pihoihoi.'

'A sparrow?' Zar snorted. 'I eat like a horse.'

Rima flapped her fingers like little wings and Omala laughed uproariously.

Zar thanked Omala, then followed Rima to a private spot where she could work on the next part of the task.

With the hair, she could taste the essence of Omala. When she was certain, she traced *Aspectu*, the rune of Farsight, before chanting out loud, '*Adefar, motumeru kono hone doyo'ni*' – Adefar, find a bone that is kin to this.

The fox-spirit caressed the lock of hair, which smouldered and collapsed into ash, then, calling her to follow, turned into a bird and soared away.

'That way!' she exclaimed, pointing towards the western hills. Impatient to be there, she burst into a jog.

Together they bounded past a group of young boys and girls learning the taiaha, the Tangato spear-club, working through vigorous movements and shouting aloud with each blow, then she and Rima passed on downstream into a swampy plain with a view of the eastern side of Rath Argentium.

Zar stopped dead and stared. This was the first time in two weeks that she'd been permitted to see the ruined city where her father's people were taking refuge. The sight struck her like a bolt: her father was in there, and Banno too, and Jesco and Varahana, all the people she cared for. Even grumpy Kemara and gruff old Vidar had become special – and there were all the young men she'd shared dances and dangerous patrols with, learning how to ride and hunt and fight together under Cal Foaley's stern, taciturn guidance, then celebrating together too. All of a sudden she missed them dreadfully.

Rima was looking at her curiously. 'You're crying,' she commented.

'No, I'm not,' Zar retorted, wiping her eyes. 'It's just the wind.' She placed her hands on her hips and shifted her gaze to the floating rock with its eerie castle perched on top and the four huge chains anchoring it to the world.

She could feel Adefar calling somewhere to the north. 'That way,' she said, turning away from the city.

'If you say so,' Rima said, unhelpfully.

Zar steamed along red-faced and breathing hard. Annoyingly, Rima drew alongside her, loping along, still fresh and relaxed.

'Are you trying to *race* me, Zarelda?'

In response, Zar put on a burst, really pumping her arms and legs, and flashed ahead – but inside a few moments Rima had run her down, although she was working hard now, too. They tore along the gully, leaping rivulets and splashing through muddy patches, until Zar's stride became giddy and uncontrolled, she tripped on the tussocky grass and ploughed into the ground.

She rolled and came up gasping and laughing. 'Enough, enough.'

'So it was a race?' Rima wheezed, bending over and panting.

At least I made her blow. 'No – I was just in a hurry.'

Rima snorted. 'Maybe you are making an escape bid?' Her tone was light, but her eyes were serious.

'As if!' Zar snorted; it honestly hadn't occurred to her. 'I was just frustrated.'

'So I thought.' Rima pulled her up, then pressed her nose to Zar's, just as she had the night they met. 'This is the place you need to be: with Hetaru and me. Only we can make you into the mahotsu-kai you are meant to be.'

It was always unnerving to be so close to someone, so Zar stepped away, covering her fluster with bluster. 'I'm *trying*,' she snapped. 'Just give me space.'

She turned and ran on at a more sensible pace this time, topping a small rise – and there she found a little cairn on newly disturbed earth, with Adefar in fox form perched atop the rocks. She pulled the stack apart – and there it was, the bone pendant.

She picked it up and handed it to Rima, grinning in triumph.

'Pai te mahi,' Rima grinned. Well done.

When Zar rose, she saw that Rath Argentium was even closer – she was only half a mile away. The sound of the gorge provided music to accompany the stunning vista.

'Where does all the water go?' she asked, as her breathing slowed towards normal.

'What do you mean?'

'Well, all that water flows in from the north, runs around the city, then goes underground, flowing south, and joins the frozen lake . . . But if that's been happening for hundreds and hundreds of years, surely this whole piece of unfrozen land should be one big lake . . .'

'Oh, that. We say, "The land drinks it." ' Rima spread her arms wide, her face lifting to the sun. 'Isn't this the most beautiful place in the world?' she boasted.

Zar thought about all the places she'd been – marble palaces in Otravia and Pelaria, the Tomb of the Golden Heirs in Shadra, or the Church of Gerda Reborn at home – and felt the gulf between them widen again. 'You know *nothing*,' she said. 'You live in wooden *huts* – you eat with your hands and wash in a river! We have marble buildings and plumbing and guns and bombards – we have books that preserve words for centuries, and musical instruments that can make one musician sound like twenty. We have proper clothing and–' She threw up her hands. 'Compared to us, you're *primitive savages*.'

It came out worse than she meant, but in her desire to defend her homeland, her tongue had run away with her. She tried to apologise, but Rima silenced her with a gesture.

'We who live in the shadow of Rath Argentium know that there are "better" ways,' she replied tersely, 'but after the Fall, we were forced to return to the land. We had all the things you speak of – look at the Aldar city: you know this to be true – but we lost them when our lives were reduced to the fight for sheer survival. We fully understand that there was a Golden Age, but it is not an age we wish to emulate, because it ended in utter destruction.'

'In Magnia, no one would reject *progress* in favour of *preservation*,' Zar told her. 'It's dog eat dog. You thrive or fail. But don't you want more from life than digging and growing and hunting – surely you want more than just this . . . *stasis*?'

Rima was looking hurt. 'You do not understand: every year, we relearn things of value – how to write, to make paper from flax; we find better ways to cook or hunt. We discover new things, or things that are at least new to us. But each new thing must be approved by the Yokei, not just for its worth, but for whether it is *safe*. Yes, we could make better weapons – but why would we, if the result is that killing becomes too easy? Our lives are peaceful and full of community. Work and labour unify us, bringing us closer to each other and to the land. We are happy.'

'*Happy*,' Zar snorted, irritated by all this damned bliss when the deadly world outside had wrecked her family. 'Don't you understand? The world is going to find you and eat you up.'

She couldn't have explained why she was perversely hoping this would make Rima angry, but the Tangato girl wasn't biting.

'If that day does come, we will face it bravely,' Rima replied.

'But bravery won't be enough! You should be arming yourselves! You should be making alliance with my father, not trapping him – you should be making weapons and mining istariol and learning how to *really* fight, to kill and win, so you're ready when the Bolgravs return, because they will. It's what they do.' She felt the bitterness overflowing.

Rima just looked at her sadly. 'There is too much anger in you.'

'*Argh!*' Zar shouted at the skies, and she stomped away, ignoring the nagging thought that she was just confirming that Rima was right.

That evening, when she heard the singing coming from the biggest community hall, her heart ached a little. But as she was cooking, batting away Adefar who was sniffing at the stewing vegetables, there was a rap on the door lintel and a colourful figure stepped into view.

At first Zar didn't recognise her fellow sorceress. '*Rima?*'

She had discarded her traditional flax bodice and kilt for a silk robe of scarlet and purple swirls, covered with lizards embroidered in green and gold thread. She wore delicate embroidered slippers and her hair had been tamed into an intricate pile of braids.

'Koni'ka,' she greeted Zar formally, bowing from the waist, her palms pressed together as if in prayer. 'You are invited to join the Hiriwa people in food and song. Please, come.'

Perhaps this was an offer of reconciliation, or maybe another attempt to persuade Zar that the Tangato ways were best. Whichever it was, she instinctively she shied away, tired from the day's exertions – until she remembered that she'd resolved to try. 'But what do I wear?' she asked nervously.

'Aha!' Rima dropped her deferential pose and pushed her way in. 'You have all you need here,' she said, pulling garments out of a bag that Zar hadn't even noticed. 'I will show you!'

For the next twenty minutes, Rima showed the Otravian how to wrap and tie Tangato garments, which slippers to choose, even how to do her hair, although she still complained that Zar wore it far too short.

When she was done, Zar was dressed in a full-length robe like a dressing gown of stiff silk. The pale greens and reds suited her more than she would have guessed, and it was embroidered with real skill and detail. It was more beautiful than anything she'd seen her mother wear back in Otravia.

'It's gorgeous,' she confessed, wishing she had a mirror to view herself properly.

'You look very well,' Rima said, 'but now you must practise walking. Like this' – she clasped her hands together, stood bolt upright – 'take small steps. No sway. This is proper for formal occasions.'

When she deemed Zar to be 'not completely embarrassing', she led her through the very quiet village to the closest of the four large communal halls. They left their slippers outside, entering barefoot into the massive smoky, dimly lit room. Zar had been envisaging something like a Norgan beerhaus, where men spent hours mingling with buxom serving maids while guzzling ale and boasting – but this was much more genteel. There were groups of people clustered together, all sitting cross-legged on the floor and sipping little cups of a clear fluid – zaki, Rima called it, a rice wine. The young people were continually bustling in and out of the kitchens at the back, serving food, constantly replenishing platters of titbits that smelled wonderful. The conversation was buzzing, and in one corner, a group sung and danced, although to Zar it looked more like gently swaying than her idea of dancing.

But when people noticed her, the conversations faltered, heads turned and voices hushed.

Rima stepped forward boldly and called out in Gengo-Magnian, 'This is Zarelda, new mahotsu-kai of the Hiriwa. Please, make her welcome.' Then she repeated the words in Tangato, before leading Zar to the middle of the long hall, where a pair of masked Yokei sat on stools before the central fire, presiding over the gathering. Rima presented Zar to them, naming the Yokei as Aidiko and Unaji, while everyone watched. Zar felt terribly self-conscious as she performed the required homages, then waited for the two Yokei to respond.

Aidiko spoke first. 'This woman is welcomed among us,' the Yokei said in her high-pitched voice. 'The coming of her kind presents a new challenge to us, after five centuries of isolation. Therefore, runners have been sent to summon the rangatiras' – chieftains, Adefar translated for Zar – 'to confer here. They will begin to arrive in three days. Our Queen asks that we prepare a feast and ready the practise-fields for our allies.'

This caused a murmur and some questions, then Unaji spoke. 'Queen Shiazar reminds us all that we must forget past conflicts. The other tribes were once Hiriwa like us; even now, our differences are few.' Then she made some signs over Zar' – *a blessing*, Rima murmured – and concluded, 'Welcome, Zarelda. Join us and learn our ways, as we learn yours.'

After some more bowing, Rima drew Zar towards a circle of diners that included Hetaru and Kamo. Around them, the evening returned to conversation, but she felt eyes on her all the time, and not all friendly. She took comfort from moments when she glanced out and met some- one's eye, usually a young woman like herself, and was rewarded with a tentative bob of the head, or a fleeting smile.

The conversation at Hetaru's mat switched to Gengo, so she could be included. Hetaru led them in asking Zar about her people, but not in an interrogative manner. At first she answered guardedly, thinking of her- self as an envoy with secrets to keep, but the discussion soon turned to the pending arrival of the chiefs and war parties from the other five tribes, how they would be accommodated, what their views might be of the interlopers in the city.

'They'll push for direct action,' Kamo opined, glancing at Zar. 'Your people would be wise to abandon their refuge and surrender them- selves to the Queen's justice while mercy is still possible.'

That didn't seem likely to Zar. She knew her father's indomitable spirit and his refusal to play by the rules. He *always* had a plan – even if it didn't always work out the way he'd intended. But in this company, she merely bowed her head meekly.

All at once the conversation broke off, for a new song had begun, one with stomping feet and clapping hands, and everyone was climbing to their feet, young and old alike. Only the Yokei remained seated, but even they were clapping along.

Rima seized Zar's hands, overriding her protests, and pulled her into the middle of a line of women facing a line of men; she found herself opposite Hekami, Kamo's son, who grinned in welcome – and suddenly everyone was stamping and clapping and the lines were advancing on each other, and Zar found herself copying the moves – stamp left, stamp right, clap and turn – then she slapped her hand into Hekami's and he turned her, first to the left, then to the right, then they were spinning and turning, stamping and jumping, and now everyone was bellowing a refrain which made the roof rattle.

Spin, turn, stamp and jump . . .

Zar felt out of time and yet carried along and the laughter was infectious, making her heart thud to life, lifting her gloom and worry for a precious few minutes. Then suddenly all the women were pressing noses with the man opposite, and she found herself nose-to-nose with a shyly smiling Hekami, feeling giddy and exhilarated . . .

. . . and wishing he was Banno.

But even that intrusion of reality couldn't spoil the moment entirely.

She remembered the trek across the wilderness to get here, and how music and song and dance had brought the travellers together. The same magic existed here. So she stayed on her feet and danced some more, getting it wrong and yet getting it right, on this first night when she began to feel that perhaps she really did belong here.

But four days later, as Zar practised her new maho vocabulary with Rima on a grassy hillside, the sorceress suddenly got to her feet and pointed to the eastern hills, where blotches of darkness stained the green slopes. 'They've come,' she exclaimed, her face anxious. 'The first of the tribes has arrived, answering the Queen's summons.' She offered Zar her hand. 'Come, we must join Hetaru and prepare.'

Her demeanour was of a soldier, readying for battle.

2

The People of the Thousand Lakes

Zarelda watched the rituals of greeting unfold with mounting tension. Over the past two days, the war-parties of the five tribes had been arriving and setting up camp outside the Hiriwa village. Now everyone was there, the five rangatiras and their entourages could be formally invited into Hiriwa lands. The whole Hiriwa tribe was here to watch this, for there were ritual challenges, songs and acts, like presenting a frond of a certain tree as a peace offering, and speeches before the throne. They would all be taking place in the open field before the giant red-arched gate that marked the entrance to the village.

Shiazar and her masked attendants had been there all day, receiving homage. Zarelda, as a novice mahotsu-kai, was entitled to stand with Hetaru and Rima, clad in the traditional style of the sorcerers. She felt horribly conspicuous in the flax skirt and bodice and cloak of feather and hide, revealing far too much white skin, covered in goose-bumps from the bitterly cold wind whipping through the valley. But she was drinking it all in, aware that no outsider had ever seen these things before – and much of the spoken words were in Gengo-Magnian, the language of ritual among the Tangato, so she could follow it all easily.

One by one the tribal chieftains came forward: the Rotomahau, the only tribe where the warriors went bearded; the Tanuahi, marked out by their blue tattoos, the Wakatoa, whose face markings were red and the Puketapu, whose tattoos were sharply geometric. The most striking – and belligerent – were the Manowai, who wore their hair shaved, but for a thin strip running from forehead to nape.

Zar craned her neck and glimpsed Onkado, who was part of the retinue of Ikendo, the Manowai rangatira. She could admit to herself, if no one else, that she'd hoped to see him; she had enjoyed their conversation at the old Summer Palace. He looked very martial, clad in leather armour with a taiaha in his hands and a bronze sword slung over his shoulder, his face set and grim, a far cry from the friendly young man she'd met. But his eyes flickered to her as he knelt and she was sure he'd winked.

Shiazar took the homage of the Manowai delegation and everyone visibly relaxed – until Ikendo, a burly, fierce-looking warrior-chief, suddenly jabbed a finger in Zar's direction, barking out, 'We would view the foreigner you harbour, Great Queen.'

Zar shrank against Rima's side, then chided herself for cowardice and stuck her chin in the air. The urge to do something defiant hit her, as she would have if she'd been singled out like this among her own people, but Rima, guessing her mood, laid a restraining hand on her arm.

Jinkatia, the Yokei of the Manowai, gestured imperiously. 'Shiazar-san, I support Ikendo's request.'

Shiazar's sister, Ulaka, shrilled, 'Let the gaikiko girl come forth.'

'Don't be afraid,' Rima whispered. '*No one* will touch you without coming through Hetaru and me.'

Zar was grateful when Rima accompanied her forward. They bowed to the Queen, then turned to the Manowai chief and his retinue, as well as the chiefs of the other tribes. It was daunting, facing that wall of dark, tattooed faces, as they *mm-ed* and *ah-ed* at her.

But she kept her stance and expression strong, and caught Onkado nodding approvingly. Though she didn't dare smile at him, not here where protocol was so complex, she was grateful.

He's rather handsome, a small part of her noted, to which she replied, *I belong to Banno.*

But what if we go to war and Banno dies? that treacherous little thought asked.

She had no answer to that, and she didn't even want to contemplate it, because if Banno died, then so would everyone else she loved.

Shiazar clapped her hands once in dismissal, and Hetaru said, 'You have seen her, Rangatira Ikendo. She is Hiriwa now, and beholden to me. Pray, do not seek to make an exhibit of my protégé again.'

Ikendo's belligerent face hardened, but clearly Hetaru outranked him, because, grimacing sourly, he bobbed his head in acquiescence. Rima drew Zar back to Hetaru's side and the old mahotsu-kai gave her an approving nod.

'What happens next?' she whispered.

'Lots and lots of meetings and speeches,' Rima replied. 'We Tangato love to talk.'

'Better that than going to war,' Hetaru said calmly, and there was no argument to that.

They fell silent as Shiazar spoke in her clipped falsetto, then the newcomers all bowed – and with that, the ceremonies were over and the mood changed almost instantly. The Queen's entourage, accompanied by the rangatiras and their attendants, mingled with the newcomers, renewing acquaintances amid much pressing of noses and chatter. Zar, finding her gaze drawn back to Onkado, finally dared to throw him a grateful nod.

'Cute, for a Manowai,' Rima murmured.

'I haven't noticed,' Zar replied coolly, looking away toward the west, where Shiro Kamigami, the tethered citadel, hung in the sky in defiance of gravity and reason.

Banno, I'm here, thinking of you, and I know you're thinking of me.

The Yokei all withdrew and the gathering became informal. Hetaru was greeted by an old woman with snow-white curly hair and within moments, the pair were chuckling away, then he called, 'Come, Zarelda meet the wisest of the kannushi – our priestly caste.'

The old woman chuckled. 'Ha! Hardly that. The oldest, perhaps.' She looked Zar up and down, then they pressed noses. Her face was so seamed that it was impossible to make out the patterning of her tattoos, but they were blue, which meant she was of the Tanuahi tribe. 'I am Akuiatala, but you can call me Kuia.'

'Kuia,' Zar repeated, as Adefar translated inside her. 'Meaning . . . um . . . "Old Lady"?'

'I am a lady, and I am certainly old,' Kuia chuckled. 'It is an honourable term. What is a "Zarelda"?'

'A warrior woman.'

'Ah, yes, I see that in you: skinny, but fierce. Hetaru says you make good progress.'

'Does he? I wouldn't know.'

'Kuia, it'll go to her head now,' Hetaru laughed. 'You've just undone my good work.'

They all laughed, but then Hetaru's smile died as he glanced behind Zar. She turned, and her blood ran cold.

Two mahotsu-kai were facing her: a man of about her father's age and a younger female, maybe his apprentice, both with their hair shorn away except for that ridge of thick hair running down the middle of their skulls, and heavily tattooed in the distinctive designs of the Manowai tribe. But that wasn't what had made Zar go rigid.

They both had empty eye sockets, their ear lobes had been sliced away and their noses had been removed, leaving just two slitted holes – yet they were watching her with piercing attention.

'So this is the gaikiko shirohada,' the older man rasped. The white-skinned foreigner.

'No. This is Zarelda of the Hiriwa,' Hetaru replied, apparently unperturbed by their grim appearance.

'Like a snowbird,' said the female, who was perhaps Zar's own age. Her nose slits pulsed wetly as she sniffed. 'She has a strange stink to her.' Her empty sockets bored into Zar's eyes and she added, 'I would press noses with you, Snowbird, but . . .'

Zar swallowed and said nothing.

In Magnia, using sensory deprivation during training was standard practice, but some fanatical sorcerers practised self-mutilation, most commonly in Bolgravia, where it was embraced. The Izuvei, they were called. Zar hadn't expected to see anything like that out here – and yet, here they were.

Pluck out thine eyes, that thou may see . . .

'Zarelda, this sad fanatic is Tatsu, and this, his apprentice Kyu,' Hetaru said calmly. 'Both names mean "dragon" in the Aldar tongue, as pretentiousness runs in their veins.'

'I think it sad that they lacked the courage of their convictions,' Kuia put in. 'It would have been a fine thing had they cut out their tongues as well.'

I guess we're not playing nicely with these people, Zar thought, a little startled. Hetaru was normally the epitome of kindness and generosity, and Kuia had seemed very sweet.

'The weak rail at the strong, when it were better they look to their own faults,' Tatsu answered, before returning his attention to Zar. 'This one is still young enough to be shaped. Come with us back to the Thousand Lakes and I will teach you *real* power, Snowbird. My bone knife awaits you.'

She shuddered, but replied defiantly, 'I would never be so sick in the head as to want that.'

Kyu laughed coldly. 'You say so now, but when you grovel for your life before some stronger mahotsu-kai, perhaps you will wish you had been brave enough to reach for more power when it was offered.'

'Are you here for a purpose?' Rima demanded. 'Or do you just enjoy cawing like crows?'

'Ah, little Rima,' Tatsu sniffed, peering blindly at her. 'You too have so much potential. But no, we are here simply to view this sorcerer from afar. What times we live in! We, who thought ourselves alone, learn that others survived the Great Fall – one wonders how we Tangato will adjust our thinking to this new reality.'

'This outside world is a place of war and suffering, we are told,' Kyu added, 'so we all must harden our hearts and embrace the Way of the Dragon to survive, as we Manowai have. Our days of peace are ending.'

With that, the two sorcerers walked away, effortlessly weaving through the crowd despite their blindness.

Rima glared after them. 'The Manowai are worse than the foreigners in the city.'

'What have they done, that you all hate them?' Zar asked.

'We do not "hate",' Hetaru replied sternly. 'But the Manowai have been trouble ever since their colony was founded. It has become a place of dissent and conniving. The Yokei have had to stamp their authority to prevent open conflict at times.'

'But they are still Tangato, like us,' Kuia added. 'And they do reflect a valid fear: we have lived in isolation for centuries, but now the outside world has found us again. We wonder what we must do to cope, especially with the riches of Rath Argentium here to lure them.'

'Ae, Kuia,' Hetaru sighed. 'It is a theme we will hear over and over in the coming days.'

'But Shiazar is Queen and she has an agreement with Father,' Zar blurted. 'She won't renege, surely?'

'She will come under pressure to do so,' Hetaru said. 'If your people are allowed to leave, then word will spread, despite your father's promises. Some believe the only way to preserve our way of life is to make sure your people never leave.'

'Something's brewing,' Cal Foaley warned the meeting after a risky scouting mission to the tribal village. 'There's been a big influx of Tangato fighting men.'

The days are passing too swiftly, Raythe thought, looking around at his leaders; there were only five days left of the truce and a crisis was looming. Food stocks were lower than they needed for any journey home, and no one wanted to leave without enough istariol to reward their many sacrifices.

'Are these newcomers here to ensure we leave?' asked Jesco. He'd left the infirmary, although his right arm still hurt to use. 'Or are they here to make sure we can't?'

'The latter,' Sir Elgus suggested grimly. 'Damn it, where's the *real* istariol? We've found a few paltry mini-seams, but there's enough of it *somewhere* to keep this region free of snow – *so where is it?*'

This was the burning question on everyone's mind, and Raythe had no answer, but Varahana spoke up. 'I've been thinking about that. In the empire, istariol is rare now, and the way it interacts with the environment remains a mystery. Out here, we have the rare privilege of studying its impact on a near-pristine place. I've barely scratched the surface, but I do have a hypothesis.'

'Then spill it,' Elgus grunted impatiently.

'I'm about to, Sir Elgus,' Varahana snapped back, 'if you'll let me. It's known that istariol radiates warmth when in the ground, but *not* after it's been mined. Heat requires energy: so where does that energy come from, and what fuels it? I've also been thinking about water: the Fenua Tangato is surrounded by ice, which melts on contact with this heated zone, creating rivers that flow mostly north to south and then freeze again at the southern border – so why isn't this whole region underwater?'

'And from this, you're concluding . . . ?' Raythe prompted.

'I'm coming to believe that the istariol "drinks" the excess water, in effect, feeding on it to grow.'

'What do you mean, "grow"?' Elgus rumbled. 'Rocks don't grow.'

'You're assuming istariol is a normal rock, but it's not a rock at all – in fact, it actually shares some aspects with plants. My hypothesis is that it spreads underground when fed by plentiful water.'

Raythe gave her a doubtful look. 'I've never heard this theory before – why is that?'

Varahana smiled. 'Because I'm smarter than everyone else' – she ignored Raythe's snort – 'or perhaps, more accurately, I'm the only scholar who's had the chance to explore a place like this in centuries. Istariol is mined out in Magnia and the steppes of eastern Bolgravia, where there are no more large deposits – so everything we know is based on old analysis or experiments using tiny samples – that's why I'm saying "theory", not proven. But what it boils down to is this: far from Rath Argentium being the place where the istariol *is*, this city is the one place in these lands where it now *isn't*.'

Raythe rocked back in his chair, casting his eyes to the heavens and really wishing he had a solid counter-argument. *But as usual, I think she's probably right.* 'Oh, Deo – really?'

Elgus groaned. 'No wonder the Queen isn't pressing her attack. She knows that all we're sitting on are old bones and broken egg-shells.'

They all sagged and looked at Raythe, who felt another weight land on his shoulders. He rolled his neck and sat up. 'Even if you're right, Mater, we can't give up. There may still be seams we've not found, so we'll keep looking.' He turned to Kemara. 'Any progress on finding a way up to the floating citadel? If the Aldar stockpiled any istariol, it would be up there.'

'And when exactly have I had the time?'

'Have you sent your familiar up there?' Varahana asked her.

'It's too far from our bodies – in a very real sense, our familiars are tied to us,' Raythe put in. 'And the Tangato say it's haunted – so perhaps it is?'

'Haunted?' Elgus sniffed. 'Is that a real thing?'

'Oh, ghosts do exist,' Raythe commented. 'Some occur "naturally", others are created by mizra.' Out of the corner of nis eye he saw Kemara flinch at that.

'How did the Aldar get up and down, then?' Foaley wondered. 'Surely they must have had some simple way to move servants and supplies?'

'Honestly? I haven't a clue.'

'In the Arcanum there was a book which described the Aldar using flying platforms,' Varahana said, 'but no one's found anything like that.'

'I've got one last mineshaft to explore tomorrow, on the north side – although Vara's theory suggests I'm wasting my time,' Raythe said, then he turned to Kemara. 'If Varahana briefed you about these plat-forms, could you look for them?'

'Of course.'

'I'll help her,' Jesco put in quickly.

'Go find a room,' Elgus grumbled.

'Grow up,' Kemara retorted. 'We're friends, that's all.'

'All right, all right,' Elgus said, holding up his hand defensively. 'It was just a joke.'

They all fell silent, until Foaley asked, 'How are our preparations for leaving?'

'We're stockpiling food, drying as much as we can, but I have to say, no one is happy,' Varahana said. 'Pretty much everyone is feeling like they'd rather just dig in here until they've extracted all the istariol, than leave with less than they'd hoped.'

'And face a full-scale attack ?' Raythe asked doubtfully.

The priestess gave him a wry smile. 'That's what you get for pulling off miracles. People begin to believe you can do it all the time. They trust you to keep them safe.'

'Speaking of miracles,' Elgus put in, 'could you use the istariol we've got to get us out?'

Raythe had been thinking along those lines himself. 'I'm carrying some I've extracted from the nuggets, just in case, but it's not stuff you use lightly. But rest assured, I'm not helpless.'

'Do you have a plan to get Zarelda out?' Varahana asked.

'I'm working on it, but if I act too soon, I'll plunge us into open conflict and I'm desperate to avoid that. I'm thinking we'll try something on the eve of the Kirra Moon, then smuggle her out with the rest of us when we leave.'

Elgus looked doubtful. 'You really think the Tangato Queen will just let us all leave?'

'I have no reason to doubt that.'

'No wonder you Otravians lost the war,' the Pelarian knight snorted.

'We lost because the Mandarykes stood down our armies and invited the conquerors in,' Raythe snapped back. He waved a hand, dismissing them. 'That's all I have to say. Let's meet again tomorrow evening.'

As they left, he pulled Jesco aside. 'Jesco, what's going on with you and Kemara? I know you – and she's a *woman*. Leopards don't change their spots.'

The blademaster gave him an awkward look. 'It's not what you think.'

'I've known you to walk away from the most beautiful women in the empire to be with some scruffy wagon guard. You're a man's man, and Kemara – fine woman though she is – is *not* your soulmate.'

Jesco's face showed rare annoyance. 'How would you know?'

'Because I've seen you in love and that's not what I see now. So what's going on?'

Jesco shrugged. 'Truth is, it's not sexual. We truly are just friends. You're right: she doesn't stir my blood, but there's still a connection. When we're together, I'm completed, somehow – and she says it's the same with her.'

Raythe was feeling uncomfortable. It made him think of the arcane: love spells and dark enchantments, the sort of malarkey the old tales trafficked in.

It's Kemara I need to talk to, he realised. *This is mizra, if it's anything.* But he didn't want to start a fight with his best friend, so all he said was, 'I suppose there's no harm to it, but you do know that you and she are the talk of the expedition?'

'I'm sure we're breaking hearts,' Jesco chuckled, 'but I swear, nothing's happening.'

'Just tell me if it gets any stranger.'

'And what did our noble leader want?' Kemara asked.

'Nothing. Just trying to work us out, is all.' He laughed. 'The whole place is.'

That was true enough – all day, all she got was, '*How did you land that gorgeous man?*' – as if no one as plain as her should ever get to bed such an angel. All her protests of innocence were met with disbelief. Not that she could blame them.

They were on her balcony now, watching the night settle over this eerie, unearthly city. For once, the infirmary was quiet: no one was dying or giving birth and her patients that day had been drop-in cases, easily tended. She'd left the ward in the hands of Sister Bea for the night, while she looked forward to a quiet evening.

But she had to sort this out first, however awkward it was. 'So – and I'm sorry to ask – but what exactly is going between us?' Sleeping with a man but not having sex with him felt decidedly strange.

'Um, well . . . you know I prefer men . . . and really, although I have made love to women before, well – I don't want sex to ruin our friendship.'

Kemara's gut reaction was relief, which she thought was telling. 'Me too.'

He grinned. 'Phew! Okay, glad we've sorted that out. Let's be brother and sister, eh?' He looked out the window, then added, 'Shall we go for a walk?'

She found her shawl, tucked the Aldar mask into the satchel she used to carry her medicinal herbs and slung it over her shoulder. Then, arm in arm, they made their way into the city, heading by mutual agreement up the slope to where the crater rim offered the best views. Overhead, the planetary rings glowed, a pale rainbow cut in two by the floating citadel. In five days, the Kirra Moon would rise and the truce would end.

'How do you think the Aldar got up there?' Jesco asked.

'Varahana said they flew, didn't she? But we've not found any of these platforms.'

'Does your familiar remember?'

She shivered. 'I've not asked . . . I feel like every time I call him to me right now, I lose a little more control over him.'

'Then don't – I don't want to go up there anyway.'

The city was bathed in bright ring-light, an eerie but beautiful scene, and as she gazed about, Kemara noticed the small circular pool at the base of the crater far below. She looked at it properly for the first time. 'Hey, see how the lake down there in the middle is a perfect circle?'

Jesco squinted, then nodded. 'Aye.'

'Nature doesn't do perfect. Now look up *there* – and tell me what you see.'

He followed her gaze and his eyes widened. 'Maybe it's just the angle of light, the way the shadows hit? But it looks awfully like there's a circular hole on the underside of that floating rock directly above that circular pool.'

'*Exactly!*'

His eyes brightened. 'Has anyone examined that little lake?'

'I don't know.' She shivered, a little reluctant now to follow this through, but Raythe was right: they needed to find a way up to the floating citadel. 'Shall we?'

'Now? In the middle of the night?'

'Come on, let's do this – it'll make Lord Vyre happy.'

They zigzagged their way down, past the mouths of mines and over drainage canals, until finally they stood at the rim of the circular wall containing the stagnant, slimy pond. There were gutters to carry the excess water into what must be the underground drainage system that also served the mines.

'Deo, it stinks,' Jesco complained. 'What if there are water boghuls?'

Kemara ignored him, instead touching her mask and watching Buramanaka form on the other side of the pond. His dark gaze was fixed on her. *What does he want?*

Jesco stiffened. 'He's not exactly cuddly, is he? Not like Raythe's parrot.'

Kemara was shocked. 'You can *see* our familiars?'

'I've been able to see them for a few days now.'

Stranger and stranger. 'Raythe should know that. We need to tell him.'

'Perhaps it's because we've been spending so much time together?' Jesco suggested.

Kemara doubted that, but for now, she concentrated on Buramanaka. '*Bura, misete kono basho,*' she ordered the familiar – Show me this place – and he flowed into her.

Suddenly she could sense the shape of the pool and realised with a burst of excitement that there was a circular stone dais beneath the surface – and that it wasn't a true pond, either, just a pooling of rainwater that hadn't flowed away because the drains were blocked.

She raised her hands, pointed to the nearest jammed gutter and traced the Aldar sigil for stone, then said, '*Bura, heisoku no zangai*.': clear the debris.

Buramanaka reached out from inside her, forcing sludge through the drainage holes, and with a gurgle, the pond began to empty. In minutes, a round dais was revealed, dripping wet and coated in slime. It was roughly six feet across, with a central plinth, and it looked intact.

Jesco gave her an admiring look. 'Let's investigate.'

They climbed over the stone parapet and with Jesco leading the way, his hand on his sword hilt, they walked through the sludge. The dais was stone, with the rusted remains of a metal fence around the outside – to keep people safe, presumably – and the stone plinth was for the controls. It was a hiko-sakuru, according to Buramanaka, which meant flying disc.

She turned to Jesco. 'So this is how they got up – although I doubt it still works.'

He glanced up at the huge rock, hundreds of yards above and blocking out half the sky. 'Let's have a closer look.'

They clambered up onto the dirty platform and went to the stone plinth in the middle, which had carved symbols on it, worn by time and damp. Kemara went to touch them, then thought better of it. 'We need to show his Lordship.'

Jesco was still looking skywards. 'She's up there – I can feel it.'

'Who?' Kemara's eyes went to the ring on his finger and she brushed it with her fingertips – and all at once, instead of Jesco, she saw a willowy woman with flowing dark hair wearing a flimsy silken dress and a beautifully wrought heart-shaped mask.

Kemara jolted in shock and jerked away–

–and the woman vanished, just as Jesco brushed his hand over one of the carved runes on the stone plinth – instantly causing the whole platform to vibrate, then wrench free of the debris packed round it and start rising into the air.

'Jesco!' Kemara shouted, staggering at the sudden movement.

The Shadran steadied her, but in that moment, their chance to leap off had vanished. Kemara hammered at the plinth where he'd touched it, but nothing changed; the dais just kept rising. In moments the ground was thirty feet below them and falling away fast. The underside of the floating citadel filled the night sky as they rose towards it.

3

Castle in the Air

Cold winds buffeted them, but Kemara barely noticed the chill, nor the incredible vista unfurling before them as they rose above the crater rim and the city spread below, kissed silver by the planetary rings.

'What in the Pit happened?' she demanded. 'I saw a masked woman – who is she?'

Jesco flinched, like a child caught lying. 'She . . . um, she appeared after I found this ring.'

'What? Then get rid of it – give it to Vyre. Gerda's sake, Jesco, who do you think you are, an imperial sorcerer?'

He closed his hand over the golden ring. 'It's mine . . . no, hers . . . *Oh Deo . . .*' He looked at her helplessly. 'We have to help her–'

'No! What we have to do is get back down,' she cried, turning to the plinth.

But Buramanaka growled inside her, and when she tried to expel him, he did something terrifying: he gripped her heart so hard that she could feel his fingers inside her chest, and hissed, *We must find her. She is my sister.*

'Who is she?' she asked aloud.

'*Shameesta*,' Jesco confessed: a name from legend: the last Aldar King's chief wife, whom Tashvariel the Usurper had coveted.

Kemara rocked back on her heels. 'Gerda's Teats . . . that ring was *hers*? You've got the God-King's last wife locked inside your soul . . . And I've got her *brother* in mine . . .'

She couldn't even begin to process that.

Jesco hugged her against him and for a minute they just stared out over the landscape, trying to think. To the southeast, the neighbouring valley had come into view, revealing the Tangato village, just a couple of miles away. There were big bonfires there, pinpricks of light, and she thought about what Foaley had said about the influx of warriors.

We have just four full days left until the Kirra Moon rises and the truce ends.

'Everything's coming to a head,' she murmured. 'We've got to resolve it all in the next few days, or we're all going to die. I think Buramanaka wants us to reach the fortress before we run out of time.'

They faced each other, looking into each other's eyes – and now she could feel Buramanaka communing with Shameesta, making promises she couldn't hear.

No wonder he was having such nightmares – or that we found peace with each other . . .

She turned her attention inwards, daring to ask for confirmation, and the mizra spirit – or more accurately, the Aldar ghost – replied in deathly tones, *I am her brother. I fought in the rebellion against Tashvariel's rule. We prevailed, but my sister died. Afterwards, I returned home, just as the storms which brought the Ice Age began. All my people died, and I perished with them. I lay there for half a millennium and felt every moment, until you found me.*

'How did she die?' she asked, not entirely sure she wanted to know.

Buramanaka's voice grew dark as night. *'All I know is that Tashvariel is said to have murdered her at the final banquet. The legends say that he served her as a dish at the meal.'*

The horror of that image overwhelmed her. 'Did you recover her body?' she dared to ask.

'No,' he admitted. *'Shiro Kamigami was deemed unsafe, so I was forbidden to ascend, and the Jaws of Ice were closing on us all. I wanted to return here when I could, but I didn't survive the freezing of the world. Now her spirit lingers above in this cursed citadel.'*

The floating rock was now filling the sky above them. She conjured light, which revealed a shaft, right where she'd suspected, just wide enough for their stone disc – and free of obstructions, thank Deo.

Moments later it swallowed them. They held hands and breath until the platform came to a smooth stop level with a floor, held in place by a stone lip.

They were in the centre of a circular chamber, facing giant doors. Jesco joined her where there was a gap in the safety railing and they looked around cautiously.

'There's another control plinth here,' Kemara exclaimed, darting off the platform, which was still vibrating, trying to rise but restrained by the lip of the shaft. She examined the runes, biting her lip. 'Any ideas?' she murmured to Buramanaka.

Before he could respond, the flying platform suddenly stopped vibrating – and instantly dropped.

Jesco fell with it–

–but he'd been holding the safety railing, and that saved him. As the platform vanished down the shaft, he clung on, howling in pain as his injured arm took his weight, his legs thrashing over the void. Kemara lunged for him and hauled him up, clasping him to her, panting and gasping. Only when she was sure he was okay did they crawl to the hole and peer through the railing – just in time to hear a mighty *crack!* – as if the stone disc had broken on impact – in the darkness below.

Kemara buried her face in her hands, shaking from the shock.

'Holy Gerda,' Jesco breathed, 'now we've done it.' He winced as he rotated his wounded right arm, then hissed as he tried to lift his limp left arm, and gasped, 'It's dislocated.'

'Here, let me. That's one thing I can do,' Kemara said.

Jesco gritted his teeth as she manipulated the joint back into place, but he stayed conscious, when many would have fainted.

'Someone will have heard that platform hitting the ground,' Kemara suggested, once her brain had restarted.

'And do what?'

'Good point.' She looked round blankly. 'Maybe there are other platforms?'

'There's only one hole under the rock,' he pointed out.

'Also a good point,' she mumbled. She took off her one piece of jewellery – a copper pendant she knew Varahana would recognise – and threw it down the shaft. 'If someone finds it, they might put two and two together. So: what do we do now?'

Buramanaka was the first to answer. *Find my sister.*

She helped Jesco rise, taking the opportunity to examine the gold ring properly. It looked plain, but when she peered closer she could see symbols of what looked like Aldar script engraved into the band. Buramanaka confirmed that it belonged to Shameesta.

'She kind of haunts it, I think,' Jesco muttered, 'but her body's somewhere up here. Maybe we're supposed to find it, and ... what's that word? . . . exorcise it?'

'I don't know anything about that sort of shit.'

Jesco gave her an encouraging look. 'We'll make it up as we go, like we usually do.' He flexed his right arm, winced, then tried the newly adjusted left arm and moaned plaintively. 'I guess I'm one-armed for the moment. At least I can use both, being ambisexual and all.'

'Your right arm was wounded just a week or so ago, so take it easy,' she reminded him. 'Best not to get into any fights . . .'

'If there's anything up here to fight after five hundred years, we're in serious trouble,' he said, giving her a shaky grin.

The smooth-walled chamber was just wide enough for a walkway around the disc. The huge double doors, the only exit, were heavily carved, but dulled with age and dirt. As Kemara examined them, she realised they were sealed with sorcery, but from *this* side, which made her wonder why the stone platform had been down below and who'd used it last – and for what purpose? But whatever the answer, the doors yielded to her opening spell, delivered through Buramanaka with an emphatic rush of energy. The locks undone, she pulled the bolts aside and pushed the door open, then sent her sorcerous light bobbing through to illuminate the space beyond.

They were at the bottom of a round stairwell that went spiralling up through the floating rock. It was ribbed by circular bannisters undamaged by time. The walls were veined with glowing green activated istariol, the element that was keeping the rock airborne, a miracle of sorcery and nature.

'Deo on high,' Jesco breathed. 'This puts *everything* I've seen in the Empire in the shade.'

Kemara was just as awestruck ... and chilled by the absolute precision she could see everywhere. Every curve was geometrically precise, every plane smooth, every joint so exact they were almost invisible. Even the great cities of Magnia looked ramshackle by comparison – and this was just the entrance.

'I don't think we should go up,' she told Jesco, but Buramanaka immediately bristled at the suggestion. *Perhaps I could send him to Raythe to warn him where we are?*

Inside her mind, Buramanaka's demonic mask scowled. *No. We must go upwards. There was supposedly another way in and out – and my sister Shameesta may be still alive.*

Her eyes went round and she glanced at Jesco's finger. 'But I thought her soul was trapped in the ring?'

That is just a trinket – a link to her. I can sense her spirit, though I can't reach it.

'But she's been dead for five hundred years,' she blurted, glancing at Jesco, who clearly could not only see Buramanaka, but hear him as well.

Perhaps not, the ghostly Aldar lord replied. *I need to see. Regardless, your friends cannot reach you here. If you wish to escape, the only means to do so lies above us.*

'You've been here before?'

Buramanaka's mask twitched into a grim expression. *No, not even I, brother of Shameesta, Vashtariel Last-King's favourite wife, was deemed worthy of these exalted halls. What lies above I know of only by hearsay.*

Kemara slumped. She'd been hoping for insights, but it looked like they'd all have to take on whatever they encountered. 'So what did you hear?' she asked the spirit.

There was so much confusion – the citadel was besieged, as best as such a place can be, then one night, all was silent: no bombardments, no fire and sorcery, no prisoners executed by being thrown down, no men on the walls. Day after day, the silence went on, until a delegation ascended. They found everyone dead, and this place was declared forbidden. No tokens of victory were ever displayed, nor bodies recovered. Nothing.

'Didn't you question that?' Kemara wondered.

Of course, but the ice storms were closing in, and we had to return home to protect our people. Within weeks, everything had descended into chaos, and of course . . . we didn't survive.

Kemara couldn't begin to imagine such times, but the fact that no one had brought out trophies of victory struck her as ominous.

She turned to Jesco. 'Well?'

'We must press on upwards, if only to escape,' the Shadran replied. 'Shameesta won't let me rest otherwise.'

'I suspect Buramanaka will not stop plaguing me either,' Kemara grumbled. 'Well then, shall we?'

Squaring their shoulders, they went through the great double doors and ascended wide stairs to the first level, where corridors fanned out like spokes of a wagon wheel, each hall studded with doors. 'The real finds will be above, but I don't like not knowing what's behind me,' Jesco murmured, leading her down one of the halls and opening the first pair of doors they came to. Kemara followed closely, her magical senses alive to changes in the atmosphere, but all was quiet.

Jesco opened the doors to reveal an armoury containing war gear, as ornamental as it was martial, racks of spears and curved swords in scabbards of wood and velvet. Tarnished breastplates were embossed with dragon designs and Aldar sigils. Graceful plumed helms, banded leather body armour and boots that were cracked and decaying – although not as much as five centuries ought to have wrought.

'Varahana's going to love this,' Jesco remarked.

Kemara picked up a long, curved blade with a long, two-handed hilt and slung the scabbard over her shoulder. 'Buramanaka uses a blade like this. He can wield it through me.'

The rest of that hall revealed more rooms filled with Aldar weapons: bows and arrows, halberds and pikes, maces and axes, all graceful and deadly-looking – and quaintly anachronistic for the lack of flintlocks and pistols. These were relics forgotten by time.

Oddly, there was no evidence of birds or rodents, remarkably few cobwebs on the ceiling, and not much dust on the floor. Kemara turned to Jesco. 'I'm no expert, but isn't this stuff too well preserved? I mean, after five hundred years, shouldn't the metal be reduced to rust and the leather and cloth be entirely gone?'

Jesco shrugged. 'Perhaps they had some way of preventing decay? The Aldar were – well, magical, right?'

They returned to the stairs, continued to the next level and found storerooms filled with empty crates, but again, nothing completely decayed. Bolts of cloth folded on shelves looked good enough to use right now. Kitchen tools and cutlery were barely corroded by the half-millennia they'd been sitting here. The level above contained large stores of old timber, sawn and treated, completely dry and still straight and true, and old saw-wheels as sharp as if they'd just been ground.

On the fourth floor they found dozens of blacksmith forges, with stockpiles of metal bars and unfinished projects of all types – half-made weapons, blades and spearheads, horseshoes, tools and dozens of other artefacts, some still silver, others a little rusted – but not enough for the elapsed period of time.

On the next level, Jesco opened the first door – and even his composure faltered. 'Deo on high, is that–?'

Kemara looked inside, and swallowed. There were twelve stacks of ingots, carefully arranged so that air could pass between them. Each bar was about six inches long, four wide and an inch thick. A quick count suggested more than a hundred ingots in each stack. The ingots were a pastel red: pure, inert, unprocessed istariol.

'*Holy Gerda.*' She tried to estimate their value, but calculations failed her.

'So Raythe was right,' Jesco said excitedly. 'We're not even going to have to dig – we can just load up and leave.'

The opposite room was identical, and so too the ten others on that level – and the dozen more on the next floor. It was more istariol than they'd ever dared to imagine, already mined and ready for transport. Kemara tucked one bar into the inner pocket of her skirts as proof. She could almost feel angry at Raythe Vyre for the way the universe seemed to conspire to help him – but it was the sort of miracle she could learn to accept.

The next floor up was an unearthly puzzle: a dozen massive glass vats of powdered istariol were arrayed in a circular formation. Each was topped with a metal funnel and piping system – maybe it was used to pump istariol powder (or perhaps a liquefied solution) up into the castle above? Neither of them had ever heard of anything like it, nor could they begin to guess its function.

In the next levels, still below the surface, they found living quarters, for servants, they guessed, looking at the size and starkness of the rooms. They had a mausoleum quality: the narrow cot beds were largely still intact, made of some alloy that had resisted time. The fabric was stiff and yellowed and the mattresses just beginning to rot through the slats beneath them. Little trinkets lay among the collapsed wooden stools and tables, and there were brittle envelopes on many of the pillows; final messages, never read.

Buramanaka exuded anger, his dark voice whispering inside Kemara's skull: *They rained down on the city below: Tashvariel's 'birds'.*

She understood: *The Usurper threw his own servants from the battlements . . .*

'Let's push on,' she whispered. 'There's nothing for us here.'

Jesco nodded wordlessly, taking her hand again as they returned to the central stairwell. There were another three storeys of servants' quarters, then a barracks level. At the very top of the stairwell was a circular roof carved with an Aldar dragon, and a doorway into a massive hall: the ground-level entrance hall of the citadel. They peered through, almost too scared to breathe, at the majestic, coldly empty vista before them.

It was hundreds of yards long, lined with pillars and alcoves, with a vaulted ceiling like a Deist cathedral but even more magnificent. Each window was filled with coloured glass, but there wasn't enough light outside to see what was depicted. The floor, a marble mosaic, was overlaid with a cover of fine dust. Heavily patterned triangular pennants hung motionless in the dry air. The walls were lined with alcoves containing what looked like stone sarcophagi, surmounted by lifelike bronzes of fighting men in archaic armour, holding axe-bladed halberds that looked chillingly lethal.

But nothing looks old enough, Kemara thought. All the cloth was vividly coloured; there weren't even cobwebs. Except for the light dust, it was as if the people had simply stepped outside moments before.

'There's something strange . . .' Jesco breathed. 'The light . . . ?'

Kemara focused on a narrow shaft of light from a small upper window that was lighting dust motes in the air – and realised that one edge of the sunbeam looked like it was trailing sparks.

'That's really weird,' she said uneasily.

I've never heard of such a thing, Buramanaka murmured inside her.

Jesco drew his sword and prodded the space before them, grunting in surprise as the tip of the blade snagged on some unseen obstruction, as if the tip were pushing slowly through invisible treacle. He frowned, pulled the blade out and swished it quite normally – then he pulled out a coin and before Kemara could stop him, he tossed it through the doorway.

Their mouths dropped open and they gaped, for the moment the coin entered the doorway, its flight slowed right down. It turned over and over, but ponderously, until at last it struck the stone floor, belling deeper and longer than could be natural.

'Huh?' the Shadran muttered, as the sound echoed through the hall, but still nothing moved, no other sound came, and slowly they let out their breath.

'Bura?' Kemara asked quietly.

The Aldar ghost appeared beside her, making Jesco flinch. *There were rumours*, he whispered. *Some said those sent up here to investigate the silence were unable to enter the citadel at all, but they declared the Usurper dead anyway, to allay panic.*

'But what's causing this?' she asked.

Buramanaka's masked visage looked uncharacteristically reflective. *I once saw a play in which the hero went backwards in time. Such a thing was impossible, of course, but my tutor said that with sufficient power, one might be able to slow down time – in a small, limited locale. Perhaps Tashvariel achieved this?*

'So Tashvariel himself may still be alive in here?' Kemara squeaked.

'And Shameesta,' Jesco added.

Kemara's every instinct was to run. In every tale she'd ever heard, Tashvariel the Usurper was insane, a psychotic killer in kingly robes who destroyed his world rather than submit to defeat. That he might still be alive up here was terrifying.

Then she had a worse thought.

'We've found some rust and decay – but not enough,' she whispered. 'What if there really is a block of "frozen time", but it's *melting*. If anyone is still alive inside it, they may be on the verge of coming out.'

Jesco let out a wordless yelp, and Kemara could feel Buramanaka almost paralysed by such a notion.

'So if we go on,' she added, 'not only do we risk facing someone we can't possibly handle, but we're probably going to freeze ourselves in time, too. If we do manage to get out at all, it might be years from now – decades, even centuries.'

All three fell silent as they contemplated that until Buramanaka lifted his masked face and gazing up, said, *If there is a sphere of frozen time, then it is melting, that is clear. The spell is breaking down from the outside. It might be that in the centre of this spell, time is still frozen, and it's at that centre that Tashvariel will be – or whoever else cast it.*

Jesco seized on that eagerly. 'Aye, it could be that if we skirt round the edges, we could find a way through to . . .' He frowned. 'To what, exactly?'

Buramanaka faced him. *There was another way in and out. The hiko-sakuru – the stone platform – was for the servants to bring up supplies. The Aldar lords used another way. The Bridge of Izanami – the Rainbow Bridge – linked the citadel to the Summer Palace, not far from here. That's the way I hope we may escape – after we have found Shameesta.*

His words brooked no disagreement, and they were accompanied by a *frisson* of sorcerous energy that made Kemara's heart palpitate. Just like on the night of Crowfoot's attacks, she was left thinking that she was as much Bura's familiar as he was hers.

She bowed her head, commended her soul to Gerda and drew the curved bronze sword she'd found in the armoury below. 'Then let's do it,' she said firmly, before her courage failed. 'Because time is apparently very much of the essence.'

With that, she summoned Buramanaka back inside her, and together she and Jesco entered the great hall, wading in as if into water . . .

. . . but thereafter, there was no discernible difference to being outside this 'bubble'. Everything – light, sound, even smell – appeared to be exactly as normal. *Because we're in a new 'time' zone*, Kemara thought, picturing layers like an onion. She noticed that the stars, visible through the windows, moved fractionally if you watched them closely, suggesting that minutes were passing like moments, while out there, time was burning away.

'We have to hurry.'

The hall was majestic, but lifeless. At one end were huge doors, perhaps leading outside, and at the other end was a raised dais bearing a huge throne, set around with many lesser seats, the lowliest of which would have outdone a Magnian king's seat of state for magnificence. The lines of sarcophagi brooded as they passed them; the bronze suits of armour above them looked on the brink of movement.

'No wonder the Aldar regarded themselves as demigods,' Jesco murmured. 'No wonder they went mad.'

Kemara agreed. Buramanaka's mood was darkening: loss, regret and anger were warring inside him, and above all was heart-rending des-peration for his sister. '*Onwards*,' he urged them constantly.

They found another cylindrical staircase, this one leading into the upper reaches of the castle, and as they climbed it, they felt the air change, and through the windows the stars outside started shifting a little faster. They were moving deeper into the frozen block of time, and slower in relation to outside.

Will we emerge to find centuries have past? Kemara wondered.

But she gritted her teeth and went on, past a floor of what looked like council rooms, then dining halls, until they reached the Aldar's living quarters. In contrast to the cramped servants' rooms, these were truly magnificent: each a suite of four to eight rooms, with banked windows, heavy drapes and furnishings of polished wood and metal. Divans crouched around old fireplaces, where tinder piled ready to light was coated in dust and doused in old soot fallen from the chimneys above. But for all the evident luxury, the place was lifeless, just an echo of the past.

Eerily, every room contained at least one sarcophagus, the lids deco-rated with relief carvings – of the dead person within, Buramanaka confirmed – with verdigris-coated masks over the stone faces. Under-neath the masks were alien visages: high cheekbones, flat faces and noses, narrow eyes and a kind of mound behind the lips that was almost feline. They were chilling, predatory, and oddly alluring – and unlike any race Kemara knew.

'I don't know how these Aldar lived with all this death around them,' Jesco murmured, prising one sarcophagus open with his dagger, then allowing Kemara to lift the lid, his shoulders not being up for the task. He fished inside and pulled out the skull. 'Look at this.'

Kemara took in the pronounced teeth and jaw-line with a sense of unease. A picture formed in her mind of men and women with dark, flat faces and teeth that could rip out another's throat.

'Screwing must've been risky,' Jesco chuckled. 'You'd have to *really* trust your lover.'

They returned to the central staircase and realised that there were only two floors left to explore. Kemara's unease had been growing; she had a pronounced sense of being watched and whispered about, but her sorcerous sight revealed nothing.

'Come on,' she urged, anxious for this slow crawl through the death of a civilisation to be over. Hand in hand again, they took the last set of stairs onto a landing with a hallway extending to the left, and yet more stairs to the right. Buramanaka had no more idea than she, and they couldn't tell if the heart of the time spell lay on this level or above.

'We should check this level first,' Jesco said. 'As quick as we can.'

Kemara sent her sorcerous light down the hallway, banishing the shadows as she led the way. The ceiling was at least five times their height and there were a dozen giant statues lining either side, *kneeling* to anyone that passed. Names she didn't know leaped into Kemara's mind. These were the Aldar Gods: Kagemori Deathlord, Kiiyan the Merciful, Shinija-Kyu the Dragon-King, Ankazo the Jade Emperor, and eight others, their shoulders and bowed heads brushing the ceiling as they genuflected in reverence.

'Every day, the god-king traversed this hall and the gods *knelt*,' Jesco marvelled.

'It must hurt to know they had an ego bigger than yours, Jes,' Kemara quipped, in an attempt to lighten the air.

'I do feel kinship to the God-Kings,' Jesco drawled. 'I think we'd have been real chums.'

They cautiously entered the next hall, this one lined with upright sarcophagi decorated with the reliefs of crowned men and women. The symbols etched above each were legible to Buramanaka, who whispered their names; Kemara didn't know any, until the last one.

Vashtariel.

'These are the coffins of the God-Kings and Queens of the Aldar,' she told Jesco, her voice filled with awe. 'Holy Gerda, they got buried in the private rooms of their heirs.'

The dead are never gone. It is right that we walk with them, to emulate their glory or learn from their failings, Buramanaka whispered. A quiet cacophony of emotions were leaking from his mind into hers – anxiety, anticipation, anger, and a harrowing despair.

Next came a luxurious living room, a dressing room full of ancient regalia and an office full of papers, before they reached a huge bedroom built around a massive canopied bed. The sheets looked disturbed, as if they'd only recently been abandoned.

Kemara was too nervous to touch them, in case they were still *warm*.

She went to the window and pulled open the heavy drapes to see where they were – and sunlight gleamed in, for, alarmingly, it was daytime again – the night had passed in what felt like half an hour. When she looked out, she saw they were facing east now; the rising sun had a comet tail and was clearly moving, an hour passing in minutes outside their bubble of time. Below was an overgrown garden, walled in by battlements that blocked off the edge of the floating rock. The snow-tipped mountains glowered back resentfully, as if insulted that this peak had somehow escaped the ground.

'You can see for miles,' the Shadran remarked. 'It's truly a view fit for a god.'

'What day is it, do you think?' she wondered.

Even Buramanaka didn't know for sure.

'I don't think the Kirra Moon has risen,' Jesco said, 'but it can't be far away.'

'You're assuming it's the same month,' Kemara replied bleakly.

No, outside only the night has passed, Buramanaka told her. *The angle of the sun is relatively unchanged.*

Reassured, they went to another window, which overlooked a view of the wall, and saw a tower housing a strange metal device: a series of interlocking curved metal strips that formed a sphere. Incredibly, it looked intact, despite having been open to the elements for so long.

That's what we seek, Buramanaka told her. *The gate of a Rainbow Bridge. We must have bypassed the exit to the outside on the way up.*

Kemara's hopes rose. Perhaps they could escape without confronting whatever lay at the heart of this lost place. 'Can we get there? We could come back later, in force.'

She guessed Buramanaka wouldn't countenance that, not with his sister unfound, but his answer ruled out her suggestion anyway.

Such gates require a key to be opened. Until we find it, this portal is unusable.

'Perhaps it's below?'

It was always kept on the person of the King or his closest advisors, Buramanaka replied. *We have no choice.*

She turned to Jesco, who looked resigned. 'Like it or not, there's a battle to be fought,' he said, his voice dropping to a dead monotone. 'Let's get on with it.'

They returned through the royal suite, past the kneeling gods to the central stair, and gazed up. The air shimmered: they were going deeper into this bubble of slow-moving time, further into the deadly unknown.

How many days do we lose outside if we ascend those steps? Kemara wondered.

But she saw no other way, for the only thing that might possibly save them was somewhere up there. Gripping the bronze Aldar sword, she placed one foot on the stairs and began to climb, Jesco at her side. With every step, she felt that tugging resistance in the air, a palpable sense of slowing time, like walking through water. When she looked at Jesco, she saw a trail of afterimages behind him.

Then came the sound of a blurred voice, deep and slow, and she looked up to see a man and a woman in tooled leather Aldar armour had stepped into view. They carried bladed halberds which were spinning slowly up to guard position, energy blazing along the shafts as they aligned spear-tips at them.

That sorcerous energy became twin blue bolts that exploded soundlessly from the tips of the weapons and lanced down the stairs, right at them . . .

4

The Challenge

The Tangato feast was a strange mix of ceremony and informality that Zar couldn't quite understand, but found herself enjoying.

There was strictly segregated dancing, performed as entertainment: lines of either men or women facing the throne and chanting songs which all sounded the same to her. A few plucked eerily high-pitched stringed instruments or tapped hand-drums, but the music was primarily provided by voices.

The tribes all kept to their own designated areas, sitting cross-legged on mats; they applauded by slapping their thighs and whooping. Each had a turn to perform, and vociferously cheered their own. Only Shiazar's people had women singing, and there was a lot of nudging and backslapping in the visiting war-parties afterwards, with the men boasting and trying to catch the eye of whichever woman had taken their fancy. Men were the same, no matter how far you travelled.

But my man is lying unconscious, five miles away, Zar reminded herself, because she was by no means immune to some of the handsome, exotic faces surrounding her.

Apart from the Queen and her Yokei, everyone here was dressed in traditional Tangato garb, the warriors in nothing more than a flax kilt and a light shoulder-cloak of feathers, leaving the chest and midriff bare. Most of the older men had hefty bellies and chests, formidable but off-putting to Zar's eyes, but the young men were lean and athletic, their bronze skin gleaming with oil.

Many stared openly at her white skin and pale hair. Some were clearly repulsed, but as many were undressing her with their eyes while whispering to each other, which made her skin crawl. She clung to memories of Banno as a barrier to all the attention.

Seated where she was, close to the throne, she was safe enough, although there was a different tension in the air here, so close to the heart of power. The Queen was like a living doll, clad in blindingly beautiful embroidered silk and masked in gold, surrounded by her resplendent Yokei advisors, and her court wove about her, seeking advantage.

She and her Yokei are half-Aldar, Zar reminded herself. *Living legends.*

She also had opportunity to study the mahotsu-kai of the other tribes: there were just seventeen of them, six senior and eleven apprentices, and they were all older than she was. Most were male, and lacking the athletic grace of the warrior caste. They snubbed her, not speaking directly to her but instead bombarding Rima with questions about her and her people. No one looked satisfied with the answers.

But to her relief, Tatsu and Kyu, the two mutilated Manowai mahotsu-kai, kept their distance, preferring instead to whisper in the ear of their rangatira, the belligerent Ikendo. Zar averted her eyes from them, although that meant also ignoring Onkado, who was attending Ikendo, much like a knight's squire.

She must have given something away, though, because Rima leaned in and murmured, 'That Onkado is good to look at, hmm?'

Zar decided not to grace that with a reply.

'But he's Manowai, and they're trouble,' Rima went on, her voice more serious now. 'The only war we've ever fought was because of the Manowai. We have a law that no sorcerer may also be a rangatira, but rumours have it that Ikendo has the maho and that Onkado is his apprentice and his heir. Some say Ikendo aspires to overthrow the rule of the queens and reassert male superiority.'

Rima clearly thought it outrageous that a man could be both rangatira and mahotsu-kai, but Zar reflected that her father was both commander and a sorcerer, and that just made him more effective. *The Tangato have some strange attitudes,* she decided. She risked a glance at

Ikendo and thought that he looked like a man with a grievance, the sort who would make trouble even in good times. Then her eyes trailed back to Onkado. *So he might be actually be a sorcerer as well? How wonderful.* He glanced up, saw her looking and his eyes flickered in both greeting and warning before looking away.

He's a potential ally, Zar decided. *I wish I could talk to him again.*

'If Ikendo is really a chief and a sorcerer, why doesn't Shiazar remove him?' she asked.

'Because it's unproven. Jinkatia lives among them for much of the year, and she says it's not true. Shiazar even sent her sister Ulaka to check, but she found no evidence.'

Zar peered at the throne, where Shiazar was conferring with her three closest Yokei attendants, including Ulaka. 'Do you think Jinkatia and Ulaka might have been deceived?'

Rima scowled. 'I doubt it. Jinkatia is the Yokei archivist. Nothing gets by her. And Ulaka is Shiazar's sister and closest confidante.'

'How are your queens chosen?' Zar asked.

'Not by bloodline but by acclamation,' Rima replied. 'The fall of the Aldar told us that hereditary titles are nonsense, that merit should be the determinant. So each queen is chosen by the Yokei from among their ranks, and reigns for eight years. This is Shiazar's third year as queen.'

'How long does a half-Aldar live?'

'Longer than us. Shiazar is young for a Yokei at forty, but she's very accomplished.'

In Otravia, Zar's father Raythe had been the grandson of the Premier, the elected ruler, and he'd been seen by all as a future political power. But the old aristocrats who resented democracy had sided with the Bolgravian invaders, so now it was a monarchy again, and ruled by the father of Luc Mandaryke, the man who'd stolen her mother away. 'My father says that electing rulers only works if those who lose are prepared to respect the vote.'

Rima gave her a sideways grin. 'We say a similar thing: "A kite with no strings is soon blown away". It means that no one who rules without the will of the people can last.'

'We thought the same in Otravia, but we were wrong,' Zar warned. 'Ikendo reminds me of Luc Mandaryke. Father thought they were friends, but Luc's family seized power by force. Now Luc's a prince, and married to my mother.'

'Ikendo can't aspire to be anything other than what he is,' Rima replied. 'Only a Yokei woman may rule. He's just a human male.' She patted Zar's arm. 'He can't touch you, nor will he change the Queen's mind.'

Evil men do what they like, Zar worried, *unless someone stands up to them.*

Her anxious thoughts were interrupted by the advent of the main course of the feast – phorus birds stuffed with trout, then cooked for hours in oven-pits, the natural stringiness of the birds overcome by the slow cooking. They smelled delicious, but unease was spoiling Zar's appetite, especially when she noticed Ikendo's hard eyes on her again.

His stare reminded her of Luc Mandaryke's: ambitious, cold and utterly lacking in empathy: someone who would sacrifice anyone and everything for his ambition.

She averted her eyes, but whenever her gaze flickered in his direction he was still watching, until she found herself fearfully glancing at him every few seconds, scared he might suddenly storm towards her.

'Ikendo keeps looking at me,' she told Rima.

Rima looked at Ikendo. Her eyes narrowed, then she splayed her left hand while poking out her tongue and crossing her eyes. 'Do that,' she advised.

'What does it mean?'

'The hand gesture tells him that he's not welcome and the tongue conveys contempt,' Rima explained, grinning maliciously. 'And the cross-eyes mean that you can't bear looking at him.'

'But he's a rangatira!'

'And also just a man. Rudeness is rudeness, whoever does it.'

Zar blinked, thinking that in Magnia a man could have his tongue ripped out for criticising a lord. But the cheek and defiance of Rima's gesture appealed, so she did it, and was rewarded by seeing Ikendo's eyes go round and his face puff up in outrage.

But Onkado was hiding a grin, then he murmured in the chief's ear and the rangatira was the one to look away.

She and Onkado shared another moment, better than the last, a communion of mutual applause. She felt a hot rush to her cheeks and her mouth twitch into an involuntary grin.

'You've gone pink as a sunset,' Rima smirked. 'Aren't you married or something?'

Zar looked away. *I'm not married, but I should be. It's Banno I love.*

She refused to look in Onkado's direction again.

Finally, the Queen rose from her stool – she was the only one not sitting on a mat – and everyone stood, then knelt. She left, and the meal was officially over. Most stayed on to wolf down final mouthfuls and converse informally, but Rima and Zar got up to leave – when the blind, nose-less Kyu blocked the way, her serpent familiar coiled round her throat.

'Ikendo Rangatira honours the gaikiko pia by his glances,' she said coldly. 'He does not appreciate her returning his honourable regard with insulting gestures.' She turned her sightless gaze on Rima. 'He says women should learn manners from a man, not a castrated boy.'

Gaikiko pia – foreign novice, Adefar translated, but Zar doubted the phrase was complimentary. Being so close to Kyu was unsettling. 'Well, I don't want him leering at me, a married woman,' she retorted. 'Tell him to look elsewhere.'

Kyu's empty sockets crawled over Zar's face. 'You should not be so quick to insult your betters, Snowbird. Ill-chosen words are not quickly forgotten.' Her serpent familiar bared fangs, then she strode away.

'Something's going on,' Zar muttered to Rima. 'No one's that smug unless they've got something planned.'

Rima glowered at Kyu's back. 'There's always trouble when the Manowai visit. Do you want to stay in my farai tonight?'

A little unnerved, Zar decided that it might be a good idea.

Rima's pole-house was bigger than Zar's, with a lush garden beneath and several beautiful embroideries decorating the walls. Zar admired them while Rima got the fire going and put on some water.

As they drank their tea, sitting cross-legged around the small fire, Zar asked, 'Can Shiazar be deposed if the other Yokei disagree with her rule?' It had occurred to her that a throne given by acclamation could be just as easily removed; she needed to know if that was possible, in case her father's treaty with Shiazar was less solid than they thought.

'That's impossible,' Rima declared, then her face clouded. 'Well, *almost* impossible. There was a Queen who was rumoured to have contemplated re-entering the city. The Yokei declared her "unwell" and she abdicated. That is how seriously we take our traditions.'

Zar thought that through. 'So what if some of the Yokei believe Shiazar's mishandled things since my people arrived?' she asked.

Rima frowned. 'It would require a serious complaint, and a four-fifths majority of the Yokei agreeing that she had misused her powers. Doing so would undermine all the Yokei stand for: continuity and the preservation of our ways. And even if the vote went against the Queen, she can refuse to abdicate and invoke the *Gishiki no Shihai*.'

'What's that?'

'The Rites of Dominance: it is one of the few occasions when ritual combat is permitted, as a proxy for all-out war. If the Queen refuses to abdicate, the Yokei will permit a martial challenge. If that were to happen, it would require a challenger to enlist two warriors and two mahotsu-kai to fight against the Queen's own champions.'

'That's barbaric,' Zar scoffed. 'In Magnia that sort of thing died out centuries ago.'

'Here, nothing changes,' Rima reminded her. 'And it's better than tribes going to war.'

'I suppose . . .' Zar remembered Ikendo's suppressed fury; he was certainly capable of making such a challenge. 'So if it did happen and Shiazar was challenged, then Kamo and Hetaru would fight for her?'

'Yes, Hetaru and Kamo would defend Shiazar to the death; with their understudies.'

Zar froze. '*You?*'

'And Poromazi, Kamo's named successor as warleader. But such a challenge has only ever happened twice in our history, and both failed. The challengers must stake their entire family as surety – if they fail, all are put to death. And the Queen may choose a Yokei to aid her side alone, so the Queen's side always has the advantage. This is to dissuade trivial challenges and ensure stable rule.'

'Does Ikendo have a family?'

'Yes: a new wife and four children by his old one. He has much to lose . . . and anyway, the Yokei will not turn against Shiazar. If Ikendo sways them, they will pressure Shiazar privately to make concessions, but they will never permit a challenge.'

'Will Shiazar be swayed?'

'No,' she said firmly. 'Remember, everything she's done has already had their approval.' Rima grinned. 'Enough of Ikendo. He is just a puff of wind from the buttocks of the world.' They shared a giggle, then she teased, 'So, what about all those hot eyes you were throwing at Onkado?'

'I was not!' Zar replied indignantly, then she saw that Rima was teasing, and flushed. 'When I talked to him at the old palace he was nice. Intelligent and kind. But that's all.'

'An intelligent Manowai? Impossible!' Rima snorted. Then she gave Zar a shrewd look. 'Are you *really* married to Banno?' She leaned in and added, 'He's back with your people now, so it doesn't really matter if you lied to us. I'd understand, and I won't tell anyone.'

Zar bit her lip, then sagged and relented. 'We're not married. We've kissed, that's all. When we were taken, I had to protect him.' She wrung her hands. 'I do love him – I really do – but he's not here!'

All the pent-up tears she'd been storing up inside came flooding out, while Rima gathered her up and hugged her against her chest. 'You'll be reunited soon,' the Tangato woman cooed. 'I promise. It's not right that you should be separated.'

'Why not now?' Zar sobbed.

Rima *tsked*. 'Hetaru and I have discussed it, I promise you, but if we allow you to re-join your people, you'll be caught in the middle if war does come. We're trying to protect you. But if your father honours his promises to leave, you'll be allowed to go with him, I swear.'

'I understand,' Zar mumbled, peeling herself away. Oddly, she felt better having cried, and to have someone to comfort her was special – she'd only had her father to dry her tears for the last few years, and he'd always been so busy.

'Thank you,' she murmured. 'I needed that.'

'All will be well, you will see.'

It occurred to Zar that Rima had never really seen just how treacherous life could be, while she'd seen her family disintegrate, spent her life on the run, moving from palaces to hovels, and watched their world descend into tyranny and chaos.

It could happen here . . . and it probably will if the Bolgravians return.

But she pretended to be reassured and they settled in for the night, taking a sleeping mat each and lying by the fire, wrapped up in blankets. Zar watched the embers die down until weariness pulled her down into sleep. But it wasn't a restful night: her dreams were of being hunted through a dark forest full of snakes and mad phorus birds and ended with Kyu sitting on her chest and readying a crooked claw to scoop out her eyes.

She jolted awake, her skin slick and her heart racing. She'd rather have pissed on the floor right there than go outside, although she badly needed to relieve herself.

It was some three hours until dawn, a scarlet stain that spread across the sky amidst distant thunder and bursts of rain carried on gusting winds. When the sun finally rose, it was greeted by horns blowing from the direction of the Queen's throne hall, and news running through the village, borne by gabbling children and gossiping men.

Overnight, the Yokei had indeed turned against Queen Shiazar, forcing her to invoke ritual combat rather than abdicate. Ikendo of the

Manowai had then laid a formal challenge against her, and it had been upheld.

Shiazar's champions, Rima among them, would have to fight for her life in the arena.

'How did you know?' Rima demanded of Zar, as they wolfed down fruit and guzzled water, a makeshift breakfast before a day that suddenly threatened far more than rain. 'How *could* you know?'

I saw it in his eyes, Zar thought. *I saw and I knew.*

5

Unravelling

At sunrise, Raythe discovered he had a problem. Varahana sought him out, complaining that Kemara's room was empty, and so was Jesco's.

Raythe yawned; he'd slept badly after being woken by a booming sound sometime around midnight. 'Did you hear it?' he asked Varahana, describing the moment.

'I can sleep through a cannonade, darling,' Varahana replied, her worried expression belying her light words. 'I can't believe they've just wandered off – Kemara's always in the infirmary by sunrise. And Jesco plays at being a rebel, but he's never been lax.'

'Maybe it's love and they're off somewhere – well, you know . . . ?' Even he thought he sounded dubious.

Varahana snorted dismissively. 'Jesco insists that he and Kemara are just friends, and I believe that. I mean, I adore them both, but Kemara is pricklish as a quill-rat, and Jesco seldom looks at women at all. Something's wrong.'

'Damn them,' Raythe groaned. 'We've got a thousand things to do right now, and only four days to do them in. We still haven't found enough istariol – and we need to get into the fortress above.'

Then Vidar, newly restored to something like health, strode in. 'Raythe, something strange has happened – come, quickly.'

Raythe stood at the bottom of the crater, staring at the broken remains of a stone disc, lying in what had been up, until yesterday, a stagnant pool. The stone disc was – or had been – about thirty feet in diameter and three feet thick, a solid slab, now broken into several pieces. And looking up from the middle of the old pond revealed a cylindrical hole in the bottom of the floating rock, hundreds of yards above.

'So whatever it is, it fell from up there,' Raythe commented – then he saw something gleaming among the broken lumps of rock and scooped up a battered copper pendant. 'Isn't this Kemara's?'

Varahana peered at it. 'Yes, that's hers.'

They all looked up at the floating rock again.

'Ah, *shit*,' Vidar groaned. 'They're up there – but how?'

'I've no idea, and I've got a horrible feeling we're looking at the only way up,' Raythe replied, yet another impossible weight settling on his shoulders. 'This stone circle must've been hidden beneath the water. I'm guessing they stumbled on it last night, and were *stupid* enough to try it on their own.'

'Can we repair it, or build another?' Varahana asked.

Raythe rubbed his eyes. 'I'll see what we can do.'

'Can we afford the time?' Varahana asked. 'Not that I don't love Jesco dearly, and Kemara too, but we've got less than four days until the truce ends.'

'I know. Has my hair turned grey yet?' He pointed to some rusted copper rods and patches of red powder among the rubble. 'See those? The platform must've used activated istariol for lift, and I'll bet there's a mechanism to mute its effect for control. I'm guessing that using it after so long burned out the istariol – they're lucky it didn't fail halfway up.'

'What exactly is "activated istariol"?' Vidar asked.

Raythe gave them the layman's explanation. 'There are two overlapping spheres of existence: the material world and the spiritual world, between which a sorcerer can mediate. Istariol has a similar quality – when it's "activated", it can touch both worlds. When that happens, it becomes, well, "slippery" to gravity, for want of a better explanation,: it can float, and support whatever it's attached to.' He pointed to the rock above. 'Like that.'

'How do you activate it?'

'Well, that's the tricky part. When a sorcerer uses istariol, it's consumed; but when it's activated, it's *altered*. That can happen naturally – which is why floating rocks used to be more common, until we mined them all out. But it can also be done deliberately – the key is exposure to copper verdigris.'

'That shouldn't be hard to find,' Varahana mused. 'There's all sorts of debris in these ruins.'

'I can use the unprocessed istariol nuggets from the mines, but it'll take two or three days for the process to take effect.'

'Then best you get busy, dear,' Varahana urged. 'I'll look after the infirmary, and Vidar, if you're up to it, you can assign a work team to fit this disc back together.'

They were about to part ways when Cal Foaley appeared, jogging down the path into the crater. 'Raythe!' he was calling, 'that dark—Ah, the Tangato girl is back. Says it's urgent.'

Raythe turned to Varahana. 'We'll catch up later.' Then he clapped Vidar's shoulder. 'How are you? Up for a run to the gatehouse?'

The bearskin eyed up the climb. 'Sure. I'm fine.'

The three men hurried out down to the bridge, a ten-minute trot through the twisting streets of the ruined city. The men at the gatehouse had their flintlocks primed, but they looked relaxed; this was Rima's third visit and they were more interested in the fact that she'd apparently ridden up on a phorus bird, which now awaited her at the far end of the bridge.

'Is there aught she can't do?' Rix Morro was marvelling.

'Stow it, lads,' Raythe told them. 'She's a sorceress, and she can probably hear you.' He turned to Tom Corday, who was commanding the watch. 'Does she have an escort, Tom?'

'She came alone,' Corday replied. Having sided with Elgus against Crowfoot, he was now seen as the much-depleted mercenary company's number two.

'Then I wonder what the problem is?' He shed his pistol and sword and called Cognatus to his shoulder before walking out onto the bridge to where Rima waited.

'Thank you for coming,' she said.

'You rode that mad bird? You're braver than I thought!'

'They're swift,' Rima said, clearly in no mood for banter. 'We have a problem.'

'*We?*' he asked. 'Why? It's still four days until the Kirra Moon rises.'

'You may have less time than that,' Rima told him. 'Yesterday evening, when all but the chieftains had retired for the night, the rangatira of another tribe, Ikendo of the Manowai, laid a formal complaint before the Yokei, calling for the deposition of Queen Shiazar. He alleged that she hasn't responded adequately to your presence here, and in doing so has failed her people and endangered all Tangato. The complaint was upheld by the Yokei, who have called on Shiazar to abdicate. She has refused.'

Raythe stiffened. 'What does that actually mean?'

'It means the Yokei have sanctioned a trial by arms, with the throne at stake.'

'Really?' He stared at her. 'That's . . . archaic.'

'It is better than the Tangato going to war with each other. Rangatira Ikendo argued that the city should have been watched more closely, that we should have attacked at once; and that istariol is sacred and allowing you to leave with any is a violation of our sacred trust. He is claiming that if you are permitted to leave, then others will return and destroy our way of life, and therefore all of your people must die.'

'And the Yokei agreed?'

Rima's voice turned bitter. 'They did, to everyone's surprise. They elected Shiazar to the throne, so for them to turn against her now shows how divided we are by the advent of your people.'

To his surprise, Raythe felt a heavy twinge of guilt. 'We truly didn't know you were here,' he reminded her.

'Ae, so you keep saying.' Rima sniffed. 'If she is defeated, Queen Shiazar must take her own life. And whoever takes her place will almost certainly enact Ikendo's proposals. Your truce will be no more.'

'But Shiazar contests the matter?'

'She does,' Rima replied. 'She contends that the sacred tapu has protected the city for centuries, and no Queen has ever guarded it closely. She maintains that you are to be trusted and we need but wait four days; and that you will honour your word and not return, nor spread our secret.'

'You can rely on that,' Raythe answered – although he was by no means sure how he could enforce that agreement.

'If you were to leave now, with no istariol, this situation could be over,' Rima added pointedly. 'Ikendo's challenge would be invalidated and Shiazar's reign secured.' When Raythe didn't react, she added, 'Shiazar is prepared to offer you land west of here, so that your people need not return to your homelands and risk exposing us.'

'That won't be acceptable to my people,' Raythe told her. 'We came here to find fortune, not settle.'

'Don't you understand? I'm trying to protect you – and your daughter! Ikendo is already leering at her – do you want her raped and murdered?'

Raythe reeled at her tirade. 'No – no, of course I don't! But if I put your proposal to my people, I won't be their leader for long. And my daughter means everything to me, but not so much to them.'

Rima made an exasperated gesture. 'Then what use *are* you?'

Good question. He ran his fingers through his hair, which was *surely* grey now. 'When will all this happen?'

'Today, in the hour before sunset. The Queen's Yokei champion, her warleader and his second, the mahotsu-kai and his apprentice will contend against the warleader and mahotsu-kai and their apprentices of the challenger: so five on four.'

'Why is it uneven?'

'To dissuade reckless challenges.'

'Barbaric,' he couldn't help saying, then he stopped. 'Wait – you said, "and their apprentice"? Does that mean you?'

Rima put her hands on her hips. 'Ae. I will fight for my Queen also.'

'But not Zar?'

216

'No.'

'Thank Gerda for that!' He had a wild impulse to arm himself with istariol and somehow burn his way into the tribal gathering, snatch up Zar in the confusion and flee. But that would be madness: he'd be blundering in with no idea what they faced, not even where Zar was, or what the terrain was. All the Tangato sorcerers and the half-Aldar Yokei would oppose him, and even with istariol, he'd be unlikely to survive, let alone succeed.

We'd fail – we'd destroy the truce, vindicate Ikendo's challenge and trap ourselves here until we're massacred. It's stupid, is what it is . . .

He looked hard at Rima. 'My daughter's life is in your hands. I pray you are victorious.'

The Tangato girl looked moved. 'I will fight for her, as I fight for my Queen,' she said solemnly. 'You should pray for our victory.'

Then she made a strange semi-curtsey, spun and bounded away as he turned his eyes skywards and murmured, '*Deo, Gerda – protect my daughter, I beg you.*'

Then he started thinking about how to tilt the odds.

The path back to the village took Rima along the edge of the ravine. To her left, the river confluence grew louder, and across that chasm, the ruins of Rath Argentium were an eerie, unearthly presence: sacred and forbidden, but now housing these foreign white-skins.

In the mythology of her people, evil goblins with pale skin lurked in the wilds, preying on the lost. White was the colour of bones, of age and decay, the hue of funeral clothes and mourning. White birds like the kotuku – the heron – brought ill-fortune.

But that's just superstition. Hetaru had always taught her to be openminded, to deal with facts, not fears. So when she'd met Zarelda and Banno, she'd put aside her shock and treated them as humans, not monsters – and when Zar's magical abilities were revealed, she'd accepted her as a sister in maho.

She is *my sister – I like her, even though she's so strange.*

But like cursed birds, Zar's people had brought fear and doubt. The Tangato had thought themselves alone in the world, but Zar said it was peopled by greedy warmongers with deadly weapons and no morality, who still fought the Mizra Wars.

I wish they'd never come.

But they were here now, and couldn't be wished away.

She wasn't sure what to make of Raythe Vyre. He appeared to be a mix of steel and cunning, one who cared for his own, which was endearing. But he had a haunted air, and he clearly regarded the fate of his country as more important than whatever destruction he wrought here.

Ikendo thinks we can erase them and preserve our safety, but Shiazar believes that where one has come, more will follow, so we must learn to co-exist.

But it was Ikendo's argument that had swayed the day. That morning, before the whole tribe, Ikendo had strode before the throne, holding a taiaha dipped in blood, and made his challenge formal. He'd spoken well, and swayed many of the tribesmen listening, even among her own tribe.

These people cannot be allowed to depart, he'd said. *Mercy is not an option – if even one slips away, they will bring back more. This cannot be permitted. They have come seeking fortune, but the wealth of these lands belongs to us. The istariol is tapu, and no one is entitled to it. It belongs right where it is. Let these foreigners be slain, to the last man, woman and child. We don't want them here, and we don't want their wars to become ours.*

The Yokei had been almost unanimous in condemning the Queen's inaction. Only Ulaka had spoken for her, and cast her vote in her sister's favour. In just a few hours, the champions would contend.

I myself must fight and kill, or I'll die.

That was itself a chilling prospect: she'd hunted game before, but she'd never killed another human. Her only consolation was that she loathed Ikendo and his Manowai retinue.

With all these thoughts churning through her mind, Rima rode on, passing no watchers today, for everyone was back in the village, preparing to witness the challenge.

She was distracted, and that was her undoing.

Suddenly her familiar, which had been gliding beside her in winged-reptile guise, shrieked a warning and the bird she rode stopped, its big head darting left and right—

—and an arrow slammed into its breast, right beside her leg, and the giant bird staggered and fell. She rolled clear, barely avoiding going over the edge into the ravine, then scrambled to her feet – but even as she tried to conjure, the air filled with cobwebs of energy. Her limbs entangled, she stumbled and fell, burning strands of energy catching her limbs. She had a glimpse of Kyu's gloating face, her mutilated visage full of malicious glee, and then dark shapes burst from hiding on the slopes of the hill-fort above her, a massive, sweaty male body bore her down, then something cracked against the back of her skull.

The world burst like a bubble, sending her out into the darkness . . .

The first Zarelda knew of something wrong was when Hekami, the son of Kamo, looking worried, hurried up to Hetaru and whispered in the old sorcerer's ear. The old mahotsu-kai then scurried into the Queen's pavilion, where she sat with her sister Ulaka, the Yokei who would champion her in the arena.

The tribe had marked out the arena for the challenge, roughly a hundred yards square, outside the village. Zar had spent that time in Hetaru's lodge, bringing the old sorcerer whatever he requested, mostly water and berries, as he prepared to fight.

Now the hour of the challenge was nigh and the crowds were gathering on this blustery, cold afternoon. A short distance away, looking very serious, Kamo and Poromazi, his second, were limbering up. Rima had been sent off on some matter by the Queen, but that had been hours ago and Zar was beginning to worry.

Finally, Hetaru emerged from the royal pavilion and approached.

'Rima is missing,' he told her. 'Searchers are hunting, but in the mean-time, you must prepare to fight in her place.'

Zar felt herself go pale. *'What—?* But I can't – I don't know how—'

'It is required that the apprentice of the mahotsu-kai fights,' Hetaru answered. 'I am sure Rima will be found, but if not, you will be with me.' He tousled her hair kindly. 'It's not what I want either, but your role will be to support me and follow my lead. I will shield you.'

'But where's Rima?'

'She was sent to the city to see your father and warn him of this chal-lenge. We've searched the entire village – including the Manowai camp – but she's nowhere to be found. Some say she's taken fright and run, but no one believes that. I suspect foul play.'

'Can't the challenge be delayed?' Zar asked desperately. Though she believed in herself and Adefar, she'd barely got to grips with her newly enhanced magic – and she'd never used it to fight, let alone kill.

'No, it cannot.' The old sorcerer pressed his nose to hers. 'We will triumph, you and I.'

It was hard to imagine Hetaru fighting anyone, and as for herself . . . But she reminded herself of all she'd been through. *I'll do my best*, she resolved. 'What do I need?'

'Is there a weapon you know?'

Father had taught her some fencing. 'Could I have one of the cap-tured Bolgravian swords?' she asked, though she couldn't imagine actually stabbing anyone.

'I'll see what I can do.' Hetaru turned and talked to a young warrior and sent him off, then faced her again. 'Now, as one who has lived a little among us, you've seen that sometimes we use contests to replace deadlier conflicts. This duel is such a thing, but the stakes are deliberately high to dissuade reckless challenges. Ikendo's wife and children are in custody – they will die if he fails. The fact they were brought here shows that he planned in advance to issue the challenge and didn't want a delay. He is willing to risk not only his own life, but those closest to him. This was planned, possibly with the collusion of certain Yokei.'

Zar felt her stomach churn, thinking about Ikendo's cold eyes, and his hideously mutilated sorcerers. 'How does the arena work?'

'The war leaders and their seconds contend on the right hand side, while the mahotsu-kai are on the left. Those who capture, disable or slay their enemies may then attack the other side of the arena.'

'So you and I are taking on Tatsu and Kyu?' she confirmed, struggling not to vomit.

They've mutilated themselves like the Izuvei of Bolgravia – they'll be too strong for us.

'Ae, while Kamo and Poromazi take on Ikendo's two warriors. But after one hundred heartbeats, the Queen's Yokei champion joins the fray. That's Ulaka. She and I have already conferred and formulated our strategy.'

To Zar, Ulaka was just a mask and name. 'Can she fight?'

'She is Yokei, and Shiazar's sister, with a deep bond of love,' Hetaru answered, touching his heart. 'The Yokei are swift and strong, and possessed of powerful sorcery. She could likely defeat Tatsu and Kyu on her own.' He patted her shoulder reassuringly. 'We will triumph, Little Bird. And Rima may yet be found.'

But there was something in his voice, a small catch, that said she wouldn't be.

'And who are the warriors on Ikendo's side?' Zar asked, in a small voice.

Hetaru looked her up and down and said, 'The shoganai is a man named Kotabashi. He will be aided by Onkado.'

Zar felt the crushing weight of destiny slam down on her.

Rite of Dominance

'Are there really no Tangato watching the far side of the ravine today?' Raythe asked.

'As far as we can see,' Foaley replied. 'They must all be at this ritual combat Rima told you about.'

Together with Vidar, they were crouched in the shadow of the two dragon statues at the far end of the bridge. Above them, clouds scudded across the late afternoon skies.

'Then let's go,' Raythe said, determined to sneak into the Tangato camp while they were distracted and try to rescue Zar.

With all the usual sentries and watchers absent, it was tempting to use every able-bodied man to launch a full-scale attack – but he had barely a hundred fighting men left so the advantage of surprise wouldn't last long, and nor would their powder and shot.

We have a better chance trusting to stealth.

'Let's go, but keep your wits about you,' he said, as they left the lee of the statues, climbed the short defile to the level ground beyond and took the path running along the edge of the ravine, moving east towards the old hill-fort from where they'd first viewed the city. Below them, the sound of the river rose as it flowed towards the confluence and the mouth of the cave that was its only outflow.

Raythe sent Foaley on ahead, as he had the best eye for tracking, but kept Vidar close. The bearskin was not fully recovered, but even weakened, he was still as strong as any other man. 'Stay calm, no matter what,' he warned him. 'The Tangato village is no place to develop the bloodlust.'

'So long as Zar is unharmed, they've nothing to worry about,' Vidar replied.

They'd just reached the viewing platform on the north side of the hill-fort when Foaley threw up his hand to stop them. Vidar went still, and Raythe called Cognatus to him.

'What is it?' he called softly to the hunter.

Foaley plucked something from the patch of trampled mud he was examining. 'There's fresh blood here, and bird feathers,' he called, 'and this.' He held up a long black hair. 'It's naturally curling. There's blood matted into it.'

'Rima?'

'She's the only one I've seen with hair like this. The men keep theirs shorter, and the women in silks kept theirs bound up – and anyway, we haven't seen any of them for days.'

Raythe cursed. 'So what do you think happened?'

Foaley was examining the footprints. 'The bird's claw tracks end here. There're signs that it was dragged to the edge of the ravine and dropped over. There's several sets of bare feet too, but they're too big for her.'

Vidar, joining the hunter, bent down and started sniffing. A bearskin's senses were far more attuned to the natural world than even a sorcerer's. He was breathing a little faster and his nostrils flared as his inner beast rose. 'Aye, I have the scent: all the blood is hers or the bird's.'

'Which direction did they take?' Raythe asked, hoping they hadn't simply brained her and tossed her into the water with her mount. He glanced back over the ravine – it was possible one of his watchers might have seen something, but they'd lose too much time sending one of them back to ask.

Foaley pointed up the slope of the hill-fort. 'That way.'

The summit was concealed by ruins, debris and years of regrowth, but when he concentrated, even he could see broken grass stems at the nearest gap in the palisade.

He dropped his voice. 'Listen, Rima is the closest thing we have to an ally in their camp, so let's investigate. She could be miles away or even dead – but she might not be. Cal, you're the expert, you follow the signs. Vidar and I will flank you, ten yards either side.'

They fanned out as he'd suggested, each picking their own path up the slope. The hill-fort was primitive, just wooden stakes driven into the ground at the lip of each terrace, which had been shaped by men centuries ago. When they'd first arrived here, Raythe's people had defended it successfully against the Bolgravians, even though most of the stakes were askew, broken or fallen. But there was still plenty of cover as they crept upwards, following Foaley's silent gestures.

Then Raythe saw a Tangato man in a cloak appear on the second-highest tier, silhouetted against the sky. He had hair like a cock's comb and was carrying a wooden spear-club.

Raythe and his comrades had immediately dropped out of sight. *One,* Raythe mouthed, holding up one finger. Foaley nodded, stringing his bow, drawing an arrow and nocking it, then giving him an enquiring look. On his far side, Vidar was hunched like a wolf about to spring.

This man could be nothing to do with Rima . . . but I doubt it . . .

Raythe strained his senses, and with Cognatus helping to enhance his senses, he heard the murmur of male voices, suffused with crude malice. *She's up there,* he decided, and gave Foaley a nod.

Foaley's bowstring sang and the Tangato man crumpled and dropped from sight.

Raythe erupted from cover, sword flashing out and fire coming to his call. To his right, Vidar howled like a wolf and bounded up, his body contorting as he ran.

Rima woke with a splitting headache. Her familiar was gone from inside her and she could feel blood drying in her hair. Her hands and legs were bound and she was roped to an old pou-mahi pole. There was a gag around her mouth too; and a leash round her throat.

Mokomoko? she called with her mind, but her reptile familiar was gone, the absence like a missing limb.

Where am I? All she could see was some kind of subterranean cavern, open to the sky and surrounded by wooden stakes. After a few moments she recognised it: the old prayer pit at the top of the hill-fort.

She cursed herself for the foolish assumption that with his challenge accepted, Ikendo would play by the rules – and then anger filled her, that he *dared* to do this. A ritual challenge was sacred: as a champion, her person was inviolable until she stepped into the arena.

Jade Emperor, she prayed, *give me justice.*

Silhouetted against the rim of the pit, she saw six Manowai warriors, all but one sitting on the lip. Two were eating; the others were talking. Only the one standing guard wasn't joining in; his attention was on the wider world. The sun was out of sight, but judging by the angle of the shadows, it was late afternoon. The challenge would soon begin.

They'll say I was too scared to fight, she seethed. *And Zarelda will be pitched in, in my place . . .*

Somehow, she had to escape. There was no sign of Kyu; she would be in the arena now, and that gave her a little hope. She examined her ankle bonds, then her wrists, but the wet flax rope was tied painfully tight. Her feet and hands were already numb from loss of circulation and the back of her head was throbbing. She tried rubbing her wrists together to see if the knots had any give.

One of the men above chuckled. 'Look, the kararehe is waking up.'

They all laughed darkly. 'Let's have some fun with her,' one burly warrior suggested.

'Are you mad?' another protested. 'She's for Rangatira Ikendo.'

'Who's to know?'

'She'll tell him, Raido. Let it be.'

Raido wasn't ready to let it be, of course; he contorted his face into a leer and called, 'Hey, kararehe, you want to play? Might be the last fun you get.'

She looked up at him and wished him dead.

It must have been a potent wish, for a moment later, the man on guard buckled, an arrow juddering in his ribcage. He staggered and fell from view. The five remaining Manowai warriors went rigid in fright as she heard a man bounding up the slope, snapping out foreign words. She knew that voice: *Raythe Vyre*.

There was another sound: a beast, snarling.

Then everyone moved, the seated men lurching to their feet, hefting their weapons – but Raido stumbled at the edge of the pit, lost his balance and fell in, landing beside her with an explosive grunt, and for a moment he lay still, his stone club tantalisingly close.

But before she could reach it, he rolled over and grasped it, staring at her face with hate – that turned into alarm when a loud *crack* sounded, the report of a gaikiko fire-weapon, and another man shrieked in agony. Above them the air filled with bestial roars, bellowed war-cries and the crack of wood on steel. Raido made a bleating noise, but he lifted his club and grabbed her hair.

'Kill me and Ikendo will *eat* you,' she gasped, praying he wasn't beyond reason.

'If I lose you, he'll have my head,' he retorted, readying his blow.

Then something fell on him, smashing him to the ground beneath a mountain of hairy flesh. Elongated jaws snapped closed on the Manowai warrior's throat and *tore*. Blood spurted, Raido jerked and kicked spasmodically, then went limp.

Rima stared, aghast. The last of the Tangato mohoao, the shape-changing beast-men, had died centuries ago, his tragic tale handed down through the generations, so she knew what she faced. She'd be lucky if he recognised her as anything other than a meal.

. . . until Zarelda's father leaped down and laid a calming hand on the mohoao's shoulder. The wild man's rage subsided, as did the animal in his face and demeanour.

Raythe Vyre pulled her gag away. 'You're safe now,' he told her. 'What happened?'

She ripped the leash from round her neck and the moment the barrier spell was broken, Mokomoko came flooding in, filling her senses and fuelling her anger.

'There's no time,' she replied, 'I have to go now—!'

In all the best tales, rescue came at the last possible moment, so Zar kept believing that Rima would burst into the arena, complaining of some plot to delay her – or her father and Kemara would appear, scattering the Tangato with fire and lightning.

But no such thing happened and the moment had come for the challenge to begin. Although she'd been limbering up and communing with Adefar, when she stepped into the arena and saw the grotesque faces of Tatsu and Kyu across the field, she felt woefully unready. Knees wobbling, bones hollow and her lungs breathless, each step felt like a fall she barely caught herself from.

Hetaru gripped her shoulder. 'Calm,' he told her. 'You can do this. You're brave enough, smart enough, strong enough. Those across the way are just wounded animals.'

Wounded animals, she echoed inside, clinging to that notion. *How can cutting yourself ever make you stronger?*

'Let's put them out of their misery,' she said, trying to sound bold.

She was very conscious of the watching Tangato; there was little empathy on their dark faces. 'This is wrong,' she heard. 'What is a gaikiko doing in the arena? Ikendo is right, we have lost our way!'

They'd rather I died, she realised – but her natural defiance reared up and she squared her shoulders. *I'll have to disappoint them.*

The tactics of the arena had been explained: her side would play for time until one hundred heartbeats had elapsed and Ulaka could join the fray. Their enemies would be more aggressive, needing to gain some advantage before Ulaka attacked.

She glanced back. The Queen's sister was a fearsome sight, clad in close-fitting leather armour that had been lacquered blood-red, with a silver mask that was something of both angel and demon. She was wielding a long-handled halberd topped with a razor-sharp blade. The air around her crackled with energy.

Just how much Aldar is there in a 'half-Aldar' Yokei? Zar wondered.

Above Ulaka, Queen Shiazar sat on her throne, wearing a red mask for the blood that would be shed, and white robes for death. Around her were arrayed the two dozen Yokei in judgemental black; and before her were Ikendo's wife and children, bound and kneeling, ready for execution if he lost.

They looked very scared.

As the fighters were introduced, Ikendo glowered fiercely at her, but Onkado was solemn; she thought his eyes were pleading for understanding – but knowing he didn't wish her dead gave her no strength at all, because today, one of them had to die.

Then Kotabashi, the Manowai shoganai, a mountain of a man, joined Onkado on the far side of the arena, preparing to face Kamo and Poromazi. A row of planted arrows halved the field, which was surrounded by thousands of tribespeople. Zar pushed away thoughts of what might happen on that side and looked towards the far end of her own side, where Tatsu and Kyu lurked, squat and hideous.

The voices of the crowd rose in anticipation, a melody to the rhythm of the pulsing drums that built to a crescendo, then fell silent.

All the world held its breath.

Then as one, the Yokei clapped their hands; once, twice . . .

Thrice.

The eight champions stepped into the arena and a single drum began a steady pulse, timing the one hundred heartbeats until Ulaka could join the fray.

The first moments were automatic: Zar snapped out, '*Adefar, habere scutum*,' to conjure a shield, while beside her Hetaru conjured his own protections, his hands trailing rainbows.

Across the field, a hundred yards away, Tatsu and Kyu strode towards her, the air around them rippling. On the other side of the field, Kamo and Poromazi took up defensive fighting stances, looking strong and confident as Kotabashi and Onkado charged.

Zar's attention returned to the pair of disfigured sorcerers and her world shrank to just this small space. *Stay alive, stay alive.*

Three years ago, Colfar's army had retreated into the Vossland deserts, where her father had shown her two scorpions fighting, mostly with their pincers, while the stings hovered threateningly above and behind. *That is how sorcerers fight,* he told her. *See the stings – those are the real weapons, but if they strike and miss, the scorpion is vulnerable. So they use their movement and pincers to try and pin their opponent in place for the perfect strike with the sting.*

She'd been a child then, her magical powers nothing but a burning desire. But she'd watched that deadly dance in fascination until the moment when the fatal strike came – and *missed*, opening the way for the blinding counter that slammed the stinger through the carapace of the errant attacker. The poison took swift toll.

Defend, stay strong, counter at the right moment . . .

So she and Hetaru huddled together as Tatsu and Kyu separated and Kyu's malicious voice filled her head. 'Yield and I won't slay you,' she whispered. 'Though I might *flay* you, to amuse myself.'

Meanwhile, subliminal voices snarled, *Attack, coward! Charge forward and kill her . . .*

Zar resisted the impulse, as Kyu unleashed a bolt of energy that smote her like a battering ram. She reeled, but steadied, with Hetaru's help.

Kyu and Tatsu continued their pincer movement, forcing Zar and Hetaru to go back to back, turning their contest into two separate duels. Kyu went at Zar, her stocky body hunched over as she pulled at the air and chanted commands. Her familiar's form overlaid hers, a bipedal lizard with gleaming red eyes. But Zar could feel Adefar inside her, her fox-faced protector, and her confidence grew with each blow she parried.

Only twenty yards separated her from Kyu now. The reaction time for each spell was shortening, each blow punching harder. She was mostly defending, holding on as the hundred heartbeats pulsed by, blocking punches of force, fending off blasts of energy and fire. But she was holding her own.

Then Kyu changed her attack, instead going mind-to-mind, and Zar's inexperience began to tell. The mutilated sorceress conjured illusions to distract her, while drawing up memories from Zar's brain of old injuries: a torn lower back from a bombard explosion; the agony of a piece of shrapnel in her arm two years ago . . .

There's worse to come, weakling, Kyu hissed, inside her head. *I'll rip your face off . . .*

Zar lashed back with flame and force, but though Kyu recoiled, she came back with worse: images of her own self-mutilation, sharpened by a mind attuned to hate and harm.

Zar realised she wasn't going to win – until Hetaru, beside her, started chanting in his deep, sonorous voice, and his protective spells welled up around her, giving respite, and then he hammered a blow at Tatsu that had the bearded mahotsu-kai staggering.

Then the heartbeat drum fell silent: Ulaka was free to fight.

Instantly, the Queen's sister sprinted their way, igniting the blade of her halberd with energy as she came. Tatsu and Kyu's assaults fell apart as they rushed to erect defensive spells and Hetaru shouted, 'Feed me energy, Zarelda – now we attack!'

Zar caught a glimpse of the other side of the arena, where the four warriors still fought, no one down, then threw herself into aiding Hetaru, as Ulaka arrived–

–and her halberd slashed round, beheading Hetaru with one screaming, savage blow.

The image of the gentle mahotsu-kai standing erect, full of righteous power, and that deadly, treacherous blow imprinted itself on Zar's eyes and brain. His frame remained upright a moment as the head spun away, then he crashed down.

Ulaka ignored her, instead pirouetting away to charge towards the four warriors, lancing fire into Poromazi's back as she hurdled the fence of arrows. The Hiriwa warrior howled, his guard went awry and a routine slash from Onkado opened his belly.

Kamo turned in shock. He missed his parry and the massive Kota-bashi battered at him. Kamo staggered, then Ulaka's axe-blade crunched into his back and he collapsed.

Zar stared in shock as all five now turned on her.

The crowd was in uproar, howling imprecations: the Queen's *own sister*, the only one to support her in this crisis, had betrayed her.

Like Zar, Shiazar was paralysed, rooted to her throne.

Breathing hard, eye sockets leaking blood from Hetaru's last blow, Tatsu crabbed forward, while Kyu closed in on Zar's other flank, yammering in malice. Zar cast about, but her brain couldn't process the fact that they'd lost and she was now going to die.

Then Ulaka was standing in front of her, flashing across the distance and seizing her sword hand, just as it occurred to Zar that stabbing herself might be the least bad option.

'Why?' Zar wailed at the serene ferocity of the Yokei's mask. 'She's your *sister*—'

'She's my *predecessor*,' Ulaka whispered back.

Then she backhanded Zar's face so hard and fast that she never saw it coming. She was still falling backwards, back arched and limbs flailing, when she blacked out.

It was a brief respite, for she woke to find Kyu sitting on her chest, her unwashed stink filling her nostrils. Adefar was gone, and so was her blade. 'Snowbird,' the sorceress gloated, 'shall we begin?'

She pulled out a bone knife with a jagged edge and seized Zar's left ear.

Then Onkado appeared behind Kyu, seizing her wrist and shouting, *'Kao!' No!*

Kyu hesitated – and Onkado pushed her off and stood over Zar, brandishing his sword.

'Step aside!' Ulaka snarled as Kyu's eyes went scarlet and her hands grew talons.

'Tomeru!' Shiazar shouted. '*Tomeru!*' *Halt!*

She rose from her throne, stepped down, plucked the bloody taiaha from the ground and threw it into the arena to signify surrender. Then she held out her arms and knelt. Four of the Yokei closed in, each seized a limb and together, they dragged her away towards her palace.

Zar realised she'd yielded early to save Zar's life – and perhaps Onkado's.

I'd rather have died . . .

'This isn't right,' she moaned. 'Ulaka changed sides.'

'Inside the arena, all is permitted,' Tatsu rasped. 'The only truth is victory.' He glared at Onkado. 'You should not interfere: the girl belongs to me now.'

'That remains to be seen,' Onkado retorted. 'The combat is over. I claim her.'

Tatsu looked inclined to argue, but something passed between them and to Zar's puzzled relief, the old sorcerer deferred to the young warrior and stepped away.

Then Ikendo appeared among them. His challenge might be vindicated, but he looked as angry as ever. 'You overstep, Onkado: this victory is mine, and she is *my* prize, not yours – mine to use or dispose of as *I* see fit.'

Zar felt her fleeting hopes of some kind of respite, of some miracle of mercy, collapse around her.

Onkado reached down and, grasping her upper arm, effortlessly pulled her upright. 'There is a saying, "Learn the Ways of Thy Foe",' he said loudly, addressing not just Ikendo, but all those watching. 'I desire her as my concubine, to learn her people's ways. Don't deny me this, *Father.*'

'Father'? Onkado is Ikendo's son? Why is that a secret?

Then she guessed: he wasn't an acknowledged son, but a bastard.

She waited for Ikendo to refuse, but the rangatira jerked his head in assent. 'Ae, take her. Enjoy her while you can.'

Onkado flushed, but raised his blade and shouted, 'Zarelda is now my prisoner.' He turned, picked out the nearest woman – Kuia, the ancient mahotsu-kai who'd been Hetaru's friend – and said, 'Have her ritually cleansed and brought to my pavilion.'

Only then did he release Zar to follow Ikendo and Ulaka as they approached the now vacant throne and the waiting Yokei.

As they walked, Ikendo and Ulaka touched hands in a way that told Zar everything about their relationship: they were lovers . . . and then her eyes flew to Onkado's face.

Is he Ulaka and Ikendo's child? Is he therefore part-Aldar?

'What in the *Pit* just happened?' Raythe breathed.

For once, Rima was lost for words.

They were perched halfway down the hill dividing the Tangato village from the plains before Rath Argentium, concealed in a clump of bushes. Raythe had his spyglass trained on the arena, which was now engulfed by tribespeople. He'd had only a brief glimpse of his daughter, surrounded by enemies, before she'd been swallowed among the crowds. She was still alive – but surely not for long.

'The Queen's sister betrayed her,' Rima choked out. 'Ulaka was supposed to help the Queen's champions.' Her usual cockiness had vanished in the shock.

He put a consoling hand on her shoulder, but she slapped it away.

'She murdered my mentor – the only person I have *ever* loved,' she snarled, tears streaming down her face. 'She's sentenced her own sister to death, too: Shiazar must take her own life now.'

Raythe was more interested in what this meant for his people: it didn't sound good. *Shiazar was someone I could work with. She restrained her people and protected Zar.* But her regime was gone, and nothing Rima said of this Ikendo boded well.

I must get back and prepare my people to fight – or to run . . .

He turned to Rima and asked, 'What will you do?'

Her face was desolate as she watched the Yokei arrayed in black before the throne wrap a gold cloth around a masked woman: a figure still dressed in scarlet armour. 'Ulaka is nominated as the next Queen,' Rima whispered hoarsely. She hadn't even heard his question. 'She did this to usurp her own sister – and all Heaven weeps.'

He laid a hand on her shoulder again and repeated gently, 'What will you do?'

This time she didn't smack his hand away. 'I don't know. They all think I'm a coward, so no one will wait to hear my words; they'll just strike me down. Perhaps it's what I deserve for my blindness.'

She began to rise, but Raythe hauled her back down. 'I *will* get my daughter back, and I'll kill *anyone* who gets in my way. If you want revenge, your place is with me.'

'Revenge is for savages,' she spat. 'You think we are so primitive, but we are better than that!' She flung her hand towards the arena. 'We're better than *this*. True Tangato are honourable – but now you're here with your treasure-hunting rabble, we're turning into all that we once rejected – because of you!'

'Maybe,' Raythe fired back, 'but those backstabbers are *winning*, and letting them get away with it won't make them stop. That is going to take backbone and brains.'

Rima looked like she wanted to spit blood, but gradually her heaving chest subsided and her rage diminished enough for her to speak again. 'You think I have none of those?'

'No, I know you've got both in spades. Please, Rima. I'm as angry as you – I'm just not so shocked. I've been stabbed in the back many a time and I know how it can break your faith in all good things. But you've got to keep believing in what's right. Remember this: those who betray send a clear signal to everyone that they are *never* to be trusted again. On their day of reckoning, they will find themselves alone. Let's bring that day.'

He offered his hand, as he would have in Magnia.

Rima stared, then she reached out and clasped his hand in a surprisingly strong grip. 'I will help get your daughter back, if you will help me kill Ulaka and Ikendo.'

'Agreed, on my heart.'

'That is sacred,' she told him, before pressing her nose to his, a gesture so like a kiss it momentarily stunned him. It transcended the handshake, turned their vows into something deeper, and he felt it.

'Sacred,' he agreed, staring into her tawny eyes and seeing not a young woman but an old soul. He licked suddenly dry lips. 'Let's get out of here, before we're seen.'

She took one longing look back at her people's village, then joined him. Together, the four of them slipped away through the trees, heading back to Rath Argentium.

7

The Secret of Seppun-Saishu

Shiazar knelt on the mat, clad in a white death shroud, staring at the gem-set bone-handled knife on the stand before her. The ritual weapon had been handed down from Queen to Queen, a reminder of the price of failure. *Seppun-Saishu*, they called it: *The Last Kiss.* Her mother had given it to her on her deathbed, where she'd lain in agony caused by her terminal illness.

Her last words to Shiazar had been, *May you never need this.* Then she'd shown her the Seppun-Saishu's secret, and died by her own hand. Outside, the Yokei had been waiting to choose a new Queen.

Soon after, Shiazar's reign had begun. Now, just three years later, it was over.

She was kneeling in what had been until now her own shrine room in her wooden palace. Above her, a bone-white statue of Kiiyan presided, serene and benevolent.

'I was blind, Great Lady,' Shiazar whispered. *So stupidly blind . . .*

A few minutes ago, the Yokei had finished stripping her, pulling off her royal silks and jewels to give to her successor, then wrapping her in the burial shroud. She only had her mask left, the visage she would be buried with, and a musubi leash round her throat to prevent her using sorcery. There was a crowd waiting outside and a gong had sounded, the sign that she must begin, lest she face the shame of execution instead.

Have courage, Shiazar, she told herself. *It's just a two-handed stab. Be brave and firm-handed and it'll only last a moment.*

Part of her – the part that desperately wanted to *live*, to have a life full of love and children and friendship like her Tangato did – urged her to flee, but that was impossible, even for a Yokei. Running away would condemn her irrevocably, before gods and men alike. The only way out of this moment was through Kagemori's doors, into the realm of death.

It will hurt for only a moment.

She lifted the knife, caressing the gems on the handle, and placed the tip of the long thin blade against her skin, just above her left breast: a breast that had never been caressed or suckled. She licked lips that had never been kissed, feeling her heart fluttering to be leaving a life only half-lived.

Preparing herself for the moment of truth, she lifted her gaze to Kiiyan's face.

Then a secret wall-panel she never even knew existed slid open and a figure in the gold mantle that signified a candidate for the throne stepped through.

'Ah, Sister,' Ulaka said. 'Just in time.'

Shiazar stared. 'What are you doing here? Tradition forbids–'

'Tradition forbids many things,' Ulaka drawled, her voice wet with malice. 'I've come to watch you die, my beloved sister.' She glided across the shrine floor and dropped to her knees, facing Shiazar from six feet away, comfortably out of reach. 'You can't know how much I've longed to see this moment.'

'I don't understand,' Shiazar said. 'I thought you loved me – as I love you.'

'What do *you* know of love, my virginal, hollow-souled sibling? You're nothing but an empty wooden puppet for those old crones to pull around: a vacuous figurehead to keep the rabble quiet. But that age is over. This will be a time of war, and my consort will rule, through me.'

Shiazar stared. 'Your *consort*?'

Then she realised the truth . . .

'Oh, Sister, Ikendo is so much more than you know,' Ulaka purred. 'Forty years ago, when Jinkatia was assigned to the Manowai, she broke the great forbidding, for she mated in secret and gave birth to a *male* – yes, I see you do understand. A male Aldar, in all his power, born to lead us back to glory. That Aldar lord is Ikendo – and he and I have mated. Nineteen years ago, I birthed him a son ... Onkado.' Ulaka's voice was overflowing with triumph and passion.

Shiazar felt the bottom drop out of her world at this ... *blasphemy*. It was the deepest of betrayals of everything the Yokei were, everything they believed, everything they stood for. That Jinkatia – who was considered their wisest – had broken the strictures transcended belief. This was the death blow of all the Yokei had ever been.

If Ikendo has been one of us all along, his face must be a flesh-mask, she realised.

'Ikendo and Onkado are anathema,' she said, in a hollow voice. 'And so are you.'

'No, Sister,' Ulaka retorted triumphantly, 'we are the avatars of a new dawn. Ikendo is a true force of nature: a storm, a runaway beast! When he lies with me, he takes me to both Heaven and the Pit. Together, he and I will change the world. The time of the Aldar is returning, through me, through Ikendo – and through our glorious son.'

The thought of black-hearted Ikendo coupling with her own sister was making Shiazar's skin crawl. 'Have you forgotten all we were taught, Sister? Men are made of violence, and their rule leads inevitably to war. Do you want us all to perish in a new Mizra War?'

Ulaka snorted. 'No, Sister, I want us to be *victorious* in a new Mizra War.'

I have to tell someone ... 'When the other Yokei realise –'

'Stupid, stupid,' Ulaka sneered. 'Why do you think they permitted the challenge? Jinkatia has rallied them to her side – to *me*.'

Then truly, all is lost. Shiazar's eyes welled up as the inevitability broke her. 'My happiest moments were with you, Sister.'

'And mine are with him,' Ulaka replied cruelly.

Shiazar hung her head, still unable to believe that someone she had loved could have proved to be so false. 'Please, Sister, take off your mask,' she whispered. 'I would see your true face again before I die.' *To see if it's really you, or some demon ...*

'If you will take off yours,' Ulaka answered, after a moment. 'So I may see your expression as the blade goes in.'

They peeled away the metal and lacquer faces, revealing the sharp, elegant planes and delicate perfection of Aldar faces. There were no 'half-Aldar', really; the Aldar seed overwhelmed all that was human in any conception. The Yokei were entirely Aldar, and Shiazar and Ulaka were the youngest: *our generation's hope for the next.*

It had been months since they'd last been barefaced together. Ulaka's visage was the more perfect and her eyes were shining in victory, but they were still almost identical. Shiazar's tattoos, those of an anointed queen, were the more elaborate, covering her chin and cheeks; Ulaka's were plainer, adorning the chin alone. The rest would come during her crowning rites.

'It's good to see you again, Sister,' Ulaka cooed. 'But Kagemori and Kiiyan are waiting, and so is my lover. Take up your blade and do your duty.'

Her malicious glee killed the last vestiges of sisterhood in Shiazar's heart. *I can't let you lead my people into the furnace* – but tradition forbade anything but her own death and the gods were watching.

Do they see my sister here, gloating and blaspheming?

She closed her eyes, prayed for forgiveness, then opened them and stared at Ulaka as she once again aligned the bone-handled needle of steel. Her shaking hand made her prick her skin, and she glanced down to see a perfect drop of blood on her breast.

Time to end this . . .

Shiazar pressed the gems on the hilt–

A metal projectile exploded from the wrong end of the weapon, punched into Ulaka's ribs and pierced her heart. Her eyes flew wide, her smugness slipping into confusion, and she slumped sideways, lips moving as she tried to invoke sorcery to save herself.

Shiazar reversed the sacred dagger and flew at her, driving the main blade into Ulaka's right eye, transfixing the brain, and Ulaka's kneeling body crumpled.

Shiazar's mother's voice echoed in her brain. *The secret of Seppun-Saishu is that it has two blades, not just one. Death is never the only choice.*

For a moment she grieved for all she'd lost, including the sister she'd loved – but not for long. There was much that needed doing.

Shiazar stripped off her funeral shroud, removed the gold robes from her sister's corpse and pulled them on, then placed Ulaka's mask over her own face before arranging the corpse in the death-shroud and covering her sister's treacherous face with her own mask. She wiped Seppun-Saishu on the underside of the mat, but reluctantly left the secret dart inside the body. Cutting it out would take too long.

She took the royal sword – the ceremonial weapon was perfectly functional – and sliced off the musubi leash binding her sorcery, then belted on the weapon and went through the panel. In the concealed hollow in the wall she found steps descending into a candlelit tunnel.

A masked Yokei waited below: her Aunt Sinagato, who she'd thought she knew. *She must have revealed this passage to Ulaka – but why not me? I suppose she's spied on me herself.*

Her broken heart turned to stone.

'Is it done?' Sinagato wheezed, sounding indifferent to the death of someone she'd cosseted as a child.

'It is done, Auntie,' Shiazar said, mimicking Ulaka's malicious tones. 'Seeing her eyes empty was a pleasure beyond description.'

'Her death was *necessary*.' Sinagato rebuked her. 'Enjoying it is not.'

'All traitors must die. That's duty, Auntie, and I take pleasure in my duties.'

Sinagato *tsked*, but nonetheless, she bowed obsequiously and turned to lead the way.

Shiazar drove Seppun-Saiahu straight through her back until the point emerged through her left breast.

Sinagato fell silently to her knees, and then onto her face in the dirt.

'I am sorry,' Shiazar told the dying woman, 'but your death was *necessary*.'

The tunnel emerged in Sinagato's lodge, next door to her own. It was empty, while outside the royal lodge, thousands waited for someone to enter the queen's shrine and confirm that the royal death had occurred and the transition of power could be formalised.

For a moment, Shiazar considered denouncing Jinkatia and Ikendo and trying to reclaim the throne herself, but she swiftly discarded the idea. Jinkatia clearly controlled the Yokei – and she was supposed to be dead; any attempt to counterstrike would be stamped down.

Jinkatia's Yokei probably won't choose a queen at all. If they were in Jinkatia's thrall enough to back Ikendo over her, knowing what he was, then of course they'd break with the unwritten law and crown a king: *God-King Ikendo, first of a new Aldar dynasty.*

Sagging a little, she realised what she had to do.

Hands shaking, she kicked off her embroidered silk slippers and shed the golden robes, leaving them on the floor, then went to Sinagato's wooden chest and took out the old woman's flesh-mask – they all used them so they could at times pass among the Tangato without the whole village bowing and scraping. She untied her hair, stroked ash through it to age herself, then mussed the long, sleek tresses. She found the plain shift Sinagato had used when moving incognito, wrapped her sister's mask and placed it in a cloth bag she slung over a shoulder, then, donning the worn sandals and stooping, slipped silently out the back door.

A gong started ringing out, marking the death of the Queen, signifying that Ulaka's body had been found, but clearly not yet identified. Shiazar quickened her step, hurrying through the deserted homes, all the while expecting an outcry, but by the time the alarm finally went up, she was already at the edge of the village.

She hoisted up her skirts and ran.

Ikendo stared in disbelief and no little fear, superstitiously aware that he was standing before an image of Kiiyan, whose mercy, as everyone knew, did not extend to murderers, and Kagemori, who knew no mercy at all.

How?

The guards at the doors – all Manowai – swore that Shiazar had been brought in here, and the Yokei confirmed it. And no one had seen Ulaka enter at all – she'd been with her aunt, Sinagato, in a neighbouring lodge.

And yet somehow it was Ulaka behind Shiazar's mask, gazing skywards with one empty eye and one blinded one, a death wound. Her heart had been pierced as well. It *stank* of sorcery – and yet his magical senses told him it wasn't.

Shiazar has escaped and my status as consort to the new queen has been erased at a stroke. His blow against the pacifist feminine tyranny that had emasculated his people was hanging in the balance.

His mind raced as he gathered his courage.

After a minute or two, he went to the royal lodge and found Kotabashi, his second, who was guarding the door. 'Bring the Yokei in,' he muttered in his shoganai's ear.

The burly warrior threw him an uncertain look. 'You want *me* to summon *them?*'

'Tell them you speak in the name of the Queen-elect,' Ikendo told him, forgiving his nerves. Traditions built over centuries didn't collapse all at once. 'And then send for Onkado. I need him here too.'

His true nature was known to only a few, though the word was spreading. It was time for deeper secrets to be revealed.

Kotabashi hurried away and Ikendo returned to the shrine room, placed the queen's mask back over Ulaka's face and waited, musing on the cruelty of fate. *I will miss your beauty and your drive,* he thought. She'd adhered to him like a second skin, seeing in him the strength and courage to propel her to the throne she so craved. They'd shared burning ambition and, whenever chance allowed, a bed. She was Aldar, lovely beyond even the words of poets, but she'd also been passion itself: an angelic body he'd used like a demon.

And she'd been his path to power as consort to the elected queen.

That plan might be in ashes. His ambitions were not. *I must seize the moment, or perish.*

Then the Yokei filed in, twenty-three masked women in silk. A moment later, Onkado followed, his face solemn and uncertain. They all stopped when they saw the body on the ground, believing it to be Shiazar.

Ikendo gestured his son to stand beside him, then faced the Yokei. 'Behold, the dead,' he boomed.

'Why are we here?' one of the elder crones asked, in a scratchy voice. 'It is not customary for us to view the corpse of the old queen. Where is Ulaka, the Queen-elect?'

In answer, he bent and removed the mask from the body.

The sight of Ulaka, dead at their feet, caused an immediate fluttering of hands and a sucking-in of their breath.

'Where is Shiazar?' one squeaked.

'Gone.'

'*Gone?*' They clutched at their breasts. 'But she can't be . . .'

'Shiazar obviously doesn't believe in "can't",' he replied. 'She murdered her sister, instead of taking her own life as the sacred rites demand. She knows that you all conspired against her, and she has slain the only one of you young and strong enough to oppose her.'

Sekana, the next youngest after the two sisters, straightened. 'I am still fertile,' she said querulously. 'I must be anointed. It is my right.' A few murmured agreement, but he could hear fear at the knowledge that Shiazar was still at large.

'You?' Ikendo snorted. 'The Tangato need youth and vitality, not your dried-up chitsu.'

Sekana's eyes flashed. 'I *demand* the throne.'

In answer, he peeled off his flesh-mask and revealed his lustrous Aldar visage. Onkado blinked, then did the same. His true face was similar to the flesh-mask, but perfected.

Two Aldar males, in a world where there were supposedly none.

Jinkatia clasped her hands together in approval of her son's boldness, but the rest of the Yokei wavered. They'd been told of his true nature, but they'd not yet seen him – and a male Aldar, as everyone knew, was a harbinger of doom. His acceptance hung in the balance.

Then his mother Jinkatia stepped to his side and proudly said, 'This is my son. The line of Queens is failing and we face foreign invaders. We need a man to rule such an age.'

Her assertion was met with stunned silence.

The day is not yet won, Ikendo thought, schooling his face into stillness. These old crones, sorceresses by blood, had chosen *Ulaka* for the throne, thinking to limit his power to that of a consort, Aldar or not. Big, bold steps were contrary to their nature. *Will they oppose me? And can I survive if they do?*

Taking his courage in both hands, he set out to batter down their resistance. 'Look at you, Sisters,' he began, 'dying out by choice. Lost and frightened, clinging to tradition while the people entrusted to you fall into decline. *We are about to face a war* – not of our making, but that of the gaikiko devils who have found us. To preserve our existence, we must wipe them out utterly. Ulaka understood this!' He jabbed a finger at the corpse beneath the two statues. 'But she has been murdered, leaving you bereft and leaderless.'

'Not leaderless—' Sekana started, but Ikendo rolled over her.

'*Leaderless!*' he thundered, and she whimpered at his naked aggression. 'Weak and craven shadows of what you were – shuffling little handmaidens – *barren prunes!*'

He pulled out his curved sword, and beside him, Onkado drew his.

'Who among you even remembers how to fight – who of you has even held a blade?' Ikendo asked. 'Who here has used sorcery to kill? Do you even know how? Your rule has been upheld by tradition and nothing else. You are a coven of paper dragons!'

As one, they hung their heads, cringing, nodding, praying.

Look upon the mighty Yokei: the remnants of the proud Aldar – I could die of shame!

'But now, here I am,' he shouted, thumping his chest. 'Born of Jinkatia, who chose to bear a male, because she saw clearly what your traditions blinded you to: that *men* are needed here. I am fertile and fecund – Onkado is proof of that. He and I will breed a new generation.

I will be your *god-king* and you will show me the fealty and loyalty you failed to show Shiazar.' He touched the sword-tip to Sekana's neck. 'Give me an instant of doubt about your obedience and you will feel my wrath. Am I understood?'

They'd arrived at the proving ground, the moment when all would be decided. Jinkatia saw it and stepped to his side, glaring at the semi-circle of masked women, silently demanding obedience.

Sekana fell to her knees and kissed his feet.

Her decision made the choice for the rest. They capitulated as one, and with quivering voices, named him King.

Ikendo had to move quickly, but he needed to be careful too: this was the village of the Hiriwa tribe, and they had loved their Queen. So he reluctantly decided to forego the days of ritual that would normally precede his crowning.

Instead, he led the Yokei out into the large gathering space before the royal domicile and summoned the other tribal chieftains and their retinues, which naturally brought everyone in the village, all in ferment.

The moment of revelation, something he'd dreamed of for forty years, was almost anticlimactic: he stepped before the massed gathering and bared his head and face, letting them see for the first time in five hundred years, a male Aldar face.

There was shock, of course – but then awe and reverence, and for most of the men, exultation, seeing in him the harbinger of a new era in which their domestic mastery would be enhanced.

As it will be, he swore to himself. *Let it be as it once was, when women served us.*

It was somewhat ironic to be crowned by a female: his mother Jinkatia placed the crown on his head, then he crowned Onkado as his heir. No one dared protest, not when legends were coming to life. He took the pledges of the tribal leaders, the humans visibly in awe of their newly revealed Aldar lord, each trying to outdo each other in their promises of service.

Every fresh moment still brought a challenge, though, whether it was convincing his loyal Manowai warriors that he was still the man they had followed, to facing down the blank faces of the Hiriwa, still loyal to Shiazar; although revealing the murder of Ulaka, and Shiazar's shameful flight, appeared to bring them round.

By midnight, the throne felt solid beneath him, but Shiazar was still nowhere to be found, and nor was Rima, alarmingly. Tatsu and Kyu, shamefaced, had shuffled in to report that their prisoner had escaped.

'The wounds on the dead indicate that she was rescued by the foreign devils,' Tatsu rasped. 'She has likely taken refuge with them in Rath Argentium.'

It was disturbing, but he wasn't daunted. Tomorrow, he would send for the remainder of the Manowai warriors to strengthen his support among these uppity, hidebound Hiriwa. Once they'd arrived, in a day or two, he'd launch his attack on the city. If Rima was there, she would be taken or killed with the foreigners.

And then there's the white girl, he mused. *Zarelda, the Snowbird.*

At the banquet, he'd admired her bearing and purposed to take her as a plaything, to see what mysteries a foreign chitsu might hold. But his son had demanded her – he still wasn't entirely sure how he felt about that.

Onkado had claimed her publicly, giving him no leeway to disagree without it looking like a rift between father and son – and while raping female prisoners was a fine way to establish dominance over a defeated foe, he'd pledged to wipe these gaikiko out, to the last man, woman and child. *And I shall.*

That decided him. *I'll give Onkado a night with her, to show our mastery. Then he will kill her.*

8

All Choices Are Evil

Zarelda heard the shuffle of feet on the floor of the lodge Onkado had been given following the shocking ascension of his father to the throne. Last night, the priestess Kuia had overseen her being washed at a bath-house, protecting her from the fierce Manowai warriors, then returned her to Onkado's lodge, but the new prince hadn't turned up and Kuia had been called away. Now every footfall presaged some new terror.

She hadn't slept much – that had been impossible with her arms bound to a pillar behind her, forcing her to sit up. Adefar was bound by an ensorcelled musubi leash round her throat, leaving her helpless and scared.

But this time the footsteps belonged to a young woman she vaguely knew.

'Ro?' she croaked.

The girl squatted beside her and spoke in breathless Tangato, but Adefar was locked away, so Zar had no translator. But she'd recognised kai – food. When she nodded, the girl thrust a wooden bowl under her chin and produced a wooden spoon.

Zar was ravenous, gulping the root mash down as fast as Ro could spoon it into her mouth. When the bowl was empty, she begged, 'Wai, tena?' – Water, please? – and Ro placed a small cup to Zar's lips. Then she grabbed the bowl and cup and fled.

Fully awake now, Zar looked around. The room was dark and the fire had burned out, but light through the gaps where the door-leather hung suggested it was dawn outside. She could hear angry murmurs, masculine and many-throated.

There's a crowd outside, she realised. *A very hostile crowd.*

Then Onkado entered – he must've found somewhere else to stay, she realised. He squatted down beside her and examined the leash which confined Adefar, then said, 'I'm sorry, I was kept away all night, but Kuia kept watch.'

Zar glared at him. 'Your people came here to bring down the Queen – when you spoke with me at the old palace, you already knew you were going to move against her.'

He dropped his gaze. 'Ae, I did.'

'Did you murder Rima so that I would have to fight?'

'No, that was Tatsu and Kyu. I was told after the event.'

'She was my friend.' Tears stung her eyes. 'Get out – I don't want your protection. I'd rather die.'

He laid a hand on her shoulder. 'Zarelda, you must be brave. Rima has escaped, and so has Shiazar. Ulaka is dead.' His voice was hollow, almost disbelieving. 'Shiazar killed her sister, then fled, instead of committing ritual suicide. We don't know where she is.'

Zar, stunned, spent a minute thanking Deo and Gerda, then, knowing she was a dead woman in any case, she said gleefully, 'That must have *really* pissed you off.'

'Ulaka was my mother,' he said in a hollow voice. 'Ae, I mourn, of course.'

'I hope the next queen decides you and your father are too dangerous to let live.'

Onkado grimaced and said, 'There is no queen any more. The Tangato now have a king.'

She stared. 'I thought the Tangato only had Yokei queens?'

He met her defiant gaze as he slowly peeled his own face off.

Her mouth went dry. Beneath the fleshy mask – *how did I not see it?* – his true face was much like the visage she knew, but the planes were subtly different: flatter, with higher, more angular cheekbones, the nose a little smaller and the mouth more prominent, and all lined with thin black tattoos. When he bared his teeth momentarily, the incisors were an inch long. His skin had a lustre of copper and gold, and his eyes – *Dear Gerda* – his eyes were yellowish and slitted; there must have been some kind of film in the eye sockets of his mask.

'You . . . you're a Yokei? A *male* Yokei?'

'Ae, but rather say, "Aldar". "Yokei" was a word adopted after the Fall, from folklore. And in truth, there is no *half*-Aldar. One is fully Aldar, or not at all.'

'But there are no male Aldar . . . Rima said –'

He silenced her with an impatient gesture. 'Forty years ago, Jinkatia, then a young, aspiring archivist of the Yokei, decided to break the strictures on breeding a male. She knew the reigning queen would forbid this, so, using the pretence of research, she went to live with the Manowai. There, she seduced a man and bore him a child: Ikendo. They kept his heritage secret using flesh-masks, and she ensured he became rangatira. She introduced her own protégé, Ulaka, to him and I was the result, born in secret nineteen years ago. My father Ikendo is the new King of the Tangato. I am his acknowledged heir.'

Zar listened in stunned silence while her eyes soaked up the sight of an Aldar, a *real live Aldar*, right there in front of her. Only his voice was familiar, the voice of someone she'd thought of as a potential friend.

I have left reality, she thought numbly. *I am still asleep and dreaming this.*

'The tribes have given my father homage,' he went on. 'The Yokei have relinquished control to him. They will no longer breed only daughters. Our tribes will reunite, ten thousand strong, and we will once more take our rightful place. Father says that the time has come for we Aldar to renew our rule of the world.'

She noticed his phrasing: 'Father says' – that gave her a little hope that he *wasn't* just like his father, and maybe not fully party to Ikendo and Jinkatia's power-plays. If he really was his own man, he might yet protect her. But if she wanted that protection, then she would have to destroy his little fantasy.

'Time for you to *rule* again? You think ten thousand warriors is a lot? I told you when we first met: there are *millions* of people in Magnia, with guns and bombards and steel, and there are *thousands* of sorcerers. They'll *annihilate* you.'

He flinched and admitted, 'Ae, I heard you. But Grandmother Jinkatia says that we will be welcomed by the elites of the world, that our superior intellect and sorcery will make us dominant again.'

'The Bolgravian Emperor bows to *no one*,' she told him. 'He cuts down rivals like a scythe at harvest.'

'This is why I need you, for your knowledge of the world.' He dropped his voice, as if he feared being overheard, and whispered, 'Zarelda, my father expects me to rape you, then hand you over to Tatsu and Kyu for execution. I don't want that.'

When she met his eyes, she read empathy, sympathy, and the courage to stand up for her. Her heart thudded painfully at the intensity of that communion: a chest-bursting, throat-clogging feeling that was physical, emotional and spiritual all at once. The only thing she could compare it to was falling in love with Banno.

Banno would stand up for me too, she reminded herself guiltily. *But he's not here.*

'Is there anything you can do?' she whispered hoarsely.

He looked down. 'I could leave you opportunity to escape; or give you a weapon to take your own life,' he said mournfully.

She seized on the word *escape*. 'Is escape even possible?'

His alien face creased in thought, then he shook his head. 'No. Tatsu and Kyu are waiting outside, and this pavilion is surrounded. I have an hour to "enjoy" you – that is all.'

Holy Gerda . . .

She shrank from him, but he hadn't finished. 'Only one other option occurs to me and that is to claim you as a bride – but you are married, and Father will invoke that if I try.'

'*A bride?*'

'Ae. If you were my wife, he could not claim you himself, or kill you.'

Her skin quivered at the thought, but her heart constricted inside her breast, because it was set on Banno, as it had been from the moment they met back in Teshveld, at the start of their epic journey. The taste of their first kiss, her very first, still lingered in her mouth.

But Onkado was here right now, shielding her from death. *Once Ikendo launches his assault, Banno will die*, the rational part of her brain argued. *Father too, and Vara and Kemara and all the others . . . If I die too, my family is gone.*

'I'm not really married,' she confessed.

He blinked, momentarily shocked. 'Truly?'

'Truly. I only pretended that to protect Banno. Rima found out, but she said nothing either. Though I think Kuia guessed,' she added.

'Can you prove it?' he asked, a trifle uncertainly. 'I mean, physically.'

She ducked her head. 'I'm still a virgin – therefore under our laws, even if I were married, it wouldn't be legally enforceable. Only consummated marriages are legal in Magnia.'

I can't believe I'm saying this . . . but I don't want to die . . . 'I'll do whatever you want,' she stammered.

Onkado gripped her hand and squeezed. 'I'm sorry,' he murmured, 'but it's the most I can do, and even then, Father may try to invalidate it. He'll be furious.'

'What do we do?' she asked. She felt very odd, suspended in a state of disbelief.

'Come with me.' He untied her and drew her upright, then kept hold of her hand shyly, in a way that reminded her that for all he was an Aldar – *an Aldar, by Deo!* – he was also a nineteen-year-old boy, only a few years her senior. It was both reassuring and endearing.

Am I really going to do this?

He led her deeper into the lodge, to a shrine room, where wooden carvings of the Aldar gods were arrayed in a circle around a circular fire-pit.

'Do you know our gods?' Onkado asked her.

'A little. Rima showed me the temple. They are not my gods.'

'Of course.' He walked round the circle, naming them: Ankazo, the Jade Emperor who ruled them; Kiiyan, Goddess of Mercy, Kagemori, the

Death God, Shinija-Kyu, the Dragon and the others. Some looked serene and kindly, others fierce and cruel. He stopped in front of the last, a blindfolded woman with eyes instead of nipples tipping her bared breasts. She bore a dagger in one hand, a flower in the other.

She joined him in kneeling, asking, 'Who is this one?'

He lifted his face to the disturbing half-naked statue. 'This is Aikoi-Joo, the Goddess of Love. She is blind because love doesn't follow logic or reason.'

That's certainly true, Zar thought, shivering at the goddess' weird gaze.

Onkado turned to her. 'When first I saw you, Aikoi-Joo spoke inside me. My people value serene, stately beauty, but I admire girls with a zest for living. An "otenbasan", we say, a woman with a man's spirit. I see this in you, and I am drawn to it.'

Zar wasn't sure she saw herself in that way – what was a 'man's spirit' anyway? But perhaps his culture didn't have other words for independent women? She knew one thing, though: she was drawn to him too.

But oh, Banno!

'Ours is an old culture and we are about to face a new world we don't understand,' Onkado went on. 'We must adapt, and I have come to believe that both my father Ikendo and Queen Shiazar are wrong. Shiazar wanted to wish you away; Father wants to eradicate you – but neither are possible. Another way must be found, and I believe that together, you and I might be able to find that path.'

She appreciated that he was offering her survival, but she couldn't see how that was going to help her father and his people. 'Will marrying me stop this war?' she asked.

He winced, but said, 'Let us deal with one problem at a time. If my father punishes you, all negotiation is gone. While you live, some chance of a new way remains.'

She bowed her head, closing her eyes, and tried to think. *I love Banno . . . I don't want to be another man's wife . . . But I want to live, and very soon, everyone I know and love will likely be dead, including Banno.*

Is that a world I want to live in? Perhaps it's better just to die?

In tales, lovers killed themselves out of grief at losing each other. To do otherwise was to betray true love.

You are your father's only child, a new voice said inside her head and the image of a fox-headed man appeared behind her eyes. Adefar was at his most alarming: naked, his vulpine head feral and dangerous. *Choose life*, he said. *Live, for me, for you, for your father's blood in you. Live.*

Adefar's uncompromising words made up her mind, giving her the strength and clarity she needed. She opened her eyes, took Onkado's hand and whispered, 'I'll do it.'

He sagged in relief – he was clearly afraid she'd choose death – then called softly, 'Kuia?'

The white-haired kannushi pushed aside the door-flap and slipped inside. When she saw Onkado and Zar kneeling together in front of the Goddess of Love, her face went through a rapid series of twitches, from anxiety to surprise to solemnity – and perhaps, at the last, approval. 'She has agreed?'

'Ae,' Onkado said, looking at Zar directly and squeezing her hand.

'And Rima was right – she is a virgin and not married?'

'Ae.'

'Then we must be swift,' the priestess said. She produced a scarlet silk ribbon and wrapped it around their wrists, all the while invoking the blessing of her gods. She spoke quickly, but her voice was purposeful.

Then she turned to Zar. 'Zarelda Vyre, are you here of your own will?'

Zar's voice was hoarse, but she managed a weak, 'Yes . . .'

'And will you take Onkado, son of Ikendo, as your husband and lord? Do you pledge him your heart, your body and your loyalty as his wife?'

A vivid image flashed into her mind, of Banno's face crumbling in pain, but she managed to whisper, 'I do.'

She barely heard Onkado's vow, just stared numbly as Kuia knotted the red ribbon. 'Then I declare you are man and wife, before the gods. It is so—'

Her voice faltered at a racket outside, then Ikendo burst in, roaring,

'What have you done?' He saw the knotted hands and screamed, '*What have you done?*'

Onkado stood, pulling Zar to her feet alongside him. 'You gave Zarelda to me, but I will not ravish an unwilling woman. Aldar honour forbids it. So I have married her, to make it right with the gods.'

'*You—!*' Ikendo clenched his fist, stepped forward and raised it—

—and Kuia stepped before him. 'This is a holy temple. Do not taint it with violence.'

For a moment, Zar was sure he'd punch the old woman instead – he was certainly contemplating it, glaring at her while his whole body shook with pent-up rage. Then he shouted, 'She's married already – Tatsu told me so.'

Somehow Zar found the courage to say, 'I was never married.'

The new King of the Tangato turned his fury on her. 'Do not speak!' he shouted, as the curtain stirred behind him and a masked Yokei appeared.

'What is happening?' Jinkatia asked, her musical voice sounding curious but unconcerned.

'I have married Zarelda,' Onkado said, 'as is my right.' He deftly unwound the ribbon binding their wrists and laid a hand on the hilt of his sword. 'I will defend my wife with my life.'

No one else spoke or moved, but Zar could feel the unspoken communication among the three Aldar like the heat of the sun: a whole silent war that she was relieved not to be privy to, until Jinkatia gave a dry, somewhat amused cough.

'Let it be,' she told Ikendo. 'We raised him to be honourable, and the girl is a mahotsu-kai, a worthy bride. If she is truly a virgin and unmarried, he is within his rights.'

Zar coloured. 'I'm not lying.'

'Examine her,' Ikendo snapped at Jinkatia. 'If it's true, I'll consider it.'

'No!' Onkado protested. 'You will not dishonour her—'

But Jinkatia ignored him, stepping past him and grasping Zar's hands. 'Sit, girl.' She indicated a stool.

Zar's skirts were hoisted and her legs parted, baring her genitals. Suddenly wondering if all the riding might have torn her, as she'd heard could happen, she begged silently, *Please, Gerda* – and tried not to flinch as Jinkatia's cold fingers probed at her nethers roughly. The examination was humiliating but brief, and it didn't kill her.

Onkado waited with angry patience. When Jinkatia straightened, he demanded, 'Well?'

'She is intact,' Jinkatia admitted.

'You'll regret this, boy,' the King snarled at Onkado, before storming out.

Jinkatia remained while Zar straightened her clothes, gathered her dignity and stood. 'Well played, Snowbird,' the Yokei said coldly, 'but being the last of your kind will bring you nothing but sorrow.'

With that, she too was gone.

Zar's legs almost gave way, but Kuia stepped in and caught her. She clung to the old woman gratefully, realising numbly that she was now married. It was such a step into the unknown, she could barely believe it was real.

'What now?' she asked in trepidation. She felt overwhelmed, wanting desperately to be alone, to pull herself together.

Miraculously, Onkado appeared to understand. 'Nothing more,' he said solemnly. 'There is no requirement that our union be consummated immediately. There is only one more thing for now: we must reveal our vows to the tribe, so all understand we are bound in marriage.'

Kuia steadied Zar before letting Onkado take her arm.

'I'm sorry it had to be this way,' he said quietly, leading her back into the main lodge, where he wrapped himself in a silk tunic, while Kuia dressed Zar in a robe of the same material before fitting a pair of embroidered slippers on Zar's feet.

Then Onkado gestured at the main doors. They could hear the crowd outside, buzzing and humming with muffled anger. 'Now, we make this known.'

She refused to cling to him, instead carrying herself as a

noblewoman would, straight-backed and proud, as they walked through the doorway and emerged, blinking, into the morning light.

Zar almost turned and fled back to safety. They were surrounded by hundreds of warriors of many tribes – but those closest were Manowai, and the moment they saw her, they started howling for blood. She felt like a sacrificial offering to their bloodlust.

But when Onkado raised his hand, they fell silent instantly.

He spoke first in Reo, and then Gengo: 'Warriors of the Tangato, know this. I, Prince Onkado, have taken this woman to wife. She is now mine, and any harm to her is an assault upon my sacred person. So I attest, before the Twelve Gods of Heaven.'

His words, and the bold, inflexible way he delivered them, silenced the crowd, who started looking at each other uncertainly. After several moments, they made what Zar assumed must be a gesture of homage, bowing over their clasped hands. She could see different attitudes to her: the Hiriwa faces held sympathy, but the other tribes were looking on her as an enemy, although their reverence for the Aldar appeared to be overriding their urge to object.

Then one of the Manowai fighting men stepped forward, beating his chest and ululating wildly, as if celebrating her subjugation.

Onkado's mouth twisted. Kindling flame in his hand, he shouted, '*Enough!*'

That small display of power silenced even the most bellicose.

'Zarelda is now wholly Tangato,' Onkado declared. 'She is a sacred mahotsu-kai, and a royal bride – *not* a concubine. Disrespect towards Zarelda is disrespect to me.'

Zar realised the tribesmen were taken aback: this was no humiliating forced marriage, a ploy to ensure Onkado possessed Zar for himself alone, but something *real*.

A path suddenly appeared between the disgruntled warriors as Tatsu and Kyu shuffled through the ranks. Their blind and mutilated face were twisted with anger, but the hideous old man said only, 'Congratulations on your nuptials, Prince. An act of nobility.'

Kyu glared silently at Zar with poison on her face, cheated and full of malice.

But with that, the pair stalked away, and Zar noticed even the most fearsome of the warriors were looking visibly relieved by that.

She remembered to breathe as Onkado led her back inside.

Only once they were alone did he take her hands. 'Are you all right?' he asked.

That he was concerned enough to ask heartened her. 'Just about,' she managed, trying hard to control her shaking.

'Then I will leave you in Kuia's care. I must attend upon my father in council and fulfil whatever tasks I am given. Wish me well.'

With that, he bent his head, kissed her hand – and left her alone.

Zar dropped to her knees, thought of Banno and burst into tears.

Varahana brought Raythe some welcome news that morning: Banno Rhamp was being discharged from the infirmary.

Raythe joined the old knight in welcoming his son home and getting him settled into the mercenaries' barracks behind the gatehouse before bringing him up to date.

When Banno learned that Zar was still a prisoner, he was distraught. 'You *have* to get her back,' he told Raythe. 'You *must*.'

'We will,' Raythe answered, though he still couldn't see how just yet. 'Elgus, I'll leave you to your son.' He patted the pair on the shoulder, then left them, returning to his lodging. He found Rima in his dining room, puzzling over a bowl of porridge.

'How do you eat this stodgy excrement?' she asked, prodding dubiously at the glutinous mess.

'You're not the first to ask,' he chuckled. 'I'm on my way to the gatehouse – they've got some wild fruits there, and Mistress Borger bakes hotcakes each morning.'

He did have an ulterior motive: he'd resolved to keep Rima in sight as much as he could, for he still wasn't sure she would be safe on her own among his people – nor that they were safe from her, although he *mostly* trusted her . . .

They walked the short distance to the gatehouse, where the morning watch was arrayed facing the bridge, under Cal Foaley's eye.

'What's happening, Cal?' he asked.

'They're massing on the far side,' the hunter reported grimly, his wary eyes on Rima.

He wasn't alone: all the men were staring – beautiful, exotic young women in outfits showing a lot of thigh and midriff weren't a common sight anywhere in Magnia. 'If they're all like that, I'm goin' native,' Miki Brond was muttering.

Raythe gave Miki a warning look. 'Mistress Rima, will you join me in the tower?'

They climbed to the top, where Vidar was using Raythe's spyglass to monitor the Tangato warriors. 'There's a bunch of them approaching the bridge,' he shouted down. 'Stand by!'

Raythe threw Rima a worried look. 'I guess that truce is already out the window.'

There were just forty men below, but they were already bent over their flintlocks. 'They're coming!' Foaley shouted, followed by the familiar sounds of men praying or shouting insults to comrades, each preparing for the fight in their own ways.

The leather-clad Tangato had strangely shaved scalps with just a narrow mane down the middle. 'Manowai warriors,' Rima muttered. 'Ikendo's own tribe.'

Foaley let them get to within forty yards, close enough that no one would miss, and then, just as the war cries reached a crescendo and they began to surge, he roared, *'Fire!'*

The next minute was murderous: the guns belched their fury and the singing lead balls cut down the leading tribesmen; those behind suddenly found themselves staggering over dead and dying bodies, the wind completely knocked from their charge. The second volley, delivered four seconds later, smashed those men over backwards. With their captains dead and all order gone, the third volley saw them wavering, and the fourth punched into the backs of the laggards as they fled. The reports echoed about the cliffs, black smoke billowed up, and the Magnians cheered hoarsely, until Foaley told them to shut their traps and reload.

Rima stared with bulging eyes while Raythe estimated the carnage: sixty, seventy dead? With as many more wounded trying to crawl away? He shifted his gaze to the far side of the ravine, where the songs and drums had fallen silent.

'How . . . ?' Rima finally managed to whisper.

Of course, she hasn't ever seen such a thing before . . .

'That wasn't me, and it wasn't sorcery,' he told her. 'Warfare has changed. Zar must have told you this: a flintlock can kill a man at more than one hundred yards. Battle isn't a duel any more. It's mass-produced death.'

He wasn't sure the Gengo language had the vocabulary for all he'd said, but she must have understood enough, for she went very quiet.

'Queen Shiazar was right,' she said eventually. 'War is too great a horror. We should not court it.'

'Let's hope your new queen is persuaded so, too.'

For a minute, all that could be heard were the shrieks and groans of the wounded and dying men on the bridge.

Then young Ando Borger pounded up the stairs and approached. 'Lord Vyre, I've just come from the fishing hole by the confluence. You've got to come.'

'What is it?'

'I don't know, but you've *got* to come. It told me to fetch you.'

Raythe gave Vidar a puzzled look, then leaned over the parapet and called, 'Cal, stay vigilant, but allow them to collect their dead and wounded.' Then he turned and said, 'Vidar, Rima, with me.'

They followed Ando east along the parapet overlooking the river. A few hundred yards on was one of the steps leading to the river below. Ando led them down to a small stone platform, where some rotting beams were all that remained of an old dock. They were almost opposite the confluence here, and the sound of the churning waters nearly drowned their voices. On the other side was the hill-fort where they'd rescued Rima.

'Well?' Raythe asked Ando, who was watching Rima with mistrust in his eyes.

In reply, Ando pointed across the river at a semi-submerged cavern. 'Look – there!'

A Tangato canoe, a narrow wooden craft with ochre-coloured timbers and a high carved prow, floated out of the cavern. No one was rowing, but somehow it carved its stately way unerringly across the swirling current. Behind the prow stood a masked figure in a dun cloak and robes, staring back at him.

Rima clutched his shoulder. 'That's Ulaka's mask,' she hissed.

Then the figure called out, 'Rima!' and she went rigid – then her face lit up.

'Watashi no Joo! Anatana no?' Rima sounded as if she was torn between disbelief and hope. *My Queen, is that you?* Cognatus translated drily.

Raythe gaped. Wasn't Shiazar supposed to be dead?

The canoe propelled itself closer and the masked figure switched to Gengo-Magnian. 'Rima, you are here? Praise the Gods!'

Looking like she would explode from sheer astonished joy, shaking with emotion, Rima dropped to one knee and bowed her head. 'It's my Queen – it's Shiazar . . .'

The masked woman turned her blank gaze towards Raythe, and called, 'Lord Vyre, to my sorrow, I find myself in need of sanctuary. Will you take me in?'

He too was stunned to reply. *The Tangato Queen . . . here . . . ?*

Her canoe scraped against the dock and Ando, seizing the prow, prompted, 'Lord Vyre?'

Raythe couldn't quite believe this was real, but he pulled himself together, stepped forward and offered his hand. 'Of course, Great Lady. Please, allow me.'

She stared at his hand and he realised that quite possibly she had never touched another human being, or at least not a human male – but then she held out a small bronze-gold hand that was smooth as a child's and placed it in his. He hadn't before noticed that she was a head shorter than him, or that her hair was streaked with grey – *Ah, no, she's run ash through it.* He helped her step from the canoe to the dock, released her and told Ando unnecessarily, 'Secure the canoe.' Then he bowed. 'Your Majesty, welcome.'

'I am a queen, but I no longer rule. I am just a beggar at your doorstep.'

He and Rima both went to protest, but she silenced them – *by removing her mask.*

Rima spluttered a protest, her face betraying her shock at what was surely a massive breach of Tangato custom and etiquette. Ando choked and went rigid; Vidar let out his breath and forgot to take another – and Raythe just stared, trying to fix this moment in his head for ever. He was looking on a living part-Aldar five hundred years after they died out.

Her skin was burnished bronze, her face a symphony, with a full-lipped mouth hinting at prominent front teeth below a small, childlike nose, and cheekbones that could cut paper. Intricate tattoos like black lace decorated her cheeks and chin. Long, narrow eyes with tawny orbs and slitted pupils pierced him through. If this was part-Aldar, he couldn't imagine that a full Aldar could be any more alien – or beautiful.

'You may call me Shiazar,' she said, in her fluting, musical voice. 'I am your servant.'

INTERLUDE (2)

Sommaport

A southwest wind had been plaguing the west coast of Magnia for the past month, making Toran Zorne's sea voyage down the coastline a trial of patience. A last gasp of autumnal winds resisted the onset of winter, blasting warmer winds full in their faces as they crawled south-southeast from Verdessa to the Pelarian coast. Some days they couldn't even raise a sail; they tried rowing, but were still all but becalmed. Even now, a gale-force headwind was whipping at Zorne's unruly hair and beard as he watched the land slither by.

I hate this coast. I hate this ship, I hate the crude, uneducated scum who sail it, and I hate Raythe Vyre for dragging me off the edge of the world.

What should have been a journey of a week had taken a month and Zorne had spent every moment fretting over what might have befallen Vyre's refugees and criminals since he'd been forced to leave them behind. *If Deo is just, they've been massacred by those primitives I saw.* But if this pursuit had taught him anything, it was not to bet against Raythe Vyre.

But that afternoon they rounded a small headland and there – *finally!* – was his destination: Sommaport. The harbour was quiet, only a couple of merchantmen and a dozen fishing vessels moored there, and few stirred on the dock as his ship sailed in. It had been four months since he'd left here to hunt down Vyre; but it had been more than two years since he'd been brought before the High-Komizar for the Western Empire and assigned the task of tracking down Colfar's only surviving general.

Now here I am, and still empty-handed. Failure was a bitter pill.

He watched stoically, ignoring the resentful looks from the human waste that passed for sailors as they brought the ship in – he'd have expected some gratitude; after all, he'd given them four months' respite from the squalling demands of their trollops and brats. Ignoring the captain, who was attempting to formally farewell him, he strode down the gangplank and pushed through the desultory flock of dockers and whores gathered to earn what pathetic coin they could.

What was the local governor's name? he asked himself. He snapped his fingers. *Yes! Veterkoi.*

When he reached the imperial blockhouse three blocks away, the dockyard stench of dead fish and sewage had faded just enough to be bearable. Zorne was aware that he looked like a scarecrow, so he wasn't surprised when the two guards crossed pikes in front of him.

Pikes are stupid weapons, except in mass combat, he thought as he broke one man's nose and felled him, then caught the other guard's pike-haft and held it across his throat until he blacked out. Then he loomed over the first man and hauled him up by his hair until he was staring into his bloodied face and said, 'Toran Zorne, Under-Komizar of the Ramki-seri, seeking admission on imperial business.'

All this was quite unnecessary, of course, but it had been too long since he'd had someone on whom he could take out his *screaming* frustration. The guard's face went ashen at his name.

When Zorne released him, he crawled to the doors as quickly as he could manage to open them.

'You didn't check my identity,' Zorne noted as he strode past. *Now, which way was it?*

He burst into Veterkoi's office to find the florid governor dandling a dishevelled dockside floozy on his knee. They were both guzzling wine and giggling as the governor fondled the woman's teats until Zorne kicked the doors open, when she squealed and fell to the floor, while the governor started bellowing in frightened rage.

'How dare you, you . . . *You—*?'

'Governor Veterkoi. I'm glad you remember me,' Zorne replied. He flicked a finger at the woman on the floor. 'You, out. And close the doors.'

She fled without even taking the time to adjust her clothes, but Zorne didn't take his eyes off Veterkoi. 'If you're at your desk, you are on duty, Governor. And you are married.'

'But Komizar—'

'*Under*-Komizar.'

'But you *deserve* to be a full komizar,' Veterkoi whined, frantically doing up his trousers. 'It is a relief to see you, sir. Was the mission to Verdessa a success? Did you find Vyre? Are my two ships—?'

'The frigate sank off Mount Lucallus,' Zorne interrupted. 'The troopship is in port, unloading. Your men are dead, as is half the garrison of Rodonoi, including their commander. Vyre is free and has been revealed as the most dangerous man alive. Only *I* can stop him.'

That last was a vanity, but Zorn was increasingly coming to see this as truth.

Veterkoi went pale. The frigate was a considerable part of the assets of his office and the lost men would mean large payments to bereaved families – not to mention the need to recruit and train replacements. His tenure here had just become a financial disaster.

As that sank in, his expression went from shock to anger and resentment.

Their eyes met and Zorne let his familiar's presence inside him fuel just the *subtlest* glimmer of praxis-light in his eyes, to remind this petty bureaucrat who was the real power here.

Try to blame me and I'll disembowel you, he didn't need to say.

Veterkoi's nerve broke, as Zorne had known it would.

'Oh Deo . . . What can I do, Komiz— *Under*-Komizar . . . ?'

'Have your best carriage and horses prepared,' Zorne ordered. 'Bring paper, ink and quills, prepare a hot bath and shaving gear, a barber, fine clothing in my size, and a chest for luggage. Oh, and your best sword and a pair of pistols, with powder and shot. And your bed – and no disturbances.'

He paused as Kemara Solus rose in his mind's eye. Perhaps there was a redheaded prostitute out here who might allow him to enact some of the fantasies he now harboured. Although it had been Moss Trimble, the persona he'd assumed during his secret life with Vyre's people, who had been obsessed with redheads, that obsession had gradually become his own . . . together with the belief that she, even more than Vyre, had to die.

I stabbed her through the heart and she rose again . . . She is an abomination.

But he'd always had something of a horror of other people's bodies. People were dirty by nature, and any whore out here would be pox-raddled and uncouth.

I don't need such creatures. I will wait for the real Kemara.

So he concluded with, 'And your best whisky. Now.'

The next morning, Zorne rose, eager to press on. The previous evening had been restorative: his hair had been clipped to the close-cropped basin-cut he preferred and his beard and moustaches were gone, although the pale skin beneath contrasted oddly with the weathered skin on his forehead and cheeks. He felt wondrously, mercifully clean, and some of the aches of the journey had been soothed away by hot water and a soft mattress.

Most importantly, he felt like he was himself again. *Out there, I became someone else . . . I turned feral, like Vyre's scum.*

Now I'm back.

He strode through the house, paused before Veterkoi's curtseying wife and simpering sons and told the gaping woman, 'Governor Veterkoi uses prostitutes. See a healer, lest he infect you with the pox.'

Then he strode past the two guards he'd beaten up the previous day, silently daring them to seek retribution, but they just looked into the far distance, refusing to catch his eye. A footman held the carriage door for him and he was pleased to see it was a fine, well-sprung piece of machinery, worthy of a governor – and *almost* worthy of him.

Veterkoi hurried after him. 'Erm, Under-Komizar . . . where is your destination?'

'That, Governor, is Ramkiseri business.' He looked up at the smartly uniformed driver. 'Take the road east – and don't spare the horses.' He slammed the door in Veterkoi's face and the carriage lurched into motion.

Falcombe, he thought, *then Rannock and southern Pelaria, and on to Otravia, and the High Governor of the Western Empire. We must claim Rath Argentium, so I need to go all the way to the top . . .*

PART 3
Shiro Kamigami

1

New Steps

Feeling a sense of the unreal, Raythe Vyre opened the door and ushered in the two women. Even though he'd warned Elgus Rhamp, Mater Varahana and Vidar Vidarsson so they would be prepared, they were still bursting with awe and curiosity.

Rima wore her usual bodice and beaded flax skirt, but he'd given her a leather cloak of his own against the cold. Her usual strut had returned; he was pleased to see her confidence restored by the arrival of Queen Shiazar.

Rima had braided and coiled the Aldar's long fine hair and Varahana had gladly parted with some robes. She still wore the red-and-white-lacquered mask – her dead sister's, she had explained – and she looked mysterious and regal: a legend come to miraculous life.

The three of them rose to their feet, their eyes widening.

'Holy Gerda,' Elgus blurted.

Varahana was more composed. 'Welcome, Majesty,' she said smoothly, drinking in the sight of a part-Aldar stepped from history. 'It is an honour.'

Vidar just stared at the vision in front of him, the vein in his temple pulsing.

Raythe had revealed Shiazar's presence in the dining hall last night, and he'd told everyone what was going on in the Tangato camp, but he'd not asked her to make an appearance then, lest that prove too unsettling. *Her presence here offers both opportunity and grave risk,* he'd told them. *I'll tell you more when I can.*

Between the shock of the Queen's arrival and worry for Jesco and

Kemara, he'd barely slept, but he felt vividly alive as he ushered her to one end of the table. 'Queen Shiazar, we don't have a throne, but may I offer you this seat?'

Shiazar coolly took in the room, then offered Rima a hand and allowed herself to be led to the proffered seat. Rima flapped Raythe away, helped the Queen to sit, then turned and frowned at the Magnians. 'Only the Queen may sit,' she announced.

'The Queen does not mind,' Shiazar said quickly. 'We are guests here, and grateful.' She indicated that Rima should take the neighbouring chair.

After a moment, the young sorceress obeyed, but she looked scandalised.

Raythe sighed in relief: he certainly wasn't going to ask anyone to sit on the floor to salve the Queen's ego, or to satisfy the demands of Tangato royal protocol.

He made the introductions then took his position at the other end of the table. 'I have asked Queen Shiazar to join us so that she might tell us what's going on among her people.'

'It is not fitting that the Queen tells such a tale,' Rima put in. 'I shall speak.' She described the arrival of the tribes, Ikendo's challenge, her own abduction and the treachery of the Queen's sister. 'But the Gods are just: Ulaka has paid for her crime. However, we are puzzled, for the banners across the ravine are a mix of Aldar and Manowai – and it was revealed to my Queen that Ikendo is a male Aldar – the first to draw breath in five centuries. We surmise that the Yokei have broken with tradition entirely and made Ikendo King.'

Raythe glanced around the table. None of his comrades looked like they understood the full significance of the regime change, and he wasn't sure he did either.

But right now, it surely means a conflict we can't win.

'Our truce has already been broken,' he told Shiazar, although she undoubtedly already knew that. 'The new ruler attacked yesterday – and we bloodied their nose, badly.'

'But now we're trapped,' Elgus growled. 'So how do we get out and get the istariol home?'

'The istariol is already "home",' Rima told him. 'It belongs here.'

The Pelarian knight grunted. 'That's one opinion, but it ain't ours.'

Raythe raised a hand to forestall an argument. 'Leaving is no longer an option, until the usurper Ikendo is deposed and Queen Shiazar restored to her rightful throne. In this, our interests are aligned.' He turned to the Queen. 'Majesty, how are your people likely to be taking all this?'

They waited while Shiazar and Rima consulted in Reo – he didn't do them the discourtesy of engaging Cognatus to eavesdrop – then Rima replied, 'We are six tribes, united by one ruler. The royal tribe, the Hiriwa, are the largest, representing four-tenths of the Tangato. If Ikendo is truly the ruler now, he'll be backed by the Manowai, who are a smaller tribe, but he must have made alliance with the other tribes. It may take him time to win over the Hiriwa, but he is Yokei and that will engender respect, despite him being male.'

'*Despite* him being male?' Elgus echoed, looking puzzled. 'Surely being male is better than–?'

His voice trailed off under Varahana's baleful glare.

'Let me explain,' Rima answered, not rising to the bait. 'The Tangato served the Aldar, as all people did, prior to the Mizra Wars. After those wars, we Tangato were trapped in these lands, surrounded by ice. Only a few Aldar remained, all of them women: the first of our "Yokei". They saved us. Since then, all of our Queens have been Yokei.'

'Only Queens?' Varahana asked. 'What do you do with male children?'

Shiazar said, 'We Yokei females are capable of choosing the gender of our child during conception. Unlike humankind, whose bodies and minds are formed of fragments of both parents, an Aldar parent of either gender will birth or sire a child who is *wholly* Aldar. Although I was sired by a human male, I am wholly Aldar, as was my mother.'

Varahana's eyes were shining. 'How wonderful!'

Elgus and Vidar were looking appalled, but luckily, neither spoke.

Raythe pricked up the courage to ask, 'Majesty, I do not intend offence, but perhaps they might understand better if they saw your face.'

Rima shot him a filthy look, but the Queen said calmly, 'Of course.'

She pulled off her mask – and everyone sucked in their breath. In daylight, and properly groomed, she was utterly stunning. Her gold-flecked bronze skin and coiled black braids shone; her amber eyes flashed beneath long lashes and her full lips were lustrous red. The delicate swirls and sigils of her tattooing only enhanced her entrancing appearance.

'Oh my,' Varahana sighed.

The men gaped wordlessly.

'Among my people, our Queen *never* shows her face,' Rima grumbled, likely the closest she could come to reproving her ruler. 'The mystery of the Aldar is sacred.'

'These people need to know,' Shiazar replied calmly. 'May I replace my mask, Lord Vyre?'

Raythe's mouth finally caught up with his brain. 'Oh! Of course – yes, thank you . . .'

'Arigato.' Thank you. She gave him a paralysing smile, and restored her mask.

He remembered to inhale. 'Right . . . so . . . your people have only ever been ruled by women?'

'That's correct,' Rima answered, still miffed. 'The Yokei chose to give birth to women, because they saw that unbridled male aggression had fuelled the Mizra Wars.'

'But women can't . . . *um* . . .' Elgus started, before very wisely shutting his mouth.

'So thought some men over the years,' Rima said, 'but the Yokei have maho in their blood. Those men who sought to usurp their rule were defeated. Now we channel male aggression into hunting, providing, building, and the martial arts. Female rule is completely accepted . . . or it was, until now,' she concluded ruefully.

'How and why did Ikendo come to be?' Raythe asked.

'He was born in secret to the Yokei Jinkatia, a revered former Queen and our Archivist,' Shiazar said, her voice stiff with disapproval. 'Ikendo's son Onkado is Ulaka's son, and therefore my nephew.'

Rima picked up the thread. 'Among our people, a male Yokei is spoken of in two ways: some prophesy that one will lead us to glory; others are certain he will be our doom. Jinkatia and Ikendo must have convinced the Yokei of the former, if Ikendo now rules. He is strong-willed, and the remaining Yokei are . . . er . . .'

'My sisters are old and pliant,' Shiazar finished for Rima, saying what she couldn't.

'Then to your people, Ikendo is some kind of saviour?' Raythe asked.

'To some.' Rima grimaced. 'Now we believe he means to drive your people out and reclaim this city, and Shiro Kamigami above us.'

Raythe thought of Kemara and Jesco, stranded above, and groaned inwardly.

'Majesty, if your people knew that you lived, would they change sides?' Varahana asked.

'Some, perhaps, but Ikendo has claimed that I have betrayed my own kind,' Shiazar replied. 'Most would see my coming here as proof of that. I believe that only his defeat will allow my safe return.'

'Then we'll make sure he fails,' Raythe said. 'Yesterday we gave him a taste of what we can do, and the same will await him when he tries again.'

'Provided we have enough ammunition,' Elgus growled, before going red, glancing at the Queen and Rima, worried that he might have said too much.

'It's all right,' Raythe told him. 'Queen Shiazar and Rima must be part of our council, for now, at least.'

'Then let me say that Elgus is right,' Vidar said. 'Raythe, we're getting damned low on powder and shot. We're making more, but we're struggling to find the ingredients – we need nitre, sulfur and charcoal for gunpowder, and lead for shot.'

'I'll see if the mines below have anything helpful,' Raythe answered;

it wasn't an adequate answer but right now, it was all he could think of. 'What about food, Varahana?'

The priestess stroked her shaven skull, which Shiazar and Rima appeared to find fascinating. 'We're building up stores steadily now. The city is rich in forage, and we're preserving bird-meat for the journey home.'

'Manpower is the bigger issue,' Vidar said. 'The walls are too long to secure: it's only going to take a few men stealing across the river to capture a watchtower and we're screwed.'

'What is "scrood"?' Rima asked, making the Norgan ranger go red.

'Ah, "not in good shape",' he managed, making Elgus grunt in amusement.

'Vidar's right,' Raythe said, 'but we do have the Rim House as a fall-back.'

'That's not going to save us, just delay the end,' Elgus pointed out. He jabbed a finger upwards. 'The only real bolt-hole is up there, in that damned floating castle.'

Rima looked aghast. 'No, you should not go there. It is haunted – all know this.'

That sounded like superstition to Raythe, but it deepened his fears for Jesco and Kemara – and also raised the final point on his unwritten agenda.

'Majesty,' he said, turning to Shiazar, 'we have two people trapped up in the citadel.' He explained about the flying stone disc, now shattered on the ground. 'Somehow, we have to get them down. Do you know a way?'

'Our people have not walked the sacred city in five hundred years, Lord Vyre,' she answered. 'We have tales, but like all, they grow in the telling. The stone platform we knew of; other tales speak of the Aldar walking on rainbows. There are old mechanisms to be found here and there that may pertain to that, but Jinkatia, our Chief Archivist, assured me that they were rusted and useless.'

'Is that the same Jinkatia who murdered your mahotsu-kai, broke your laws, engineered your overthrow and intended your death?' Raythe queried drily.

Shiazar stiffened, then admitted, 'Ae, the same. But it is likely she told the truth. Five centuries have passed, after all.'

'Then our only recourse is to repair the stone platform. I believe that Jesco and Kemara are up there right now, and I doubt they've got much food or water.'

'Rima and I may be able to aid such a repair,' Shiazar offered, making Rima scowl.

'I would be grateful,' Raythe said. 'Right, let's get busy. Varahana, food and the infirmary; Elgus and Vidar, powder and lead. I'll work on getting Jesco and Kemara back – if there's another attack, send for me instantly.'

Elgus and Vidar looked grateful to escape the unsettling presence of Queen Shiazar, but Varahana lingered, gazing at both foreign women, so different, yet of the same lost culture.

Raythe waited until the men had gone before asking, 'Majesty, I need to know the worst. What will Ikendo do to Zarelda?'

'I am sorry, but most likely she will be killed.'

Raythe hung his head. 'I feared as much.'

'You would be foolish to attempt a rescue,' Shiazar added. 'Ikendo is an Aldar, far beyond the power and prowess of even the most skilled mahotsu-kai.'

Raythe conjured a flame on his right hand. 'I'm not helpless.'

Rima snorted. 'You're as weak as your daughter.'

She swirled her hand and fire burst into being, trailing her fingers like comet tails, then changing it to vapour and then to a rainbow of light, a subtle display of skill and strength that left Raythe unnerved. He'd seen highly renowned sorcerers with much less talent. Clearly, she was well beyond him, though she looked to be no more than twenty.

He wasn't too proud to ask. 'How do you *do* that?'

Rima smirked. 'Your daughter learned fast.'

Did she just? 'Of course: she's a Vyre. Would you show me? As a guest gift?'

Rima put her nose in the air. 'Will you give me a flintlock and show me how to use it?'

Touché. 'I'll see what I can do.'

'Then so will I.' Rima threw him a challenging look. 'It's not for the faint-hearted.'

'I'm not faint-hearted. But can you at least explain where I'm going wrong?'

'It'd take too long.' She turned to the Queen. 'Majesty, do you wish to rest now?'

'I am not tired. Lord Vyre, will you show me the city? It is a place I have longed to walk. Rima can make a start at the stone platform – I'm sure I won't require a chaperone.'

Rima looked appalled again, but Raythe stammered, 'I am at your service. Varahana, could you please show Rima the stone platform? We'll join you shortly.'

The priestess curtseyed and murmured, 'Deo on high, I envy you,' as she passed.

'I'm sure you'll find Rima just as fascinating,' Raythe whispered back.

Varahana winked. 'Isn't she, though?' and led the Tangato girl out.

Raythe turned back to Shiazar and unthinkingly offered the Queen his arm. Then he froze before her blank, masked stare. 'Uh, I'm sorry,' he stammered. 'I'm unused to your customs.'

The Queen folded her arms inside her sleeves and inclined her head. 'Your informality pleases me. We Yokei do not smile enough – and of course, no one sees when we do. I feel that if I'd seen my sister's face more often, I would have seen her treachery coming.' She indicated the door. 'Please, show me the city that has haunted my dreams.'

For Raythe, the next few hours were enchanted.

As they walked, Shiazar explained that to her, Rath Argentium was a tantalising lure: always in sight, always unattainable – so now she wanted to see *everything*: from the gatehouse and walls to the broken statues and overgrown buildings of the lower blocks, right up to the grander ruins on the rim. The miracle that they could actually converse in a shared tongue was wonderful, even though many new words had entered both vocabularies in the intervening years. She asked many questions and he quickly became accustomed to the fluting cadence of her voice and her a dainty short-stepped gait that looked like gliding, as if she was made of light and air.

It was midday by the time they reached the rim wall overlooking the crater. The gusty wind was cold and clouds scudded low overhead, at times engulfing the tethered rock above. She surprised him by removing her mask again, sighing as the sun and wind kissed her face. 'I love it when I can do this,' she sighed, eyes closed and chin lifted towards the sun.

He couldn't look away from that entrancing sight: the angular features and the beautifully wrought tattoos on her cheeks and chin that accentuated both her differences and her loveliness. Then he became burningly conscious that he was staring, so he looked away and asked, 'How long have you been Queen of the Tangato, Majesty?'

'Just three years. My reign was to be for eight, and then I am permitted to breed.'

'With a Tangato man?'

'Ae.' She gave him an arch look. 'Those are the only men available to me, and they are very fine.' Then her voice took on a bitter tone. 'Although it appears my sister could not wait, for she lay with Ikendo and I never even knew she gave birth during her absence.'

'It hurts when someone close to you betrays your trust,' he said with deep sympathy.

'You have felt this pain also?' Shiazar asked.

Raythe *never* told strangers his secrets, but found himself explaining about his wife and Luc Mandaryke, and how he'd stolen his own daughter and run. 'Mirella told me she married Luc to protect us, even though he – once my best friend – was now an enemy. I still can't say whether she made a dreadful sacrifice, or if she betrayed us for power and status.'

'And you still hope to free her?'

He looked away. 'It's a foolish notion . . . but yes, I still hope for that. But it's been four years, nearly five. Then I found an explorer's journal that hinted at istariol, followed the clues and ended up here.'

'But the istariol isn't yours,' she reminded him.

'We didn't know your people were here – and our need is great. The whole of Magnia is being crushed by Bolgravia. We need only enough to make a difference at home.'

'We both know that won't happen,' Shiazar replied. 'You've found us and now more of your kind will come, maybe this year, or in ten years hence. It is inevitable. In this sense, Ikendo is right: we must prepare to confront the world. But I will not begin that process with a massacre. Such acts only beget worse deeds.'

He was grateful, but principles counted for little against the belligerent, entitled greed of the Bolgravians – and most Magnians, in truth. She was a child of a different time, a different way of thinking. *I've brought the big ugly world here, and it'll crush her.* Another layer of guilt and fear piled onto his shoulders, but he squared them. *I have to find a way through this that saves her people as well as mine.*

'Life is a maze, but we can find its centre if we try, as we say in my lands,' he said.

She looked at him and smiled. 'Thank you, Lord Vyre. You encourage me.'

Her smile, radiant in the sunlight, caused him to blurt, 'Majesty, in our tales the Aldar are beautiful beyond comparison – but the stories don't do you justice.'

Then he went utterly red, for sending his tongue racing ahead of his brain.

She replaced the mask on her face. Sounding more amused than offended, she said, 'Often the exotic can appeal more than the familiar. Among my kind, Ulaka was the acknowledged beauty.'

The mention of her treacherous – and now dead at her hand – sister cooled the air faster than the northerly wind. Raythe bowed and indicated the path back to the bridge district. 'Majesty, the midday meal awaits, then we'll go and help Rima.'

Then he cast his eyes upwards and silently prayed for Gerda and Deo to protect Jesco and Kemara, to give them strength and sustenance up there in the clouds.

Be safe, my friends, he wished. *We'll come for you, I swear.*

Varahana laid her ear against Vidar's bare chest and said, 'Breathe.'

The big Norgan inhaled deeply, then let it out in a slow gusty breath.

He was lying on the largest cot in the infirmary, being tended in Kemara's absence by Varahana and her Sisters of Gerda. They were fortunate that there were no serious new cases right now, just the usual cuts, sprains, broken fingers and toes, impending births and new pregnancies.

Vidar's chest was a huge shaggy expanse, with an aroma of good honest sweat. And his lungs had finally stopped gurgling with each breath. *He's right*, Vara thought, *he does heal fast*. But she didn't lift her head immediately, luxuriating in being close, before sitting up.

'I declare you completely cured,' she reported. 'Now get out of my hair,' she added with a wink.

He laughed and took the liberty of stroking her scalp. 'I knew I was in good hands.'

He was never so bold as to voice it, but she knew he was in love with her, although she couldn't think why. She was a book-obsessed, opinionated priestess; he was a taciturn man of the wilderness, and their infrequent conversations were very one-sided. But she liked what little he said, and the way he listened. And though she was far from a helpless hollyhock, she liked his protective care. Those times he'd rampaged in to guard her, she'd felt like a queen, with a knight-errant at her beck and call.

'Well, it was mostly Kemara who saved you,' she said briskly, conscious that the two Sisters on duty were all ears. 'Get your shirt on and get out, you lazy lump. You've taken up too much of my time already.'

But she knew he had heard the smile in her voice.

He dressed, and went to the window. 'Raythe's back,' he noted. 'With the Queen.'

She joined him, staring out at the two figures making their way down the winding cobbled road that led down from the Rim House. Grey-clad Raythe, rangy and animated, his hands waving about as he spoke, while the masked Queen had her hands clasped inside her sleeves, her lacquered face immobile, but clearly listening.

A real Aldar, stepped from the pages of fable.

Varahana dearly wished she could examine her – she had so many questions. What's an Aldar's physiology? What do their teeth look like? Their organs? What about her eyes? What do they prefer to eat or drink? How does their control over their baby's gender work? *I could study her all my life and never run out of questions.*

She suddenly realised she was thinking out loud and stammered into silence. Vidar gave her a wry smile. 'Aye, she's quite something.' But his eyes were purely on her.

Varahana went red and tried to divert the conversation. 'Raythe is being *very* attentive.'

Vidar chuckled. 'Who wouldn't be?'

'He's always been drawn to the mysterious and unattainable. His wife Mirella was quite the beauty, but her father set her on a pedestal. Raythe had to fly to the rings and back to win her. And in the rebellion, Tami declared that no man was good enough for her; so Raythe – grieving and angry about Mirella – set out to win her. I think it was a mix of him trying to prove something to himself, and at the same time, to wound Mirella; it was complicated. When he wants something, he's quite charming.'

'Weren't you unattainable enough for him?'

'Too unattainable.' Varahana sighed, then shook herself. 'We've both moved past that.'

'Did you–?' Vidar began, then he – great craggy lump that he was – blushed. 'Sorry, none of my business.'

She looked up at him. 'True. But the answer is no. It was touch and go, bad timing as much as anything. I was newly ordained, and took too long to come round – by the time I'd realised my feelings, he'd moved on to Tami. I renewed my vows, but we remained friends, which was, I am quite sure, the best outcome for us both.' She smiled. 'If not, I might not be here.'

'Then it's a good thing,' Vidar said. 'We need you.'

By which she knew he meant, *I need you.*

'Yes,' she answered carefully. 'I have a congregation, and they need me to keep my faith, so they can keep theirs. So I must keep my vows and retain Deo at the centre of my life.'

'May they bless you,' Vidar muttered. 'I guess I'd better get back to my duties.'

He lumbered off, and she felt a familiar hole open up inside her.

But there were dressings and splints to check, remedies to brew and bandages to wash – and a sermon to plan. There was no time for regret, and perhaps that was for the best.

Night-time was the worst, now they'd run out of beer and hard liquor. After a life of going to bed drunk, Elgus Rhamp had to face down his ghosts sober these days. It made him miss Tami, or anyone else who might've helped him keep the shadows at bay.

But he had his son back, and that made it endurable.

The lads were calling Banno 'Hole-head' because of the trepanning, but it was all good-humoured. Banno was popular, and pleased to be out of the infirmary. Father and son were sharing a house in the knot of dilapidated but largely intact houses he'd commandeered for his mercenaries.

Watching his only remaining child wolf down food lifted his spirits, even though right now, he was telling him about the shit that had happened while he was unconscious.

'Aye, so we had to hang 'em,' he concluded, watching Banno's appalled face. 'Crow and Thom an' all. They sent kragging *Skavid* to kill ye.'

'Holy Gerda,' Banno breathed.

'So there's only 'bout twenty of us,' Elgus went on. 'Tom Corday's my new second, then there's Falgram, Semus, Aramak, Dando, Hadric and his Norgan mates. Even Miki's a veteran now and he's useless as tits on a bull. Mind, fewer to share in the haul, I guess.'

'Can we get still out?' Banno asked.

'Not with wagons and womenfolk and kids in tow,' Elgus muttered, not quite meeting his son's eye. 'Fact is, the only chance of surviving this mess is for a small group to slip through the Tangato lines and head for the glacier and the way south.'

Banno sat up urgently. 'Father, we *can't* do that.'

'Why not?' Elgus kept his voice low, after checking again to make sure that no one was near enough to listen. 'There's been a leadership change among the Tangato and the new man – if you can call an Aldar a "man" – is going to hit us in force any day. We've got to get out before then.'

'No,' Banno replied firmly.

'You got the "honour" bug, boy? Vyre's daughter been corrupting you?'

'What's wrong with having some common decency?' his son retorted.

Elgus leaned forward. 'I'm all for it, until it gets me killed. Folks in our line got no business with fair play, boy. That gets you shoved into the front line of a charge uphill into cannons, or trapped in the rear-guard protecting Lord Whatshiskraggingname as he flees. Come tomorrow or the next day, ten thousand screaming tribals are going to massacre us all.'

'But Zar –'

'Forget her, lad! She's likely dead already – her throat slit, if she's lucky. Just pray they left her virginal before doing it.' The pain on his son's face hurt him, but the boy had to move on. 'Forget her,' he urged. 'We're getting out, as soon as we can.'

'Then you're going alone,' Banno said firmly. 'I'm bloody well ashamed to be a Rhamp.'

'That right? You too good for your own kin now, are you? You and me are the last Rhamps left, but I tell you this: I can breed more.' He jabbed his finger into his last son's chest. 'You get yourself right in the head, boy. We leave tomorrow night.'

In any other situation, Kemara was sure they would have been dead. She and Jesco were halfway up the stairs, approaching what they guessed must be the banquet hall, the centre of all the strangeness and danger here, if Jesco's dreams were to be believed. When the two guards appeared above them and bolts of energy flashed from their halberd tips, they were caught cold.

But a strange, miraculous thing happened as the two energy bolts blossomed and seared towards them: they left their foes' weapons *slowly*, and though they sped up, their frantic lurch towards the balustrades was easily in time, allowing the sorcerous blasts to slash past them to scorch and break the stonework below.

It was all about *time*.

The two guards, both flat-faced, graceful Aldar, were deeper into the time-stasis spell than Jesco and she were, which was why they were moving slower – so their next volley was easily evaded. Their movements were ponderous – but as she and Jesco approached, those advantages began to shrink.

Seeing that, Jesco ripped out his dagger and threw it.

To Kemara, it looked like his spinning blade started like a blur, then slowed – but to the female guard, it must have been the opposite: a quiver in the air, barely seen, that was impossible to evade. It thudded into her throat, hammering her backwards. She clutched helplessly at the hilt as her blood sprayed everywhere.

Then Buramanaka took over and Kemara conjured a vivid, crackling blast of her own mizra-energy which struck the other guard before he even saw it coming. For a moment he was limned in purple sparks, then he jerked into a dreadful dance as his leather armour and skin blistered and burned. Convulsing in the grip of the blast, he emitted a low, ululating sound that must be his death scream, distorted by the time lag.

By the time they reached the two Aldar, both were dead.

Jesco gave her an amazed and relieved look, then yanked out his dagger. 'Deo on High,' he breathed, 'for a moment there I thought we were screwed.'

He wiped the blade on his victim's tunic, then they went on, pushing against that eerie feeling of resistance until they stepped out onto the uppermost floor of the tethered citadel.

Two more guards, both male, were stationed before a set of huge double doors. Their faces blanching in alarm, they started charging – but as before, their exaggeratedly slow movements gave Jesco time to go backwards, retrieve the halberds, then hurl first one, then the other into the guards' chests. To Kemara, it looked ridiculously slow, the weapons taking twenty seconds or more to strike – but to the guards, Jesco must have looked like a blur of motion – and then the spears slammed through their breastplates and spitted them.

In the time it took to cross the threshold and reach the banquet hall doors, the sun vanished from the windows and darkness fell. There were weird murmuring sounds coming from within, and something that sounded like a drawn-out scream, slowed in tempo so much that it reverberated like a bass note on a musical instrument, vibrating on into eternity.

They looked at each other, steeling themselves for what was to come.

Then Jesco took the handle of the right-hand door and yanked it open.

2

Hammer Fall

The chosen ones set out after the evening meal, travelling through the night. Ikendo, the new Aldar King, and Onkado, his son and named heir, led the small party. Neither wore Aldar or flesh-masks, so the awe of the warriors accompanying them was palpable: they were legends, come to life.

Six Yokei attended them, those young enough to fight if need be. Aldar aged slowly, but half the Yokei were more than a century old, the equivalent of fifty human years in terms of physical capacity. Jinkatia led them: she had demanded they alter plans and make the journey, after glimpsing strange lights inside the floating citadel through a captured Bolgravian spyglass.

'Our enemies are ahead of us,' she told Ikendo as she set in motion this journey to the fabled gate-spheres, the entrance to the Bridge of Izanami, the Aldar God-Kings' path from Lake Waiotapu to Shiro Kamigami.

'If the whiteskins occupy Shiro Kamigami, we are imperilled. But there is a way up.'

Ikendo had agreed to take only twenty warriors, as Jinkatia said the Bridge of Izanami's capacity was limited and it might become unstable if too many tried using it. He left his shoganai, Kotabashi, in command of the warriors surrounding the ruined city, with orders to begin pressing the gaikiko from midday. Once they'd got the defenders of the gatehouse to commit, they should then strike them in force from elsewhere, dividing their meagre forces.

For Onkado, it was a fretful journey. He worried constantly about Zarelda, fearing that his absence endangered her, despite her status as his bride. But all he could do was assign Kuia to look after her and station some trusted men to protect both women.

The small party arrived at the old Summer Palace just after midnight and set up camp in the plaza housing the giant metal interlocking spheres, the gateway of the Bridge of Izanami. As they ate, they watched Jinkatia and her Yokei get to work. The Archivist produced a small puzzle-ball, which she placed inside the base of the mechanism, and it began slowly whirling to life, spinning faster and faster.

Onkado watched absently, despite the miracle on display. All he could think about was Zarelda – he'd first met her in this very place. By every standard he knew, she was the opposite of beautiful. An ideal Tangato woman had curves, long, lustrous black hair, golden skin, a heart-shaped face and the grace of a dancer. Zar had a small nose and a pugnacious visage. She was as skinny as a rake and moved like a boy. Her skin was pale as the belly of a slug, her cheeks were freckled and her straw-coloured hair was cropped short.

But she had a way of drawing his eye, and she carried herself like a fighter. She was a prisoner of an alien people, yet she'd survived and adapted without compromise. And she had a palpable sense of mirth bubbling just beneath her surface that intrigued him. He wanted to be with her. He wanted to make her laugh.

Naturally, his father was furious, which was why they weren't talking right now.

He wanted her served up to Tatsu and Kyu, to be made an example of, Onkado thought resentfully, *but I will never allow that. In time she'll become a valued member of our tribe, someone who can guide us in the days to come, especially when the barbarians she warns of return.*

It was strange to be at odds with his father and grandmother and in agreement with Shiazar, the enemy, on such a matter – but as one of his tutors had told him once, no one had sole ownership over being right.

And there was another, more carnal thing; Zarelda was his wife now, and while it was a necessity to protect her, he couldn't deny that she stirred him. He wanted to taste her – although he refused to take advantage of their current circumstances.

One day, when we're more equal, I will court her properly, he promised himself.

He mused on that – until he noticed that the whirling mechanism had begun to glow, lighting up the square, and the Yokei's chanting had become triumphant.

His father roused from his reverie and looked his way. 'Marrying the girl was foolish,' he declared, their first words in hours.

'Killing her would have been more foolish,' Onkado retorted.

'You'll regret it, once the novelty of white flesh has passed.'

'Her skin-colour had nothing to do with it.'

Ikendo snorted disbelievingly. 'At least when you're done with her, it won't be hard to disentangle the liaison. As a gaikiko, she has no rights among us.'

'Her people marry for life,' Onkado snapped back. 'Get used to her.' Then he went on the attack. 'The Magnians number in the *millions*, Father. We cannot defeat them – we can only make peace and reach an accommodation that will allow us to survive.'

Ikendo's face hardened. 'We are Aldar, the rightful lords of this world. They will bow down before us.'

'Zarelda says –'

'I do not care what the gaikiko says. Now be silent, for I would see this.'

Onkado bit his tongue and turned away from his scowling, angry parent.

His father's life had been spent waiting for this moment of triumph, resenting every passing hour that he was not in power. *Four decades I've wasted, waiting for what is mine by right*, Ikendo used to rant – but even now, when he was getting what he'd always desired, the resentment remained, together with the desire to lash out and punish.

At least it's no longer constantly directed at me . . .

The humming of the spheres had taken on a deep, musical resonance and the light around it began to shimmer through all the hues of the rainbow. Onkado momentarily forgot Zarelda, awestruck by the spectacle.

Jinkatia and her Yokei shrieked out an invocation – and suddenly the nimbus of light about the whirling mechanism deepened in colour and texture and a spear of rainbow light shot across the sky, straight towards Shiro Kamigami, floating in the sky somewhere in the darkness to the northwest.

It's working, Onkado thought in wonder. *It's really working.*

Ikendo stood. 'See, my son: we are Aldar, the true heirs of God-King Vashtariel. All creation bends to our will.'

Jinkatia came to join them, while the rest of the Yokei continued their invocations. 'It has begun,' she said. 'The mechanism was completely drained, so it will be hours before it is usable, my son.'

Ikendo scowled, but bowed his head – only for his mother did he quell his anger. 'Our enemies will see the light and know your purpose.'

'That is unavoidable,' Jinkatia said dismissively. 'Patience, and the citadel of the God-Kings shall be yours.'

Ikendo grimaced impatiently. 'Kotabashi is commanded to begin his attacks at midday,' he noted sourly. The victory will belong to him.'

'But the ultimate glory will be yours, my son,' Jinkatia said soothingly. 'All things will be yours.'

There was a giant hammer hanging over the city, blocking out the sky where the floating citadel should have been, and Raythe knew it was about to fall. Everyone was screaming, but no one knew what to do – they were all imploring him to save them . . .

Then he woke, sweating and breathless.

Holy Deo! Well, that dream wasn't hard to read, he thought dully, forcing himself to lie down again. The night was still pitch-black, with dawn hours away.

He concentrated his mind on better things and this time when he fell back to sleep, he dreamed of a glorious summer, the last before the

Bolgravian invasion, when he'd taken Mirella and Zar on a picnic to Lake Parindel in Otravia. For a moment he was back there . . . then that dream turned evil too, as his wife and daughter dived into the lake and only their clothes floated up. He had to dive after them, had to rescue them . . .

'*Milord—!*'

He jerked up, panting hard. 'What?'

At his door Xan Lynski, the duty guard, hissed, 'The chica wants to see you.'

'*Tangato,*' Raythe replied waspishly. 'Say chica again and you'll find yourself running round the city in punishment.'

He stumbled to his basin and buried his face in the cold water, blearily towelled it dry, and threw on clothes. A couple of minutes later, dressed and armed, he stepped into the hall.

Lynski, his back to the door, was facing Rima, who was leaning opposite, one foot pressed against the wall, revealing a bare thigh. That, combined with her uncovered waist and the swell of breast, left Lynski not knowing where to look.

He patted the young man's shoulder. 'It's all right, Xan, she really is on our side.' Then he faced Rima. 'Yes?'

She peeled herself off the wall, planted both feet and pointed a finger skywards. 'If you want to get up there, we need to act now. We're running out of time.'

'What do you mean?'

'Come and see.'

She led him to a balcony at the back of the building and they looked up. Dawn was lighting the sky, but the planetary rings were clearly visible – and there was also, impossibly, a rainbow in the sky, rising from the southwest – but it was *straight*, not curved, and it was striking a tower on the battlements of the floating citadel. It was still pale, but becoming more and more solid by the minute.

Raythe stared up at the spear of coloured light and blurted, 'What is it?'

'Proof that I was deceived like an innocent,' Rima fumed. 'A few days ago, I took your daughter to the old Summer Palace to show her the ruins. I was surprised to find Jinkatia there, but she said she was researching – she was our Chief Archivist, and of course I trusted her. Now I know why she was there.'

'Which was –?'

'The Summer Palace is ten miles away, but the Aldar built a sorcerous device to enable swift travel between there and Shiro Kamigami: the Bridge of Izanami, they called it, from an old legend. Jinkatia told us all it was inoperable. Clearly she lied.'

'So Ikendo can send people up into the fortress above us, via that rainbow?'

'Ae – judging by the light, it will soon be usable.'

Raythe thought of Jesco and Kemara, stranded up there. 'Why would they wish to go there now? Why wouldn't they concentrate on defeating us down here first?'

Rima hesitated, then admitted, 'There are weapons up there that can blast fire down on you – similar to the "cannons" you have described to me, but much worse. Ikendo probably fears that you'll reach them first.'

'*Aldar weapons?* Why didn't you tell me earlier?'

Rima put her hands on her hips. 'Because it wasn't relevant: the Bridge of Izanami didn't work and I thought you couldn't reach the fortress above.'

And because you didn't like the idea of my people controlling the weapons up there, Raythe thought. *I can't blame you for that.* They were allies of necessity at best – *but allies, nevertheless.* 'Then we have to get up there and prevent him from seizing control.'

Rima's expression was sour, but she nodded. 'Ae.'

The spear of coloured light was thickening and becoming brighter as he watched, despite the onset of dawn. 'I don't know how long that'll take to be ready, but we can't afford to wait and find out,' he muttered. 'I've got to repair that stone disc in the crater and get up there.'

I'll need istariol and copper rods, and I'll need help.

'We need to rouse everyone,' he told Rima. 'If that Izzy-bridge will be ready sometime soon, he'll attack at the same time. It's the sensible move. We've got to be ready for both. Wake Queen Shiazar and ask her to meet me at the bottom of the crater. We need your help.'

'My Queen is not at your command,' she said crossly. 'But I will do as you ask.' She turned on her heel and jogged away.

Raythe looked up again, marvelling at the way that beam of light stood out against the backdrop of stars and the planetary rings: a sight of real beauty – but also one of menace.

This is the day when everything will be decided.

He went downstairs to the nearest occupied house and hammered on the door, shouting, 'This is Raythe Vyre. Wake up, wake up – assemble in the dining hall. I will talk to everyone. Pass it on.'

Within the hour, just as the sun rose, everyone except those manning the defences had assembled: fewer than two hundred, with another fifty-odd on the walls. They'd lost sixty or so of those who'd started the trek, to sickness, battle or treachery, and now the remainder faced a massacre. They were cold, hungry and scared.

He picked out faces: Mater Varahana, standing with her Sisters of Gerda; Cal Foaley and his chief hunters; Elgus Rhamp and his remaining mercenaries, clustered together in the far corner; Gravis Tavernier and Lynd Borger, unelected leaders of the tradesmen, artisans, labourers and their families: all staring at him anxiously, but also with a certain blind trust. They'd survived so much and he'd pulled them through some impossible situations, so he supposed they were all expecting another miracle.

I'm not sure I can deliver one this time.

But he had to try.

'What's 'appenin', Lord Vyre?' Gilly Walsh shouted as Raythe stood and faced them.

The hall went quiet.

'Good morning to you all. Today will be a long day, and a hard one. As you know, we're sheltering the Tangato Queen and her friend Rima, because the Queen has been overthrown for *not* attacking us. I want to stress this: the Queen and Rima are friends and allies. Do *not* hinder them in any way: they are aiding me, and that means helping us all.'

He let that sink in, saw the exchanged looks, the stress of accumulated fears.

'If she's deposed, what's that mean for the truce?' Gravis Tavernier asked.

'It means we don't have one,' Raythe told them bluntly. 'They tried our defences yesterday, but they've got plenty of men, and there'll be further attacks today.' He held up his hand before the resultant moan turned into outright fear. 'We held them off last time without losses and we can do it again, but it needs everyone to contribute.' He rattled off tasks, from manning the defences to support roles carrying the wounded back to temporary infirmaries behind the gatehouse, to running messages. Anyone unable to fight in some way would guard the children and the infirm within the Rim House, their fall-back position.

'That's all very well,' Elgus Rhamp called out, when Raythe was done, 'but what's the end-game?'

Raythe concealed a grimace. The question wasn't entirely welcome, but it was fair, and people needed a hope to cling to. 'The citadel,' he replied, pointing upwards. 'We've learned that there are Aldar weapons up there which could turn the tide. I'm going to be working with Queen Shiazar and Rima on finding a way up.'

Voices rose, buzzing with nervous excitement. 'What's that rainbow-coloured light mean?' someone called out. 'Don' look natural t'me.'

'It's not,' he admitted. 'The Tangato are trying to get to the citadel first – but they won't.'

'Can ye trust 'er Majesty?' Gravis wanted to know.

I hope so, was the real answer, but, 'I believe so,' was what Raythe said. 'Most of you know that Kemara and Jesco are up there right now, so we'll bring them back down, along with the Aldar weapons. All we need is time – and that's the thing that's passing while we talk. To your stations, everyone, and Gerda be with you.'

The morning passed in a blur. Raythe found himself bouncing from gatehouse to infirmary to the southern watchtowers, giving encouragement and making decisions, so it wasn't until nearly midday that he was able to join Rima and Shiazar, who were reconstructing the stone platform using earth-sorcery. He'd already deployed Gravis Tavernier to work on powdering istariol from the nuggets they'd accumulated in the mines, mixing it with water and copper verdigris, the first steps in 'activating' the precious mineral. But it was a slow process and he didn't expect results for some hours yet.

He reached the bottom of the crater. Shiazar was prowling round and round the stone disc, which was partially reformed. As they approached, Raythe realised that she was directing her powers silently at the fractured stone. He glanced at Rima. 'Um, does she have a familiar?'

Rima gave him a condescending look. 'Of course not. The Yokei are made of sorcery.'

Holy Gerda. He paused to stare in admiration – and a little envy – of such innate power. *The Aldar were tyrants, but I can see why we lumpen humans worshipped them . . .*

Then the Queen lifted her mask and her lovely face met his gaze with a smile that stopped his breath. 'Good morning, Lord Vyre.' She spread her hands, showing him the platform. 'I can do no more until we are ready to place the hollow copper rods into the stonework and run the activated istariol into them. I am only a queen, not an engineer.'

'Only a queen', he thought wryly. 'They'll be ready soon. Lynd is working on the copper rods and our master brewer Gravis is overseeing the blending of the istariol powder and verdigris.' He looked up at the rainbow-coloured shaft of light, clearly visible against the blue skies. 'How much time do we have?'

'I know not, and the activation process can't be hurried,' Shiazar said calmly. 'We must let it take its course.'

It was hard to let anything take its natural course knowing Jesco and Kemara were trapped, Zar a prisoner and the Tangato were massing across the bridge, but he forced down his impatience. 'Fine. I need to do the rounds, but I'll be back in an hour or two.'

He left them to it, hurrying up and out of the crater and down to the gatehouse where Elgus Rhamp had the morning watch on high alert.

When Raythe appeared, he strode to meet him. 'Mornin'. Those dark—uh, *Tangato* – are getting frisky, but there's no sign of their King, so we don't think an attack's imminent.'

'He's probably still having brekkie and a cuppa,' Raythe quipped. 'Be ready, though. They won't just sing and dance all day this time.'

He took his spy-glass and scanned the massed warriors, dreading the sight of Zarelda bound and on display; or worse still, her corpse. But she was nowhere to be seen, and that was no relief either. *She's been with them for another whole night. Gerda, protect her . . .*

Zarelda jerked from sleep to the sound of a stealthy footfall behind her. She rolled over in the dimly lit lodge Ikendo had commandeered for Onkado. She'd slept fearfully, watched over by Kuia, who'd been dozing by the fire, but now she was gone, too.

She was expecting the person slipping into her room to be Onkado, but instead she saw a hunched-over female figure and for a moment was horribly sure it was Kyu.

'Who is it?' she squeaked.

'Just me,' Kuia answered, lighting a taper which revealed her wrinkled face and white curls. Dim light gleamed round the canvas blocking the door and she heard the sounds of the village waking up, wary and subdued.

It's morning, Zar realised. *Onkado didn't return.*

She was thankful he'd honoured his promise that he wouldn't sleep with her, but his non-appearance was worrying. 'Where is he?' she asked.

'Prince Onkado has accompanied Ikendo and several Yokei on a secret mission,' Kuia reported. 'They left last night. The King's shoganai, Kota-bashi, commands the assault today.'

A secret mission? An assault? Zar sat up, coming fully awake. 'Today?'

Kuia knelt beside her and took her hand. 'I fear so, my dear – but Onkado instructed me to stay with you. I'll protect you in the temple.'

I have to escape and warn Father, Zar thought wildly – then she calmed a little. Knowing her father, he already knew about it.

'How are you feeling?' Kuia asked.

'I don't know,' she groaned, drawing her knees up and wrapping her arms round them. The last few days had been the most traumatic she'd ever experienced, worse even than that terrible day when she'd been snatched from her home by her father and they'd fled Otravia.

I've just married an Aldar to escape execution and torture. Banno and Father and all my friends are about to be attacked. How am I supposed to feel?

Kuia took her hand. 'You probably feel that you've chosen the cow-ard's way out. You haven't. It takes courage to live, Zarelda, and Prince Onkado protected you from his own father. I believe you chose well.'

'You know nothing,' Zar retorted, though she was grateful that the old woman condoned her decision, even though her marriage vows weighed on her like an anchor.

I swore to be his, body and soul, before all his gods . . .

'I need to eat,' she said weakly.

Kuia draped an arm around her. 'I understand, child. Onkado instructed you should be given every comfort. Come with me. We can eat at the temple.'

Zar put on her normal Tangato bodice and flax skirt, then Kuia wrapped her in beautiful embroidered silk robes, so heavy with thread they weighed her down like armour. When they left the lodge, two Hiriwa warriors, men Kuia knew, closed round them and escorted them to the temple, where lines of fighting men were filing in to pray for the blessings of the gods, a sure sign that they expected to be fighting that day. Their wives and children were with them, and Zar saw plenty of fearful tears, fervent hugs and awkward farewells. It reminded her of the pre-battle rituals she'd seen during the rebellion.

She and Kuia were served food in the kannushi's private rooms, then Zar was left alone while Kuia prayed at length. By mid-morning, the temple had emptied out and the fighting men were all gone, so Kuia deemed it safe to take Zar to a bath house.

'It will relax you,' she said kindly.

But when they emerged, they found their Hiriwa guards gone and two Manowai waiting. 'We are assigned to protect the new Princess,' one said.

'By whom?' Kuia asked, while Zar looked around anxiously.

'By King Ikendo,' a harsh voice cut in, as Kyu's mutilated face loomed from the shadow of the building. Her empty eye sockets regarded Zar coldly. 'The King has commanded that I escort the gaikiko witch today, for her own protection.'

Zar's skin went cold. 'Onkado said nothing of this.'

'Onkado is not King,' Kyu replied imperiously. 'Where are you going?'

'The bathing house,' Kuia replied. 'This is unnecessary. Prince Onkado placed his wife in my care.'

Kyu sneered. 'The gaikiko is a sorceress – what would you do if she tried to escape? Ask her nicely to stay?' She stalked up to Zar and lashed a thick leash around Zar's throat. Her noseless, eyeless face was even more revolting up close, her breath meaty and foul. She spat her spell and Zar felt Adefar shrink into the leash, leaving just enough connection to translate. 'There,' Kyu smirked. 'Try to escape and your own familiar will throttle you until you pass out.' Then she clicked her fingers and the two Manowai guards stood to attention. 'Bathing, you say? Let's go.'

Zar had lost all desire to bathe now, and so had Kuia. 'We will return to the temple,' she protested, but Kyu overruled her.

'No,' she said flatly, 'we will ensure the Prince's new bride is as clean as a newborn.'

'I don't think–' Kuia began.

'You're not required any more, Priestess,' Kyu snapped.

'I will not let her out of my sight.'

Kyu's face contorted into an ugly smile. 'The more the merrier,' she said, relenting in such a way that the invitation sounded like a threat. 'Lead on.'

They're going to kill us both, Zar realised as she followed Kuia to a bath-house built over a stream filled with thermal springs. Everyone they passed took one look at Kyu and found something else to do.

On the way, they had to pause to make way for a long line of jogging warriors, mostly Manowai, heading northeast. Those who saw Zar nudged their fellows and some sneered, but most looked deep in thought, probably about the fighting to come, and barely noticed her.

'Where are they going?' she asked Kuia.

Surprisingly, it was Kyu answered. 'They are heading for the north side of the city,' she boasted. 'You gaikiko have fewer guards there. We will slaughter them.'

Kuia touched Zar's arm, perhaps to warn her not to answer. 'I know you'll grieve, but it will be over quickly.'

The thought that it was all happening so soon almost paralysed Zar – but it also kindled new resolve. *I have to warn Father.* Although how, exactly, when she was probably going to be throttled or drowned in the next few minutes, she had no idea. It took all her courage not to collapse in dread as Kyu and her guards led Zar and Kuia on to a small, pretty pole-house set over a steaming stream which fed their baths. There were kiln-heated stones to increase the pool temperatures. There was a queue of people waiting, but the moment Kyu appeared, confronting them with her eyeless glare, most hurried away.

The mahotsu-kai snickered contemptuously, then hammered on the door.

The aged matron opened the door with a smile that vanished the moment she saw Kyu and the two Manowai warriors. 'But . . . this is a woman-only bath-house,' the matron protested.

'Clear the premises, old woman,' Kyu barked. 'Don't make me say it twice.'

She didn't need to: the other bathers dressed hurriedly and fled. Zar shared another fraught look with Kuia, but the kannushi appeared to be paralysed by Kyu's presence.

One of the guards put his hand between Zar's shoulder blades and propelled her into the small lobby. The other blocked Kuia at the door, which Kyu slammed shut in her face.

'The three of us wish to bathe,' Kyu told the matron.

The old woman looked piteously at Zar, then squeaked a warning as her daughter appeared from the bathing room, clearly terrified of what might befall them both.

'Is a pool ready?' Kyu asked. When the hostess nodded mutely, she barked, 'Then get out. I'll look after things from here.'

The matron grabbed her daughter and fled back into the living quarters, leaving Zar alone with Kyu and the burly warrior, who was looking at her like she was prey. Kuia was kept outside, protesting ineffectually.

Zar put her back to the wall, trying to breathe.

'Undress,' Kyu told her. 'Do it, or I'll have Doba here do it for you.'

She was shaking so badly that undoing the clasps of her skirt and bodice were almost beyond her. To her horror, the beast of a man also shed his clothing. Towering over her like a dark mountain he glared at her. 'Ugly,' he commented, staring at her skinny white body. 'Like an insect larva.'

Kyu indicated the bathing room. 'In there.'

'Zarelda?' Kuia's voice called from outside. '*Zarelda?*'

She went to answer, but Doba seized her from behind, clamping his hand over her mouth and lifting her off her feet. He kicked open the door to the bathroom, hauled her through and carried her down the steps into the steaming stream running beneath the house. Zar tried to grasp at the door frame, but Doba was too big, too strong, grunting like a beast as she thrashed in his grip, sending water splashing in all directions, and she couldn't so much as make him slip as he forced her down into the water.

He held Zar's head just above the water as Kyu came to the edge of the pool, smirking. 'Onkado's stupid gesture means nothing,' she said. 'Ikendo rules, not the Prince, and he commands your death.' She nodded at Doba. 'Use the musubi leash so that it looks like it throttled her during an escape bid.'

There was no time to react, for Doba kept one hand over her mouth and used the other to seize the rope-thick leash and twist it round her throat, closing her windpipe as she thrashed in vain. Doba sank down into the warm water with her, pulling her under as her vision blurred, her eyes stinging in the hot water.

Even knowing she was doomed, she fought on, thrashing desperately – then her flailing hand brushed a burning hot rock at the bottom, one of those used to keep the water hot, and with her last strength, she grabbed it and slammed it over her head into Doba's face.

She felt it strike home, his grip gave way and she slithered free. Finding her feet, she exploded upwards, hammering the stone into his bloodied face again, crunching his nose – and to her awed disbelief, he reeled and fell, striking the back of his head against the stone lip, then slipping silently beneath the churning surface.

For an instant, Kyu was frozen in disbelief as Zar gasped in a mouthful of air and planted both feet, then she pulled back her hand and hurled the rock, aiming for the middle of Kyu's face, but Kyu threw up a hand and deflected the stone with her forearm. Then the musubi leash round Zar's throat tightened suddenly, cutting off her air as the spells preventing escape were triggered.

Zar's lungs emptied and her legs gave way. She fell backwards and went under. The water swirled, bubbles filling her sight – along with the vacant face of the unconscious Doba. Darkness crowded in as she sank.

Looking up at the silver-lit surface, she saw a leering Kyu was just inches from the surface, peering in for a better view of her death.

And Zar let it happen, deliberately emptying her lungs . . .

*

... following a desperate flash of inspiration. *Your own familiar will throttle you until you pass out*, Kyu had said: a restraint compelling Adefar to prevent her escape – but to pass out here, underwater: that was to *die*.

No familiar could let their bonded master die . . . and as Zar began to black out, the contradiction unknowingly built into the spell became its undoing.

Inside her, Adefar went mad, the fox-faced man screaming inside her brain – then the leash round her neck loosened and the spell binding her power frayed and failed.

She immediately slammed her feet into the bottom again, bending her knees, then erupting through the surface and hammering her forehead into the middle of Kyu's face. She hit right where her nose should have been, breaking the bones around the nose and eye sockets and sending the mahotsu-kai reeling back on her haunches. As she convulsed, Zar found the rock she'd thrown earlier and slammed it down on Kyu's skull.

The sorceress collapsed like a sack of potatoes, then splashed into the pool, going under and not rising again.

'Holy Gerda,' Zar wheezed as she crawled up out of the hot pool and lay on the side, panting as hard as she could, trying to force air down her tortured throat while Adefar slipped properly into her. The pool turned pink as Kyu and Doba's blood flowed from their shattered faces. They slipped to the bottom, unmoving.

She's a sorceress, she might yet live . . .

But to kill in cold blood wasn't something she had ever thought she could do, not even if she had a sword or a gun, which she didn't. All she had was the stone, and she doubted she had the strength to lift Kyu up and out of the water so that she could strike her.

She'll drown in a minute, she told herself.

Watching fearfully for any sign of life, she staggered to the pile of clothes and dressed before flopping into a seat to take stock. Neither body in the pool moved. She could still hear Kuia remonstrating with the warrior outside, her voice furious, the man's contemptuous.

She wanted to scream, to cry, to curl up in a ball and wish it all away – but she couldn't, because this was her one chance to get away and warn her father.

The other warrior is outside and I can't guarantee defeating him ... Kuia's trying, but she's on Onkado's side, not mine: she'll protect me, but she won't let me escape.

Praying she'd given Kyu enough time to drown, she went to the door through which the matron and her daughter had escaped and steeling herself, gently eased it open. The two women in the next room gaped fearfully when they saw her. They had to have heard the struggle – the walls were flimsy in Tangato houses – but that it was Zar who'd survived, not Kyu, clearly stunned them.

Well, it stuns me too, she admitted to herself. *But I have to give them a reason not to scream and raise the alarm ...*

So she put her finger to her lips and with Adefar's translation, said, in Tangato, 'Kyu and Doba want to be left alone. Understand?'

The matron nodded fearfully. 'Not disturb them, no.' Zar thought she read sympathy in the woman's eyes, as if she guessed the truth.

'Ae, not for an hour,' Zar told her. Then she took off her silk robe, which was far too conspicuous, and gave it to the daughter, saying, 'This is yours now.' She took a rough hide cloak from a hook on the wall, draped it round her shoulders, and with a finger to her lips, unlatched the back door and walked out.

Inside a minute, the bathhouse, where Kuia was still kicking up a very vocal fuss, was a hundred yards away, obscured by other houses.

Another five minutes, and Zar entered a copse of trees that backed up against the edge of the village. She chose a path which took her into a low gully and off the skyline. No alarms had yet been raised, her prayers answered ... for now.

It was nearing midday and the marching warriors she'd seen earlier were probably only an hour or two from launching their attack on the city.

Father's people will be mostly facing the bridge – an attack from the north might not be seen until it's too late.

With that fear uppermost, she began to run, following the stream towards the waterfall which fed into the ravine surrounding Rath Argentium.

Raythe looked up anxiously as the distant drums rolled over the crater rim above. It was midday: the Tangato build-up in front of the bridge was clear, but there had been no fighting yet, and they'd had no sign of Ikendo.

The rainbow of light still speared out of the southwest, striking the floating citadel above. It was glowing vividly, despite the sunlight, and Shiazar was worried.

'Jinkatia told no one it still worked, but I've read of them,' she'd told him. 'When it appears completely solid, it is ready for use. That will be soon.'

I'm needed at the gatehouse, but I have to be here.

He'd been rotating between the cavern where Gravis was making the activated istariol, Lynd Borger's makeshift smithy in a building beside the Rim House and here at the stone platform, helping Shiazar and Rima to fuse the final pieces of stone into place – and he could *feel* time running out.

Everything I've heard about Ikendo suggests decisiveness: he could strike at any moment.

Raythe had also been gaining an insight into just how weak he was, compared to the Aldar Queen and the Tangato sorceress. Rima might be almost half his age, but she could conjure in any way required, proteus, mundeus or menteus. And the Queen was even more imposing, because she required no familiar. *And as well as Ikendo and Onkado, there're another twenty-odd Yokei out there who can do the same.* He was ridiculously overmatched.

'What do those drums mean?' he asked Shiazar.

The Queen, masked and regal, looked up. 'It's a call to arms. An attack is imminent.'

He wavered again, longing to run to the gates, but there was more to do here. They needed to help Jesco and Kemara before it was too late – and maybe, if it could be done, the citadel's weaponry might be brought to bear: that would change the tide. He decided he was in the right place for now.

Standing back, he examined the platform critically. They'd been labouring all morning, rebuilding the shattered stone disc, and now the slots were ready for the copper rods and activated istariol. 'Are we ready?' he asked Shiazar.

She was masked, her expression hidden but her voice certain. 'It's ready. I'll be riding it too, so I wish it to succeed as much as you. Shall we inspect the istariol, Milord?'

Despite the impending crisis, he found the Queen endlessly fascinating. As they went, he asked, 'My familiar gives me the energy I need for sorcery – how do you cope without one?'

Her mask tilted his way. 'I am Aldar and our powers are innate, as natural as breathing. I am a conduit for the energy; it takes little from me.'

'I am deeply envious,' he confessed. 'Even my daughter is stronger than me now. Do you realise that the knowledge that the maho is superior to both praxis and mizra is potentially worth more than all the istariol in your lands?'

'So if I give you that knowledge, you'll relinquish your claim to the istariol?' Shiazar enquired archly.

'Um, I'd need to think on that. I may have over-enthused . . .'

She laughed, a tinkling sound like the high notes on a xylophone. 'I admire enthusiasm. But I understand the process is dangerous and even if successful, it can incapacitate one for days, so you're better to make enquiry of Rima after this current crisis is done.'

That quelled his impetuousness, but not his curiosity. 'But how–?'

Shiazar made an impatient gesture. 'I'm at your service, but *later*, Milord.'

They reached the nearest mine tunnel, where Gravis Tavernier was bent over a large tray of istariol and water flecked with blue-green copper verdigris. He and the four children helping him looked mesmerised by the fluid, which was rippling constantly as the lighter particles fought to the top, fused with the verdigris and were then dragged back down.

'This is incredible,' the innkeeper exclaimed. 'I've never seen aught like it.'

'*Amazing*,' the wide-eyed children chorused – then they saw the masked Shiazar and went rigid with awe.

Gravis looked up too and squawked, 'Ah, yer Maj'sty–' His tufty grey hair was almost standing on end in fright.

'Kon'ika, Master Tavernier,' Shiazar replied, in stilted Magnian. 'How does it proceed?'

'I, uh, it proceeds well, ma'am,' Gravis stammered. 'It be workin', I reckon . . . brewin' up like a bitch, as we say in . . . *Oh Gerda* . . . Pardon me tongue, Majesty–'

'It's all right, Gravis,' Raythe put in, examining the festering brew with interest. 'Her Majesty is very impressed. But we need more verdigris.'

Gravis shouted and the children scrambled to bring more of the greenish-blue powder they'd been scraping from ancient statues and water fittings, mostly, as well as some they'd manufactured from soaking untarnished copper in a fluid Raythe had put together.

At first the new flakes floated on the surface, but when Shiazar began to conjure, they began to swirl before vanishing beneath. The mixture turned violet . . . and then larger lumps of green paste rose through the liquid and floated an inch above the surface.

Gravis and his young aides watched awestruck, and Raythe was just as impressed, for he hadn't known that one could speed the process. 'It is an education to watch you, Milady.'

'Oh, I'm learning too,' she answered graciously. 'Now, about the copper rods–'

A sharp *boom*, like the crack of a bombard, crashed over the city and cut off her words.

They all hurried to the mouth of the cave and looked up – and saw a chilling sight: the rainbow spear of light had turned opalescent and was now shining brighter than the planetary rings at night.

'Your Majesty, does that mean what I think?' Raythe murmured.

Shiazar nodded. 'Ae. The Bridge of Izanami is complete.'

'How long will they take to get to the citadel?' he asked, thinking, *She said it was ten miles away earlier, so perhaps three hours, at a brisk walk?*

She crushed his hopes. 'Such devices propel their users. I would say twenty minutes.'

Holy Krag—

He whirled and rushed back to the istariol, snapping, 'Damn it, we *have* to speed this up – Majesty, please, *anything* you can do. Gravis, stay here and gather all the floating green istariol and bring it to the platform. I'll get Lynd—'

Then he heard shouting and ran to the entrance, where he saw the blacksmith running down the crater path, clutching long copper rods, and Rima was sprinting to join them from below.

Then the rattle of musketry rose over the rim, from the direction of the bridge.

Shit – they've started! Dear Gerda, what I wouldn't give to be in two places at once—

But that was impossible. The real question was what to do next. *Do I let the Queen and Rima go alone to the fortress above – which will mean that no matter who wins, the fortress is in Tangato hands?*

Or do I trust Elgus and Cal to hold the bridge without a sorcerer's help?

Damn . . .

During the rebellion, caught up in the unceasing dilemmas of command, he'd made decisions like this time and again, always knowing that even if his choices might prove to be disastrous, they had to be made.

He turned to Shiazar as Rima reached them. 'Majesty, you and I will ascend to the fortress, if we can get this platform to move. Rima, report to Elgus Rhamp at the gatehouse.'

His motives were transparent and Rima said angrily, 'My place is with my Queen. You protect your own people.'

He faced Shiazar. 'Your Majesty?'

The Aldar woman studied him, then said calmly, 'As you wish, Lord Vyre.'

Rima's face twisted in shock. 'But your Maj—'

'*Rima*, I will be safe. Go now, and make your ancestors proud.

The Tangato girl gave Raythe an acid glare. 'My Queen's life is in your hands.' she said, before turning and surging away up the slope.

Raythe turned to Shiazar. 'I suspect it's my life in *your* hands, Majesty. Thank you for backing me.'

'You're welcome,' she said formally, then she bowed and hurried back into the cavern and the bubbling trays of istariol.

Raythe shouted, 'Gravis – if you and the children spill a drop, I'll turn you all into kragging toads.' Then he turned as sweating Lynd Borger lumbered up with the copper rods. 'Lynd, come on – and *run*.'

They pounded down the slope to the broken platform while the Bridge of Light above pulsed and the wind brought the sounds of battle.

Something was missing inside him, but Banno Rhamp couldn't say what. Fearing for Zar was the obvious thing, but it was more than that. Ever since Rima's club had cracked down on his skull, he'd felt trapped in a half-life, his alert moments dotted between long blanks of blurred waking hours he couldn't remember, or dreamless sleep.

I couldn't protect Zar, and now she's surely dead, he thought, over and over again. *When Crowfoot revolted, I was helpless, in the hands of others. I'm less than a man . . .*

Maybe he was being too hard on himself, but it was how he felt. His head was fuzzy and his thoughts scrambled. And now a hopeless battle loomed, one in which he was desperate to prove himself, but in all likelihood no one would survive to notice whatever he did.

Only Deo will see me die . . .

Caught up in his misery, he barely noticed his father prowling below, shouting orders and encouragement. The men manning the gates looked heartened, or were pretending to be, but Banno found himself wishing it was already over – then came a booming *crack!* and the rainbow spear of light above turned almost solid. For a moment, everyone went silent, then the questions burst out–

'What is it?'

'It's a spell–'

'No, no, it's a sign. An omen, I tell ye . . .'

Then Elgus pounded up the stairs, shouting, 'Lad, look there!'

He wasn't pointing at the bolt of light, or even the bridge: but across the ravine, away to their left, where a slender figure with short pale hair was bounding along the cliff-top path like a frightened deer, pursued by a cluster of Tangato warriors. She was wearing just a bodice and beaded skirt, her pale skin gleaming in the sunlight.

It's Zar–

Banno's heart thudded to life. *'Gerda Alive!'* he shouted. 'ZAR! ZAR–!'

Somehow, she heard him, but just as she looked up, another group of warriors appeared, cutting her off from the bridge. A few of the men on the walls fired their flintlocks, causing the Tangato to flinch despite the range, and that bought her a moment to evade her nearest assailant, right at the edge of the cliff.

'ZAR!' Banno leaped from the turret to the next level down as more men fired across the ravine, but at two hundred yards, accuracy was impossible. He reached the outer parapet and barrelled along the walkway, trying to get level with Zar, still calling her name.

She must have heard him, because he heard her shriek, 'NORTH SIDE–!'

Then she dodged the converging men and hurled herself off the edge of the ravine, arcing like a comet, then plunged head-first into the churning waters below.

A moment later, three Tangato followed her.

Banno whirled and screamed at his father, *'NORTH SIDE – THEY'RE ATTACKING THE NORTH SIDE!'*

Then he dropped his flintlock, ditched his sword belt, took a deep breath – and threw himself out into space.

3

Dig Your Own Grave

Elgus Rhamp twisted around, caught between emergencies. The sentries beside him were shouting, 'Men on the bridge! Men on the bridge!' but far to the left, where a watchtower overlooked the confluence, a fire-arrow had been launched into the air.

And his son's last words as he hurled himself into the river were echoing in Elgus' mind.

Northside . . . What did he mean by that?

As a soldier, his first responsibility was the defences he'd been assigned; much as he hated to abandon his last surviving son, Banno was on his own. But if the north side of the city was breached, that was critical.

Elgus sent a fervent prayer to the god he didn't believe in as he pounded down to the barricade below, grabbed Cal Foaley and shouted, 'It's not just here – the docks at the confluence have signalled and Zarelda Vyre says they're also attacking the north side . . .'

'Zar?' The hunter's eyes narrowed. 'How?'

'I don't know or care, but if she's right, that's where they'll hit hardest. No way these bastards would try the bridge for real, not after last time. This is just a feint.'

Foaley bared teeth. 'They've got enough men to make every attack dangerous.'

Elgus read his indecision: the hunter was more than capable, but he had always worked alone and was unused to making snap decisions involving others.

But I'm not.

'We'll hold the bridge lightly,' he told him. 'Send half a dozen men to the docks; that'll be a feint as well. I'll take sixty men straight up and round the crater to the north side.'

'Good,' Foaley agreed, 'but *I'll* take the men to the north side. You couldn't shift your fat arse up that hill fast enough.'

Elgus glared – then chuckled as he realised Foaley was both joking and serious. 'Sure, I'd rather face a thousand tribals on my own than climb that kraggin' hill anyway. Get ye gone, man!'

Foaley bared teeth in a sort-of grin, then began pulling men out of the lines. He sent the first small group to the docks, then picked his sixty. As they headed off in a clatter, Elgus took control of the remainder, almost all his mercenaries and a bunch of Teshveld villagers.

'The tribals are coming, boys,' he roared. 'Tool up!'

'They're Tangato,' some skinny villager retorted. 'Raythe Vyre says so.'

'Yeah?' Elgus snorted. 'While they're fixing to kill us, I'll call them what I kragging like! Look to your priming and get your reloads ready. The Pit's opening, and we'll be filling it.'

The motley mix of villagers and mercenaries gave him anxious looks, but they got busy, while behind them, a mix of young men and women – *women fighting, for Deo's sake!* – stacked up the reloads in readiness.

Then a movement caught his eye and for a second his heart almost stopped, seeing a Tangato right behind them. Then he recognised the sorceress, Rima, who'd appeared behind the gatehouse, breathing hard. Rima waved and pressed through the crowd of labouring men and women, ignoring the alarm she caused, and joined him.

'Sir Elgus?' she panted. 'Lord Vyre thinks you need my help.'

He eyed her up: just a native girl barely out of her teens, wearing nothing but a grass skirt and a wrap to hide her teats. *But she's a sorceress . . .*

'As long as you're up for killin' yer own kind,' he growled.

Her eyes narrowed, but she replied, 'I'll do what must be done.'

'Then get up that tower and help the lads keep that bridge clear o' tribals.'

She scowled at the contempt in his words, but obeyed without another word. He followed, because the tower was the best vantage point, wondering if she really was here to help, or to undermine them. *One wrong move and I'll put a ball in the back of her head*, he resolved.

Across the bridge, he heard the Tangato bellow their war-cries. For a moment he missed the steadying hands of Crowfoot and Bloody Thom, but they'd dug their own graves.

Time to dig mine.

Banno hit the water like a sack of potatoes, but at least it was feet-first, with his nose pinched and a mouthful of air. But the shock of the frigid water almost caused him to empty his lungs, and his boots and clothes immediately dragged him down. As the dark churning swirl buffeted him head over tail, sucking him downwards, he fought off his boots and shirt, then clawed his way back to the surface, almost out of air.

He'd learned to float as a child, but never really to swim, and he fell swiftly behind the quartet of heads bobbing along ahead of him. The one in front was blonde, though, and adrenalin blasted the fog from his mind as he went thrashing after them.

Then an arrow scythed past his face; he looked up and saw another shaft rip past him from the south side of the ravine: Tangato archers.

With a squawk he twisted and dived again, keeping his eyes open to scan the clear but darkened water. The current was slackening where this western river was surging towards the confluence with the eastern river. He had a dagger in his belt scabbard . . . but Zar and the Tangato were drawing further away.

Then he remembered that there was a whirlpool where the rivers met and disappeared into an underground tunnel that wouldn't emerge for five miles.

Anyone who goes in there will die . . . and Zar will reach it first.

He redoubled his efforts, kicking furiously and windmilling his arms, desperate to reach her before her pursuers, but the exertion was telling and Varahana's warnings about not overdoing things were loud in his head.

I could die in this torrent, he realised, but he fought on. *If I do, it'll be for her.*

Zarelda tried to engage Adefar as she dropped, but she hit the water before she could articulate any spells, and then it was impossible beneath the water. The impact ripped her bodice and skirt away as she plunged deep, naked in the blackness and fighting shock from the cold.

But her father had ensured she knew how to swim, and water was an element she'd always loved, so she didn't panic but flowed on downstream towards the landings . . . and the confluence.

Then she saw a dark head behind her, and after him three more, further behind. The nearest was a Manowai warrior with blazing eyes and murder on his face. But it was who she'd seen across the ravine that filled her mind.

Dear Gerda – that was Banno!

She'd had only one thought: to reach the bridge and warn her father – but of course there were watchers, and she'd been running for her life. Now she was being swept towards the treacherous whirlpools of the confluence, a place even Adefar feared . . .

Bobbing up and gulping down some air, she tried paddling while shrieking instructions to Adefar, but he couldn't follow her intent and she couldn't shape hand-signals and swim, so for now sorcery was impossible – and her pursuers were closing in.

She risked a glance back and saw the nearest Manowai swimming powerfully after her. He had a bone knife in his teeth, hands like scoops and he'd reach her in a second—

—so she did what she hoped was the unexpected: she plunged underwater, reversed and went straight at him, slamming into him before he saw her. His eyes bulged as she ripped the knife from his teeth and stabbed it into his chest. He shrieked into the water, clutched at the wound as blood gushed everywhere, then she kicked off him and thrashed away with the knife still in her hand, both appalled at herself and exulting at the same time.

Another man came at her, his tattooed face a mask of ferocity, but she clamped the weapon between her own teeth to free her hands, and dived, going *down-down-down*.

The dead man was already floating away, trailing blood, but the next man had followed her into the depths. Running out of air, she kicked away and rose like a leaping salmon, streaming towards the surface . . .

. . . then his hand closed on her ankle, and as they broke the surface, she grabbed for the knife – but he grasped her wrist, twisted – and the blade fell from her hands. Then he thrust her under before she could inhale, and suddenly she was drowning, her mind shrieking and Ade-far wailing–

Then the warrior's head jerked amidst a spray of blood, she clawed free of his suddenly limp grip and shot up, bursting from the water as the echo of a gunshot filled the ravine. Fifty feet above her on the city walls, a long gun barrel was venting black smoke.

But two more dark shapes were closing in and there was no way up the cliffs here.

Gerda, help me, she pleaded as she dived again, swimming with all the strength she could muster, somehow staying ahead of the third Tangato . . . then she saw a terrifying sight ahead: a long silvery funnel beneath the surface, thrashing like the tail of a snake as it sucked in floating debris: the maelstrom at the heart of the confluence. The current was dragging her towards it, but as she turned and fought her way sideways, her remaining pursuers converged on her.

Two lead balls speared through the water on either side of the nearest chaser, but he was coming at her too fast to evade. Almost spent, she lashed out with her feet and caught him, cracking his head back, and using that momentum to surface again. The roar of the confluence was deafening, the tug of the current almost more than she could resist.

But was that a fishing platform, just ahead?

'*Zar!*' someone shouted, and a rope came snaking down and hit the water. She lunged for it – but a brown body burst up from below and wrapped itself round her, pulling her under again. She thrashed in his grip as the silvery whirlpool opened up below them –

Father! Banno! her mind screamed . . . and then, unexpectedly, treacherously, *Onkado!*

The man holding her was naked as well, and now she could see his youthful, frightened face: Hekami, Kamo's son – and he had just realised the maelstrom was going to swallow them both whole.

He stopped grappling and instead, still clutching hold of her, began to kick frantically for the surface, pulling her with him as her strength waned.

The tail of the whirlpool flicked past their legs, but they pulled free of its tug and exploded up through the surface, gasping for air, clutching each other's shoulders, eyes widening in exultation, as if this were some mad childhood dare they'd just accomplished.

She realised they'd come up within reach of the old docks, jabbing her hand at it and shouting, but Hekami only spoke Reo. He caught her meaning, though, and she realised he was, despite everything, trying to help her. He pulled her along as she did her best to help, then together they managed to get hands onto the stone platform and haul themselves up.

Then they just lay there, stark naked, their sheer exhaustion and relief at being alive making them oblivious to shame or embarrassment. Her heart kept on thumping as she tried to slow her hyperventilating . . .

Then boots crunched right by her head and she looked up, seeing two silhouettes appear from the stairs – and then another shape hauled itself up onto the platform from the river, bare-chested and wheezing.

She and Hekami suddenly realised his peril. They sat up, she covered her breasts with one arm and blinked at the men. 'No, don't shoot!' she gasped. 'He saved me!'

Two gun-hammers clicked, and the newcomer rose and stood over Hekami, water streaming from him as he drew a dagger.

It was Banno.

'You bastard,' he roared, raising his blade as Hekami, flinching, tried to flee.

'No!' she shrieked, trying to rise up and protect the Tangato boy – she liked him, and he'd pulled her from the maelstrom . . .

. . . as Hekami sprang . . .

And perhaps in reflex, Banno's blade slammed down into his back – then one of the guns roared, a lead ball punched into Hekami's side and the impact pitched him into the river . . .

Zar wailed as Banno roared in triumph, and Hekami vanished into the depths in a cloud of bloodied water.

The path opened fully with a deafening boom, the whirling spheres turning so fast they became invisible to the naked eye. Peering along it, Onkado could see that a tunnel of light had opened, a perfect circle running straight and true up a gentle slope towards the citadel of Shiro Kamigami ten miles away.

When Jinkatia stepped into that whirling mechanism, Onkado cried aloud, fully expecting to see his grandmother chopped to pieces, but a moment later she was inside, turning triumphantly and beckoning. She'd always been a source of awe and terror in his life, but at that moment, she was a goddess.

Ikendo didn't hesitate, striding past the other five Yokei and stepping through the hole in creation to stand beside his mother, where he went down on one knee and kissed her hand. The quailing warriors pulled themselves together and cheered lustily as Onkado followed.

It was a frightening experience, placing his life into their hands, but with head held high as befitted a warrior prince, he stepped into the swirling opening. He felt a breeze pass right through him, chilling him to the core – and then he was with his grandmother and father.

For once, there was approval on Ikendo's face.

Even the Yokei were scared, Onkado sensed, cowering behind their serene masks, held together only by Jinkatia's determination. But they and the twenty terrified warriors filed onto the path, and Ikendo drew his curved bronze sword and indicated the sloping path.

'Onwards to victory,' he said.

Onkado suspected his father had one eye on the histories that would be written of this moment, the songs that would be sung.

They began walking, a strange and giddy sensation, as if an unfelt tailwind was sweeping them along. Rainbow light flashed as they passed. In seconds, the roaring mechanism was left behind and the only sound was the rush of air hurtling them across the sky.

It was probably half an hour, but it felt like no time at all to Onkado before they were losing momentum and he was stepping through a metal ring three times a man's height and onto a turreted tower on the outer walls of Shiro Kamigami.

By all the gods – we're here . . .

As his father caught him by the shoulder and steadied him, he looked up and saw the exterior of the citadel, a tall, elegant building with many curves and flourishes, pure Aldar work. One tower in particular drew the eye: covered with a relief carving of a giant Aldar lord, standing like a sentinel, staring out over the southern reaches of the Fenua Tangato. It was weathered, stained by time, but enduring.

Looking back and down, he saw the edge of the floating rock upon which the castle was built, and the land far below. It was a vertiginous sensation, to see the expanse of the lost city of Rath Argentium. A rattling, cracking sound reached his ears from the gatehouse and the great bridge, where dark shapes were swarming forwards. The attack had begun.

He'd not seen the gaikiko fire-weapon in action yet, but those who had spoke of noisy metal tubes that hurled round metal balls so fast that they could kill at a huge distance. After what Zarelda had told him about her people's weaponry, he'd argued against the attack, but his father had refused to listen.

Father only ever listens to Kotabashi, and now sixty men are dead. But we are ten thousand and they are just a few hundred, the scouts say, so we will triumph. I just pray that the cost is not too high.

He had to hope that the grief of losing her people wouldn't blight his new wife's spirit, but his inner voice taunted, *How can she come to care for me, after my people slaughter everyone she knows and loves? Father is right – I'm just a foolish boy.*

He silenced that inner voice angrily and focused on what was happening around him. Seeing Jinkatia and Ikendo were helping the Yokei and Manowai warriors to dismount through the portal, he hurried to help.

Once they were all safely standing on the tower, Jinkatia touched a stone panel on the wall and the tunnel of light faded, revealing a smaller sphere of interlocking rings that began to slow in their spinning, the energy powering them fading away.

Everyone was looking around in awe, even the masked Yokei, their expressions hidden but their gestures hesitant as they all took in the sweeping panorama below and the ancient, moss-covered castle above. Jinkatia herself seemed stunned, as if even her gigantic dreams had failed to prepare her for this moment.

'This is your triumph, Mother,' Ikendo said. 'You brought me into the world for this.'

'You are the heir of Vashtariel,' Jinkatia said firmly. 'Welcome home.'

While his father put fist to chest and bowed his head, marking the moment, Onkado studied the exterior of the fortress. Sunlight shone on a raised walkway overlooking gardens long gone wild. The citadel itself was strangely difficult to look at, the light on it blurring oddly. He'd heard the tales of mass murder and madness in the last days of Tashvariel the Usurper, and not even Jinkatia knew what might await them up here, for no one had been inside the forbidden citadel in centuries.

Ikendo motioned Onkado to his side, formed up the warriors in a loose circle around the Yokei and called them all to attention. 'Take off your masks,' he commanded the Yokei. 'The ancient Aldar went barefaced up here, in the heart of their realm. We are here to reclaim it.'

They were reluctant, until Jinkatia removed her own mask, revealing her flat, timeless features and graceful tattoos. Her hair might be tinged with grey, but only a few crow's feet about the eyes hinted at her age. The Yokei unwillingly followed suit until all were bare-faced – and the Manowai warriors, overcome with awe, dropped to their knees, smiting their chests and declaring that they would die protecting their Aldar lords.

I pray it won't come to that, Onkado reflected, *but this place is said to be cursed.*

'Kindred,' Ikendo said grandly, 'this is Shiro Kamigami, the Citadel of the God-Kings. Below us is Rath Argentium, our ancestral home. To rule down there, we must rule up here, so let us make it our own.' He turned to his mother. 'Jinkatia-san, tell us what you know.'

She raised her head. 'Several nights ago, our scouts reported a loud sound from within the city. I believe that something large and heavy fell from this rock into the crater – perhaps a natural event, but it is also possible that the gaikiko invaders below have found a way up here. I have looked from afar and seen strange lights from within, for the first time ever. There were other means of egress to allow goods and servants to move between the citadel and the city: I believe the gaikiko invaders have found one.'

'Shiazar knows of these things,' Yokei Bekinta muttered. 'She will come here.'

'And we will slay her,' Ikendo interrupted. 'We will search this castle from top to bottom, as swiftly as possible, and I will have her head before this day is done.'

'Ae, we must move swiftly,' Jinkatia agreed. 'I have studied the old maps and have some understanding of the layout. This walkway will take us to the ground floor of the castle. Below are several levels – the servants' quarters, stores and armouries – and above-ground are the Aldar living quarters. The last Aldar to come here described the castle as "perilous and strange", but she gave no explanation. But in all likelihood, all we'll find are old bones – and perhaps Shiazar and her gaikiko allies.'

'What of the renowned defences of this castle?' Ikendo asked.

'Ae, those tales are true,' Jinkatia said. 'It is said that the Aldar rained fire down on the armies below, and that the key to those defences is in

322

a secret chamber. We must seek that out and secure it, before our enemies do.'

The warriors took that in nervously, fearful of being caught in the
midst of a sorcerous battle. Ikendo reassured them – he had always
been better with his fighting men than his wife and his son – while
Onkado sidled up to Jinkatia.

'Grandmother, we will need to divide our forces, enough to deal with
the gaikiko, if they're here, while the others seek the hidden chamber.'

'I agree,' she replied, giving him an approving look. 'We Yokei train to
fight in threes, which is why there are six of us. My three will accompany
you and your father; the other three will seek and destroy Shiazar.'

'And the foreigners,' Onkado cautioned. 'Don't forget they are led by
a sorcerer.'

'A poor one, I am assured,' Jinkatia replied. 'His daughter, your
"wife", was pathetic when she joined us. Vyre will be similarly weak.'

Onkado wasn't reassured – Zarelda had spoken of her father as a
seasoned commander – but he bowed his head.

Ikendo joined them. 'We will proceed indoors as planned, Mother.'
He faced Onkado. 'This is our moment, Son. Our greatest test. Make me
proud.'

Do I ever manage that? Onkado wondered.

Ikendo took the lead – no one could ever question his bravery – and
everyone drew weapons and followed, winding their way through the
gardens to the citadel, where massive double doors yielded to Jinkatia's
touch.

As they swung open, a vast hall was revealed: a massive open space
with a throne at the far end, with high stained-glass windows on either
side, through which light played strangely, as if the sunlight was flowing through it too slowly, lending the hall a strange lustre. When
Onkado focused on a long, thin beam of light from a narrow upper
window, he could almost swear that it trailed a sparkling luminesce. He
noticed something similar as his father led the way in, as if he was
trailing a tiny tail of light behind him for half a second.

'Was that a breeze?' Ikendo asked, and his voice sounded strange.

Jinkatia stopped, looking round with a troubled, puzzled expression, mirrored by her fellow Yokei. 'Grandmother?' Onkado asked.

She gestured for quiet, and her fingers trailed soft sparks as she did. The other Yokei saw and flinched, and the scared warriors clustered together.

'What is it?' Ikendo asked, coming to a halt.

'Let me think.' She motioned everyone forward, but her face remained troubled.

As they went deeper into the hall, it felt to Onkado like walking into a faint breeze – but the air wasn't moving at all, judging by the motionless old banners and cobwebs – which weren't nearly as decayed as Onkado thought they should be after five centuries. Old sarcophagi were arrayed in alcoves along the walls, topped by life-size bronzes of armoured Aldar warriors, coated in dust and yet eerily poised on the edge of motion.

Ikendo led them to a central staircase, halfway down the hall, where he stiffened. 'Look,' he said, pointing to obvious disturbances in the dust.

'Two sets of footprints,' Onkado said, dropping to his haunches to see. 'One a full-grown man, the other a woman, judging by the size and the shape of the soles. They came from over there' – he gestured to a large doorway to the right – 'and they went up these stairs. They haven't returned, at least, not this way.'

'Just two?' Jinkatia murmured, looking upwards into the twilit gloom. No sounds floated down and nothing moved. 'And they've not returned?'

'No,' Onkado confirmed. 'Raythe Vyre and Shiazar, perhaps?'

'Why just two? And why are they still up there?' Ikendo wondered out loud.

'Perhaps they've only just beaten us here?' suggested Unaji, Jinkatia's apprentice. 'Perhaps they split their forces? So only two came this far and there are more below?'

It's possible, Onkado thought. 'But what about this?' Looking at Jinkatia, he flashed his hand across his face, leaving a trail of afterimages.

His grandmother looked unusually anxious. 'I can only deduce that this citadel has been placed under a temporal interdict.' When Onkado and Ikendo looked blank, she murmured, 'Think of it as a place frozen in time.'

Ikendo looked baffled; despite his heritage, he was impatient with deep thinking and complex matters.

But Onkado thought he understood. 'Then by entering it, we could lose hours, maybe days . . .' A chill thought struck him. 'Maybe *years*?'

Jinkatia nodded unwillingly, then turned to Ikendo. 'Great King, I counsel that we go no further, until I can investigate.'

Ikendo's simmering anger resurfaced. 'Are you saying we've come here for nothing? He pointed up the stairs. 'Our enemies have gone ahead of us. They may seize control of the citadel. We must press on.'

Jinkatia gave him a vexed look, but Onkado wasn't surprised: his belligerent, impatient father had been waiting for this moment all his life and he wasn't going to stop unless the threat to life and limb was clear and obvious.

Fighting down his own misgivings, he walked to the doors from where the dusty footprints emerged and peered down into a cylindrical stairwell. All was dark and quiet, and when he passed his hand across his face, there was no trailing afterimage.

'It's all clear here,' he called, examining the doorway. There was a faint film of light in the doorframe. 'The "time interdict" begins here. I believe the lower levels are free of it.'

Giving his mother a vindicated look, Ikendo took charge. Turning to Sekana, who was leading the other trio of Yokei, he said, 'Take your group downwards, checking from level to level. We will wait here while Jinkatia seeks a way to break this spell.'

'And if we encounter any of the gaikiko?' Sekana asked.

'You will kill them.' He turned to the captain of his warriors, Noroda. 'I place the lives of these Yokei in your hands.'

Noroda put his fist to his chest reverently, then mustered his men and led Sekana and her two Yokei out of the door Onkado had examined.

Onkado re-joined his father and watched, fascinated, as Jinkatia, Unaji and Eni faced the stairs, raised their hands and prepared an exploratory spell to better understand what magic they faced, and how to destroy it.

That started him wondering whether they should, a question no one else appeared in the least bit interested in.

It was no task for haste, but they were out of time. Trying to ignore the distant musketry echoing round the crater, Raythe forced himself to be precise and patient as he and Shiazar filled each copper rod with activated istariol. They had to hold on to them carefully to prevent them from shooting upwards into the air before they could be locked into the spoke-like grooves in the repaired stone disc. It took only a few minutes, but with the fate of the city at stake, each minute felt like hours.

'Last one,' chirped Gravis, as he and Lynd lowered the final rod into position. Then the four children helping them *oo-ed* and *ah-ed* as Shiazar gestured and the stone flowed in to encase them securely.

'Now the plinth, please, Majesty,' Raythe said tersely.

Shiazar had already repaired the control plinth, inserting more of the copper rods to channel energy into the activated istariol. Now she gestured and the big lump of shaped stone rose and floated back into place on the dais, leaving the blacksmith and the innkeeper gazing at her in awe and admiration.

'Could use yer skills in me smithy, Maj'sty,' Lynd remarked.

Shiazar, her expression hidden, replied, 'If ever I should find myself needing employment, I shall bear it in mind.'

Lynd ducked his head shyly, and Gravis snorted.

She has the common touch, Raythe mused. *I like that . . . although I doubt she cares what any of us think.*

Out of the corner of his eye, he caught the great arched shaft of light winking out. 'Did you see that?' he asked Shiazar anxiously.

'I did,' she replied calmly. 'It means they've either finished using the Bridge, or it failed. I suspect the former.'

Holy Gerda . . . so we're likely to face the enemy up there, and sorcerers at that.

There was no point in summoning some armed men to accompany them; no one could be spared from the attacks on the gatehouse.

Shiazar and I are going to have to suffice until we find Kemara and Jesco.

Gravis and Lynd backed away as Shiazar gracefully ascended the platform and touched the control panel. The platform shook, then rose a few inches. 'It's holding together,' she noted. 'Lord Vyre, are you coming?'

Yet again he found himself thinking, *My people are down here and they need me – but if I don't go up there, we cede the keystone of the defences . . .* But Rima was at the bridge: the decision had effectively been made when he sent her. All he was really feeling right now was fear.

Damn it! He hurdled onto the rising platform just in time, landing in a sprawl, then he rolled over and shouted back to Lynd and Gravis, 'Get everyone to Rim House – we'll be back as soon as we can.'

'Aye,' the men shouted, staring back at him, wide-eyed and amazed.

The vertiginous rise took his breath away, so he backed from the edge on hands and knees, wondering if he'd just screwed *everything* up.

Only Kemara and I can meld, he reminded himself. *She and I working together saved us on the beach, and in the glacier. She's the one I have to find . . .*

He looked up at Shiazar. 'Can't this thing go any faster?'

Shiazar surprised him by laughing merrily, then pulling him upright with surprising strength. 'It has only two speeds,' she remarked, with dry irony. 'Up and down.'

Noting they were still clasping hands, he awkwardly withdrew his. 'Erm, sorry, Majesty.'

'You are the first male I have ever had physical contact with,' she said, her mood still strangely amused. 'I shall probably have to be ritually purified on my return.' She gazed out and added, 'Were you having second thoughts about coming?'

'I still don't know if I should have gone to the gatehouse,' he admitted.

'You chose rightly,' Shiazar replied. 'The weapons of Shiro Kamigami can destroy an army. Everything that matters will be decided up there.'

'Maybe, but without me, many will die who should have lived.'

Shiazar lifted her mask as she faced him, perhaps so that her lustrous face might enchant him. If so, it was working. 'I respect your care for them,' she said. 'It speaks well of you. But our main enemies will be up there. We Yokei train to fight in pairs or trios – it is a holy bond we call heito, a state of equality and oneness. To overcome whoever Ikendo and Jinkatia have sent up there, you and I must be hitoshii – equals, fighting as one. You are accustomed to war, but I am not. I need your experience and courage now.'

Raythe sensed that he was being offered something profound, that meant more to her than he could begin to guess. But he was never going to refuse. 'I'm your man,' he told her.

'Perhaps you are?' she said, her expression disturbed, then she replaced her mask and looked away. 'Thank you . . . Raythe.'

What just happened? he wondered. *What did that mean?*

But the rock above was growing ever larger, the circular hole opening like a devouring throat. He pulled his eyes from it as volleys of flintlocks sounded, and saw smoke billowing from the gatehouse facing the bridge, far below. There were tiny dots on the span: Tangato men, creeping forward. But the numbers were too few for them to punch through, unless the defenders ran out of powder.

It's a feint, he realised suddenly. *Does Elgus realise? And where will the real blow land?* He went to the eastern edge of the disc, saw smoke and flashes on the river . . . and then he glanced north and saw more tiny dark shapes massing across the river – and a fire-arrow shot into the air from somewhere upslope: the alarm signal.

They're coming in from the north too – does Elgus realise? Did he see the fire-arrow?

But the dark hole beneath the rock swallowed them, cutting off his view and plunging them into darkness.

He desperately wanted to turn around and go straight back down, but instead, he clung to Shiazar's words: that being up here was just as vital, and maybe even more – and that those below knew what to do. *Basically, we trust the plan, and each other.* It was the tale of every battle he'd ever fought in.

Shiazar conjured light, illuminating the smooth inside of the shaft they were ascending, and they saw the landing above coming closer and closer. Then she snapped, '*Watch out–!*'

Three masked women had appeared at the edge of the shaft, staring down at them. A moment later, before Raythe could ready Cognatus, a torrent of brilliant, deadly light coruscated down.

4

The Hourglass Shatters

For Zar, the next few moments were a nightmare. The men with the guns she could now see were Ando Borger, who looked aghast, and Guy Jagisson, one of Elgus' mercenaries, who'd fired the shot. But it was Hekami's face she still saw, contorted by shock as he fell into the river.

Then Banno threw himself onto her, crushing her against him and gasping in relief, while Ando pulled off a coat and draped it over her shoulders, all the while babbling about how Banno was a hero for killing that *Tangato bastard* and saving her.

'He was rescuing me,' she wailed, but all that came out was sobbing and retching. *I'm safe*, part of her was trying to say, but she just felt sick, remembering Hekami's face, his shy smile, and how she'd danced with him, and that moment just seconds ago, when they'd escaped the flood and thought themselves safe.

They were on an old stone dock at the foot of the cliffs, directly opposite the maelstrom where the two rivers that protected Rath Argentium met before plunging into the underwater tunnel. And gunfire was echoing down the ravine, calling them to war.

'My love, my love,' Banno kept saying – until he caught sight of her tattooed chin and his face went pale. 'What have those animals done to you? Your face is ruined!'

Ruined?

Suddenly, she felt trapped and angry. *I'm not 'ruined'*, she thought, shoving him away and retching up river water until she could finally shriek, '*Hekami saved me, not you!*'

The three young men stared at her blankly.

'Who do you mean?' Banno blurted.

'Hekami – he rescued me and you killed him!'

'He was attacking you,' Banno replied, bewildered. 'I saved you.'

'She's hysterical,' Guy put in. 'Women get like that—'

'I'll kragging give you hysterical, you moron!' she raged, smacking away Banno's hands, fighting her way into Ando's coat and belting it, then stomping to the stairs – and suddenly she was pelting up them, howling inchoately at the cruel stupidity of Deo or Fate or just this damnable world, where good people died in wars that pigs like Ikendo started.

As she ran, arrows began to whistle around her, fired from the opposite cliffs, and she heard Ando and Guy yelp and come running after her. A voice bellowed from somewhere above, shouting, 'Oi, you lot – move it! We're falling back to the Rim House. Hurry it along – the Tangato are attacking everywhere.'

Zar kept on climbing, hearing pursuing feet and not wanting to face them, but Banno was stronger and faster. He caught her at the top of the cliffs, pulling her into the lee of a wall as the archers sought the range.

'What's wrong with you?' he shouted in her face. 'He was an *enemy*—'

'No, he was my *friend*,' she shouted back, struggling in his grasp. *'Let me go!'*

'Zar!'

'Stop it!' she raged, slapping blindly at him.

Then he *hit* her – his right hand smacked across her left cheek, rocking her back against the wall, just as Ando and Guy arrived. Her vision blurred with tears and her cheek burned and throbbed, and the shock of it stunned her.

'That's what you gotta do,' she heard Guy say. 'Hysterical, I tell yer.'

Ando told Banno, 'It's okay, you had to, to shock her out of it . . .'

But realising what he'd done, Banno's face crumpled. He reached for her, blurting apologies, but Zar couldn't face him, couldn't even look at him.

Instead, she ran, and this time he didn't follow.

The suddenness of the attack had caught everyone by surprise and now a column of around eighty women and children, many overburdened with possessions, was spread out along the main thoroughfare.

Varahana was at their head, trying to keep them moving. When they finally reached the crater rim, the priestess leaped onto a plinth where an old statue had once stood and pointed east towards the Rim House, the blockish mansion they'd designated their fall-back position. 'There it is – hurry now!'

Vidar appeared, and jumping up beside her, said, 'Vara, we saw a fire-arrow on the north side–' He broke off and flung out an arm. 'Look – there's another–'

She saw the smoke trail rise above the far rim and realised the Tangato must be outside the northern walls. Turning back to the column of refugees, she screeched, *'Move!'*

Even as they reacted, Cal Foaley and a group of armed men came running up from the gates, overtaking the old folk, women and children.

'Vidar,' the hunter called, 'with me!'

'North side?' Vidar asked, and when Foaley nodded, he seized Varahana by the shoulders. 'It's likely their main attack. I'll be back when I can.'

Varahana was momentarily petrified. *Dear Gerda, he's a bearskin, going to face an unknown foe.* Everything was happening at once, all the fragile tendrils of the new life she'd planted being uprooted. 'Take care,' she urged him. 'Stay calm and–'

He swallowed her up in a bear hug and kissed her mouth, fiercely and hard, drowning her reflexive protests. She struck at his shoulders, struggled . . . and then kissed him back, because he needed it.

And she did too.

When neither could breathe, he pulled away and stared down at her, clearly uncertain whether he'd broken their relationship or cemented it. She didn't know either, but his arms felt wonderfully safe.

But she smacked his shoulder again. 'Let me go, you fool. I have to get this lot inside.' And to make sure he didn't misunderstand, she added, 'Don't you *dare* get killed.'

She didn't want to release him, but they were on a plinth and dozens of oldsters, women and children, not to mention Foaley's fighting men, were all staring up at her, their sworn virgin priestess, with gaping eyes and open mouths.

'If we get out of this, I'll kiss you all,' she shouted. 'Now go – with Deo's blessing, *go!*'

Vidar cast off his furs and joined Foaley at the head of the column, and they stormed away westwards around the lip of the rim, while the refugees went east, towards the Rim House.

'Deo, Gerda, be with us,' she prayed, while thinking, *At least five thousand against barely two hundred and fifty . . . only Deo can save us now.* Then she cast her eyes skywards. *Or maybe, Raythe Vyre . . .*

Vidar found himself loping along with his heart pounding in exhilaration. He hadn't danced in a lifetime, but with the taste of beautiful, sophisticated Varahana on his tongue, he could have pounded out a Ferrean jig right then and there.

I was living just to do that. But that was just a small, easily sated part of him – the rest wanted to savour many more years to come, with her beside him.

How and when he'd fallen this stupidly in love with a priestess, he couldn't say. But he'd never met anyone like her: erudite, drily funny, wise and brave – and something about her face made his heart beat faster. Even her shaven scalp accentuated her mystique. And now, out here where they made their own rules, who knew what the future could be?

If they had a future at all.

Don't you dare get killed, she'd told him.

Foaley caught him up, panting, 'Slow down, big man. You're leaving us behind.' Then he gave him a sly grin. 'Pleased to see some religious devotion from you at last.'

'Kissing a priestess is an old Norgan pre-battle tradition,' Vidar lied. 'How'd you get here so fast? Those fire-arrows only just went up.'

'We got warning – Vyre's daughter's escaped.'

Vidar clenched a triumphant fist at the unexpected tidings, but in truth, it was a small drop of good news in an ocean of trouble. 'If it's any kind of real attack on the north side, there'll be thousands of them – we'll not be able to hold the walls against so many.'

'Our job is to find out what we face and delay them if we can,' Foaley said grimly. 'Elgus Rhamp's got the bridge and he'll do the same. But it's all just playing for time. Without Vyre, we're screwed.' He cast his eyes upwards to the massive floating rock. 'I just hope he sees the shit we're in and comes back. Whatever's up there is worthless if we're all butchered down here.'

'I hear you, but if Raythe's gone up there, it's for a reason.'

'He's pulled us through so far, I'll allow that. Jus' hope he ain't run out of miracles.'

So do I, Vidar prayed.

They led their column to the northern edge of the crater rim and looked down the slope. Unlike the southern side, where they'd found many largely intact dwellings, this section was entirely ruined, as if some terrible wind had scoured it, leaving bare slopes of shattered rock down to the walls and a broken bridge over the river-moat.

Hurrying towards them were the three north-side duty sentries, led by Rix Morro. The scout was red-faced and frightened. 'Hey, Rix,' Foaley called. 'Was that your fire-arrows?'

'It was.' Rix pointed back down the slope. 'Hundreds of 'em, coming right after us.'

They all squinted and saw the first Tangato pouring over the walls and into the streets.

'Just hundreds?' Vidar asked hopefully.

'More like thousands,' Rix admitted. 'They had wicker boats – they piled across the river in no time. We was lucky to get out.'

'Do we fight 'em here?' the mercenary Falgram asked. The crater rim had a wall all the way round, but there was nowhere to retreat except down into the vast pit behind them.

Foaley glanced at Vidar, who was shaking his head, then faced his squad. 'Lads, there's just sixty of us. It'd be foolish. The agreed rallying point if we're breached is the Rim House. That's where we're pulling back our people now. Our job's to make sure everyone gets inside.'

'Trap ourselves outside, ye mean?' complained Matty Varte, who had a history of running from fights. 'We've got better odds playin' hide and seek with 'em in the ruins.'

'You plannin' to sneak off again?' Vidar growled. 'Like at Frozen Bay?'

A hostile murmur rose round them and Varte blanched. 'Nah, I'm wi' you lads.'

'Good. Here's what we do,' Foaley said. 'We give 'em a few long-range volleys from here to slow them down, then peel off in tens and go back round the rim in a fighting retreat – and then, yes, Matty, those what can't get into the Rim House can harass them all they like. I'll captain the rearguard.'

They all knew there was every chance of being cut off from the comparative security of the Rim House – but these men were mostly hunters; they'd see the blockhouse as a death trap anyway. Without another word, the men obeyed, spreading out along the wall facing down the northern slope, and readying their weapons.

'What are you thinking, big man?' Foaley asked Vidar.

'That when we leave, we're going to have to run like the wind.'

'Aye. Now listen, *bearskin*, you'll go after the first volley. Don' want you getting blood-riled and ploughing into them.' He winked. 'I don' want t'have to explain to Varahana.'

Vidar grinned crookedly, still buoyed by her kiss. 'I appreciate the concern, but I'm calm.' Foaley did have a point, though. 'How about I pull out with the second-last group.'

Foaley snorted, but accepted the compromise. 'Done.'

The first Tangato warriors were beginning to emerge from the tangle of ruins far below, mustering at the bottom of the rubble-strewn final slope. 'Here they come,' someone murmured, and along the line hammers cocked and arrows were nocked.

With a ragged cry, the Tangato burst into the open and charged.

Raythe should have died. He was caught cold, despite having Cognatus inside him, unable to react as the blasts of energy erupted from the trio of masked figures above.

But Shiazar extended her right hand and instantly a canopy of pale light welled up, catching the bolts of light and absorbing them in a burst of sparks. Her shield rippled at the impact, but it held off the flurry of blasts as the platform rose and the range shortened.

There's the benefit of not needing a familiar, Raythe thought, then Cognatus responded and he shouted, '*Habere scutum!*' and joined his shield to hers. The next few seconds were like watching a forest fire from underwater, the shield rippling and remaining strong.

'*Praesemino!*' he shouted to Cognatus. Readying a spell, he wished Kemara was with him, missing the meld they shared.

A moment later, the stone disc crunched against the stone rim at the top of the cylinder and he glimpsed Shiazar slamming the palm of her hand against the control panel – but his sword was drawn and he blazed blinding light through the curtain of energy, designed to dazzle and blind. Catching a glimpse of a masked face, he adjusted his swing, just as the silk-clad figure's hands conjured fresh fire, but his falchion was already crunching into her left shoulder blade and she went down, the flames in her hands withering.

A second masked woman spun in his direction, but she was no trained warrior: she saw, she processed, she reacted . . . but all too slow. He was driving his sword through her breast before she could conjure; the mouth of her mask spraying blood as she crumpled.

The third masked woman would have had him, but Shiazar appeared beside him, and with a gesture, she hurled the Yokei against the jagged wall behind her, shattering her spine and the back of her head. The body slid off the rock into a heap.

Shiazar's face contorted at the sight, and Raythe realised, *She's killing her own, her last few precious kindred.* 'I'm so sorry—' he began, but her austere, lovely face was implacable.

'They know who I am, and they struck without warning.'

Out of curiosity, he pulled the mask from the nearest body to reveal an older version of Shiazar, with cobweb lines on the brow and wide, shocked eyes. He closed her eyes.

But there was no time for remorse, for no sooner had the sorcery subsided, than five armoured Tangato warriors burst through the doors. Shiazar met them with more blasts of unseen force, allowing Raythe time to refocus Cognatus. He unleashed his own bursts of lightning as the warriors tried to rise, killing three instantly. The two remaining dived to one side, then fled. He could hear voices shouting from somewhere ahead.

The dead men had strange hair, shaven at the sides, leaving a long narrow mane down the middle. 'Ngati Manowai,' the queen said tersely. 'Rebels, as always.' There was sympathy in her voice, but no regret.

Formidable, he thought. *A true warrior queen.*

'We need to keep moving,' he told her. 'We mustn't give them time to regroup.'

Queen or not, she obeyed, pausing only to replace her mask. As it settled on her face, it altered to something like a dragon, and purple flame kindled in her hands.

Don't know if it'll put them off, he thought, *but it scares the shit out of me.*

They strode through the doors the warriors had retreated through. Raythe's senses blared, but his shielding spell broke the arrows that slammed down, then Shiazar blasted indigo flames at the shadowy archers, cutting three down and sending the others into terrified retreat up a circular staircase.

'Do we follow?' she asked.

'Aye, we follow.' Hopefully, Jesco and Kemara would find them.

Looking up the stairwell was dizzying: there were at least a dozen levels radiating from this central shaft, each with a ceiling some thirty feet high. The air was bitterly cold and there was a layer of dust, but far less decay than he'd expected. There was no time to puzzle over that, though: they could hear their enemy above, regrouping. They ran, sucking down deep breaths and preparing for more violence.

On the last stair below ground level, their enemies struck. They'd been joined by two more Yokei, who sent their energy bolts alongside the arrows of the Manowai warriors, forcing Raythe to inch forward, shielding as best he could to deflect the shafts flashing around him.

But Shiazar abandoned gravity entirely, instead launching herself over the stone balustrade and onto the inside wall and lightly – improbably – running up the curving surface.

She hurdled the barrier at the top of the stairwell effortlessly, her blade flashing among their attackers, making the onslaught of arrows falter, which gave Raythe the respite he needed to charge, blasting flame ahead of him at anyone who appeared.

Bursting through two burning warriors, he saw a brightly robed Yokei turn his way. Her white mask looked deathly and her burst of force-energy smashed him back, leaving him sprawling helplessly on the stairs – until Shiazar landed behind the woman and beheaded her, then turned to face another of her kind, similarly armed – and the blows became too swift for Raythe to follow.

He was scrambling to his feet when four more Manowai archers closed in around the two women and took aim.

Ah, shit . . .

'Watch out–!' he shouted.

Two turned at once to face him and he blasted them over, then just as the other two archers released their shots, he threw himself at Shiazar, barrelling into her and pulling her down in a rolling tumble that took them to the ground. He lashed out with a boot and tripped one archer, then brained him with his hilt.

A sword's tip sliced his right cheek and clanged into the stonework and he looked up along the blade at another masked Yokei – but Shiazar *shrilled* and a massive burst of kinetic energy pushed the Yokei backwards, giving Raythe time to parry a warrior looming over him armed with a long wooden spear-club. Raythe surprised him with a slash to his groin – the man folded onto him, while Raythe twisted away – just as one of the downed man's comrades loosed an arrow that plunged into the dying warrior's stomach instead of skewering Raythe in the side.

Shiazar somersaulted a fresh trio of men rushing in, cutting one down from behind as she landed, leaving Raythe distractedly wondering how many decades of practise it would take before he and Cognatus could manage such a move. He rallied just in time to throw up a shield that prevented being incinerated by the last remaining Yokei – who was cut down by Shiazar a moment later. The remaining Manowai fled howling.

The top of the stairs looked like a charnel house, the dying moans of those breathing their last echoing from the walls.

For a moment, he and Shiazar stood there panting for breath in the cold air foetid with the stench of blood, voided bowels and bladders. He was wondering if the Aldar showed any emotion at all when Shiazar wrenched her mask from her face, her perfect heart-shaped face now greyish-green, and vomited over the marble floor.

He was grateful to have got past that years ago. 'Happens to us all,' he told her, although it wasn't entirely true. Some loved this gruesome work, but they were considerably less human than she was.

'I'm sorry,' she mumbled, spitting to clean out her mouth.

'You realise some poor bugger's going to have to clean that up?' he said, hoping to lighten the moment, but she just looked at him with haunted eyes.

'I'll do it myself,' she said after a moment.

He rose and looked around. The remaining Manowai had fled through open double doors into a giant hall and vanished. 'Majesty, if you're ready, we really need to keep at it.'

She shuddered. 'We've killed so many . . . and either of us could have died a dozen times.'

'Aye. But we didn't.' He offered her a hand up. 'We won't.'

She took his hand – hers was smooth, delicate and cool, despite her exertions, and rose, then she reached up and touched his cut cheek. She used her bloody fingertips to trace a scarlet line from temple to chin across both her cheeks.

She looked beautiful, vulnerable and terrifying all at once.

These things matter, he thought, daubing a blood mark onto his own cheek, remembering similar moments on other battlefield, where life and death often came down to the bond you had with those alongside you.

'Thank you, my hitoshii,' she breathed. 'We fight well together.'

'I've never seen anyone like you,' he confessed.

'My sisters are older than me and I am the only one who took swordsmanship seriously.'

'I'm not comparing you to them, but to people like Jesco,' he told her.

Shiazar considered, then said, 'Ikendo will be stronger and faster again.'

On that daunting thought, they headed for the great hall, striding through the doors into the open expanse. Raythe instantly noticed a strange blurring of the light, a warped quality in the distant shouting of the retreating Manowai and the sense of walking against a subtle wind. Inside him, Cognatus whined unhappily.

And then he heard a distant cry, echoing down through the marble halls of the ancient citadel: a woman's scream, a howl from the very depths of the Pit, that echoed on and on.

Kemara and Jesco stared into the banquet hall of Tashvariel at a scene of utter madness.

This was where everything – all the strangeness and the warped passage of time – radiated from: *right here*, where the truth about what really happened to Tashvariel the Usurper was still being played out.

'*Holy Gerda*,' Kemara blurted, gripping Jesco's hand.

Tashvariel's last days had been the subject of so many stories, legends, plays and books, despite the fact that no one in Magnia knew the truth. Cannibalism, depravity, murder and madness were always the prevailing themes, the Usurper's last hours related with horror, abhorrence and glee: how he poisoned all his comrades by making them eat the venom-laden flesh of Shameesta, the woman who refused his love and died for it.

Of course it was nothing but fantasy.

The last God-King wasn't dead.

None of them were.

Kemara stared at the nearest revellers – half-naked male and female Aldar, dancing, caught in mid-air halfway through a gyrating leap. Dozens more beyond them were held in the strangest postures by the freezing of time. A trio of fiddlers caught in mid-stroke had backs arched and faces set in concentration as their single note went on and on and on . . .

As she watched, everyone moved by the *faintest* amount, the afterimage imprinted on the air, adding to comet-tails of light several feet long, plotting where they'd been all these centuries.

Beyond them was the end of a long banquet table where a gorgeous Aldar woman sat, skirts hiked and legs splayed, her head tossed back in abandon as a kneeling man pressed his face to her groin. Behind them, feasters gnawed at haunches of flesh or guzzled wine hanging in the air on the way from glass to mouth. On the floor were another naked man and woman coupling, intent only on each other.

But in the middle of the table lay the half-gutted carcase of a naked woman lying on her back with her belly sliced open and her entrails pulled out. One breast had been sliced off; the other was in the process of being butchered by a mad-eyed man wielding a huge carving knife. Her eyes were bulging and her mouth emitting a high-pitched scream that never ended.

Shameesta.

The tales were true, but with a dreadful twist: it was still happening, right now . . .

Jesco gasped when he saw her. The ring on his hand was glowing like a star. Kemara's eyes flashed to the far end of the table, where an Aldar man balanced on the arm of the royal throne like a perching bird was peering at a contraption beside him: a foot-tall hourglass in brass fittings filled with gleaming sand – which had almost all passed through to the bottom. His face was contorted with absolute glee, the look of someone who'd accomplished some dark feat beyond any and all but him.

This was Tashvariel, she had no doubt; she didn't need Buramanaka's inner snarl to confirm it.

He wore a crown, but looked more imp than king, more Pitlord than ruler.

Kemara was no scholar and she'd never heard of such a spell, but what was happening was clear: the hourglass controlled this time spell. The magic radiated out, onion rings of time, layers within layers, so the closer you were to it, the slower time passed.

And at the centre was Tashvariel, for whom virtually no time at all would have passed.

Whoever came here couldn't penetrate it, so they locked it off and called the job done.

What a gamble Tashvariel had taken, to secure himself in this place and hope that by the time he emerged, his enemies would be gone, frozen or starved by the dreadful mizra-storms he'd unleashed, bringing on the Ice Age they were still enduring.

But it worked, she reflected. *His enemies are dust.*

Remembering how the levels below had been preserved, with only a fraction of the dust and detritus she'd expected, she surmised that the spell must initially have encased the whole floating rock, perhaps even the air around it, but over the centuries it had retreated until now the effect was barely perceptible, except *right here*.

She turned to Jesco, whose eyes were still fixed on the butchered woman on the banquet table. His whole body was tensed and coiled,

ready to use all his strength to throw her off him again and go charging in.

'No, Jesco—' she started, but he hurled her away, compelled by the
ring he wore, his link to a woman who'd spent five centuries caught in
one hideous, appalling moment of savage contempt and cruelty. Roaring in fury, he charged, his outline blurring as he plunged into the
layers of time, afterimages of him forming in his trail.

Kemara's eyes flashed back to Tashvariel . . . as the final grains of
sand in the hourglass fell and everything in the banquet hall burst into
motion . . .

5

As Below . . .

Varahana stationed herself at the Rim House gates, shouting instructions as her people filed in. They were all trying to be brave, for everyone knew this would be their last stand.

The infirmary patients had arrived and the Sisters of Gerda were busy bedding down the sick and preparing for the wounded. A clutch of anxious mothers herded curious children away from the doors, while those who would be fighting started fortifying the windows and stacking up powder, shot, bowstrings and arrows.

Shouting for all and sundry to stay clear, Gravis Tavernier trundled in a barrel of gunpowder. Little Rosebud helped her mother Angrit to lug in bundles of blankets while Ray Groff, Maddy's brother-in-law, hauled in a cart bearing the newly widowed mother and her baby. The noise swirling around them all was heightened by dread; every now and then the distant gunfire made them all stop and stare, fearing the worst.

'Deo and Gerda are with us,' Varahana shouted. 'Get inside, and anyone who can use a weapon, get ready. *Hurry!*' She gazed northwest: Foaley's men were retreating around the top of the crater rim, but for the rearguard, who were still firing . . . no, now they were running too . . .

Vidar, if you're there, run like the wind.

Moments later, a wave of dark shapes broke up and over the northward rim of the crater, too many to count. Some pursued the Magnian men, but most poured down into the crater, seeking to get to the Rim House as quickly as possible.

Oh Gerda, there's thousands of them . . .

It confirmed what she already knew: that the Rim House was no haven, just a prolonging of the end.

But Raythe and the Aldar queen were still in the sky somewhere, and some hope was better than none, so she clung to that and shouted, *'FASTER! THEY 'RE COMING!'*

If this is a feint, it's a damned convincing one, thought Sir Elgus Rhamp, watching the Tangato press forwards along the bridge from his vantage atop the gatehouse. Thrice they'd tried to rush the gatehouse, but they hadn't come close, and now they were having to step over the bodies of their comrades cut down in the earlier waves.

Unfortunately, that was a drop in the ocean.

Sometimes a feint became a real assault: he'd experienced it from both sides. The blood rose, the defence was maybe less than feared, and suddenly it was all on.

He glanced at the woman beside him: Rima of the Tangato, clad in just a beaded skirt and bodice, looking like some primaeval war goddess. By Deo, she fought like one too, if you ignored the fact that between skirmishes she alternately threw up or wept.

'You married?' he asked her gruffly, as she readied herself to unleash more sorcery from her deadly hands. Her bare flesh gleamed like gold and she had all the curves a man could want.

She gave him a *krag-off* look and growled, 'What's it to you?'

'Name your price,' he offered. 'Anything at all.'

She snorted in amusement. 'Get lost, old man. You've got nothing I want.'

Then the Tangato on the bridge screeched out their war-cries again, and the next wave came in hard, mad-eyed savages, to his eyes, the biggest mob of them yet. They were screaming something that sounded like *Man o' war.*

That they surely are . . .

345

'Keep up your work,' he told Rima. 'I'm going to steady the lads below.'

He hurried down the steps to the broken gates, barricaded and lined with flintlocks, with a rank of archers behind firing up and over. Tom Corday was marshalling them, calling the volleys. Right now, to the cry of *'Reload, reload!'*, the young folk huddled behind the gunners were working like pitmen, hands blurring and faces sooty in the hazy smoke as they readied weapons and passed them forward.

'Tom,' Elgus shouted over the din, 'we got enough powder for this?'

'Twelve more volleys, give or take,' Corday, his new second, reported tersely. 'We're cutting 'em down, but more keep coming.'

'Then hold fire 'til they're closer. Gotta make every shot count now.'

Corday nodded bleakly and swung away to relay the command. Elgus stepped back and watched the gunmen – with Rima above – break up the next wave, but they didn't go far, just turning at the bridge's apex and massing again.

He did some numbers in the only field of mathematics he knew: rates of fire and casualties: *Three volleys to break an attack . . . that's just four sorties . . . Just half an hour – and then what?*

Looking to the rim, he could see the last of the oldsters, women and the children pouring into the Rim House, a bulky silhouette on the skyline. They only needed a few more minutes. *We'll hold for five more minutes, then go.* Then he cast his eyes skywards. *Raythe, if you're still breathing, get your kragging arse back down here.*

Pounding along with the last cluster of men to retreat – because that was how it had worked out, after all – Vidar realised that they were going to be cut off. *Damn, but these Tangato move like the wind.* The Rim House was still a quarter of a mile away, but the ferociously athletic tribesmen were storming through the crater and flowing just as swiftly up the south slope . . . towards Varahana.

'Run, lads!' he shouted, falling into step with Foaley. 'Cal, we've got to pick it up!'

Foaley glanced down into the crater and swore. 'We ain't gonna make it. You push on – I'll grab a few of the lads and slow down the buggers behind us.' He peeled away, reeling off names as he did so. All of them were hunters, men who could hit a deer's throat at a hundred paces. Those named stopped running and gathered round him.

Vidar took the rest on, shouting, 'Pick up the pace: it's a race to the Rim House!'

They were all sweating like pigs now, but they'd trekked hundreds of miles to get here, building up their fitness, always determined to keep going, harder and faster. Vidar roared them on as they converged with the Tangato in the crater below.

The Rim House was looming ever closer.

Damn, it's going to be close . . .

Cal Foaley's picked dozen closed in around him, each taking stock of terrain and fields of fire. Each had his flintlock and bow, with two or three quivers, forty to sixty arrows apiece.

'What's the game?' young Tasker Corbyn panted. His father Gan was too breathless to speak. Tyl Moffit was here too, with Jami Pick and Rawleston Sorly, the best archers in the expedition. Even Matty Varte looked resolved.

They might not be the sort to stand shoulder to shoulder, Foaley thought, *but they know how to kill.*

'We play to our strengths,' he replied. 'We hide here, give 'em two volleys when they pass, then melt away so we draw them after us. Then it's hit and run: every enemy who doesn't reach the Rim House is a victory. There's twelve of us, so I'm expecting two hundred kills.'

Tyl Moffit whistled and Matty Varte winced.

Rawleston Sorly just grinned. 'Let's play.'

They disappeared into the grounds of the big mansions where the Aldar lords had once lived. Foaley picked an arch with a grilled iron gate, rusted but intact, giving him plenty of stone around him, and a path to retreat into the tangle of undergrowth and ruins downslope.

He cast a glance upwards at the floating rock, wondering where Ray-the Vyre was, then lined up his first shaft. The trick was not to think of the oncoming Tangato as humans, just targets.

'Lads,' he called to his unseen comrades, 'ready?'

A chorus of steady voices murmured, 'Aye.'

He waited until the running Tangato came into solid range, then, calling, 'Now—' he drew and fired in one fluid motion, sending his shaft soaring alongside eleven others in a shallow arc and plunging into the approaching runners. His target went down; his second shaft was nocked by the time the first struck. The Tangato recoiled and began to scatter, but not before the second volley had slammed into them. Then he snatched up his flintlock and fired, as other guns barked, spraying smoke and shot. The Tangato crashed to the ground, decimated again – but more were coming up behind.

'Right, lads – shift!' Foaley called, then he turned and ran, seeking a new vantage from which to hunt the deadliest game of all.

Naturally, the five minutes Elgus needed to secure the retreat didn't go peacefully. Almost immediately, even more Tangato began flooding onto the bridge.

The first rush was half-hearted, the few dozen hotheads burning for revenge swiftly mown down. Hoping that was it, Elgus shouted up the stairs to the top of the tower, 'Rima, get your brown arse down here, now!' Then he turned and faced the young folk doing the reloading. 'Finish the one you're on, then go: get your skinny butts up to the Rim House! *Go!*'

Some shot off like rabbits, but others protested, declaring their willingness to stay, which made him proud, but also annoyed the shit out of him.

He brandished his sword at them and roared, 'Don't question my orders! Think you're a kraggin' hero? Feck off, you bloody kids!'

The rest of them ran—

—as Tangato cries echoed through the ravine and they came

hammering along the bridge again, hurdling their own dead to get to the gatehouse.

Seeing Rima, he waved her in beside him and they shouldered themselves to the front line. With Tom Corday calling the volleys, he fired flintlocks alongside his men while she blasted out fire spells. Again, the Tangato reeled back, but not far, and still more were coming up now.

Elgus drew his trusty old broadsword. It might be a museum relic, but it was heavy and comforting in his hand. 'Got work to do, old girl,' he told the weapon, polishing the pitted blade on his sleeve. Rima gave him a sniffy look, but he just grinned. 'Sure I can't persuade you, lass? I tell you, I can make a woman moan for three hours straight.'

'Complain, more like,' the nearest man, Vass Blaegar, snorted. 'Shoulda heard his wife whine about him.'

'I'm not for sale,' Rima said coldly.

'Aw, we're just kiddin', girlie,' Vass replied. 'Elgus is harmless – if you'd seen his weenie, you'd know that.'

'Vass, you half-pricked turd, whaddya you know?' Elgus snorted. 'If'n I got my todger out, I could swat them tribals off the bridge,' he boasted, and a volley of ribald elaborations on that theme had the whole line cackling.

Rima looked at them all – sweaty, covered in grime and reeking of gunpowder smoke, but grinning maniacally – and shook her head. 'You're all crazy.'

'That's how we get through it, lass,' Elgus told her. 'You either laugh or cry.'

'Or die,' appended Vass.

'Amen to that,' Elgus agreed. 'So, how much jus' for a kiss?'

But that had to wait, for another horde of shrieking warriors was storming forward . . . and reeling back. But that took another four volleys, and afterwards most of his men were blinking away smoke from streaming eyes and coughing, staggering back from the barrier to find breathable air.

'Krag, that lot got close,' Elgus heard someone mutter – or maybe they shouted; the gunfire was deafening them all. He checked the powder and shot remaining: there was too little to hold off another full rush.

Krag it all, this is it . . . A priestess had once told him that every day of life was just a dress rehearsal for the day you died. Or maybe she'd been an actress – he couldn't quite remember.

As they reloaded, he walked among them. 'Right, lads, who's married?'

Twenty-odd hands went up, mostly villagers, just a few of the hunters and trappers. Tom Corday was among them, having recently married one of Gravis' whores. *Lucky prick.* 'You lot pull back next,' he told them.

'That why you're so keen to marry the chica?' Vass snickered.

Elgus grinned and winked at Rima. 'Din' work, did it? Heartless bitch.' Then he surveyed those who hadn't raised their hands and saw Larch Hawkstone among them, who wasn't married but was bedding Angrit like they were. *Deo's mercy, do you deserve mercy, you imperialist prick?* But little Rosebud was a cherub . . . 'An' those of ye who might as well be married, raise your hands too.' A few more complied – but Hawkstone didn't look up. 'Oi, Larch, I'm lookin' at you. You get back to Angrit, hear me?'

The former imperial borderer hung his head, but after a moment, he nodded. His reluctance told Elgus that the man really had changed for the better. He turned to Corday. 'Tom, take these lads up. Let 'em fight to protect their own.'

They all fell silent and stared, some with hope on their faces, others with dread.

'We'll be following,' Elgus said firmly, 'soon as we stand 'em off one more time.'

'Nah, let's all go now,' Tom said, in a low voice. 'It'll be five minutes before they realise we're gone.'

It was tempting – damn, but it was – but it was also wrong.

'They'll know inside ten seconds and be on our heels,' Elgus said.

'We've gotta buy time, and that's all there is to it. Tom, you're my named second. The lads'll follow you.'

. . . if Banno and I don't make it back . . .

Corday swallowed, then saluted and turned, already rapping out orders. Men shook hands, those departing calling out stupid things like, 'See you up there!' to mask the grim reality.

'Feck off,' Kortenberg called after them. 'An' when you're next inside your wife's fanny, say hi from us.'

Men, Elgus thought, grimly proud. *Crude as Pit-scum, but it masks the fear.* Which reminded him . . .

'And you, Witch,' he said to Rima. 'This is men's work.'

She scowled. 'I can do anything you can and more.'

'You're not one of us, girl. Go and find your Queen. Go on, feck off.'

She stared, then touched her hand to her heart, turned and was gone.

Watching her behind as she loped away was probably going to be the last good thing he enjoyed in this life, so he watched those long, lithe legs, the curve of her waist and that taut rump until she vanished. He wasn't the only one.

Elgus saluted Tom Corday and the men as they trooped off after her, then turned to face those who remained.

'Buggered if I wanna run up that blasted hill anyway,' he joked. 'You lads ready for this?'

Are you ready to die?

'Yeah,' they drawled. 'What's the play?'

'Fire every gun, cut the bastards down. As soon as they break and run, we'll leave under the cover of the smoke. Make for the Rim House. We'll smack 'em over up there, with Lord Vyre and his sorcery.'

It made for a good story.

They did their preparation, stacking up flintlocks, getting arrows ready to pluck up and fire. Blades were loosened and prayers muttered. Then that kragging sonorous Tangato chanting began again and someone called, 'Here they come!'

Elgus poked his first long-barrelled gun through a gap in the barricade at the dark shapes surging towards them. The stone span was covered in bodies, in some places two- or three-deep, but this time the advance was slower, and they saw figures in feather cloaks among the half-naked warriors.

Sorcerers, Elgus guessed, his blood chilling. But they were buried deep in the press, well-shielded. *Even barbarian sorcerers know to hide behind real men*, he thought bitterly. *Just like at home . . .*

Then the Tangato broke into a run, howling, '*Man o'war! Man o'war!*'

'Fire!' he yelled, squeezing the trigger. The long gun bucked, spouting flame and smoke, as all round him, flintlocks cracked in a deafening roar. His ears ringing, he shouted, 'Next, next—' as he dropped his weapon and snatched up a reload. The space outside the barricade was already thick with black smoke, making the shapes charging forward hazy, but when he roared 'Fire!' they were still cut down.

Then something hammered into the barricade and he was battered backwards, amid an eruption of bodies and debris, coming smashing down on his left shoulder. His senses reeling, he came to a sliding halt, his gun gone but his hand already closing on his sword hilt. His left arm wouldn't respond and bones crunched when he tried to flex it.

Broken and dislocated, krag it.

Sound came in waves as he staggered to his feet. Ged Kortenberg was lying on his back, his neck broken, and young Semus lay by the broken barricade with a jagged wooden splint embedded in his belly. As Semus tried to rise, a Tangato burst through the smoke and smashed an edged stone club down on his skull.

Elgus rose, drew his broadsword and shouted, '*Fall back, fall back!*'

A few were still emptying the last of the flintlocks and drawing steel, shouting in defiance, though Elgus couldn't hear a thing. He could see though, as the Tangato poured through, hammering their wooden spear-clubs against good Magnian steel. Polished wood could break limbs and skulls; the pointy bits did the rest.

Then the first one reached Elgus, a big man in his prime, naked to the waist and covered in tattoos, tongue out and eyes like saucers . . . but a badly chosen overhead blow was still fodder for any trained sword. Elgus stepped to one side and gutted the fool; then spun and thrust his blade through some stupid kid, caught the wrist of the next man and hacked him down, then turned . . .

. . . as the world turned to treacle.

A man and a woman faced him, he grey and grizzled; she a squat troll – but those differences aside, they were identical, with that 'man o'war' strip of hair, tattoos everywhere else, and a series of hideous deformities . . . no, these were *mutilations*, like those kragging Izuvei: no noses, ears hacked off too, and empty sockets . . . but still they *saw*.

As hearing returned, he heard the man rasp, 'Elgus Rhamp–'

Both gestured and an unseen blow slammed into his kneecaps. He felt them shatter and went down howling, his blade dropping from limp hands . . . Except that he never quite fell, because the woman made another gesture and he was held erect and dragged towards the pair.

Even the other Tangato backed away.

'I am Tatsu,' the old man said, speaking Gengo-Magnian. 'This is Kyu.'

Elgus dropped his hand . . . towards his dagger. 'Wha–?' he panted through the agony. 'What you want? To gloat? Well then, feckin' gloat all you want. Raythe Vyre's gonna wipe you out.'

Please Deo, make it so.

'The white mahotsu-kai?' Tatsu laughed. 'I think not.'

'Do we need this one for anything?' Kyu asked. 'Or can we play?'

'There's no time, my darling,' Tatsu answered. 'We must find the girl.'

Kyu licked her lips hungrily. 'Oh yes, *her* . . . She really should have made sure I was properly dead.'

She tinkled with grotesque laughter, then turned back to Elgus.

He snatched out his dagger and lunged–

–but Kyu deftly stepped aside and he fell, the dagger snapping on the cobbles at her feet. She slammed down on his back, smashing his face into the stones, then insanely strong hands gripped his skull and wrenched sideways. Inside his neck, there was a snapping sensation, followed by numbness.

As his vision went black, he thought he saw Banno, clasping Zarelda Vyre to his chest. He tried to say something, to bless them, but nothing came . . .

Varahana hurried to the outer wall of the Rim House, measuring angles and trajectories with her eyes. To her left were twenty or thirty men, tearing towards her around the rim – and her heart thumped as she recognised Vidar among them, his shaggy mane streaming behind him.

But on the slope of the crater below was a ragged wave of Tangato, pouring upwards – and Vidar's men and the enemy were both barely two minutes away. And *still* the old men, women and children were filing into the Rim House, so *still* they couldn't close the gates.

Then a column of exhausted men staggered up from the bridge, hands and faces powder-blackened and sweaty. She strode to meet them. 'Tom, what's happening? Is the bridge lost?'

'Not yet,' the mercenary replied hoarsely. 'There's a rearguard still holding.' He looked around. 'That Tangato bint here? Rima?'

Varahana shook her head, 'No, I've not seen her. Where's Elgus?'

Corday's head bowed. 'Leading the rearguard.'

Dead then. Varahana sighed, but there was no time for grief. 'Then get your men to the rim wall – now!'

Corday, one of the better of his kind, went to argue. 'But my lads are blown, and–'

'Tell me later,' she snapped. 'Right now, I need you, right here!' She snatched her flintlock pistol from her belted sash and shouted, 'Follow me!'

Miraculously, they obeyed, pouring past her to the rim wall.

'Oh, shit,' someone breathed, gazing down into the crater at the tide of men streaming up towards them. They were barely a hundred yards away.

'Load up! Load up!' Corday bellowed. Hands blurred and prayers were raised to the unheeding heavens, while behind them, the non-combatants bustled along. There were still a few to get inside . . .

Vidar's men were only a minute away – but the Tangato horde were closer, and they weren't slowing down.

'Lads, take aim!' Corday shouted, leaping up on the wall and brandishing his sword. 'On my sig–'

Then he choked and spun as a shaft from below slammed into his shoulder and knocked him to the ground. Dozens more arrows whistled up, but the rest flashed overhead or broke against the wall. Then with a mighty roar, the Tangato horde hurtled into range.

Krag it . . . Varahana leaped up in Tom's place, lifted her pistol and shrieked, '*READY!*'

An arrow whisked past her shaven scalp.

'*AIM!*'

She sighted on a leading warrior, a savage brute with a mane of black hair, his skin covered in black tattoos. Another shaft snagged in her robes and tore them, grazing her left calf. She barely noticed.

'*FIRE!*'

The guns blasted out their loads and the Tangato reeled, bodies dropping – including, somewhat to her surprise, the man she'd aimed at. *Someone else probably hit him*, she told herself. *Deo forgive me! Gerda, steady my hand!*

'*Reload, reload,*' she called.

Then her heart thudded as she saw two dozen of the wives and daughters pouring into the line, armed with the reloads. Larch Hawkstone gaped as Angrit shoved in beside him, snatching his flintlock away and giving him a loaded one, then bending to reload the first. But a lot of the women shouldered blown men out of the way and took aim themselves.

'*Fire, girls, fire!*' Varahana shouted, insanely proud, and a ragged volley punched into the attackers. The Tangato recoiled, then came again, but by then Corday's men had reloaded and fired as well, cutting down even more.

The Tangato, miraculously, staggered back to reform.

Then Vidar's arms encircled her and he lifted her from the top of the wall. 'No actual reason to be up there, Mater,' he told her. 'We can hear ye just fine from down here.'

Despite his levity, she could see the veins in his temple throbbing, a precursor to his bearskin rage. 'Thank you,' she murmured, and then, 'We have to get inside.'

'I know, but right now, if we turn our backs, we're dead.' Then he turned, shouting, 'Reload, but hold fire! Reload and hold!' His shoulders began to hunch over and his voice to growl, terrifying her.

She obeyed with the rest, jerking her hands through the routines of reloading while shouting, 'Deo is watching,' because she could *feel* her god's eyes on them. 'This is where Gerda faced down the God-King: *let's make her proud!*'

She saw the fear and resolve and felt terribly scared, and incredibly alive.

'I love you,' she told Vidar, who turned and gazed at her in wide-eyed wonder.

Then with a roar, the Tangato charged.

'*AIM!*' she shouted, loud as a clarion.

More arrows flew, arced and hammered into the Magnian line, flying among them like stinging bees, but the wall took most. Even so, Vara-hana saw young Sheena Grigg flung backwards with an arrow in her left eye, and others slumped and fell, but grief was for later. She roared out, '*FIRE!*' and again the guns spoke.

And again the advance crumpled, but still more came on, and this time she heard Vidar howl and her heart lurched. An enraged bearskin had no control; he would charge an entire army.

'Vidar!' she shouted, 'stay with us!' She had no real hope that he heard her.

'Bayonets and blades!' she heard Tom Corday croak – on his feet again, his face white, ignoring the arrow jutting from his shoulder. She took up the call as she reloaded.

Then the Tangato burst through the smoke, eyes streaming as they hit the wall, seeking a hand-hold, seeking a foe – but sharpened steel thrust out and hacked down, severing hands, piercing chests and faces.

Then the women who'd been reloading abruptly stood and unleashed one last point-blank volley, Varahana with them, thrusting out her pistol two-handed and blasting away the face of the young warrior below her. All along the line that unexpected burst of fire broke the Tangato momentum, leaving space for blades and bayonets to cut down those who hadn't already staggered back into the smoke, repulsed again.

Vidar grabbed her shoulder and she flung herself at him. 'You held back,' she babbled. 'You held on!'

'I heard you,' he replied, then he thrust her towards the Rim House gates, shouting 'Go! Go!' and now they were all running. The dead had to be left, but the wounded were half carried, half dragged along. The Tangato came after them, but they were inside the Rim House grounds before the first appeared over the wall. Vidar hung back, shooting one of the lead men, and was last through the big front doors as they slammed shut.

She met him, kissed him hard, then shoved him away, her brain a fever of unresolved thoughts and emotions. He called something lost in the clamour that only her heart heard, then ran for a window, shouting for a reload.

Gerda, spare him, Varahana begged Heaven, as she found dozens of interested faces, mostly the women of the expedition. A few looked outraged, but most were grinning.

'Never quite knew why priestesses couldn't wed, myself,' Perya Baine commented. 'How else she gonna 'vise us 'bout men an' fuckin', eh?'

Varahana was grateful, but she wiped Vidar's taste from her lips firmly. Being a priestess was all she had time for right now. 'Get ready!' she shouted. 'This is our fortress and our temple! *No one gets in!*'

There were Tangato voices all round them and Banno was spinning left and right, trying to recognise where he was, but he'd never been here before.

As long as I'm climbing, I'm going the right way, he reminded himself. *But where's Zar? Gerda Alive, why did she run off like that?*

Because you hit her, his conscience replied. *And you can't find her because you stood around like an idiot instead of chasing after her at once.*

He'd lost Ando Borger and Guy Jagisson when a war-party of Manowai warriors had poured up the road behind them, forcing them to split up and hide. Now he was creeping through the ruins, jumping at every sound.

More voices came, and moments later a group of warriors with scarlet tattoos jogged by, heading uphill. Once they were gone, he set off again, creeping along behind a row of tumbledown brick houses, thinking, *Get to the Rim House – that's where everyone's going.*

Another block on, he found an open space before a ruined temple-like building with an archway gate. There was a giant gong beside it, hanging from one rusty chain and flanked by a pair of ancient stone statues clutching bronze halberds that were turquoise with verdigris. The burned-out temple lay behind. A broken fountain in the middle of the square overflowing into the gutter made him realise how parched he was from the exertion of the climb and the constant fear of discovery.

He scanned the other entrances to the square and was about to risk a drink when he saw a fair-haired, furtive head bob up on the far side of the fountain rim. He was about to call out, when two shapes detached from the shadows to his left.

Zar immediately ducked down, but a male voice rumbled out Tangato words sounding like an invocation of Death, then loudly called out, '*Zarelda.*'

Tatsu's voice rolled out across the square, and Zar froze. 'Come out, Zarelda,' he went on in Gengo-Magnian. 'I have a surprise for you.'

A moment later, a second shape appeared behind him: the hideous Kyu. 'Surprised to see me, Snowbird?' Kyu crowed. 'What *fun* we'll have.'

Zar shrank against the side of the fountain, her heart thudding in dread. *Her familiar must have saved her – I didn't allow enough time . . .*

She cowered, numb, stricken with fear. All she had on was Ando Borger's coat, and though the day was still, it was bitterly cold. All the fight drained from her, as if she were already succumbing to some courage-sapping spell.

'No point hiding,' Tatsu rumbled. 'We know exactly where you are.'

'Ae, the spirits see everything,' Kyu cackled. 'I can see your scared little face, I can hear you breathing and smell the stink of your fear.'

They advanced across the cobbled stones – then Tatsu bellowed triumphantly, turned and gestured.

With a yelp, Banno was thrown out into the open and sent tumbling across the time-smoothed stones. He shouted frantically, *'Zar, run!'*

But that was now the one thing she couldn't do – however furious she was with him, she couldn't leave him to die.

The spirits see everything . . .

Zar had been horrified when her dad had told her the theories behind the Izuvei way of sorcery and self-mutilation: that removing a sensory organ could enhance magical perceptions. An Izuvei was said to be able to see like a hawk, hear a pin drop a mile away, smell a perfume worn a week ago. Instead of physical senses, they joined their awareness to the spirit-beings clinging to all life, attuning themselves completely to the spirits' perceptions. Even so, to remove all three senses as Tatsu and Kyu had done was virtually unknown, and regarded even by other Izuvei as going too far.

But Father taught me that their strengths are also their weaknesses . . .

This pair certainly had power far beyond her own. Fear was almost paralysing her, but she had to try something – and a plan of sorts was forming.

'Adefar,' she whispered, thankful he was already within her, 'anabolgium, nunc.'

The veil spell welled up, hiding her from the spirits as she crept from the shadow of the fountain. She stayed low as she darted to the temple gate, knowing she couldn't interfere with the pair's vision for long. In the open courtyard, Banno, bruised and bleeding, was drawing his dagger, preparing to sell himself dearly.

The two Manowai mahotsu-kai hissed, their faces jerking as they uttered counter-spells, ripping at the veil that had momentarily made them blind to her.

Blind, but not deaf . . .

But that stolen moment got her close enough to the rusted chain holding the old gong at the temple entrance. '*Perfringo quod catena!*' she murmured, and left the rest to Adefar.

Hearing her words, the two sorcerers spun her way, blue fire gathered in their hands – but the chain snapped and the old gong smashed down on the cobbles, belling out a deafening, echoing *clang* that made the air ring. It was barely endurable for a person with normal hearing, but the two Manowai sorcerers, hyper-attuned to sound to compensate for their momentary loss of vision, went rigid and *screamed* . . .

And Zar shouted, 'Banno, now!'

Banno rose, dagger in hand, while she dashed to the nearest of the guardian statues and wrenched the bronze halberd from the crumbling stone fingers. It came away, so heavy it almost threw her onto her back, until Adefar filled her with energy and she turned and flew at the Manowai mahotsu-kai.

Banno rose as Zar cried out and stormed towards the two screaming sorcerers.

The man recovered first, although blood was running from his puckered ear holes, and he whirled upon Zar, hate contorting his hideous face.

Banno pulled back his arm and threw his dagger, straight and true.

The blade thudded to the hilt in man's back, cutting off whatever spell he was forming – and the woman choked as well, almost as if sharing his pain . . .

Both Tatsu and Kyu convulsed as Banno's thrown dagger struck home, then Zar raised the massive bronze halberd and crunched it down on Tatsu's head. The blade might be ornamental, but it was still metal, and very heavy, and it broke his skull open like an eggshell. His hideous face split as he crumpled to the cobbles. The force of the blow had badly bent the haft, but the sorcerer was already dead.

Beside him, Kyu was screaming as if her heart had been ripped out. Falling to her knees, her empty sockets staring blindly, she moaned, '*Kao* . . .' Then her own skull caved in – with exactly the same death wound that Tatsu had suffered – and she fell on her face, just as dead.

'*Holy Gerda*,' Banno blurted, grabbing at Zar and pulling her away.

Zar's mouth was working, but nothing came. Finally, she blurted, 'A life-link – they shared life and longevity – but you both have to avoid a death blow. That must be how she revived when I thought I'd killed her . . . I've only ever read of it . . .'

Banno was gaping at her, and looking at her as if scared that she might be just as monstrous.

'I'm not like them,' she stated, as firmly as she could. 'Now come on, we've got to go.'

Banno went to follow, then stopped, his face earnest and his voice plaintive. 'Zar, I'm sorry, I'm so sorry – I thought that Tangato was try-ing to kill you – I *didn't know*,' he babbled, the words tumbling from his mouth in a great gush of remorse.

She waited for the words to tail away, then fixed him with a glare. 'You *hit* me.'

'I didn't mean to . . . but Pa hit Ma all the time–'

She knew that in many families, *giving her a tap* was how you dealt with 'hysterical women'. Why she'd thought Elgus Rhamp's son might be different, she had no idea.

Even when Father learned that Mother had betrayed him, he never raised a hand to her.

But there was also a good man inside Banno Rhamp, she was con-vinced of that.

'I don't forgive you,' she snapped. 'You've got a lot of ground to regain.' Then she softened her tone and added, 'But you *can* regain it.'

His face lit up with the fragment of hope she'd tossed him –

–until a Tangato warrior appeared at the edge of the square, and moments later, a crowd of Hiriwa warriors, familiar faces to Zar, surrounded them. To her surprise, they were led by old Kuia – and by Rima.

'Zarelda,' Rima exclaimed, 'Kiiyan is truly merciful!' Then she saw the bodies of Tatsu and Kyu and her face creased into a savage grin. 'Well done, indeed. Hetaru is avenged.'

Banno had shrunk back at the sight of the warriors, and Zar moved quickly to protect him. 'Rima, Kuia, Banno might not be my husband, but no one may touch him.'

Kuia nodded. 'For now, child, at least until all is resolved. Your people have retreated to a house on the crater rim, but they're surrounded.' Then she looked up at the floating rock above, chained to the ground but now throbbing with unseen energy. 'Ikendo has ascended into the skies, and Rima says that your Father and Shiazar are also up there. All will be resolved by those above.'

6

. . . So Above

As the final sands fell in Tashvariel's hourglass, there was a sudden rush
of sound as the room before Kemara burst slowly and woozily back into
life and motion. The afterimages shortened as the half-naked dancers
began to pirouette, the musicians sawing on their instruments produced
deep, uneven tones; a singer's voice rang out, her voice slowed to a dron-
ing bass note, and the woman enjoying her lover's tongue moaned in
slow release, tossing back her hair in a languid billow of locks.

And Shameesta, half-butchered but somehow still alive, continued
to scream.

Far below her, Kemara heard feet hammering on the stairs, but all
her attention was on Jesco as he exploded into the tableau as it came to
life, shoving the first dancers aside and whipping out his sword.

For a moment the Aldar revellers continued with the acts they had
been caught up in when time froze: dancers danced, topers drank and
sexual partners went on with their pleasures – but then everyone faltered and heads turned, *seeing* each other – and the miraculously arrived
Jesco, rampaging through them. Kemara saw confusion and shock, and
the realisation that somehow, they were freed. Her first fearful thought
was that these were the confidantes and friends and lovers of the Usurper,
the man who had triggered the Ice Age and destroyed civilisation – until
she saw that freed of the spell, most of the revellers were now staring at
their hands, or gazing about in blank confusion, or beginning to vent
insane gusts of harsh laughter, and she had a dreadful thought . . .

*What if the five centuries wasn't just a few moments for them at all? What if
they've endured every single moment, trapped in all but motionless bodies?*

Her eyes flew through the crowd again, following Jesco as he bullocked through the faltering dancers towards Tashvariel, perched like a mad bird on the arm of his throne . . .

. . . as the Aldar King saw her, his hand still on the hourglass, and his face cracked into a manic grin.

If he flips it again, I'll be trapped here for the rest of eternity, Kemara thought, so amid the confusion, she did the only thing she could think of, conjuring energy and blazing it down the room, straight at the hourglass itself. She struck it full-on and it shattered, the glass and sand exploding in every direction . . .

And every grain of hourglass sand took flight, growing exponentially as they flew out, transparent bubbles that passed through Tashvariel and his throne and then on and outwards – and where they struck a moving person, that person froze for as long as they were enveloped.

But Jesco was still rampaging forward. An Aldar man with a sword tried to stop him, but got caught in one of the bubbles, allowing Jesco to cut him down as he passed. Then the Shadran vaulted onto the banquet table, scattering the revellers. Half-dressed Aldar noblemen lunged for weapons or tried conjuring sorcery as the birdlike man on the arm of the throne stood, balancing on one leg, and shrieked with laughter.

Something had changed. It was almost imperceptible if one wasn't paying attention, but Onkado had felt it. Pounding up the stairs behind his father, encountering that headwind of time and trailing afterimages, he felt a shimmer as if the whole world had begun to unravel – and then Ikendo fell and Onkado tripped on his trailing leg.

The headwinds vanished, along with the trailing light of their afterimages.

They hit the stairs hard, but their greaves and armour protected them, then they were up again and running, their warriors following with Jinkatia. From above came a clamour of lurching music, voices raised in fear, and one drawn-out, agonised scream.

And from behind them came a shout of alarm.

'They're behind us,' one of the warriors called, and when Onkado glanced over the balustrade, he glimpsed a pale-faced, grey-clad man with a rough mop of dark hair, running after them.

Zarelda's father?

'I'll deal with them,' Jinkatia snapped, coming to a halt and turning. 'Press on!'

Ikendo grabbed Onkado's shoulder. 'You are ready, my son?'

'Ae, Father. But what's above us?'

Ikendo bared his teeth. 'The scum who collected around Tashvariel: ancient relics to sweep away.' Then he rose and stormed upwards, while Onkado quailed.

That's the Usurper he's talking about – and a court full of Aldar!

But he still followed, because quite clearly, this was going to be victory or death.

'What the –?'

Raythe looked about warily as a strange prickling sensation rippled through him – and all at once the odd, muted noises from above resolved into recognisable sounds: hammering feet, shouting, and the dreadful, agonising scream of a woman.

He and Shiazar broke into a run across the dusty marble floor of the great hall and onto the stairs leading upwards, taking two of the wide steps at a time. Steel in hand, he was conjuring as he ran.

Then someone shouted in Tangato and Cognatus translated, 'They're behind us!' Other voices, low and terse, responded, all of them from above.

Another set of Tangato, he thought grimly. *Another uphill battle.*

He glanced up the central shaft of the stairs and saw, three levels and sixty feet above, a flat-planed male face, tattooed and alien: an Aldar, like Shiazar. It blinked at him as if in recognition, then withdrew, but others appeared, dark Tangato faces this time, and all had bows with arrows nocked.

He jerked aside from a shaft that flashed past his nose, conjured shields and yelled a warning to Shiazar before pressing on up the curving stair to the next landing. Two Tangato archers were waiting, kneeling and ready, and they loosed just as he saw them—

—but even as the arrows left the bows, something rippled through the air from above and everything went *strange*. Giant, contorted bubbles, like huge droplets of water, emerged from the ceiling and washed over the archers, and their arrows and bodies slowed, allowing Raythe a fraction of a second to read the arrow's flight and sway aside just as it erupted from the bubble again. It flashed harmlessly past his ear.

'Stay out of the bubbles!' he shouted to Shiazar as he vaulted onto the balustrade to avoid the descending shape. The archers tried to react, but while they were caught in the shimmering orb of air and time, he was to them just a blur of motion, somehow able to dodge an arrow in flight before reaching them in the blink of an eye, just as they came free.

He hammered his blade into the point where shoulder blade meets neck, then spun, glimpsing Shiazar running up the underside of the curved stairs – *how?* – to avoid another time bubble so she could blast purple light at the second archer. He collapsed, jerking spasmodically.

Then another bubble flashed downwards, and this one caught him. Everything round him blurred . . . until Shiazar gripped his collar and pulled him bodily out of it, all the while shielding him from arrows and a storm of fire from the landing above.

Gerda's Teats!

He scrambled up, added his shields to hers, then drew his pistol, cocked the hammer and shot an archer, before they ran on up the stairs, just in time for another bubble of time to envelop their foes, turning battle into murder. Raythe and the Aldar Queen lunged into the bubble to kill with impunity, first scything down a trio of helpless men, then diving to avoid a pair of sorcerous bolts that arced with weird slowness from above, unleashed by a masked Yokei on the next landing.

'Jinkatia,' Shiazar shrilled, going straight up the outer wall towards the other woman, while Raythe dealt with a pair of Tangato swordsmen running in from his flank. He parried one, and as a bubble hit the other, who froze, he slashed the man's throat, shouting, '*Cognatus, lumis!*' before drilling a narrow beam of light into the first man's face, blinding him for an instant, enough to rip his blade free and stab it home.

But more and more bubbles were streaming through the air now, too many and too swift to dodge, and time came and went in blurs as he did what he could, manoeuvring a Tangato into one, stabbing as he went rigid, and sweeping on.

At last he returned to the foot of the final staircase, where Shiazar was locking blades with the masked woman – Jinkatia, he presumed.

'Shiazar!' the Yokei shrieked. '*Outcast!*'

The deposed Queen slashed at her in fury, unseen spells crackling all round them, but she still found time to shout, 'Raythe, go!' and threw her arm upwards.

He hesitated, then thought of Jesco and Kemara and ran up the final steps.

It was the strangest fight Jesco had ever been in, and he'd had a fair few over the years. All he could see was the stricken, gutted and still some-how horribly alive Aldar woman in the centre of the table: Shameesta, chief wife of the last God-King and the unrequited object of Tashvariel the Usurper's obsession. She had spent five hundred years as the victim of the most horrendous cruelty, butchered and served up at the Usurp-er's death banquet. Ever since he'd picked up her ring, her voice and her face had filled his dreams.

But it's happening now *– and here she is, right here, still dying.*

And therefore, still alive.

In he charged, although whether to save her or to end her agony, he didn't know; the only thing that was clear was that this was where he had to be, and anyone who got in his way deserved to die.

Because these are the bastards having fun watching her suffer for eternity.

Some of them still had her flesh in their mouths as he hacked his way down the table, dispatching these sycophantic followers of the sick creature sitting on the throne. It took a while for him to see that few were actually defending themselves: most were in shock, and some were even turning on their lord with rage and hatred on their faces.

Surely for them it's just been moments? Aren't they his friends?

But he took no chances as he rampaged through them. Most died before they could react, too drunk or dazed or broken to realise the danger. Some fought, but they had their backs to the stream of time bubbles radiating from Tashvariel, while Jesco could see them coming. He couldn't evade every one, but they all hit his foes first, slowing them down enough that he could dodge blows and kill with near impunity.

He had no idea where Kemara might be: his eyes were only ever on the next body, and the next, until he reached the man butchering Shameesta, currently frozen in a shower of time bubbles. He'd barely moved in the time it had taken Jesco to traverse the room.

Jesco leaped at him, howling in rage, but the butcher, caught between killing the dying queen and defending himself, did nothing.

One mighty blow – and the butcher's head parted from his neck in a slow-motion arc, sending blood spraying across the air, drops hanging where bubbles caught them, while the butcher collapsed in a wet mess.

The nameless killer folded and fell, trailing afterimages, and at last Jesco found himself face to face with Tashvariel the Usurper, now standing at the head of the table, still grinning maniacally. He had one hand raised to block a beam of light that was striking his palm harmlessly. The other held a pocket-sized hourglass.

But then a hideous gurgling coming from Shameesta drew Jesco's gaze down to a sight sufficient to destroy the strongest mind. Vashtariel's chief queen had been eviscerated, pieces carved off her, yet somehow – by sorcery and the butcher' skill – she had been kept alive for the entire hideous experience. Pieces of her flesh were roasting on the hot plate beside the table, clearly carved off thighs, breast and arms. But her flawless face was untouched, contorted into a rictus of agony and terror.

He'd seen enough horror in his life to fuel a million nightmares, but the sight of her torture paralysed him.

She was speaking his name, and the ring on his finger burned . . .

Kemara knew she'd never catch up with Jesco as he went off slaughtering his way down the table, so she concentrated on protecting him, following him so she could cut down anyone who survived the trail of carnage he was leaving.

She knew little of fighting, but she was a vessel for Buramanaka's centuries-old hatred of these people, with all his skill and fury at her disposal. She didn't know these people, but he did: fellow Aldar nobles, for whom power and manipulation were a game, and lives taken just part of keeping score, all part of Tashvariel's usurping of the throne: callous, self-serving and as close to pure evil as she could imagine. Avoiding the oncoming bubbles of paralysing time, she blasted fire and hacked with her blade, taking lives and careering on.

Once close enough, still running, she unleashed a bolt at Tashvariel, putting everything she had into it.

He caught the blast on his palm without flinching, even though, being at the epicentre of everything, he was palpably still caught up in a slower version of time. He glanced at her and smirked, then pointed at Jesco – and his intention was clear.

She was still a dozen yards away, but unless she acted, Jesco was dead.

She did the only thing she could: ignored Tashvariel and struck at Jesco, using a bolt of kinetic energy to hammer him out of the time bubble holding him. He fell off the table an instant before Tashvariel's beam of dark light carved through the bubble and out the other side, through the head of an Aldar behind it, then the chest of another before bursting against the walls. Both Aldar disintegrated before her eyes, turning to ash.

With a look of mild annoyance, the Usurper conjured again, losing her among the dozens of revellers who still staggered about . . . but clearly not caring, because he sent something like whirling blades of air scything through the room. Everyone who was upright and didn't see it coming was slashed in half at the waist, but Kemara ducked beneath the table, landing on Jesco and holding him down as the air-blades tore through the revellers, spraying clouds of blood everywhere. Above the dreadful hiss of unseen blades, she heard Tashvariel shrieking with laughter. A moment later a pair of headless Aldar crashed down on her.

She froze, holding Jesco immobile and trying not to breathe as the cacophony fell away to just two sounds: Tashvariel's polished shoes clipping languidly along the wooden table, and Shameesta's unending scream.

'Well then,' the Usurper chirped, in the Aldar tongue, 'what have we missed?'

She was sure he was about to turn on her, but footsteps sounded at the doorway, stealing Tashvariel's attention. Her eyes flashed to the entrance, her heart in her mouth, to see who'd come.

Onkado and Ikendo went stride for stride up the staircase, leaving their remaining escort behind with Jinkatia. At the top they found two dead Aldar guardsmen, and another pair dead outside the double doors of the banquet hall, which were open, revealing a scene of revelry turned to absolute carnage.

Here was Tashvariel's infamous banquet hall, a long, narrow room with a massive table running its length. Half-clad drunken Aldar lords lay dead and dying, disembowelled or decapitated or cut in half, though a few at the edges of the room were still crawling, vomiting as they went. It was impossible to say how many Aldar lay within, but it must have been dozens.

Halfway down the table stood a lean, birdlike Aldar, in rich robes stained with food, drink and blood, wearing a crown in a lopsided fashion: Tashvariel the Usurper, Onkado realised – it could be no other. The destroyer of his own empire and half the world of Shamaya with it, standing here alive as if five hundred years of human suffering had never happened – as if it all meant nothing.

He saw them, blinked, and asked in ancient Aldar, 'Who are you?'

Ikendo drew himself up and replied, 'I am Ikendo, heir through fourteen generations of Prince Lochiel, child of Vashtariel the God-King. This is my realm, and I reclaim it.'

Onkado, of the same lineage, was struck dumb with terror at his father's reckless words.

But he's the Usurper, Father – he thinks it's all his!

Tashvariel reacted like a parent whose child has made some amusingly outrageous declaration, his eyebrows lifting and his grin widening, as he advanced along the banquet table, peering at them quizzically. 'Lochiel? *Your* realm? *Really?*'

He reached the end of the table and leaped down, landing like a dancer and preening. Behind him, those still able were stirring dazedly. Onkado realised they were all Aldar . . . except for a red-headed white woman, lying battered and bloodied in a pile of bodies. The floor was awash with blood, still pumping from the dismembered bodies of the revellers.

How can a white woman be here? he wondered.

But then Tashvariel spoke again, the enchantment of his voice eclipsing all other thought. 'Lochiel . . . he survived, did he? Nasty little toad. I can see I have a lot to catch up on.' He clicked his fingers, and Onkado felt his limbs lock. He strained against it while his eyes flickered sideways, and he saw his father do the same.

'I don't think I need both of you for that, my "heir"', the Usurper sneered.

He made a slashing movement with his hand.

And Ikendo's body crumpled, the head rolling off the neck in a spurt of scarlet and thudding to the ground, while Tashvariel's mad eyes focused on Onkado.

No, no! Onkado's mind screamed. His father might never have shown him love, but he'd been the pillar of his life, his drive and will to seize life the dominant force that shaped him. He convulsed, howling inside, but couldn't break free . . .

As he strained, the Usurper reached out and caressed his cheek like a lover. 'I'd much rather have that conversation with you, pretty one.'

Raythe took the stairs at a run, feeling more like a murderer than a hero as he carved through the last Manowai warriors, taking advantage of the bubbles of slow time paralysing them from behind. At last he reached the top of the stairs and ran past two fallen Aldar soldiers, and two more in the lobby before the huge doors.

He had no idea what to make of the scene before him: there were two heavily armoured Tangato before the banquet hall doors, which were wide open. One lay decapitated, the other stood frozen, facing a tall, skinny Aldar, with a crown sitting carelessly on his shock of golden hair and a look of amusement on his face, who was crooning over the frozen warrior like he was about to kiss him. Behind them, all was carnage, a banqueting hall full of bodies and twitching, bloodied figures.

Tashvariel, he thought dazedly, focusing on the crowned Aldar. *He's alive.*

Then the Usurper looked over the Tangato's shoulder and saw Raythe.

'Ah,' he breathed. 'Someone else who wants to play . . .'

He touched the young warrior's temple and he crumpled to the floor, motionless, then pointed lazily at Raythe, a dark violet vortex forming on his fingertips.

Dread broke Raythe's paralysis, even as from somewhere in the banquet hall, a familiar mind touched his: Kemara Solus, reaching for a meld. Energy began to blaze between them, giving him the impetus to lift his blade and shout, '*Cognatus, ig—*'

That was as far is he got. Tashvariel clicked his fingers and everything *stopped*.

Everything, from the crawling Aldar inside the hall to the flames on the candles to the dust motes in the air. All sound ceased for him. His body was rigid and unmoving. Even the smoke stopped drifting.

Everything was still – except Tashvariel himself.

The Usurper advanced on Raythe with a curious look on his face and a small tornado of purple light still dancing on his fingertips. 'A human . . . so your kind survived?' the Aldar mused. 'How useful.'

Raythe couldn't even strain against the spell; his body simply hung there. But his mind didn't stop working, and in that moment he gained an insight: in this pocket of space and time that Tashvariel has created to preserve himself, the chemistry of matter had been slowed to barely perceptible interactions – but awareness had remained: of identity, of thought, of the passage of time, because brains function so rapidly that cognition had continued, albeit more slowly. For five hundred years, those in the banquet hall had been physically frozen, but probably able to think at something like their normal rate: to ruminate and reflect, but unable to move and change and grow. Whether it was deliberate or an oversight or just the limit of the spell, he had no idea, but it was horrifying.

He doubted any of them had been left sane; including this terrifying being – if he'd ever been sane to start with.

But it also represented his only hope, because the meld that had formed between him and Kemara was continuing to bloom and blossom, even as he strained to move.

And now power was surging between them . . .

Kemara felt time clamp round her like a vice, everything locked down . . . except the meld she'd tried to initiate with Raythe, the praxis-mizra bond they'd formed on the journey. It had saved them from the Bolgravian Empire on multiple occasions and now it represented their one hope, so she channelled all her pent-up rage through it and let Buramanaka have full control. His armour and sword and mask formed around her as she broke from the cloying cobwebs of paralysis, launching herself at the spindly Aldar lord's back, just a dozen paces away.

But even as she did, he turned and saw her. 'You,' he snarled, seeing Buramanaka, ignoring the stiffly rigid Raythe Vyre and playing with the inky storm in his right hand. The hourglass in his left began to glow.

Shiazar planted her feet, took a strong low stance and swept in. Jinkatia parried, gestured and battered her backwards, a fall she turned into a somersault, and leaped back at the older woman, faster and more athletic. Glimpsing an opening, she almost fell for it before realising it was a feint, instead lurching back and taking a slash across the face that dented her mask.

'Clumsy child,' Jinkatia admonished. 'I thought I'd taught you better.'

They traded more blows, circling again as the muted clamour above sharpened and grew in volume. Shiazar's anxiety grew. *Raythe needs me up there* . . .

She went in again, kicking off a wall and hacking sideways, but Jinkatia crabbed aside and blocked ferociously, then riposted at her neck, a blow she barely blocked.

'Too impatient, child,' Jinkatia taunted. 'Your mind's up there, when it needs to be here.'

She's right . . . Shiazar slowed herself, taking a fresh stance: Jinkatia deserved all of her attention – after all, she was the one who'd taught her to fight.

'You're siding with the invaders, Shiazar,' Jinkatia observed. 'Have you no shame?'

'You started destroying our culture forty years ago,' she retorted, 'when you whored yourself to beget a son. And all the time you pretended to be my *dearest* aunt?'

'If I hadn't been forced to step down at the end of my term as Queen, none of this would have been necessary,' Jinkatia replied. 'Ikendo would have ascended the throne decades ago and we'd have met these invaders with all the power of the Aldar.'

'It's not their destruction we need, but their friendship.'

'You're an innocent and a fool,' Jinkatia sneered. 'Between races there can be no friendship, only the rivalry of predators.'

Shiazar darted forward, feinted left and went right – as a bubble of slow time passed through the roof, heading straight for her. She rolled away from it, taking a slash on her left calf as she did, barely blocking another combination, but managing to riposte enough to limp backwards. Blood was running freely into her shoe, making it slippery within.

Then Jinkatia gestured and a wall of force hammered Shiazar backwards – into the bubble.

She hung there, trying to parry a savage slash, but Jinkatia blurred and then stood before her, pushing her blade tip into the bubble towards her heart, leaving Shiazar no chance of countering . . .

. . . just as the bubble burst apart and time resumed.

Jinkatia's stab punctured her skin, scraped her rib and slid in slowly, because Jinkatia was barely pushing, thinking Shiazar helpless and wanting to be sure of the kill – or more likely, to slow the moment for her pleasure – until her thrust struck a rib and stuck, inches above Shiazar's heart.

But Shiazar's blow had retained its momentum, and once freed, it carved onwards, through a space Jinkatia no longer occupied – but the blow pulled her body round, twisting herself off the tip of Jinkatia's blade and giving her the chance to slash again, just as Jinkatia realised her peril. She tried to drive her sword home, but it just gouged Shiazar's side as she whipped her body through a full circle, her blade whirling until it met the Yokei archivist's neck.

Jinkatia's head jerked sideways as the blade lodged in her spine. Her limbs lost all strength and volition and she crashed downwards on her face, convulsing, choking as blood gushed from her mouth and neck.

Then she went still, visibly emptying of life.

Shiazar fell to one knee, both to regain balance and to take in this moment of grief and fear, and to accept the burning pain in her calf and chest. If the Chief Archivist had thrust harder, her heart would have been pierced and she would be the one lying on the floor in a pool of blood.

But she hadn't.

And now the sounds above had fallen into an ominous silence . . .

She rose, sucked in a deep breath and looked up the stairs, seeing no sign of Raythe Vyre, just two dead Aldar in archaic armour sprawled at the top. Howling silently as her wounded calf was forced to work, her left foot slithering in her blood-wet shoe, she limped up, reached the top and turned.

A skinny, birdlike Aldar in a crown was grinning madly at a frozen Raythe Vyre.

Tashvariel – however impossible it was, it had to be him. *Time, time – it's all about time.* He stood in a transparent bubble of light that enveloped the entire doorway to the banquet hall and reached halfway to her.

Ikendo and Onkado were lying motionless at his feet – but no one was moving, except the Aldar lord, who was examining Raythe like a specimen.

She was terrified he'd turn on her, but something had grabbed the Usurper's attention: he turned away to the banquet hall, where a scarlet-masked, flame-haired woman in lacquered Aldar armour had appeared. Tashvariel was conjuring dark fire in one hand, while holding an hourglass in the other.

She had no idea who the woman was: that she was an enemy of the Usurper was enough. She knew herself inferior to the Usurper as a sorcerer, but delicate spells were the easiest ones to wreck, and what Tashvariel was doing had to be some of the most exacting sorcery possible.

So she hit it like an avalanche.

Counter-spells were general disruptors; in the heat of combat, no one could read the exact spell they faced and counter it precisely, but it was possible to disrupt, quickly and easily, and that was what she did. Although Tashvariel's spell was the strongest she'd ever come up against, she was Aldar – and her strength was enough.

The bubble burst and the Usurper spun in her direction, his sly face suddenly shocked – just as Raythe broke free and lunged, and the redhead bludgeoned at Tashvariel from the other side.

Surely the Usurper should have died right there – but he moved like a striking snake.

Raythe thought himself dead, but somehow the time bubble came apart and his restored momentum threw him into a lunge with his curved falchion, while Kemara, masked and fearsome, chopped at the Usurper from behind.

But Tashvariel somehow twisted between them and spun away, sending a burst of energy from his left hand that forked and struck them both. It was agonising and brutal, shocking through Raythe and sending his limbs into a palsied dance.

If they hadn't been sorcerers, with some residual protections, and if the spell hadn't been divided between the two of them, he would have died – but the meld still crackled between them, their unique union of praxis and mizra which had destroyed a warship and melted a glacier. It was too much energy to hold inside, so they unleashed it, pure and deadly, in a torrent at Tashvariel.

The Aldar lord's look of sly complacency evaporated, but still he managed to shield, a translucent half-sphere that caught the flow of molten energy and forced it to go around him. His own attacks faltered, though, and then vanished as he was forced back, all his strength going into self-preservation.

And still the Usurper fought. He was a dim presence behind his shields now, not yet able to counter, giving ground as he was driven back into the corpse-strewn banquet hall, which was filling up with sickly smoke as bodies burned all round them.

It became a war of attrition. Raythe couldn't keep up this draining assault, nor could he afford to let it lapse, not when he didn't know how long Kemara could endure. Chillingly, Tashvariel was now able to push back, creating an unbearable level of force between the combatants . . . the first to falter was going to face a backlash that could level buildings.

Then Tashvariel's shield came apart and he was slammed back into the stone wall, bones in his hips and spine audibly breaking, then he went sliding down the stones and sprawling, his limbs thrashing like a demented spider. He tried to rise . . .

. . . and failed as the broken bones grated and gave way.

Kemara – or maybe Buramanaka – roared in triumph, storming forwards as the Usurper flopped to the ground, but one skinny arm rose, holding an hourglass. He flipped it, and suddenly another bubble began to form, washing over Kemara as she lunged in . . .

'No!' Kemara screamed, realising exactly what she was seeing – the beginning of another bubble of frozen time, one that might last years or even centuries. But while Raythe, flinching, went backwards, she went in, feeling resistance as time slowed . . .

Tashvariel looked up at her, his face breaking into a triumphant leer – until her blade shattered the hourglass on the way to lodging in the Aldar's chest. The bubble winked out as Kemara drove it in deep and twisted, then she wrenched it out and swung again.

That gurning skull dropped and rolled away as the pumping gouts from the neck stump turned the carpet scarlet.

Kemara sagged to the ground, panting in utter, absolute relief.

The meld came apart, Raythe's legs gave way and he began to fall – until a masked figure stepped in and caught him. Queen Shiazar put her shoulder in under his armpit, wrapped an arm round his ribs and held him up until his legs could take his own weight.

He held on, grateful just to be breathing. It was a sensation he knew well – the relief of having survived when he could so easily have died. Without realising he was doing it, he kissed her mask, on the forehead.

'Lord Vyre?' she said formally.

Oh Deo, he thought numbly, mumbling, 'I'm sorry.'

'He does that,' Kemara croaked, looking up at them with a crooked, weary smile. 'Soon as the fight's over, he snogs the first woman to hand. Tried it on me last time.'

Shiazar disentangled herself from Raythe – somewhat to his regret – and asked, 'Mistress Kemara, I presume – how did you react?'

'I punched him,' Kemara replied, wondering how the masked woman knew her name.

'She did,' Raythe admitted. 'Sorry.' He tottered to Jesco and knelt. 'Jes? Jes?'

The Shadran stirred and his eyes flickered open. He saw Raythe and gurgled, '*Sha — Sham . . . ees . . . ta.*'

A cloudy, hazy form appeared above the butchered woman in the middle of the banquet table which flowed into an upright shape and formed in the air above Jesco. It didn't look like Raythe could see her, but Kemara saw her touch the ring on the Shadran's finger, and suddenly she was more substantial: a beautiful Aldar woman, her face clear but her body just a ghostly blur.

Jesco flopped, going limp, but his chest rose, then fell.

Then the ghostly woman turned to Kemara – or rather, to Buramanaka inside her.

Abruptly, he wasn't inside her at all, but holding Shameesta, his sister.

Kemara dared not move.

A few seconds later, Shameesta faded and Buramanaka slowly peeled off his mask, revealing his true face to her for the first time: grim, sorrowful, noble, with all the beauty of an Aldar.

'*Redi-san?*' he said in a pleading voice.

'Noble Lady' – the first time he'd ever shown her such respect.

She knew what he asked. '*Anata wa jiyūda, Buramanaka,*' she replied. 'I abjure you. Go.'

It was like having her marrow sucked from her bones, but she'd been through it before, the day she rid herself of her first mizra familiar. This was easier, because Buramanaka wanted to go, unlike the other. She still almost fainted, lurching to one side and falling to the floor.

'Kemara?' Raythe asked, puzzled by the half-sensed exchange.

She waved him off. 'I'm fine.' *Relieved, really. He's gone with her: brother and sister, together at last.* She could feel good about that, she decided, if nothing else.

Raythe stared around the banquet hall, numbly taking in the carnage. Most of the Aldar were dead, but a few clung on, all wounded, with fractured or lost limbs, bleeding profusely, and their minds were clearly gone. None were likely to live. They just stared about them numbly, unable to comprehend. It was pitiable to see, despite who they were and what they'd once been.

Raythe went to one of two prone fighting men at the entrance to the hall, the Tangato men – and realised that no, they too were Aldar, but in Tangato armour. The elder one was decapitated, but the younger still had a pulse. 'This one's alive.'

Shiazar joined him. 'The dead one is Ikendo, so this must be Onkado, his son,' she said. 'Perhaps that's useful.' She looked round, a queen in the hall of her ancestors, the place of legend that had haunted her people for five centuries, a piece of frozen time that had effectively paralysed her people as well, for fear of what was done up here, and what had been unleashed. 'It's everything the tales said, and worse,' she breathed.

Raythe was struck that even bloodied and holding a sword, she looked regal and glorious – or maybe that was just the post-combat blood pounding through him. Regardless, he was in serious danger of falling under her spell entirely, which would be madness.

So he gouged his fingernails into his palm until they hurt, to clear his head, then said, 'Come on, we've got a war to stop.'

7

The Best of Both Worlds

The Tangato were massing outside the Rim House, crouched behind the garden walls and probing for a weakness, when something like a hammer of thunder – like one of the Old Gods of Norgania might have wielded – sounded above them. Light burst over the city.

Varahana, on the ground floor, was giving a Final Blessing to a room of terrified defenders when the sound crashed over them and she flew to the window. A dark circle was descending from under the floating rock, and something riding it was shining a brilliant white light.

What–? Varahana thought, and, '*Raythe?*'

Then a shrill female voice clarioned out over the city, a string of words she couldn't follow, but the Tangato outside all stood up, looking towards the sky.

A moment later, she heard Raythe Vyre, amplified by sorcery to the voice of a god, shouting, '*CEASE FIGHTING! WE HAVE A TRUCE! CEASE FIGHTING!*'

Apparently, miracles did still happen.

'Look at you, descending from on high,' Kemara remarked, with her old sarcasm.

Raythe was too nervous to respond. How the Tangato warriors below reacted now would determine everything.

As the platform sank into the crater, he checked again on Jesco, sitting with Kemara in the middle of the platform, wrapped in a cloak they'd found above. The Shadran looked utterly shattered – and the healer was just as drained – and she no longer had a magical aura. He couldn't begin to imagine what it was like to lose one's familiar.

And it's her second time, he reflected. He'd never heard of such a thing.

But for all that, there was a peace in her face that he hadn't seen before.

At the edge of the platform, Shiazar was standing impassively, once more masked and immaculate. At her feet knelt the male Aldar, Onkado, now a hostage to his tribe's obedience. She also held Ikendo's head, gripped by his hair. A grisly trophy, but necessary, she said, if she was to reassert control.

As Raythe had feared, by the time they were in any position to tend the surviving Aldar, they were beyond help. The last to die, a young woman, passed away as he tried to staunch the blood flow from a lost arm – she had no idea what was happening to her. The banquet hall was a nightmare that was going to haunt them all.

As they descended, the Queen kept exhorting her people to come down into the crater to meet them, her magically amplified voice booming over the city – and wonder of wonders, they were obeying, streaming down the slopes with faces upturned, wide-eyed with wonder.

But Raythe couldn't read their mood . . .

He peered up towards the Rim House and saw his own people emerging guardedly, not cheering or waving, just watching and hoping.

As they landed at the bottom of the crater, a sea of brown faces crowded in, tattooed and warlike: warriors who just ten minutes ago had been trying to kill his own people. Now they were gazing in awe as Shiazar held her trophy aloft, with the kneeling Onkado at her feet.

'Ae, Ikendo is dead,' he heard, over and over. 'The King is dead. Shiazar has returned.'

Raythe pulled Kemara to her feet, and then Jesco. 'Don't touch your weapons, no matter what,' he told them. 'We're in their hands now.'

Shiazar turned to Raythe and motioned him forward. The sea of Tangato murmured, some in anger, but most in curiosity. Reading their mood, he dropped to one knee, because it might be what her people needed to see.

It worked, and he heard cautious approval of the foreigner giving homage to their ruler.

'Rise,' she told him, her voice grateful – and faintly amused. Then she addressed her people again. 'Ikendo is dead,' she shouted in Tangato, Cognatus translating for Raythe. 'Jinkatia, who betrayed our nation – our entire culture – is also dead, and so are too many others.' Her voice caught with emotion. 'But we have given peace to the unquiet spirits who haunted Shiro Kamigami.'

The truth would be just too confusing, but everyone understood ghosts. He heard approval in the reaction of the warriors, and many began a keening wail, an unearthly sound that filled the crater. Only the Manowai warriors were now visibly harbouring doubt – but they were gazing at Ikendo's severed head and their kneeling prince, fearful of what was to come.

In Tangato legend, a male Aldar would be either saviour or a harbinger of doom, Raythe remembered. The former option had now been forcibly removed.

'Ikendo's war is over,' Shiazar told them. 'But I have concluded that he was right in one key matter: we, the Tangato, are the heirs to this place, and if we are to survive the inevitable arrival of the outside world, we must lift the tapu on this city and reclaim it.'

Raythe looked at her in anxious surprise as she went on, 'Ikendo's mistake was to believe we must also make war on the foreigners inside our city. He forgot that these people know what we will face. He did not care that they, like us, are afraid of that world, and of the tyrants who rule it. He should not have made war on these people but made them his allies. This, I have done.'

Raythe glanced at her masked face. *You have?*

'This man is Lord Raythe Vyre,' she went on, placing one hand on his bowed head. 'He is rangatira of the Ngati Magnia tribe. He has knelt to me and offered service.'

I have?

But as plans went, it was one that he could get behind.

'I bequeath them the bridge district of Rath Argentium,' Shiazar went on. 'We are at peace with them now, and they are free to come amongst us, as we are free to go among them. In return, he has pledged to teach us of his people's ways, and learn ours.'

This was met with caution, not approval, but no one dared voice disagreement.

Raythe took that as a win.

Shiazar turned and signed for him to rise, then pressed the nose of her mask to his uncovered face. Behind the mask, she winked impishly. When they faced the crowd again, Raythe saw confusion . . . and cautious approval. Despite the fierceness of the warriors all around them, the prospect of peace was being greeted with relief, not frustration.

Life is genuinely precious to these people, and too many have already died today – but Deo only knows how it'll go down with my people. Hopefully, they'll prefer it to a massacre.

'What's going on?' Kemara asked. Without her familiar, Shiazar's words were gibberish.

'I'll tell you in a moment,' Raythe replied. 'Just look harmless and follow my lead.'

'I am bloody harmless,' Jesco groaned. 'I'm a lump of tenderised lamb.'

'Hush,' Raythe hissed, for the Queen was speaking again.

'Rangatira Vyre must now go to his people and explain the terms of this truce to them,' Shiazar told the gathered warriors. She gestured, indicating a line straight up the slopes to the Rim House. 'Please, make a path for the rangatira and give him the honour he is due, as a slayer of the haunted ones above.' Then she turned to Raythe. 'We will speak again soon, Rangatira. Go to your people.'

'Deo knows how I'm going to convince them of your little plan,' he muttered.

'I'm sure you'll manage,' she said drily. 'Expect an invitation to celebrate our alliance very soon.'

He bowed, then asked, 'And my daughter?'

'Is free to re-join you.'

He sagged in relief. 'Thank you again . . . um, my Queen.'

He gestured for Jesco and Kemara to follow and they clambered from the platform, then hobbled to the gap which had appeared in the wall of faces. He didn't see a lot of friendship or welcome, but he did see obedience to Queen Shiazar, and perhaps even respect: a testament to her authority, but also perhaps a recognition of their feat. The floating castle had been haunted for half a millennium, and they'd just been told that he'd played a part in freeing what was a holy place to the Tangato.

Their whole lives are about to change – and so are ours.

They climbed up through the crowd, which flowed round them to press closer to their Queen. He still feared for her, worried some Manowai fanatic might seek revenge, but she was Yokei, an Aldar, and that appeared to override all else in their culture. And, of course, she'd won, and her usurper and betrayers were all dead.

The three of them trudged up the slope unhindered, left the Tangato behind and clambered up to the rim, where the wall was lined with pale faces, waiting anxiously to learn their fate. Varahana was there, with Vidar. He saw Cal Foaley, Tom Corday, Lynd Borger, Gravis Tavernier and so many others.

Then Raythe thought of those he *couldn't* see: Xan Lynski, Semus Rygor and Miki Brond, among others, and most of all, the bluff face of Elgus Rhamp.

He might be still alive, he hoped, but he doubted it. Elgus had been holding the bridge, and someone would have had to lead the rearguard. *We returned too late for some.* He was surprised to feel a pang of genuine regret for the old snake.

'What's happenin', Milord?' someone shouted.

'Peace,' he told them. 'We have peace. What we have, we hold.'

He expected probing questions about what he might have surrendered for this respite from death, but instead he was bear-hugged and

back-slapped and cheered and wept over, passed from body to body,
face to face, with much weeping. Behind him, Jesco and Kemara were
given the same embraces.

Life, it appeared, was worth more than gold. *Who knew?*

Afterwards though, he had to explain the deal, which wasn't easy:
pledging to stay here, off the map and out of time, wasn't the journey
anyone had signed up for. But back in Teshveld, he'd somehow con-
vinced this bunch of villagers and recluses to join his trek. He'd saved
their lives, he'd found the mythic Rath Argentium and he'd stopped a
massacre.

Frankly, I reckon I can sell these buggers anything . . .

To prove him right, they listened, then shouted agreement and
cheered him to the heavens. That didn't mean that half of them wouldn't
try and make a run for it later, but for now, dissent was well-buried.

The Ngati Magnia, he mused. *What a thing . . .*

'But will we still be rich in the end?' Gravis wondered, after Raythe
was done speaking.

Lynd Borger answered, 'Gravis, that don' matter any more – I mean,
what's "rich" anyways? This place, it's out of a fable, eh? We're living a
dream – a scary one, but ain't it amazin'? Ne'er happen back home.'

'I think we can make a better life here than anywhere in the empire,'
Relf Turner added. 'Being rich back there just puts a target on your
back. We're better off here.'

'I guess so . . .' Gravis sagged. Then he brightened. 'Tell ye what
though. That beer I laid down when we first arrived? Reckon it should
be about right ready fer broachin'. Just' let me get a tavern set up,
and . . . hey, d'ya reckon them Tangato fellas drink?'

Raythe left them to it. He had what he needed for now; the details
could wait.

First he sought out Varahana and Vidar, to hear their accounts of
what he'd missed down here while he was among the god-kings and
myths, and get the full tally of who'd died. Eventually, they ran out of
words and he looked up to find that it was only midday.

'Feed me,' he said to Varahana and Vidar. 'Feed me before I faint.'
Then I'll go and find Zar . . .

There was music and dancing at the Rim House already, for all it was only two or three hours since peace had broken out in the wake of Shiazar and Raythe's magnificent return.

My father was never one to make a quiet entrance, Zarelda thought proudly.

She'd watched it all from a perch on the rim wall, surrounded by the Tanuahi tribesmen. By now, most of the Tangato had left the city, seeking food and turning their mind to burying the dead – hundreds had been slain, especially at the bridge.

And then Shiazar will want them to resettle the city, Zar thought. It was a daunting task: they'd have to repair and rebuild and come to terms with an entirely different way of life, all the while ensuring their crops were still tended and harvested before winter.

We're supposed to go from fighting over this city to sharing it, but how in Shamaya is that going to work?

During the battle, Kuia had kept her and Banno together, hemmed in by warriors. She'd wanted to comfort Banno, who was glassy-eyed at the news of his father's demise, but his actions at the river below still hung between them.

As did another awkward fact.

I married Onkado – and he's still alive.

She knew her father or Queen Shiazar could annul that in seconds, that it needn't matter a jot: she'd been coerced, there had been no choice, and it had never been consummated – and what's more, Onkado was now a prisoner who'd more than likely be executed.

But he didn't want this war either, she thought guiltily. *He stood up for me when I was alone, and he saved me from Tatsu and Kyu. He doesn't deserve to die.* Just as imperative was the fact that she didn't want him to die – not when there was so much in him to admire. She tried to pretend it had nothing to do with the shattering of her rosy view of Banno, but she knew better. *There's something between us that I'm not sure I want to lose.*

But she didn't have to decide anything now, she decided.

'Zarelda,' Kuia interrupted. She pointed west along the crater rim. 'Your father.'

Zar stood, feeling utterly unready, as the most important man in her life approached. She wanted to run to him, but her limbs felt too hollow to risk speed, so she just walked with Banno, not touching, until her father swept in and lifted her from her feet and held her, shaking and weeping as she did the same.

'What did they do to you?' he murmured, withdrawing enough to examine her face. 'I've been so scared.'

'It's all right,' she answered. 'There were some who protected me.' She met his gaze. 'Prince Onkado, for one. He saved me when I was condemned to die.'

Her father took that in with a troubled frown. 'How? And why?'

She took a deep breath to forestall the confession a moment longer, still wondering if this was foolishness. But no, she was wilfully determined to see it through, even if it was just to make Banno see that he would have to *fight* if he wanted her.

'He told Ikendo that I was a sacred mahotsu-kai sworn to the Hiriwa tribe and that harming me would be an offence against the gods. When his father refused to listen, he married me in secret, so that I would be untouchable.'

'He *married* you?'

She wasn't sure she'd ever heard her father snarl like that before.

'It was never consummated,' she said quickly.

'Then it can be annulled and—'

'Aye, if I want it to be.' She met his gaze stubbornly. 'I have told Kuia and Rima to tell Queen Shiazar about this. As he protected me, so I protect him. According to Tangato law, he can't be executed without my blessing.'

388

Banno looked at her like she'd just stabbed a knife into his chest. 'Married?'

All at once she felt unutterably cruel. He wanted her, he loved her, they'd kissed and made promises . . . But he'd also killed Hekami at the river, and he'd struck her.

He wasn't forgiven . . . not yet.

Raythe looked from one to the other, then asked, 'What is it you wish, Zarelda?'

What his eyes said was, *Think twice, and commit to nothing. We can work this out.* Typical Father, but also sound advice. This was too hard for her, right now.

'I don't want anything, except for Onkado to be treated fairly,' she replied. 'And I want to stay in the Hiriwa village tonight.' *Safely out of everyone's reach, so I can think.*

'What?' Banno exclaimed, but her father looked like he understood.

'Of course,' he said. Turning to Banno, he asked, 'Could you give us a moment, please?'

Banno went to protest, then remembered he was talking to a sorcerer, the leader of their expedition, a famed general – and the man he still devoutly wanted to be his father-in-law. Wisely, he clammed up. 'Yes, sir,' he said, backing away.

'Is this true?' Father murmured, once Banno was out of earshot. 'You swear Onkado rescued you?'

She felt like the ground beneath her feet was shifting, but it was the truth, so she maintained it. 'He saved me and I owe him.'

'And Banno?'

She bowed her head, knowing that her father didn't wholly approve of Banno anyway. 'I'm not sure any more.'

He tousled her hair. 'We've all been through a lot,' he sighed. 'And right now, he's grieving his father. Let's all take a deep breath, get some rest and things will look clearer in the morning. Are you sure you'll be safe in the village?'

'Kuia and Rima say so.'

He looked doubtful, but he gave her a wry smile. 'Well, I am the rangatira of the Ngati Magnia, so they'd better treat you damned well, or they'll have me to answer to.'

She smiled shyly and touched his chin. 'Are you going to get tattooed?' she teased.

He frowned. 'I'm still angry about those marks they put on you.'

'Don't be,' she told him. 'I forget they're there most of the time. And they're quite pretty in a good light, once you're used to them.'

'There are ways of removing them, and once we're back in Otravia–'

'Dad,' she interrupted, 'we're not going back to Otravia. Not ever. You promised the Queen.' She made a gesture that encompassed the vast ruined city, the floating citadel above, and the lands around them. 'And anyway, this place won't let us go.'

He began to protest, then he looked at her and his face took on a timeless, wise look she knew so well. 'Aye, well, you may be right.' Then he winked and asked, 'What do you think of Queen Shiazar?'

While no one was giving away much about what had happened, other than the Queen had fought alongside her father in the citadel above, she knew that something profound had happened up there. And the way the Queen had killed Ulaka and escaped was very much the sort of thing her father would do. 'She's brave, clever, resourceful, and she cares about people,' she offered. 'And she seems to get her way in the end.'

Her father's clever face creased into a wry smile. 'She certainly does.'

'A bit like you, *Rangatira* Vyre.'

He laughed and hugged her again, then drew back. 'Be safe in that village. Some of them may still harbour grudges. I'll visit you as soon as I can.'

She noticed that Banno was still waiting, hoping for some sign that she'd speak to him. But all at once she was too tired to deal with all that, so she just nodded noncommittally and turned to the waiting Kuia.

'I'm exhausted,' she said. 'Please, take me home.'

Kemara watched Jesco play his fiddle for the dancing crowd, missing him a little. Nothing had been said, and she knew they'd remain friends, but without Buramanaka and Shameesta, they'd never have quite the same bond again.

I'll miss that, even though it was scary. But he won't have much time for me any more.

She smiled to see Jesco himself again: the showman, at the centre of the party, sawing on his fiddle and singing while Milly Cranville played poor Norrin's harp and everyone else sang along, clapped or danced.

But she also felt a bleak sense of emptiness settle back inside her. Whatever they'd gained, all she'd done was lose. *No more sorcery . . . Mizra is damaged magic, and I'm a damaged sorcerer. Any more of it will likely kill me.*

She finished her bite of whatever it was and trudged away, nodding and fake-smiling to those she passed, who were talking nine-to-the-dozen about how close they'd all come to death. She was happy for them all, but there was no way she was going to share her own tale.

Her feet dragged her west along the rim wall, seeking peace and quiet. The bodies had been dragged away, but bloodstains remained here and there.

Shiazar and Raythe's truce will hold for now – but for how long? And do I really want to live here for the rest of my life?

She looked around, down into the depths of the crater, out over the ruined city to the plains beyond, up at the floating rock above, blocking out half the sky. The planetary rings glowed and the stars twinkled, as did the torches of the celebrating travellers. It was familiar and foreign, and beautiful. She decided that she could get used to it.

Here, I'm still the midwife and healer. I have a place. Back in the empire, I'm a fugitive, living on borrowed time. So perhaps I really am better off staying.

It was something to cling to.

'May I speak with you?' a half-familiar female voice said.

She started as a woman stepped out of the shadows. 'Rima?'

The Tangato sorceress was wrapped in one of her people's short feather cloaks that did nothing to hide her lithe, shapely frame. She looked as wild and lovely, as dark and mysterious as a Shadran jinn.

'I wanted to see if you were well. You've lost your familiar – that must be painful.'

Damn right it is. But it's also a relief. And it's none of your business.

But the Tangato girl had a perky, likeable face, and Kemara found her habitual guarded hostility didn't rise as it usually did, so she decided that she could open up – just a little.

'Sorcery scared me,' she confessed. 'I won't miss it.'

That wasn't entirely true, though: Buramanaka had been terrifying, but his potency had been intoxicating – and there had been the addictive pleasure of clicking your fingers and changing the world. How she'd live without that, she didn't know. But she had to, because more mizra would kill her.

Rima pursed her lips. 'You Magnians are a puzzle to me. On one hand there is Raythe and Zarelda and their pathetic praxis – and then there's you. My Queen noticed that you used the same warped, dangerous magic that drove Tashvariel to madness. You each have the worst of both worlds. Don't you realise there's a middle way?'

'Mizra and praxis are polar opposites,' Kemara replied, puzzled. 'There is no middle.'

'Between two places, there is always a middle, which can be the best of both worlds, not the worst. Do you want me to show you? We've already helped Zarelda.'

'But mizra is all I know.' *Mizra, with all its rage and terror.* 'Maybe I *can't* be anything else.'

'So thought Zarelda about her praxis. You are a mahotsu-kai and you have a sacred gift that should not be squandered. Let me be your guide, if you'd like to learn a new way.'

Kemara's native defensiveness asserted itself. 'Why would you do that?'

'Because helping others is what people do. Our worlds have collided: let us try to find the best of them both.'

The best of both worlds. Kemara couldn't help but smile as a little sunshine broke through her inner gloom. 'Yes,' she found herself saying, to her own surprise. 'Yes, I would like that.'

Epilogue

Mandaryke

The lines of supplicants went out of the doors of the mansion and around the block, queues of the disenfranchised, the wronged, the hopeful. But just as many were the sorts of greedy chancers who polluted places of power all over the empire: men and women with an *angle*, a scheme to rob their fellows, requiring a patron and protector in high places – for a mutually beneficial arrangement, of course.

But Toran Zorne didn't need to queue, for the word *Ramkiseri* opened all doors.

In this case, it was a discreet back door to that mansion in Kalla Vista, the richest part of Perasdyne, the Otravian capital. The man who met him was the secretary to the Imperial Governor of the Western Empire, a local Otravian, which was a rarity in the empire.

The secretary, a balding man in his fifties with sharp, shifting eyes, led the way up via the servants' stairs, to a room where no fewer than four armed soldiers patted Zorne down for weaponry. He amused himself by picturing the moves required to kill them all.

I could do it in three seconds, he estimated.

Then the secretary said, 'Lord Mandaryke will see you now.'

Lucallus Mandaryke was a sculpture come to life: blond and muscular, and perfectly attired in Bolgravian grey. He was just thirty-four, but was arguably the most powerful man in the western empire, depending on how one judged the relationship between him and the Otravian Premier.

As the Premier was Luc's father, the question was largely academic.

He marched in, visibly impatient, juggling priorities, but Zorne ignored that; there was no one this man needed to see more than him.

'Ah, Zorne.' Mandaryke came to greet him with hand outstretched, his grip firm and confident. 'Welcome, take a seat. Would you like a drink?'

'No, thank you, Milord. And I will stand.'

The Governor smiled wryly. 'Always the upright servant of his Imperial Majesty.' He rounded his desk and sat in his padded leather seat, adjusted his cuffs and asked, 'Is he dead?'

Zorne kept his face impassive. 'No, Milord.'

'Then why are you here?'

'Because a greater opportunity has arisen, Milord.'

'An opportunity? Master Zorne, I hired you as an assassin, not as a businessman.'

'You won't regret hearing me out, Milord.'

Mandaryke frowned. 'I have the Ambassador of Pelaria awaiting me, and the Countess of Senphalia is expected presently. You have five minutes.'

Zorne calculated. 'I'll need fifteen.'

The Otravian's face hardened, but he nodded. 'Fifteen.' He steepled his fingers, leaning forward. 'Speak.'

Two hours later, when all had been told and the most obvious questions asked and answered, Luc Mandaryke walked round the desk, pumped Zorne's hand and guided him to an armchair. His face was animated, his gait now that of an excited boy. 'Rath Argentium,' he crowed. 'The seat of the Aldar God-King itself! Gerda's Teats, Zorne . . . !'

He went to the window, staring out but clearly not seeing.

He's dreaming of floating citadels, and his own arse on the imperial throne . . .

'And Raythe's led us right to it . . .' Mandaryke shook his head, bounced to his desk and pulled a bell-rope. Then he pressed a glass of the finest Ferrean whiskey into Zorne's hands. 'I insist. And tonight, you dine with us. I'm not letting you out of my sight.'

A minute later, a glittering woman swept in, her honey-gold hair girded with diamond-studded gold chains, her emerald gown perfectly moulded to her hourglass figure and her face made up like an exquisite doll.

'Luc, darling, what is it?' she purred, barely noticing Zorne – then her hand went to her mouth. *Master Zorne—?*'

Luc smiled cruelly. 'Oh, don't fret, my love – your former husband still breathes, and so does Zarelda. In fact, we're going to visit them, with ten thousand of my best friends.'

She blinked. 'Why do we need an army? This man was supposed to spike Raythe's lying heart and bring my Zari back.'

'We need an army, because we're going to conquer new lands and explore the legends of old. Pack your bags, my love. I'm going to take you to the citadel of the God-King.'

THE END

ACKNOWLEDGEMENTS

I once saw the wonderful Gillian Welch (an American folk singer) play live, and she introduced the show saying, 'We are a band, called *Gillian Welch*.'

In the same spirit: 'David Hair' is actually a team name, because writing is a team sport.

On awesome agency duties are Heather Adams and Mike Bryan, who open the doors and spread the gospel to the gatekeepers at the publishing houses. Thanks heaps, much love. Also thanks are owed to Jon Wood of RCW for stepping in when Heather stepped away in late 2020 to embark on an academic adventure.

The team gatekeeper (i.e. publishing editor) is the wonderful Jo Fletcher, whose crew at JFB/Quercus UK keep things editing tight at the back and supply the art, promotion and distribution. Without them, you would definitely not be reading this book.

Closer to (my) home, thanks to the long-suffering test reader team of Kerry Greig (who also plays the role of wonderful wife and sternest critic), Paul Linton and the aforementioned Heather and Jon.

Cheering us on from the side-lines are friends and family, especially my parents, Cliff and Biddy, my children Brendan and Melissa, and myriad others, but special mention to Felix and Stefania, who bring some European culture to the whole thing. My thanks to you all.

Stay safe, be healthy, be kind in these troubled times.

David Hair
Wellington, New Zealand
2021

Hello to Jason Isaacs. Tinkety-tonk and down with the Nazis.

Read on for a preview of
Sorcerer's Edge

Book three of
THE TETHERED CITADEL
Trilogy

by
David Hair

Prologue

Servant of the Greater Good

From the balcony of his suite in the Mandaryke family mansion on Kallavista Heights, Toran Zorne could see the beating heart of Perasdyne, the capital of Otravia. The greatest city of the western empire, its famed boulevards lined by oaks, was gilded by autumn's touch, basking in the afterglow of another prosperous day.

Thriving under imperial rule, Zorne mused, *dissent silenced, the scum cleared from the streets. Every Threat to Order has been quelled, and the Greater Good allowed to prevail.*

It had been nearly five years since the Otravia Republic had surrendered to the oncoming Bolgravian forces. After initial victories, the country had fallen from within, imperial sympathisers, led by the Mandarykes, betraying their own people to side with the Bolgravians. Zorne remembered it well. He'd been assigned to covert operations within the capital, specifically, the assassination of dissidents working against imperial rule. The lists of known republicans whose voices should be silenced had been supplied by Mandaryke's people, enabling his team to reap a deadly harvest and easing the transition to the new Bolgravian-sympathetic rule.

In many ways, I helped make Luc Mandaryke the man he is.

But that was the past and the question now vexing his mind was altogether more problematic: *what will Mandaryke do next?* So long as he continued to serve the empire, all was well. But should he choose to put ambition ahead of his duty to Bolgravia, he would no longer be a servant of the Greater Good, but a Threat to Order.

'Master Zorne?' a voice called from behind him.

Zorne had detected the servant's approach several seconds before, assessed any potential threat and dismissed it. 'Yuz?' he replied curtly, deliberately using Bolgravian to unsettle the man.

'Governor Mandaryke requires you attend his meeting,' the servant said uneasily. He was a veteran, one who'd witnessed his nation's 'disgrace', and faithful servant or not, his loyalty could never be taken for granted. Zorne had noted the way his facial features tightened when he heard any foreign accent.

He hates me, he despises his master, and he's possibly a spy for the rebel faction.

'What is your name?' Zorne asked, staring at the man.

'Rofort, sir,' he replied, dropping his eyes, dislike now tempered by uncertainty, even fear.

'Have you served the Governor long?'

'Fifteen years, sir,' the man answered. The sideways shift in the man's eyes told a story, of fear at having his doings looked into. Zorne mused on the different ways he could kill him. *Dagger to the throat, or slam the back of his skull onto one of the balcony spikes . . . or just pitch him head-first over the railing?*

Luc Mandaryke wouldn't question his action, for a Ramkiseri, a member of the Bolgravian Secret Service, answered only to the Imperial Throne. Zorne had been a law unto himself for most of his career, a right he'd earned.

But whatever guilty secret Rofort harbours is more likely just some misappropriation of coin or abuse of status, he decided. *I'll recommend his dismissal so that he can contemplate his fall for years to come.*

That settled, Zorne turned his mind to the meeting he must attend: another duel of civility, prestige and innuendo he'd rather avoid. But duty called, so he examined his reflection in the bank of windows – not through vanity; he was unmemorable, he knew, and took pride in it. An impassive, clean-shaven face with iron-grey eyes framed by cropped brown hair looked back at him. An unsettling visage, when he wished, and that suited him far more than being handsome. He decided he'd pass muster as he was.

'I know the way,' he told Rofort. 'Dismissed.'

He waited until the servant was gone, set the little traps that would indicate if anyone entered the room in his absence, then wound his way through the guest wing to the central stairs.

'Under-Komisar Zorne,' the doorman announced him as he entered – and the room stopped. The novelty of meeting a known Ramkiseri was rare, though all senior officials would – unknowingly – have at least one in their household, monitoring them for the empire.

Zorne surveyed the large room. These people would be his companions on the road ahead, his allies in name, but each and every one a potential traitor nevertheless. Not least his host, Luc Mandaryke, who was at the centre of the gathering, of course.

The Governor, the highest representative of the Bolgrav Empire in Otravia, cut a flamboyant figure. Blond, square-jawed and handsome, big but athletic, he was famed as a gentleman sorcerer and noble, and the man Otravian virgins dreamed of, so it was said. He was wearing embroidered velvets so intricate that he looked like a walking tapestry.

His face lit up with calculated enthusiasm as he turned to Zorne. 'Ah, the man himself!' he exclaimed, as if Zorne were the missing piece in a puzzle he'd been battling to complete. 'Toran, my friend, come and meet the crew!'

His wife was standing beside him. Mirella Mandaryke was honey-blonde and exquisitely beautiful, despite being in her thirties and a mother. Her dress was all delicate pastel hues, looking more confectionary than cloth, and dripping in jewels that glittered incessantly in the lamplight. Only her face didn't shine: she wore a sour look as she contemplated Zorne.

Because of me, her husband is whisking her off the edge of the map – although it is not my fault he refuses to leave her alone here in Perasdyne. Zorne had no sympathy: Mirella had chosen her bed. With Great Houses came great risks, and House Mandaryke was the greatest in Otravia. *And leaving her here would indeed be foolish. She's a serpent.*

Despite his distaste, he went to her first, kissed her reluctant hand, clicked his heels and bowed. 'Milady, you are as fair as the first day of spring,' he recited, a line from a hackneyed old poem. Then he turned to face the adherents Luc had assembled for the mission. 'My lords.'

'Toran Zorne, you know my father by reputation, I'm sure,' Luc said, stepping aside and introducing a vision of his own future: a stout, balding giant with broken blood vessels in his cheeks and a sour, suspicious manner. 'Premier Rodias Mandaryke, this is Komisar Zorne.'

'Under-Komisar,' Zorne corrected by reflex, making Luc smile wryly. He suspected that the nobleman deliberately inflated his rank to amuse himself. 'I am honoured, sir.'

The Premier – officially the ruler of Otravia, as long as he did what the emperor wanted – puffed himself up, unable to resist the flattery. 'So you're the man who lit this fire? House Mandaryke thanks you, Zorne.'

Touching the premier's hand was a slightly queasy experience, because treachery disgusted Zorne, even when it benefited his emperor. Men who betrayed their own country could just as readily betray another.

We should have beheaded these traitors as soon as they'd given us what we wanted.

But this was not the time. Feigning camaraderie, he turned to the next people in line.

'Toran Zorne,' said Luc, 'this is Ferdan Verdelho, imperial Courser.' Verdelho, a dapper man with fashionable moustaches, was dangerous: there was an ages-old rivalry between the Coursers, who were emissaries of the Imperial Court, and the Ramkiseri.

Luc introduced two generals; one in Otravian red and the other in Bolgravian grey. 'This is General Nemath Torland, who'll command the Otravian division, and General Romoi Lisenko, who'll lead the imperial division.' It was mandatory that any military operation in a vassal state be at least half Bolgravian.

'Zorne,' said Nemath Torland, one of Luc's drinking comrades. They'd met already, and Zorne knew that Torland disliked him. The feeling was mutual.

'*Under*-Komisar,' Romoi Lisenko greeted him. Zorne knew him by reputation as a blusterer and a dilettante. It troubled him that Mandaryke had chosen such a poor imperial commander for this expedition, fuelling his fears that the governor was planning to use this mission to further himself, not the empire.

Zorne kept his face neutral. 'My lords.'

He was more interested in meeting the sorcerers who would accompany the mission. All Ramkiseri were sorcerers as well as trained assassins, and rival magicians were always a concern. Tresorov and Drusyn, the two senior Bolgravians, wore military robes of deep maroon; the elder was a hollow-eyed man with lank silver hair and the junior an effete youth who looked like his senior's catamite. He didn't know either, which also troubled him. There would be five more Bolgravian military sorcerers with Lisenko's division, but they would be novices, beneath everyone's notice.

Mandaryke really is stacking the deck with his own cards.

His unease grew when he turned to the final guest, the Otravian sorcerer. Non-imperial forces were only allowed one per division and she was clearly powerful, though unlike the Bolgravians, whose auras radiated energy, hers was like a hole in space that sucked warmth away. She was young, but her long hair was grey and her skin had a deathly pallor, enhanced by her white clothes: her skin scarcely contrasted with the blanched cotton fabric. Her eyes were violet and empty.

'This is Lady Teirhinan, of the Imperial Otravian Order,' Luc Mandaryke told Zorne, his voice suitably solemn. 'We are honoured that the Order saw fit to lend us their best.'

Zorne knew the name, of course. Everyone did. *Teirhinan Deathless.*

Some say saint. Most say madwoman – but not to her face.

He'd heard that she'd killed then resurrected herself, to enhance her power. That was not theoretically possible, but in her presence it was hard to deny. He bowed over her hand, but didn't touch her. 'An honour,' he murmured, meeting her chilling gaze and recognising a kindred spirit.

'Master Zorne,' she replied, her voice was scratchy, her breath foul. 'Your reputation precedes you.'

Does it? Zorne didn't like having a reputation. Self-effacement was a defining credo of the Ramkiseri.

Sensing his discomfort, Luc Mandaryke stepped in. 'Take a glass, my friends. This is a solemn moment. Otravia and Bolgravia, working together to right a wrong and avenge an entire generation of people who have suffered at the hands of an egotistical maniac.' He gestured and servants appeared with trays of sparkling wine.

Luc Mandaryke faced the circle and raised his glass. 'Five years ago, when my father and I signed a treaty between Otravia and Bolgravia, there were dissidents who failed to see the wisdom of alliance, preferring a hopeless, vainglorious war. Fortunately, sense prevailed and those fools were forced to flee.'

And thus the victors rewrite history, Zorne mused cynically.

'We have hunted down those traitors, and now just one remains unpunished,' Luc continued. 'And now we know where to find him.' He raised his glass. 'Let us drink to the imminent death of Raythe Vyre.'

As they all drank, Zorne watched Luc's wife, trying to read her, but she was clearly well-used to hiding her thoughts.

You were married to Vyre, and you betrayed him for Mandaryke. That makes you Otravia personified.

She sensed his gaze, met it coolly, then looked away, leaving him none the wiser.

Ever since Zorne had arrived with his tale of lost peoples, a legendary city surmounted by a floating citadel and Raythe Vyre, utmost secrecy had prevailed. Mandaryke needed an army to seize Rath Argentium, and that required the cooperation of the Bolgravian military. But all Luc had told the imperial court was that Raythe Vyre had been found in Verdessa and a military expedition was required to defeat him.

If we even breathe the words 'istariol' or 'Rath Argentium' every nation will seek to intervene, Luc had told Zorne, which made sense: istariol, the mineral that enhanced sorcery, was the most valuable commodity in existence. But Zorne worried that Mandaryke wanted it all for himself. Every day he wondered if he should inform his Ramkiseri masters, but Luc had asked him not to, 'friend to friend', and Zorne had so far acquiesced. He was the only non-Bolgravian governor permitted by the empire, an anomaly that had always worried Zorne. *I know they helped us greatly, but we should never have left these traitors in charge. The entire ruling class should have been massacred, starting with the Mandarykes.*

Luc lowered his glass, and gestured toward the far doors, that led to his banquet hall. 'Let us dine, my friends,' he said grandly. 'We have a long journey ahead of us.'

PART ONE

Stranger Here

1

Trust

Trust is hard, Raythe Vyre remembered reading once. *None of us are self-sufficient, so we must lean on others, placing our lives into their hands. How well do you know them? Just because you've shared food, laughter or a bed doesn't mean they wish you well. But you have to trust someone, because solitude is impossible. We are social animals, and only survive by banding together.*

Some days he wondered whether he shouldn't try disproving that theory by living at the bottom of a cave – because at times, involving himself in all the big and petty turmoil of daily life just didn't seem worth the risk of having a blade – metaphorical or actual – thrust into his back yet again.

My wife slept with my best friend, who betrayed our country and everything I love. I've fought an empire and lost, and even out here, beyond the known world, I've been repeatedly deceived.

He wasn't sure why he felt so gloomy, the morning after a miraculous victory, but everything came with a cost, and that triumph had been hard won. Too many people had died; of the nearly three hundred who'd set out on this mad journey into the unknown, barely two hundred remained. Most of the losses had been men, who'd borne the brunt of the fighting, leaving many woman alone with children to feed. He could hear them wailing and sobbing below.

But the real reason for his morose mood, he decided, was that they'd all followed him here for nothing. He'd promised them riches and freedom, but instead, here they were, stranded, with nothing to show for all their blood, sweat and belief.

I've failed them, which is pretty much the same as betraying them.

That was why, he reluctantly admitted to himself, he was currently hiding on the roof of the mansion they'd called Rim House. Dawn had yet to break, although light had begun slowly creeping across the sky, fading the planetary rings.

The previous day his little group of Magnian refugees had survived a battle against the Tangato tribes that should have destroyed them. If he looked down from the roof, he could see bodies lying in the grounds and piled up beside the crater rim fence, where the fighting had been fiercest.

Instead, he looked up. Silhouetted against the pale glow of the rings was a dark rock hanging in the air, tethered by four massive chains rooted in the ground on the lower slopes of the hill. Atop that floating rock, out of sight from this vantage, was a citadel, Shiro Kamigami, where another battle had been fought, a sorcerer's duel against the deadliest foe imaginable.

Shiazar, Kemara and I prevailed – just. We won the chance to move forward and fight another day.

The after-images of that insane battle against a mad Aldar lord, in a place where time fluctuated and the past had come to life, still haunted him. He wondered dazedly if he would ever sleep again.

But the sun would rise soon: life went on, and his people were his responsibility.

Groaning as his joints clicked and creaked from the cold, he stood, clutching at the rail fencing off the roof, and reflected ruefully that though he was nowhere near forty yet, he was no longer a young man. But he shoved aside that unwelcome thought and gazed out over the ruined city, marvelling anew at the view.

Rath Argentium had been the seat of the Aldar Kings, a city built upon a hill so full of istariol that the peak had broken away and now floated above, leaving a massive crater he could see right down into. The outer slopes had been uninhabited for five centuries, but the Aldar had built well; many of the buildings were surprisingly intact, despite the passage of time.

Beyond the city were plains, forests and hills, rivers and lakes – but for less than a hundred miles in each direction, for this miraculous, impossible land was deep within the Ice Wastes, thousands of miles from civilisation, here only by grace of the istariol in the soil, which had kept the earth warm enough to prevent it freezing. That had allowed the Tangato, a lost tribe, to survive the Ice Age that had gripped the rest of the planet.

Raythe had brought his people here seeking that istariol, but it looked like they'd never leave. Last night, to stop the slaughter, he'd agreed peace terms with Queen Shiazar of the Tangato. It meant they would join the Tangato nation – and never leave.

I still don't really know how I feel about that . . .

He was profoundly grateful to have survived, and to have found a way to save his people, but it was a high price to pay, relinquishing everything they came here for – their dreams of istariol and wealth, and returning to their homelands as free people. Now they'd never go home again.

Dear Gerda, did I do the right thing?

The Goddess had no answer for him, but light feet on the stairs brought him back to the present. He turned, not sure who he was expecting, but was still surprised when a dark-skinned woman wearing a flax kilt and bodice and wrapped in a feather cloak appeared. Her black hair billowed around her lively, pugnacious face.

'Rima,' Raythe exclaimed, worried some new emergency had arisen. 'What is it?'

The young Tangato grinned at his worried expression. 'There's no problem,' she answered. 'The Queen asks that you attend upon her at noon. There's much to arrange.'

'That's the truth,' he sighed. 'We must recover our dead and prepare them for burial, secure food and water and move back into the buildings we were using before the fighting. That's assuming they don't just shoot me for bargaining away their right to go home. They'll take some convincing.'

'My Queen believes strongly in your ability to talk.'

Feeling damned with faint praise, he asked, 'How does the Queen fare?'

'She has reclaimed her throne, Ikendo is dead and his son Onkado imprisoned, and the people are praising her for ending this conflict and asserting authority over your kind. Some lament that she arrived in time to save your people, but most are just pleased to see peace return to our land.'

'That's nice,' Raythe drawled. 'Is Zar all right?'

Last night, with the fighting over, he'd been briefly reunited with his daughter. He'd expected her to re-join him after months as a prisoner, but instead, she'd chosen to return to the Tangato village. She'd also announced she was married to Onkado, son of the man who'd usurped Shiazar's throne: a man of *Aldar* blood.

Onkado did it to protect me, she'd told him. *It's not been consummated.*

Rationally, he understood, but he was angry at himself for failing to protect her.

'Zarelda is well,' Rima reassured him. 'Midday, just over the bridge, *Rangatira* Vyre.'

Shiazar had made him rangatira – the chieftain of his tribe, the Ngati Magnia – but he didn't yet know if that was a gift or a curse. 'I'll be there,' he told her.

She bobbed her head and was gone, and Raythe turned to watch the dawn and prepare himself for the arguments and anger he'd face today.

'My Queen believes strongly in your ability to talk . . .'

It was all right for Shiazar: she was Aldar and was revered, bordering on worshiped, by her people. His Magnians viewed dissent against authority as their Deo-given right. But that attitude also made them resilient and adaptable, virtues they'd needed on this journey.

Thinking about the Tangato Queen and her Aldar blood was its own maze of miracles. Though she was the child of an Aldar woman and a Tangato man, the concept of being part-Aldar didn't really exist: any-one with Aldar blood was Aldar, a being made of sorcery. She usually wore a mask, but he'd gazed on her inhumanly beautiful, timeless face and been entranced.

She was also a courageous woman, dedicated to both of her peoples – her fellow Aldar, the Yokei; and the Tangato, who'd once served the Aldar. He'd seen her fight and she was glorious and brave, truly a legend come to life.

Just then, the sun broke through the eastern hills, bouncing shards of fractured colour on the unseen ice sheets beyond the rim of the unfrozen lands before sending shafts of light across the landscape, a sight to dazzle even his tired, jaded eyes.

Then Magga Kern's roosters crowed and a baby cried in the rooms below, setting off others.

It was time to re-join his people and face their music.